THE SHAMELESS HOUR

The Ivy Years # 4

SARINA BOWEN

Rennie Road Books

Cover image: e g o r r / iStockphoto

Cover design: Tina Anderson

Get more *Ivy Years!* Sign up for the mailing list at
http://SarinaBowen.com/theivyyears

The Shameless Hour is a work of fiction. Names, places, and incidents are either
products of the author's imagination or used fictitiously.

ONE

September

RAFE

It had been two hours since I blew out twenty candles on the cake Ma made for me, but my ass was still parked in a chair at Restaurante Tipico.

It was always hard for me to get away from the Dominican joint that my extended family ran. I needed to be on a train headed back to Harkness College. But here I was at table seven in the back corner, rolling silverware for the evening rush, the same way I'd done my whole life.

"One more and then I'm gone," I said to Pablito, my sixteen-year-old cousin. "I have seven o'clock dinner reservations. If I miss the four-thirty train, I'm screwed."

"Big date tonight?"

"Yeah, it's actually her birthday, too."

"No shit?" Pablito grinned as he applied yet another of the self-adhering bands we used to hold the napkin around the knife and fork. "So I'm going to sling food all night and go home smelling like the fryer. *You're* getting a nice dinner, a bottle of wine and then" — he made a lewd hand motion — "some happy birthday to *you*."

Jesucristo. I was not about to share the details of this evening's plans with Pablito or anyone else. "At least you got an hour's worth of labor out of me." I set a silverware roll on top of his pile.

"Don't forget your present," he said, casting an eye on the vintage money clip my mother had given me for my birthday. It was sterling silver with an art deco design. "I know why your Ma chose that for you."

"Yeah?" I tucked it in my pocket. It was no mystery why Ma gave it to me. I loved old things. She'd chosen well, and I'd thanked her.

"No place to hide a condom." Pablito snickered.

I had to grin, because the kid made a good point. But looking out for a dozen younger cousins was a part of my life, so I felt obligated to add, "You're not supposed to keep them in your wallet, anyway."

"Eh." He shook his head. "Like it would matter."

Check please. I could *not* talk about sex with my sixteen-year-old cousin. Not today of all days. I tossed one last silverware roll onto the pile and stood. "*Tengo que irme.*" *Gotta run.*

He returned my fist bump. "Go on, then. Back to the good life. Don't think of us, the little people."

I cuffed him on the head, then ran into the kitchen to kiss my ma goodbye.

She wished me a happy birthday, and I thanked her for the cake and the present. "Bye. I need to go. I'm taking Alison out tonight."

She eyed me for a few seconds. "*Sé bueno,*" she said finally. *Be good.*

Cristo. I could swear sometimes she had telepathic powers. When my mother got pregnant at nineteen, my so-called father had married her. But when I was a few months old, he'd gone back to his people in Mexico for a family funeral. And never came back.

Since then, it had been just the two of us — plus about three dozen aunts, uncles and cousins — but my mother had always impressed upon me that sex made babies and that good boys had a responsibility not to get girls in trouble.

My mother would *not* approve of what I had planned for tonight.

"I'm always good," I told her. True statement. I planned to be very careful with Alison. Every single time. (I hoped there were many times.)

Before I left, my mother unleashed one last bit of Catholic guilt. She asked if I was coming home for my cousin's christening in November. (I wasn't sure.) She reminded me they were short-handed at the restaurant (a familiar guilt trip, since I'd decided to go to college outside of the city) and she told me to have a happy birthday.

That last thing I could do.

I kissed her cheek one more time and ran out of there.

The Metro-North train from 125th Street wasn't crowded, and I got a seat to myself. After watching the grit of New York transform into the green of Connecticut, I pulled out my phone to call my girlfriend.

"Hi," she answered sounding a little breathless.

"Hi, angel. Happy birthday."

"Happy birthday yourself!" I could hear her smile coming through the phone.

"I made the four-thirty, so we're still good for seven o'clock."

"I was just thinking about you," she said in a quiet voice.

"Yeah?" I hoped she meant it in a good way.

"I love you, Rafe."

Alison had said those words before. But there was something so serious about the way she said them now. "I love you too, Ali."

"Tonight is going to be great."

Warmth bloomed inside my chest. There had been too many moments during the past six months when I'd doubted Alison's feelings for me. It was just so gratifying to hear she was looking forward to taking the next step.

"I can't wait," I whispered. "I hope dinner doesn't take too long."

She giggled. "See you soon."

The train pulled into the Harkness, Connecticut station at six-fifteen. I ran the mile to campus because it saved me seven bucks, clearing the doorway of suite 301 in Beaumont House with just a half hour to get ready.

Unfortunately, both my roommates were home and bickering in the common room as usual.

When I passed them with my towel, they were arguing about politics, and when I came back freshly showered and shaved, they were arguing about tomorrow's Giant's game.

"You want some action on the game?" Mat asked me as I headed for my closet.

"No thanks."

He turned his attention back to my roommate, Bickley. "Come on, fancy boy," he taunted. "Bet me on the Giants. A hundred bucks. That's like pocket change for you."

"I will consider your wager," Bickley countered, "if you shave that bit of ridiculousness off your lip."

Alone in the bedroom I shared with Bickley, I chuckled. It's not like I had time to witness the latest episode of The Mat and Bickley Show. But Mat's experiment with facial hair *was* pretty hideous. Of course, the louder Bickley made this point, the longer Mat would keep his weird little 'stache.

"I'm not shaving it off," Mat argued. "Tonight, when I have Devon's balls in my mouth, I'm going to scrape it against his shaft."

Cue a disgusted groan from the common room. "You arse-hole," Bickley spat. "No thank you for that image."

"Then quit yapping and bet on the football game, sissy boy,"

Mat said. "The spread is three and a half in favor of the Giants. I'll even give you an extra point, okay? But only on a hundred bucks. No more."

I rolled my eyes at this bit of salesmanship. Mat was a complete shark, and I was pretty sure that betting against Bickley was a major source of his income.

There was a silence while my roommate tried to decide whether there was a catch. Bickley was my soccer teammate, but as a Brit he didn't have a lot of experience with American football. But he had trouble admitting that he wasn't an expert at, well, pretty much anything.

The ego on Bickley? It was so large it had its own gravitational field. And the chip on Mat's shoulder? It was as vast as the Grand Canyon. Between the two of them, I rarely had any peace.

"Give me the spread plus two," Bickley countered in his clipped, aristocratic accent.

"Plus two? Forget it. I'll call my bookie instead."

"Well..." Bickley was about to cave. I could hear it. "Fine. Plus one on a hundred dollars. As soon as I look up the spread, you have a deal."

"Seriously? If I tell you it's three and a half, it's three and a half." Mat's voice was full of irritation. But that was normal for him. Mat was a prickly guy. "Only a dick would lie about the point spread."

"Trust but verify," Bickley replied.

"You douche canoe," Mat grumbled.

"What? You don't want my money?" Bickley asked. "Ah. The point spread is indeed three and a half." (His clipped British accent made it come out like *hauf*.)

Mat was silent for once.

A minute later, Bickley appeared in the doorway to our little room. "I feel good about this one," he announced. With his designer jeans, polo shirt and preppy haircut, my roommate looked like a J. Crew ad come to life.

"Awesome," I deadpanned. Not only was I sick of listening to these arguments, I had my own stuff to think about tonight.

"Where are you taking Alison?" he asked.

"The Slippery Elm."

"Nice. Be sure to order the sweetbreads. They are a delicacy."

"Wait — what the hell are those?" Taking dining advice from Bickley was nearly as risky as betting on football with Mat. The guy bragged about eating whale blubber in Japan and Haggis in Scotland. "Aren't sweetbreads the calf's balls, or something?"

"Pish. They are a gland and very buttery." Bickley closed his eyes, smacking his lips with appreciation.

"I'll take it under advisement." The fancy restaurant lost its appeal all of a sudden. I was nervous enough about tonight without having to worry about which fork to use, too.

"Hopefully, I *won't* see you here later," Bickley added. "I know you bought earrings for Alison. But I hope she gives you the kind of gift that can't be wrapped in a box."

"I always wanted a pony," I quipped, trying to steer Bickley away from this topic.

He flopped onto the bed, a gleam in his eye. "At brunch this morning, I heard your Ice Queen's roommate say that she was staying away from their room tonight. This bodes well for you, sir."

"Does it now?"

"Come on. You can tell Uncle Bickley. Are you going to finally shag that girl?"

I was, unless she'd changed her mind. "That's none of your business, dude."

"Very well. But I need to know if I can bring my date back here later. At least tell me that much."

Bickley, to his sorrow, did not have our room to himself very often. Since I'd slept alone every night of my life (so far) his trysts usually happened elsewhere. When he did bring a girl home, they had to finish up at a reasonable hour. This made for the occasional awkward departure, where I kept my eyes on Bickley's fancy television screen while he led his girlfriend-for-the-night out of the room.

My roommate had a whole lot of what everyone else called casual sex. In my head, though, those two words didn't fit together. To me, there was nothing casual about getting naked with a girl. My sexual experiences — as limited as they were — had been intense. The first time my high school girlfriend let me touch her was an experience that was burned on my soul. The sounds she made, the heat of her body. The potent look in her eye when she...

Dios. "Casual" was not the right word at all.

I wanted all of that with Alison. And more. And the fact that I was supposed to have it all tonight? Mind-bending.

"Er, earth to Rafael."

"Um," I said stupidly. "You can have the room. If I come home, I'll crash on the couch."

"I hope it does not come to that."

So did I.

"Do you need one of my suit jackets?"

"I'm good, thanks." I'd rather wear my old one than borrow from Bickley. He'd probably lend me some Armani number that cost two grand, and I'd have to worry about wrinkling it. I didn't need any extra reasons to feel jittery tonight.

The suit jacket I slipped on was the one I wore to church with my mother. It was a vintage 1940s blazer that I'd found in a Harlem thrift shop.

Funny how I was wearing my church jacket for the date where I would lose my virginity. And the next time I wore it would probably be to confession. Now there was a fun little irony.

I opened Bickley's dorm fridge and grabbed the bottle of champagne I'd stashed there. The bottle went into a gift bag that I'd bought, along with a gift for Alison (silver earrings) and a gift for me (a box of condoms.)

With a wave to Mat and Bickley, I left.

The commute to Alison's door took sixty seconds. Harkness

College had twelve "houses." But these were misleadingly named. Each house was a big stone or brick residence for several hundred students, with its own dining hall and library. Alison and I were both in the beautiful Beaumont House, with its gothic spires and slate flagstone walkways. As I strode across the courtyard, it impressed me, as usual, that Harkness students had been walking this path for a century. Ma had wanted me closer to home, and she meant well. But attending Harkness was an incredible opportunity, and I wasn't about to feel guilty about it.

At Alison's entryway door, I shivered as I peered into the little diamond-shaped pane of glass set into the oak. It was the third week of September, and we were having an early cold snap. But my chill? It was not due to the weather. Suddenly, I was nervous as hell.

Someone appeared in the entryway on the other side of the door. On a Saturday evening, there was always plenty of traffic in and out, as students returned from dining halls, libraries and coffee shops to get ready to party. So I wouldn't have to call Alison to come down and let me in.

"Hey man." The guy who opened Alison's entryway door was in my French class. "Big date tonight?" He eyed the gift bag in my hand with a smirk.

"It's her birthday," I said quickly.

"Ah. Have fun," he said, holding the door.

"Thanks. See you Monday," I called as he walked away.

I stepped into the echoing stone stairway and began climbing the stairs. I loved this old stairwell, with its marble steps and its ironwork railing. Students had climbed these stairs to their rooms when jazz was still a brand new word. I didn't hear any jazz right now, though. From behind the first door I passed came the sounds of a single-shooter video game. In the thirties, you might have heard the strains of somebody's "wireless." Or maybe a Victrola.

I was a bit of an antiques nut, which was kind of weird for a guy my age. But thinking about vintage audio equipment took my mind off my nerves. I was sweating just from climbing two flights up the curving stairwell. So when I reached Alison's floor, I kept climbing. There was an odd little landing about ten steps further on. I set down my gift bag there, taking care to keep the bottle of champagne upright.

Removing my jacket, I took a deep breath. There was really no reason to be nervous around Alison. We'd been seeing each other since last spring, when we were both freshmen. We'd taken things slowly with our physical relationship. I was always ready for more, but Alison told me straightaway that she was a virgin, and when I admitted the same, she seemed enormously relieved.

I was patient with her, even though it was sometimes frustrating. There was a lot of kissing and cuddling on the couch. But she seemed to have a whole lot of sexual tripwires. One minute we'd be making out, and then suddenly she'd push me away. Not only did I always go home horny, I went home confused. And the confusion was by far the more painful condition. I didn't like wondering what it was about me that didn't quite do it for her.

After a couple of these awkward endings, I'd tried to get her to tell me what was wrong. But she'd just say, "I'm not comfortable," and then change the subject.

And what kind of an asshole pressures his girlfriend for sex? I wasn't going to be that guy.

There was a whole lot of good stuff between us, anyway. Alison always got my jokes, and I loved the way her face went soft when I paid her a compliment. I did that often, too. Because Alison was pretty great. She was smart and funny, as well as gorgeous. With all that fine, blond hair framing her face, when I looked at her, the word *angel* would pop into my head.

My mother said that Harkness College had given me an unhealthy attraction to pretty white girls. "What you need is a nice Latina," she'd say. "Someone who will never look down on where you come from."

Mostly I ignored my mother's prejudice. But sometimes it was hard not to worry, or to read too much into Alison's reluctance to get me naked. At Harkness I was surrounded by people who had a lot more money than I did, including Alison. I worried sometimes that she thought I wasn't good enough for her.

That was probably just paranoia.

Summer vacation had separated us. I spent the month of June working in my mother's restaurant, and trying not to die from heatstroke on the subway platform whenever she sent me on errands. At night, before I went to sleep, I'd lie on my little twin bed in our cramped apartment and talk to Alison on the phone, while the window unit blew cold(ish) air across my mostly naked body.

There was never any phone sex, of course. But I loved the sound of her soft voice in my ear, telling me all the things she put up with as an intern at the San Francisco art gallery where she worked. "I miss you, Rafe," she'd say. "I was thinking about you when I was serving coffee to a table of old ladies. They'd asked for decaf, but I gave them all high-test by accident, because I was remembering that letter you'd written me on the old typewriter, instead of paying attention to the coffee."

That made me laugh and miss her all the more. So I kept the old-fashioned letters coming. And the weeks flew by.

In July, Alison had called me, all excited. "Do you remember that international program in Ecuador that I applied to?"

Of course I did. After she'd been wait-listed, she'd cried a puddle onto the shoulder of my Harkness sweatshirt.

"A spot opened up! I'm leaving next week!"

"That's awesome," I'd said, feeling happy for her even though I knew I wouldn't get to talk to her for six weeks. The Ecuador trip was an immersion program, and students weren't supposed to speak to outsiders the entire time.

So that had sucked.

Needless to say, three weeks ago, when she'd finally stepped off the Connecticut Coach from LaGuardia airport to start our sophomore year, I'd been desperate to see her.

That first night back, I'd asked her to sleep in my bed for the first time. "I am not ready to let you go yet," I'd told her. "Just stay with me. It isn't a ploy to get your clothes off. And Bickley isn't back until tomorrow, anyway."

Her face had softened. "Okay, I can do that," she'd said. I was actually stunned that she went along with it, because whenever I'd suggested she spend the night before, she'd turned me down.

But not this time. I'd given her one of my T-shirts to wear, and she'd looked sexy as hell in it. Of course, when we'd settled into my bed together, my body had gotten big ideas all its own. So I'd rolled onto my back and pulled her head onto my shoulder.

She felt terrific in my arms. I'd loved holding her, sneaking kisses here and there. "This is nice," I'd said.

"Yes it is," she'd agreed. We were silent for awhile before she said, "I know you've waited a long time for sex."

I was so stunned she'd brought up the topic I hadn't said anything for a moment. "S'okay," I choked out eventually.

"We have birthdays coming up," she continued. "Maybe that should be... a big night for us."

Again, I was too stunned to answer. A few beats went by before I managed to agree with her. "That would be incredible," I finally whispered.

"I think it will be." She rubbed my chest with one hand, massaging a slow circle on my pec. Meanwhile, my dick hardened into something approximating an iron bar, just on the possibility that she was actually suggesting what I thought she was suggesting.

I slept very little that night. And for these past two weeks, whenever I kissed Alison goodnight, I became comically horny.

And now? I was hiding in a stairwell, practically splitting out of my skin with nervous anticipation.

Three and a half floors below me, the entryway door slammed. I heard footstep. Someone was jogging up the stairs.

That woke me up. I took a moment to fold my jacket over my arm and pick up the gift bag again. After giving myself the once-over, I began to quietly descend the stairs, as if it were perfectly normal for me to come from that direction. If I passed whomever was climbing, I'd give him a calm nod. *Everything is fine, there's nothing to see here. Just your average twenty year old on his way to get his V-card stamped. Carry on.*

But I didn't get the chance. The climbing footsteps stopped, and I heard a sharp rap on a wooden door. Then, the click of a door opening. "Surprise!" a guy's voice called.

Weirdly, the guy's voice seemed to originate from Alison's doorway. I'm not sure why, but I took the last three or four stairs at a slow, stealthy pace. Just as Alison's startled voice said, "Oh my God! What are *you* doing here?" the guy came into view.

He was tall and thin, but my attention went straight to the shiny Rolex hanging loosely on his wrist. I'm from New York City, so I could spot those at a hundred yards. Mr. Rolex was a rich boy.

"I *told* you I wanted to see you again. And what better time than on your birthday?" He stepped into Alison's room, disappearing from view.

Some kind of gravitational force drew me down the last steps quickly enough to wedge my foot between the door and its frame. The view I saw next was sickening. Mr. Rolex had wrapped his arms around Alison's waist, and was liplocked to the girl.

My girl.

"What the fuck?" I said, pushing the door open. And since the question was reverberating through my mind like a gong, I said it a second time. "What. The. Fuck?"

Alison's arms shot out to her sides, as if she'd just received an electric jolt. Mr. Rolex let her go and turned around. "Who are you?" he asked, his eyebrows disappearing into his hundred-dollar haircut.

"Who am I? I'm *the boyfriend*." I was sputtering with indignation, but I couldn't stop talking. "The boyfriend since last April. That's... five months ago. Almost six." As if an accurate accounting really mattered.

Alison's mouth kept opening and closing, like the goldfish I used to keep in a little bowl on the window sill in our apartment.

Mr. Rolex was not so quiet. And he looked almost as surprised as I felt. "The *boyfriend?* We were together for *six weeks* in Ecuador, and you never mentioned a boyfriend."

At least I wasn't the only one interested in getting the accounting right.

"I *told* you I wasn't looking for a relationship," she whispered in his direction.

"But you never said *why*. I guess that makes me an idiot." Mr. Rolex actually had the balls to look sad about it.

Now that I'd been standing in the room for almost a minute, other little details were making themselves clear to me. Mr. Rolex had a bouquet of roses in one hand.

Flowers! I forgot flowers. To strew on the bed.

Wait. There wasn't going to be any strewing. Or any bed. My feeble brain could barely wrap itself around the vastness of this problem. It was just so *unexpected*. I'd never wondered if Alison had someone on the side. Even if we'd never been naked together, we'd been *together*. For a long time.

I stood there, slack-jawed, my silly little gift bag in my hand, realizing I'd missed something important. "If she didn't want a *relationship* from you," I asked Mr. Rolex, "then what did she want? A Scrabble opponent?" My face began to heat as truth smoldered in my chest. "A study buddy? A foot massage?" I turned to face her directly. "Tonight was supposed to be the night we both lost our virginity, Alison."

"Well *that* is not quite possible," Mr. Rolex sputtered.

That's when my heart really hit the deck. Alison had been saying that she wasn't ready for sex. But she just didn't want it with *me*.

My humiliation was like a many-tentacled monster — squeezing me everywhere at once. I let out one more hot breath, then spun on my heel.

"I'm sorry, Rafe," she said as I wrenched open the door. "I'm so sorry."

I'll bet. Her door slammed behind me as I left. It slammed hard. Hard enough to wake the ghosts of students who had lived in Beaumont House when it was still new.

Chapter Two

TWO

BELLA

The new hockey coach had just blown the whistle, calling the third practice of the season to a close.

Now my boys were streaming back into the locker room, dropping helmets and gear all over the benches. With red faces and sweaty hair, they peeled off their layers, seconds away from heading for the showers.

I planted myself in the middle of the room, clipboard in hand. Putting two fingers in my mouth, I gave a whistle loud enough to echo off the tiles. That got their attention. "Guys, listen up! I need two minutes of your time!" It got quiet enough for me to speak normally. "First of all, unless your mother is dropping by later to clean up after you, used towels go into the hamper when you're through." I aimed this message at the freshmen. They always needed some schooling at the beginning of the year.

"Now," I continued, "I only got seventeen health forms back. That means seven of you need to get that sucker back to me, or you won't be allowed to suit up for next week's preseason scrimmage against those punks at Quinnipiac."

"Punks!" someone yelled, agreeing with me.

"Finally — I'm putting in our gear order *tomorrow morning*. So, if you have any equipment failures, I need to know ASAP."

Davies, a senior defenseman, turned his giant, naked body in my direction. He put a hand over his bare chest in mock surprise. "Who are you accusing of *equipment failures*, Bella? My fragile male ego can't take that kind of insinuation."

I gave him an eye roll. "Your equipment is top notch, Davies. But if you come to me next week needing a new stick, it will be you who's paying the extra coin for overnight shipping."

"My stick is in fine working order," he smirked.

"Nice. You can give me a demonstration sometime."

"Wait." He stuck a hand in the air. "Can you get some more of those extra-wide skate laces?"

"Not a problem," I said, making a note of it.

I scanned the room, looking for anyone else who might be trying to get my attention. My gaze came to rest on the freshmen whom I'd housed together at lockers in one corner of the room. One in particular was sneaking looks in my direction. "Guys, don't be afraid to ask for what you need, okay? Better to let me know before it's too late."

"Mouth guards?" asked the newb I'd caught watching me over his shoulder. His name was O'Hane, and he had a baby face and a sprinkling of freckles across his nose. He'd turned only his head in my direction, keeping his private parts facing the locker.

"We stock the basic ones in the supply closet, but if you want something special you have to tell me which model."

"Okay, thanks," he said. "And..." I waited for him to spit it out, but instead he turned toward his locker, grabbed a towel and wrapped it around his waist. Then he came over, arms crossed protectively. "Is there a sporting goods store nearby?"

"Well..." Harkness was not a big town, and the shopping options within walking distance were limited. "There's nowhere to buy gear, if that's what you mean. Not unless you have access to a car." And most of us didn't, because parking was scarce here, too. "Shoes and sweats are easy to find, though. What are you looking for?"

His cheeks pinked up. "Gear. Can I see the catalog?"

"Of course." I handed it over, tapping a toe while he flipped through the pages.

He stopped near the back of the book, a frown furrowing his youthful brow.

"Problem?" I asked.

Nervous eyes flickered up to mine. "I need," he dropped his voice so low I almost didn't hear the last part. "A cup."

"Oh, honey, that's easy." He might not know it, but dicks were one of my specialties. I took the catalog from his hands. "Which brand are you used to?"

His face reddened further. "Can't remember," he said, studying the floor. "I accidentally brought my, um, little brother's instead of mine."

Ah, freshmen. They weren't used to taking care of themselves. "The one you have doesn't fit? Your cup runneth over?"

He barked out a nervous laugh. "Yeah. But the ones in the catalog don't look the same."

"Eh. It's not rocket science. Are you wearing it in compression shorts or in a jock?"

"Shorts."

"Do you want your dangler to point down, or are you used to tucking it up at the top."

"Down," he said to the floor.

I cuffed his shoulder. "No problem, O'Hane. I've got you covered, so to speak. I'll order it for you."

"Thanks," he said in a strangled voice, then headed for the showers.

Our new coach was next to walk by. "Coach Canning!" I called, halting him.

"Yeah?" The new guy was a lot younger than our retired coach. He had a sort of grumpy edge to him that I did not appreciate.

Some people don't realize that gruffness wasn't necessary to earn respect.

I gave him a friendly smile nonetheless. "I'm putting in my equipment order first thing tomorrow. If you need to add anything, you can email me tonight."

"Thanks," he said, snapping his gum. "Hey, should you be in the locker room?"

"Um," I checked my watch. The barbecue didn't start for another half hour. And I wasn't in charge of the party. That was sissy work. "Is there somewhere else I'm supposed to be right now?"

He frowned. "No, I meant... the guys don't mind?"

That just made me stare at him. *Seriously?* "Coach Canning, the players are in the locker room. I can't get them what they need if I'm not here, too."

"Yeah. That's true," he said, an unreadable expression on his stupid, grumpy face.

"Don't forget," I said slowly, "female journalists have been permitted in locker rooms since before I was born. Including *this* locker room."

He stared me down for a long beat. And then he walked off without another word.

I stood there for a minute wondering what had just happened. As the student manager for our kick-ass men's hockey team, I solved the players' problems, and I moved people from point A to point B on schedule. I was good at it. Sure, it was a job that was *usually* held by a guy. But there was no reason it *had* to be a guy. All that was required was a good attitude and an all-consuming love of hockey. That was me. Surely Coach Canning would realize sooner or later that I *lived* for this job.

Anyway, it was time for the annual barbecue.

Though for the first time, I didn't quite feel the level of excitement that usually came with the rush of hockey season. These were my closest friends. In a few weeks' time, we'd spend every weekend traveling the Eastern Seaboard together, playing teams from Maine to Newark. I'd get to watch every game from the bench, which was just about the coolest thing in the world.

Even so, tonight I felt... down. Hopefully a beer and a pulled-pork sandwich could fix it.

~

A few hours later, I stood in our retired coach's backyard, still feeling strangely wistful. All the rituals of Coach's annual barbecue had held up tonight. Vast quantities of meat were eaten. Potato salad and coleslaw were consumed. Beers were drunk. This year there were *two* coaching speeches—one by our retiring Coach (in which he quoted several dead presidents,) and one by the new guy. And, as always, there were cupcakes for dessert, because Coach's wife liked them.

But I was still chased by an unexpected sadness.

In the first place, there was an undeniable hole in my heart where last year's seniors had been. I could hardly believe we were starting the season without Hartley and Groucho and Smitty. That just seemed wrong.

Not only did I miss them, but the progression was suddenly terrifying. Because this was *my* last year. How was that even possible?

I glanced around Coach's darkened yard with fresh eyes. A year from now, most of these players would be standing here again, celebrating the start of yet another season. But where would I be?

The truth was that I had no clue. None at all. Until now, I hadn't let it bother me. Four years had always seemed like a long time. So whenever my family prodded me with questions about my lack of plans after graduation, I'd found it easy to brush them off.

Rather than worry about the future, I'd immersed myself in a fun major (psychology) the best sport in the world (ice hockey) and my favorite people (hockey players). But now I felt as though an excellent book was coming to an end, and the slim stack of remaining pages in my right hand felt entirely insufficient.

With the party easing towards its conclusion, I wound up standing with the dates. There was Amy, our new captain Trevi's girlfriend, and also our goalie Orsen's date, whose name I had not caught.

"Who are you here with?" Orsen's new little friend asked me.

It wasn't the first time I'd gotten that question. I opened my mouth to explain that I wasn't with anyone, but catty Amy beat me to the punch. "She's here with *everyone*," she snickered.

Lovely. Amy was one of the girlfriends who'd never liked me. "I'm the team manager," I explained. I wouldn't dignify Amy's cattiness by getting irritated.

"Oh," the newcomer said. "That must be exciting."

"I hear that it is," Amy practically hissed.

I tried not to roll my eyes. A lot of the girlfriends didn't know what to do with me. They didn't like how often I saw their boyfriends naked. They didn't like wondering if I'd ever *been* naked with their boyfriends. The price of being me was that my reputation often preceded me. As a matter of fact I *had* hooked up with Trevi once, before he'd met Amy. But it was so long ago I didn't even remember the details.

The Amys of the world pissed me off sometimes. But tonight I kept my cool, because you can't let the mean girls win. "It's a great job. The bench is the best seat in the house for the games," I said. If anything *should* bother the girlfriends, it was my game-day privileges. Because hockey was awesome and they were missing out.

A few feet away, Trevi and Orsen were deep into an argument about the Bruins' prospects this year. "You can't say that there's a hole in their lineup," Orsen argued.

"You're right." Trevi chuckled. "It's more like a gaping void."

"Boys," I jumped in. "The gaping void is here." I held up my empty beer bottle. "Who wants another?"

"I'll get 'em," Orsen said. "Coach'll probably kick us out soon, anyway. It's almost ten." He strode off toward the beer table.

"What's shakin' Bella?" Trevi asked, draining his beer in preparation for the next round.

"The usual. Trying to get the freshmen settled in. Trying to pick a topic for my senior thesis. How about you? Is it true that the Blackhawks are taking a look at you?"

Trevi grinned. "They're lookin'. Doesn't mean they'll kneel down and pop the question."

"I've got a good feeling about it," I told him with a friendly squeeze of his arm. Amy's face contorted, as if she'd swallowed something bitter. But I was excited about his prospects whether she liked it or not. There were several scouts circling the team. My guys had made a lot of headlines last year, finishing the season in the number-two slot in the country. The NHL was definitely going to be snapping up some of them.

See? Everyone had a plan but me. Or, if not a plan, at least they had a dream.

"Hey guys!"

I turned my head to see one of my former dreams walking into Coach's yard. Michael Graham was the second guy I had ever really fallen for. And — because I had a perfect record for romantic disaster — the second one to break my heart.

"We missed you at practice today," Trevi said, speaking aloud what I had been thinking. "Don't know why you had to take up sports writing when I could use you on the blue line."

My favorite ex-defenseman just grinned. "I had a blast today."

"Doing what?" I stood on tiptoe to give him a kiss on the cheek, careful not to lean in too far. I didn't want to get trapped in a memory. The feel of his skin against mine was a craving I'd struggled to overcome.

He gave my back a friendly pat before continuing. "I spent four hours on the river with the crew team. I *thought* I was just there to watch, but one of the heavyweights had a knee that was bothering him. So the captain said, 'Dude, get in here. We'll show you what crew is all about.'" Chuckling, Graham grabbed his stomach. "Fuck. Rowing is hard. My abs will never be the same."

Not too long ago I would have offered to kiss it and make it better. Unfortunately, somebody else had that honor these days. I plastered a smile on my face. But my heart gave a little swerve, because the guy just looked so freaking *happy*.

Gone was the broody Graham I used to love. He'd been replaced by this lighthearted creature who was almost unrecognizable to me but for the familiar bulky muscles and his icy blue eyes. The Graham I'd known hadn't smiled at everything that moved. He was dark and a little jaded, like me. But these days he was practically *glowing*.

Was there *nobody* else in the world who was confused about life?

"How does your D-squad look this year?" Graham asked Trevi.

"Is this on the record?"

"No, asshole," Graham said with a chuckle. "Just some friendly conversation."

Trevi grinned. "They're young but scrappy. I like these freshmen. I really do."

We all turned to glance over at O'Hane and the other frosh, who had gathered near the beer table. "They have good foot speed," I remarked. "I especially liked that kid Hopper at practice today."

"Wait," came a new voice. "Who does Bella like? I need this intel for the season-opening bets." Big-D, a senior defenseman, lumbered up to our circle and put his hands on his hips. "There's a pool going on which freshman Bella goes home with first."

Trevi's girlfriend tittered, then slapped a palm over her mouth. *Lovely.*

Again, I kept my bravado, even though his comment grated on me. It was true that I'd had a lot of sex with hockey players. (One at a time, usually.) But the players weren't saints, either. And nobody was starting a betting pool about any of *them*.

Double standard, much?

I wasn't the only one who didn't like Big-D or his comments. Beside me, I sensed a spike in Graham's blood pressure. "You ass," he hissed. "Don't start that shit or I'll—"

"No you won't." I planted a hand on Graham's chest. "Let it go, man. Everybody knows that Big-D only talks smack about me because I won't take *him* home again. Once was plenty."

Big-D's mouth hardened, but I wasn't afraid of him. I let go of Graham and gave Big-D an evil grin. "You should know better than to offend the team manager. You might get the shittiest hotel rooms on every road trip from now until April. Your skate blades might not get sharpened, and your meal vouchers could get lost."

"I was just *teasing*, Bella." He gave me a self-conscious smile. "You wouldn't do that."

"Wouldn't I?" *Try me.*

"Tough crowd here for a Saturday." Big-D shook his enormous head, as if we were all just a little too touchy. Then he turned and ambled toward the house.

"I hate that fucking guy," Graham said after Big-D had gone.

"He's just really insecure," I said. It was true, too. Big-D wasn't a pretty boy like Graham, or witty, like Trevi. And he didn't have Orsen's natural warmth. He was harder to love, and he knew it. As a result, he lashed out, making himself into an even bigger ass.

Did I mention that I was a psych major?

The truth was that people were always going to talk smack about me because I didn't hide the fact that I'd had more than a few sexual partners. Girls who played the field got called names. I knew the drill.

Also, while we're being honest, I *had* been scoping out the rookies earlier, pondering the fresh offerings. Last year I went home with a freshman from this very event. Proximity to the hottest athletes at Harkness was an important perk of my job.

"What do you think of the football team this year?" Trevi

asked Graham, changing the subject. Because a good captain knows when to defuse.

Graham began to talk about quarterbacks. I wasn't much of a football fan myself. So I tuned him out, tipping my chin toward the sky to look for stars. Harkness was located in a rather industrial part of Connecticut, and usually there's too much light pollution to see them.

Not for the first time tonight, I felt my attitude sag. The temperature was dropping fast, hinting at winter's approach. The chill seeped into my core. I stepped closer to Graham, who draped an arm around my shoulder. I appreciated the gesture, but it didn't really solve the problem. The empty feeling I was working tonight was bigger than a friendly hug or the beers I'd drunk.

The caterers began to take down the beer table, signifying the end of the season-opening barbecue.

My *last* season-opening barbecue.

The year stretched before me felt like that giant hourglass in the Wizard of Oz, ticking down while Dorothy panics.

Behind me, a group of hockey players began to laugh hard over some joke I'd missed. Their jolly voices echoed into the night, making me feel more alone.

Chapter Three

THREE

RAFE

After my quick departure from Alison's room, I did not go home.

For a couple of hours, I walked aimlessly around campus. In an angry haze, I passed the rare books library, its peculiar stone walls rising like monoliths over my head. I passed the monument to students who had died in every war since the Revolution. I kept going, passing the graveyard and the hockey stadium.

My mind was a continuous loop of anger and confusion. Where had I gone wrong?

My phone rang in my jacket pocket. I almost didn't look. There was no way I could talk to Alison right now. But when I drew out the phone and answered, it was only the restaurant, wondering if I still needed my reservation. "I'm sorry," I told the maître d'. "Our plans have changed."

Had they ever.

The temperature dropped even further, and it became surprisingly bitter for a September evening. My hands were cold, I hadn't eaten supper and it was probably time to go home. Walking the streets wasn't answering any of my questions, anyway. I'd been a good guy, and a good boyfriend. My only sin was stupidity.

I stomped back to the Beaumont House gate, where I had to wind through a clot of students who were on their way out to some party or another. I would be alone tonight, having blown off all my soccer buddies to spend my birthday with Alison.

And for what?

Numb, I climbed another stone staircase toward my second-floor room. I unlocked our door, bracing myself to make some sort of explanation for tonight's disaster. "We broke up," was all I was willing to say about it.

Although the lights were burning, our common room was empty. My eyes swept around the room, taking in the signs. Both of Bickley's crystal goblets sat on our coffee table, dregs of dark red wine in their bottoms. I turned to eye our bedroom door. It was shut.

There was no flag on the doorknob, but Bickley was expecting me to be gone tonight. So I would have to proceed with caution.

I stood very still, listening. The faint strains of slow music could be heard, probably from the bedroom I shared with Bickley. Yet the other bedroom door — leading to Mat's tiny single — was also shut.

I shrugged off my jacket and dropped it on our posh leather sofa. While most common rooms were decorated in the style of Early American Squatter, ours was exquisite. It was all Bickley's doing. He was the son of an honest-to-God British peer, and the family had some serious coin. The furniture he'd bought for our dorm room had cost several times the value of everything in the tiny Manhattan apartment I shared with my mother.

Alone in this opulence, I perched on the edge of the leather seat, unsure how to occupy my time. What does a guy do on the night he finds out his so-called girlfriend gave it up for some rich dude in a tent in Ecuador? Watch a little TV? Play a few video games?

Ritual suicide?

From our bedroom came the sound of moaning. *Figures*. It was just the soundtrack I needed tonight. Where was the universal remote, anyway? I needed that sucker, stat. I felt around between the couch cushions, but couldn't find it.

Then, from Mat's bedroom, I heard grunting.

No freaking way. Both my roommates were getting it on? Was the universe trying to tell me I would *die* a virgin?

Frantic now, I got down on my hands and knees, peering under the couch, desperate for the remote. Bickley had set up his complicated video system in a way which required the remote and a NASA-style checklist of instructions he'd taped to the wood paneling on the wall.

Unfortunately, the sexual soundtrack continued in stereo behind me. My frustration rose a hundredfold, until my hands were shaking with irritation at every fricking thing in the world.

My foot connected with the stupid gift bag I'd been dragging around all night, almost toppling it. I gave up. Grabbing the bag, I stood and stomped out into the stairwell, letting the door close behind me. Not that I had any idea where I should go. I was pretty tired of walking around in the cold. So I sat right down on the stone staircase, like the loser that I was.

All I had going for me was a bottle of overpriced wine. I lifted that puppy out of the bag. Owing to my lengthy walk, the champagne was cold. Or at least cold*ish*. I probably should have just tossed the whole gift bag into the first trash can I'd found. But what a waste, right?

Welp. Time to get drunk on champagne. I trapped the bottle between my knees and tore the gold foil off the top.

A little gust of cool air traveled up the stairs. Someone had come in the entryway door below me. Slow footsteps began the upward trudge. Whoever it was would soon appear, probably wondering why I was sitting there twisting the wire thingy off a champagne bottle in the freaking stairwell.

See the World's Biggest Loser right here, ladies and gentlemen! Step right up!

I tossed the wire into the bag and put my hand over the cork. It wouldn't do to put my own eye out. This night was pretty tweaked already, but if I'd learned anything, it was that things could always get worse.

"Well *hello* there."

I looked up to see my favorite neighbor approaching me on the stairs. "Hey, Bella." It figured that the sexiest resident of Entryway F would be the one to witness my pathetic little scene in the stairwell. *Dios.* What's one more humiliation?

To be fair, Bella had always been kind to me. Even now, she gave me a bright-eyed smile. Instead of continuing her climb toward her room on the fourth and highest floor, she took a seat beside me on the stair, folding her hands. "Throwing yourself a private party?"

"Yeah. But if I can get this open, I'll share." I angled the bottle away from our faces, and slowly let up on the cork.

Nothing happened.

"Can I give you a hand?"

Yet another embarrassment. Clearly, the kind of guy who knew how to uncork champagne was not the kind of guy whose girlfriend would cheat on him.

Bella smiled at me, and that smile packed a punch. I'd always had a thing for Bella, not that I'd admit it out loud. I'd noticed her last year, when I was just a lowly freshman. There was something so *lively* about her. Bella had a perpetual sparkle in her eye, and color on her cheeks — the kind you get from laughing, not makeup.

She and I didn't get acquainted until move-in day this year, when I'd helped her carry a couple of boxes up the entryway stairs. She was a senior and had a fourth-floor single under the eaves of the building — a room with slanted ceilings and a window that looked like Hansel and Gretel might have peered out of it. "Great room," I'd said, setting the boxes down. I loved the heck out of the Harkness architecture, where no two rooms were the same.

Old things. I couldn't get enough of 'em.

"It's kind of a hike, though," Bella had panted while I'd tried not to notice her chest as it rose and fell beneath her Harkness Hockey T-shirt. Standing there in her room on Labor Day, I'd felt suddenly conscious of our proximity to one another. Some girls dressed to look sexy, with short skirts and tight-fitting tops. Bella managed to exude sex appeal wearing sporty clothes and no makeup.

She'd always turned my crank, even though I found her a little intimidating. Not only were we entryway buddies, she and I were taking the same Urban Studies course this semester. I noticed her more often than I cared to admit.

And now? We were going to drink together. I'd been planning to make my pity party a private one. But I could use a friend to distract me from my misery. If only I could get the bottle open.

Bella waited with a patient if slightly amused expression on her face. "Have you done this before?"

"Is it that obvious?"

"Can I give you a tip? Try twisting gently."

"Twisting?" The instructions I'd dug up on the internet this afternoon hadn't said anything about twisting.

"Trust me. I'm very good with my hands." She gave me a playful nudge with her elbow.

My neck heated, as it always did when Bella used innuendo. And she used plenty of them, so I really should get over myself already. But Bella was sexy in a way that always made me break out in a sweat. The way she looked at me made me overly conscious of my body, and all the ways it might be put to use.

Theoretically.

Moving on.

Hunkering down to the task at hand, I gave the cork a gentle twist the way she'd told me to. Under my palm, I felt it begin to give. Half a second later, a satisfying pop echoed through the entryway, and the cork flew into the air, ricocheting off an oak moulding before crashing back down onto the stairs.

Bella put both hands on her knees and laughed. "Not bad for a virgin."

Holy...! My heart skipped two or three beats. Was it *that* obvious? Was I marked in some way? Was I *GLOWING LIKE A BEACON?*

She got up to retrieve the cork, and then handed it to me. "Here you go. A memento to celebrate your first time."

Oh. I blew out a breath. She was only talking about the champagne bottle, *estupido.* My shoulders relaxed a fractional degree. "Here," I said, handing her the bottle. "You can have the first sip."

"What a gentleman." Bella took the bottle and tipped it carefully to her mouth. She took a sip, but then had to wipe her mouth quickly when the foam rushed over the bottle's lip. She laughed. "I'm fine with the whole down-and-out vibe we have going on here. But next time we're slumming it in the hallway, I'll bring bourbon." She passed me the bottle.

"Sounds like a plan," I said, taking a sip. Even though my heart was bitter, the wine was not. It was magnificent.

"Why are we out here, if you don't mind my asking?"

My chuckle was dry. "My room is a little crowded right now. Not the common room, but..." I just shook my head.

Bella giggled. "Really? Both your roommates are getting busy?"

"Yeah." I cleared my throat. "The hallway seemed like the place to sit until the walls stop shaking."

"I would probably have asked if I could join in." Her eyes twinkled at me. "But that's just me."

I managed to smile instead of swallowing my tongue. I'd been raised in a home where sex was just not talked about. It's not like I'd ever made a conscious choice to be a prude. I just didn't know how not to be one.

Bella stood. "Come on, then. You can tell me the rest of your sob story upstairs."

"What?"

She beckoned. "I have furniture. And also glasses." She hefted the champagne bottle and picked up my gift bag. "On your feet." Then, without waiting to see what I'd do, she turned and walked up the stairs.

FOUR

BELLA

For a second I wasn't sure if he was going to follow me. But after a moment of hesitation, I heard Rafe trudging up the stairs behind me. That was good, because I really did not want to be alone tonight, brooding over all my uncertainties.

The staircase wound up into the eaves of the old building, growing narrow at the top. Up here there were just two rooms — mine and another single, its door ajar. Strains of classical music could be heard from a stereo within.

"Evening, Lianne," I said in the direction of my neighbor's door. "I have a friend over in case you wanted to join us."

Silence.

I smiled to myself. I'd been deliberately vague about what it was Lianne might join us *for*. Generally I considered myself a nice person. But Lianne's distaste for my personal life had rubbed me the wrong way since move-in day.

My neighbor didn't approve of the frequency with which men turned up in my room. Her serious frown could often be seen through her open door as I passed by with one of the hockey players who sometimes shared my bed. Both our rooms opened onto a tiny, shared bathroom, and Lianne had once gotten an eyeful of a bare-assed guy in our shower. Her mouth had zipped into a straight, disapproving line.

Lianne thought I was a total slut.

For her part, Lianne seemed to live like a monk. Not only had I never seen her with a guy, she didn't seem to have friends at all.

"Goodnight," I called into the crack of her open door.

There was no response.

Whatevs.

Unlocking my door, I propped it open for Rafe. Then I dropped his shiny paper bag on my bed and fetched two dining hall glasses from my desk drawer. I poured the champagne slowly, tipping the glasses so that it wouldn't fizz up. Into my glass, I only poured a little, since I'd had a couple of beers already. His I filled to the top.

Rafe followed me into the room a moment later, shutting the door behind him. What a hottie he was, with big dark eyes set into a handsome face. Rafe was a soccer player, and he totally had that soccer look. He wasn't as bulky as the hockey players I usually hung around with, but he carried his muscular body in a way I found absolutely sexy.

Also? There was something to be said for guys who could run for two hours straight. Endurance was an excellent trait in a guy...

Rafe glanced around. "Your room is so cool. I love the slanting ceilings."

"Mmm," I said noncommittally. Those ceilings could dole out a vicious bump to the head — or to other body parts — if you weren't careful.

I handed a glass to Rafe, and then sat down on the bed, my back to the wall. "Sit already," I told him.

Rafe's eyes darted around the room for a second, and I saw him doing the math. Aside from the bed, my desk chair was the only other option. And it had about seven books stacked onto its seat.

"Right here," I told him, patting the space beside me. I

needed this tonight — a chance encounter with an obviously lonely guy. A distraction.

A hook-up, if I played my cards right. And I always played them right.

"I don't bite," I assured him. "But I do want you to tell me why you're all dressed up, carrying around a bottle of bubbly and..." I picked up the bag in my free hand and dumped it onto the bed. Two things slid out: a small box with a fancy ribbon around it and an unopened box of condoms. *Uh-oh.* "Huh. Looks like you had a big night planned. What happened?"

Sitting down beside me, Rafe groaned. "It's too embarrassing to talk about."

Aw. "I'm sorry. I'm quite familiar with humiliation, actually."

He glanced up quickly, surprise on his face. "Challenge."

"Seriously? My humiliations could arm-wrestle yours to the ground one-handed while singing Queen's 'We Will Rock You.'"

"No way." Rafe's sexy eyebrows lifted. "Of course, now I'm desperately curious."

"What do I win if I'm right?" I had a few excellent ideas, of course.

He touched his glass to mine and took a sip. "I'm sharing my champagne either way." He touched his glass to mine and took a sip. "Tell me your tale of woe."

"You first," I demanded, just to see what he'd do.

"*Dios.*" He rolled his shoulders and undid the top button of his dress shirt, exposing a V of bronzed skin. "You only get the short version. I was dating a girl since last spring. But she spent the summer at a program in South America."

"Wait!" I grabbed the bottle off my desk to top up his glass. "I remember her. That snooty blonde? Alison with one L."

His eyebrows shot up. "Yeah. That's the one."

"Go on."

He sighed. "She's back from the summer, right? I thought everything was good..."

I picked up the condoms off the bed. "They must have been good."

Rafe dropped his gaze. "Tonight we were having a birthday celebration."

"Whose?"

He lifted those espresso-colored eyes. "Both of ours, if you can believe it."

"Get out of town! You two have the same birthday?" This story kept getting better and better. And I hadn't even heard the punchline. "And happy birthday, Rafe."

"Thanks. But before you decide that she and I were meant to be, let me get to the part where her boy toy from the overseas program abroad shows up tonight with flowers at the same time I walk in."

Jesus. "Seriously? She's two-timing you?"

He nodded, miserable. "He's all, 'Hi baby! Surprise!' And I'm, like, 'Who are you? I'm the boyfriend.' And he says, not in so many words, that he's the fuck buddy."

"Oh, Rafe!" I grabbed his hand and squeezed. "You poor thing. What did you do?"

He just shook his head. "Got the hell out of there. Good riddance."

"Well..." I hated to see my hook-up prospect go up in smoke. But it was a rule of mine never to hook up with someone who was already involved. And maybe all was not lost with Rafe and his little preppy queen. "Maybe she thought you weren't supposed to be exclusive while she was away. Could it be a misunderstanding?"

Rafe's expression darkened. "Not a chance. Things were *very* clear that we were waiting for each other. And she let me believe that she had."

"What a bitch!" I said with a little too much glee.

"That's exactly right. I mean... she knew *exactly* what it would mean to me. She *knew*. And the guy she cheated with..." He gave his head a violent shake. "She could have slapped me in the face and it wouldn't have been any clearer."

"Why? Who was he?"

"Never met him before. But some rich dude in a fancy suit. Your basic nightmare."

I let out a hoot of laughter. "Rafe? Did you just quote *When Harry Met Sally* to me?"

His gaze slid into mine, and a slow smile began to overtake his face. "I might have. My mom really likes the chick flicks."

Aw. "And a good son watches them with his mother once in a while, right? Just to be nice. Not because they're funny as hell."

His smile grew, and I felt more than a flutter. Because that smile? It was blindingly hot. "That's right. Just doing my duty." We just sat there, taking each other in for a minute longer. And I couldn't help but fixate on his lips, which were a dark, rosy red. I wondered what they'd feel like sliding against mine.

That's how it always was with me. I loved men and their variety. The texture of their hair made me want to run my hands through it. Rafe's hair was coal black and shiny. I imagined it would feel soft as it slid through my fingers. And that muscular chest was calling to me. Last week I'd seen him out jogging shirtless, and he had a set of abs that was tight enough to bounce quarters off of.

Just thinking about it now made me wonder about the scent of his skin and whether those abs would clench when I touched him.

I liked men, and I liked sex. A lot. I gave Rafe's hand one more squeeze. "I'm sorry your girl was cheating."

"I am *such* an *idiota*."

"Betrayal always makes you feel like that." *And I should know.*

"This just pushes so many buttons for me, though. My mom, for one, will not be surprised."

"She didn't like Alison?"

Rafe grimaced. "They never met. But Alison comes from money. She was this fancy California girl, you know? I always thought it didn't matter to her, though. We hit it off right away last year. We had fun together. But she's sleeping with Mr. Rolex."

"And you," I pointed out. It seemed possible that Rafe was taking this whole social divide thing a little too far.

Rafe looked down at his hands. "Not today," he mumbled. "Though I guess it's better to find out first, I guess."

"Not hardly!" I yelped. "If you're going to have your heart broken, at least you could get sweaty first. Instead, you get betrayal with a side order of sexual frustration."

He sipped his wine, a stoic expression on his face. "Nobody ever died from sexual frustration."

I was pretty sure I'd come close a few times, but I kept that to myself. "There must be some way you could get revenge," I teased him. "Let's steal her phone, and break up with her fuck buddy via text message.

He chuckled. "You are evil."

"Only when it's deserved. And revenge is very cathartic." I mimed someone texting on a phone. "Sorry Mr. Rolex, but you're just not that good in bed. I'll call you if I'm feeling desperate."

Rafe shook his head. "At least I can return the earrings." He tossed the little jewelry box back into the gift bag. "Couldn't really afford them. But I wanted to get her something nice. I thought we were going to be together for a long time."

"And that is why I do not do relationships." *Because some nice person like you comes around to remind me why it's a bad idea.*

Rafe cocked his head to the side. "How's that working for you? I think it's your turn to tell me an embarrassing story. Because I'm pretty sure I'm winning this bet."

"Not hardly." The truth was that my humiliation could dance the cha-cha around his. But I'd already decided to keep the worst of it to myself. Instead, I was going to tell my *second* most humiliating tale.

"You don't have to tell me if you don't want to. But I'd never repeat it."

He wouldn't, either. Rafe had one of the more trustworthy faces I'd ever come across. There was something serious in his expression that I didn't often find in men our age.

With a fortifying gulp of champagne, I told him about the ugly morning I'd had last January. "I have a friend, but he and I used to be friends with benefits. We'd stopped fooling around a year earlier, though. His decision. And he never really said why..."

I got lost there for a second, picturing myself in Graham's room, removing his clothes. We were usually drunk and giddy. Getting Graham's jeans off his body when he was wasted wasn't easy. But I was happy to do it. Graham only liked to have sex when he was trashed. That should have been a clue. Maybe there were other clues, too. But I never saw them. I'd always had a blind spot when it came to Graham.

Rafe was waiting patiently for my story to continue. I'd *never* talked about this. Not with anyone. But there was something steady in his expression that made it possible for me to go on. "I was hung up on him," I admitted. I'd never said that out loud before, either. And it wasn't easy. College was too early, in my opinion, to get all swoony over a guy. That never worked out.

But still, I'd hoped.

"Even though we weren't fooling around anymore, I always thought that some day we'd get together and stay that way. Because he understood me in a way most people don't. We were such close friends, too. We told each other everything. At least that's what I *thought*."

I had to swallow hard then.

"You really don't have to tell me," Rafe said gently.

Christ. I obviously wasn't as good at putting a brave face on things as I imagined. I cleared my throat. "I walked in on him hooking up with somebody else."

"That sucks," Rafe said softly.

I held up a hand. "That's not the point. I never thought he was celibate after we stopped fucking. The problem was that I walked in on him with a *man*."

Rafe's eyebrows shot up. "Oh. That's not where I thought this story was going."

"Me neither." I gave a nervous laugh.

"Maybe it was just a one-time thing. Or maybe he's bi."

I shook my head. "It wasn't. And he isn't. He has a serious boyfriend now. They're ridiculously happy together. And when I saw them that morning..." I broke off, because it was impossible to express. I just *knew*. All of a sudden, I understood what I hadn't wanted to see before. For all the sloppy, drunk sex we'd had, it had never meant a thing to him.

That awful day last winter, it was stone sober wake-up-next-to-the-one-you-love-and-grab-each-other sex that I'd walked in on. And when I saw Graham kissing Rikker, there was more passion and tenderness on his face than I had *ever* seen there before.

People could say what they wanted about all the recreational sex I'd had. But I *knew* what love looked like. I'd probably stood there thirty seconds longer than necessary that morning, just trying to process my own disappointment.

I let out a big sigh. "I *never* made him as happy as he is now. Not even close."

"That sucks, Bella."

"It really did. But it was the lying that killed me. I thought we told each other everything," I said, hating how pathetic it sounded. It's hard to admit you're just in someone's periphery when you imagined you were closer to the center of their world.

"He should have leveled with you. But maybe he was afraid."

But not of me, I argued to myself. I liked to think of myself as bulletproof. Things that bothered other girls (like being called a slut behind my back) didn't bother me so much. Graham's heartbreak hadn't been so easy to brush away. He had never belonged to me. But it had been a shock to know he never would.

Also, I considered myself an excellent judge of character. But *twice* now I'd fallen in love with people who were incapable of loving me back.

Since then, I'd stuck to sex and kept my unreliable heart out of it.

Unzipping my hockey jacket, I shrugged it off. "To add insult to injury," I added, "I was in such a hurry to get out of there that I caught my jacket on the door handle." I showed Rafe the pocket. "And it tore. I still need to get it fixed."

Rafe took the jacket out of my hands and inspected the rip. "This isn't so bad. It just needs a few stitches. You should do it, though, before the edges get too frayed."

"True. I'll take it to that dry cleaner's on Chapel Street tomorrow."

"And let them charge you twenty bucks for a half-inch repair?" Rafe looked appalled. "Don't you have a sewing kit?"

I did, as a matter of fact. "Sewing on buttons is the most I can manage."

Rafe gave me an eye-roll, which most men can't really pull off. On his chiseled face it looked sexy. "Whip it out, then. I'll mend it."

"Seriously?" I slid off the bed and went over to my desk. In the very back of the drawer, behind the highlighters that I never seemed to use, I found my tiny sewing kit. "I bought this on the street corner in Chinatown just because I liked the little silk pouch. Not because I know how to sew."

He took it from my hand. "Where are you from?"

"New York City."

Rafe raised his eyes. "Me too. What part?"

"Guess."

He chuckled because I'd put him on the spot. New Yorkers were very opinionated about their neighborhoods. "Well, you don't dress prissy enough for me to guess the Upper East Side." He measured me with his eyes. "So... I'm going to go with the West '70s. How did I do?"

I gave him my biggest smile. "You're half right. Because I went to school on the West Side. But I grew up in a townhouse on East 78th and Madison."

"Wow." His smile was wan. "But where are your pearls?"

"Very funny."

"Your turn," he said, fiddling with the sewing stuff. "Where am I from?"

"Staten Island," I teased him.

"*What?*"

Now we were both laughing, because I'd just named the least fashionable corner of the five boroughs. And I was glad I had, because it meant I got to see even more of Rafe's hot smile.

"Just kidding, okay? How about Red Hook? That's my guess."

"You are not even close." He picked up a needle. "I'm from Washington Heights. My family runs a Dominican restaurant." He looked at the needle in his hand. "These are pre-threaded. That's handy."

"How is it that you know how to sew?"

Rafe shrugged. "My mother made me learn the basics when I was a little kid."

"Show me," I demanded.

His long fingers held up a needle with black thread dangling from it.

"Is that going to look okay against the gray?" I asked.

"Sure is," he said. He wrapped the free end of the thread around the tip of a finger, then rolled it against his thumb, revealing a knot on the end. He slid the jacket onto his lap, dipping the needle's tip into the pocket and anchoring the thread. "Okay, see that?"

I peered into the pocket. He'd tucked the knot into the crease where it was almost invisible. "Yeah?"

"If you make the stitches shallow, they won't even show on top."

That didn't mean a thing to me. But whatevs. Rafe bent over my jacket for, oh, about seventeen seconds before tying another knot and asking me for scissors.

"Aren't these scissors?" I asked, pulling a tiny pair from the sewing kit.

He grinned. "My pinky finger won't even fit into those. You'll have to do it."

He passed me the jacket, and I bent down to find the torn seam now lying flat against the fabric in almost the same way it had before it ripped. Rafe had zipped the tear shut as if by magic. I opened the pocket to find a pristine row of stitches almost too small to be seen with the naked eye. "Holy crap. How did you do that?"

"I'm good with my hands," Rafe said, a flare in his dark eyes.

The expression on his face made heat blossom in my belly. *Oh, baby*. I loved a boy who could turn my own jokes back on me. I wondered what he would do if I kissed him. My pulse kicked up a notch just thinking about it. "Thank you, Rafe. Really."

He shrugged, folding his arms over his chest. Even though he was wearing a dress shirt, I could see the outline of his biceps flaring against the fabric. "It's the only part of your shitty story that I can fix," he said in a low voice.

Oh, this guy! How any girl could cheat on him was beyond me. You had to wonder if the girl also kicked puppies just for fun. Without thinking it through, I lifted a hand to the muscle joining his neck to his shoulder, giving him a little squeeze.

Beside me, Rafe stopped breathing.

My fingers drifted upwards, past the collar of his dress shirt and onto his neck. He was warm and solid, and I didn't want to stop touching him.

Rafe turned his chin two or three tiny degrees in my direction, improving the contact with my hand.

I rose onto my knees, the jacket sliding onto the floor, forgotten. Rafe watched me, and the moment stretched out between us. I loved this part — the crackling tension when "will we or won't we" became the only question in the room. "Rafe," I whispered. "Maybe there's a part of *your* shitty day that I can fix."

He swallowed roughly, and his gaze dropped to my mouth, but he didn't make a move. Instead, time seemed to slow down, and I saw Rafe's awareness of me engulf him. His body went quiet, and his eyes darkened.

For several beats of my heart, I let him get used to the idea. When I slowly put my other hand on his chest, he made a small grunt of surprise. Still, he didn't move a muscle. He just watched me with hungry eyes.

"I've always thought you were sexy," I whispered, pressing my palm against his pec. "Seems like a good time to tell you." It was the God's honest truth. And the truth, I'd learned by now, was the sexiest thing ever.

He obviously agreed with me. Because that handsome face dipped closer. And then Rafe's surprisingly soft lips skimmed mine on a sigh. He stopped at the sensitive corner of my mouth, his lips making the gentlest nibble on mine, before he pressed, warm and firm, against my mouth.

My heart practically stopped at the way he'd silently asserted control. *Holy macaroni.* He didn't grab me or anything. He didn't need to. It was a subtle takeover. I received a slow, insistent kiss. And then another. His chest shifted ever so slightly toward mine until I could feel the heat pouring off his body, and I had no choice but to press my breasts against him as he deepened the kiss.

I heard a rather eager little moan. And realized it had come from me.

Two of Rafe's fingers cupped my jaw. His other hand whispered onto my waist with a pressure so light I almost didn't know it was there.

The man was barely touching me, and I was already feeling a little desperate for him. I parted my lips beneath his. And the first glide of his tongue over mine made me even achier with longing. He tasted like good wine and sex. My fingers gripped the cotton of his dress shirt. *Slow down,* I coached myself. But the intense vibe I was getting from Rafe made that difficult. We'd both had a bad day. It only made sense we'd both want to work that out with some energetic sex.

Who wouldn't?

Smiling against his mouth, I shifted onto his lap. As I relaxed my body onto his, he let loose a groan of longing.

I felt it *everywhere.*

"Bella," he rasped between kisses. "*Me matas.*" Anyone who grew up in New York could translate that. *You're killing me.*

Holy hell. I wanted him to whisper like that again. Maybe all night. My mind filled with erotic ideas. Rafe uttering Spanish curses into my ear while he pressed me up against the shower wall. Rafe's tan hands on my pale breasts...

Meanwhile, he kissed me senseless. You can learn a lot about someone by how they kiss. Rafe wasn't fast or sloppy. He was a very *focused* kisser. Each glide of his lips against mine was purposeful and so *potent*. It was wonderful, but it made me hungry for more.

Hoping to move things along, I began unbuttoning his shirt, revealing more smooth skin. Before I'd reached the bottom button I had to bend down and kiss his throat.

He tasted as good as he looked.

Rafe tipped his head back and sucked in a deep breath. Now I had him fighting for self-control, and it was beautiful to hear. Quickly, I divested him of the shirt so I could run my hands all over his tan six-pack. Muscular arms wrapped around me. His touch wasn't quite so polite now. He held me close, kissing me hard, taking greedy pulls from my mouth. His big hands slid down to my ass, and he pulled my body even nearer to his, until I was close enough to feel through his trousers just how well I'd revved him up.

It was absolutely glorious.

As we made out, his hands slipped up the back of my shirt, fingers splaying across my skin. That was nice, but I was not a patient girl. So I grabbed my shirt tugged it over my head. That seemed to break Rafe's reverie. He didn't dive back into the kiss once I'd disentangled myself. Instead, he took a moment just to look at me. His dark eyes measured my body with an intensity I wasn't used to. I might have wondered if he'd found some flaw, except that his hands continued to worship my skin, sliding around my ribcage, slipping up to cup my breasts, which were still trapped inside my bra.

"Take it off," I begged. "Actually, take *everything* off. And I want you naked, too."

His eyes widened. And for a moment I was sure I'd blown it. Too much, too soon. But then he took a deep breath. "Are you sure?" he asked, his voice rough.

"Do I look unsure?" I reached behind my back and unhooked my bra, tossing it to the floor.

He let out another groan. And then those gorgeous hands slid up my ribcage, cupping my boobs. And Rafe dove back into my mouth, his kisses deep and bossy.

Heaven.

Eventually, he tipped us both onto the bed, shoving one of his muscular legs between mine. Otherwise, he didn't escalate things. It was if he had all the time in the world to kiss me. He held me snug against him, the way you'd hold a treasure close to your chest. And his free hand made lazy circles on the small of my back, sometimes dipping down to cup my ass.

It was divine, but I wanted more. He still had too many clothes on. I wanted my hands on the impressive erection that had been teasing me through our clothing since the first moment I climbed into his lap. So I worked a hand down onto his fly and popped the button on the trousers he was wearing.

He broke our kiss to watch me while his breath sawed in and out of his chest. His gaze suggested that I was the most serious topic on earth, and he was going to study me and write a paper about me later.

Under that penetrating gaze, I worked his zipper down until the fabric of his dress pants gave way. I slipped a hand down his perfect abs and into his trousers. He gasped when I dipped my hand beneath the waistband of his boxer briefs, my hand grazing his cock. Then he yanked his clothes down off his hips to give me better access.

It's bad form to ever crack a smile during the Big Reveal, but I couldn't help but grin. "*Jesus*, Rafe. You're *gorgeous*. Where has this been all my life?" I love dicks and not just the big ones. His was truly exquisite — long and thick and uncut. A perfect bead of precum glistened in his slit. I bent my body at the waist so I could lick it off.

Rafe's stomach clenched violently when I touched him with my tongue, and he let loose a whispered litany of sexy Spanish cursing. "Mmm," I sighed, taking him into my mouth. I loved his taste and the heavy feel of him on my tongue. And the urgent noises he'd begun to make. Rafe was a sexy beast.

Two strong hands reached under my arms, and I was hauled upward for more demanding kisses. As he held my ass in his hands, I could feel him pressing between my legs. I flexed my hips, desperate for a little friction. He let out a groan and the sound of it ricocheted through my body, like a pinball, lighting up everything it touched.

"*Tan hermosa*," he whispered, breaking our kiss, dipping his head to reach my breast. He gentled his kiss, his tongue barely swirling around my nipple.

"More," I whispered, practically squirming against him. There was something about his restraint that made me want to crack through it. Fortunately, his fingers slid down into the waistband of my knit pants. That long hand ran slowly down to the edge of my tiny underwear, then stopped to tease my belly. *Noooooo! Keep going, hand!* I took his mouth in a kiss, hoping to encourage him.

His hand slipped downward again, his fingers finally sliding into the slippery desire that I'd accumulated just for him. *Yessss!*

And that's when I felt Rafe's restraint fall away. We moaned together, our tongues tangling. Everything was heat and motion. I kicked off my pants, and he helped. We pushed all the last bits of clothing off the bed.

Side by side now, he held me as if he were trying to eliminate any distance between our bodies. Shaking hands skimmed my waist, dipping low to tease my clit, then retreating again. Even now that he was hard and leaking for me, he still did not rush. This beautiful man was worshipping at the altar of me.

And his girlfriend cheated on him? She must be an imbecile.

FIVE

RAFE

When I was a kid, I could sometimes go swimming at the public pool on 173rd Street. Above the surface of the water, it was over-crowded, loud and crazy. But when I dipped my head underwater, the world hushed, and I was lost to pure sensation.

Losing myself with Bella was just like that. The world shrank down to the size of her mattress. As I caressed her, reality was muffled by her smooth, creamy skin and the sound of our breathing.

I knew that if I stopped to think about it — if I popped my head back above the surface — the real world still waited, loud and disapproving. But she and I were swimming alone together, hands stroking, tongues teasing. I did not want to come up for air. Ever.

At some point, Bella sat up. So I sat up, too. Then she handed me the box of condoms. Somehow, even though I was drunk with lust, I managed to tear it open. They came out in a string — the way the bodega on our corner used to have a chain of red lollipops hanging over the cash register, and the cashier would tear the next packet off if you wanted to buy one. I tore off a condom and let the others slide to the floor.

I handled the packet carefully, not wanting to tear the latex inside. But the packet did not open on the first try.

"Let me," Bella whispered. The feel of her hand stroking my dick practically erased my ability to respond, let alone hear.

I handed the condom over to her, too turned on to care that I wasn't man enough to get the job done. I flashed back to the whole champagne-bottle incident. An hour ago, I'd had no idea where this night would lead me.

Still didn't.

It seemed impossible to believe that sexy Bella and I were naked together right now. That she was kneeling beside me, one hand on my hip, the other one fitting a condom over my *pene*.

"Is this your usual brand?" she asked softly, using two hands to roll it down. "It's kind of tight. Seriously, you should buy the next size up. And I'm not just saying that."

I didn't answer, because I didn't want to admit that there *was* no "usual brand" for me. There was nothing at all *usual* about this moment. I didn't even want to think about why.

With a tug on her hands, I pulled Bella onto my lap and kissed her again. As long as I had my mouth on hers, I didn't have to think. More sensation, *por favor*. More action, less talking.

And no thinking. Maybe not ever.

Bella straddled me willingly. So willingly. She curled one of her pretty hands around my waist and let me plunder her mouth again. *Cristo*. The way she touched me was incredible. I'd never felt my own desire mirrored back to me like this. With Alison, I'd always been *coaxing* her. But Bella arched into me. When I touched her, she pressed closer. When I groaned, she joined the chorus.

This. This is how it was supposed to be. Bella's enthusiasm had obliterated all of my caution. She wanted me. And I could no longer think of any reason why I couldn't have this.

Our kisses were bottomless. I leaned back against the wall

behind me, the sound of my heartbeat throbbing in my ears. Bella reached down between our bodies, wrapping her hand around me again. This time, the condom prevented me from feeling very much. That was probably a good thing. When she'd stuck her hand down my pants earlier, I nearly came like a fountain.

"I like you right here," she whispered.

I only groaned. I liked her anywhere at all. As long as she didn't stop kissing me.

She reached over to grab a pillow, and I had to lean forward so she could jam it behind my back.

Then she put her hands on my shoulders.

Then she rose up on her knees.

Then? She lowered herself down on my aching dick.

Caliente, I thought immediately. It was so warm inside her. I let out the breath that I didn't even know I was holding.

"That's more like it," Bella whispered, pushing her hips forward. Her cheeks were pink, I noticed. And those beautiful rosy nipples were right there in front of me, shamelessly asking for my attention. I took both breasts in my hands and circled the nipples with my thumbs. "Yesss..." she hissed, moving her body against me.

I had never seen anything so erotic. All my senses stood at attention as that beautiful girl began to ride me. I felt the tickle of her hair on my shoulders. And the brush of her smooth belly against my abs. The only thing keeping me in check at all was the condom's tight grip.

Bella was exquisite, and I couldn't quite decide whether to watch her or kiss her. So I did both as well as I could. Her gaze began to go soft and unfocused. She moaned into my mouth. And her hips flexed faster than they had before.

Dios.

I couldn't hold still any longer. My hips jacked off the bed to match her rhythm. And time slowed to a crawl as Bella's breath stuttered. "Oh, fuck," she panted. Then she slammed her mouth down on mine and moaned.

The sound of her climax was so fucking beautiful. It had been a long time since I made a girl come. I'd forgotten how that felt — to make someone whimper as if she were helpless and I was the only one who could save her. Only this was so much better than any of the furtive make-out sessions I'd had in high school. Bella was soft and draped all over my naked body, her back heaving, her *tatas* rubbing against my sensitive skin.

She dropped her face into my neck. "*Whew*. Sorry."

"No," I whispered, cupping the back of her neck. "That was magic."

"You're going to have to take the wheel." She lifted her face and kissed me once. "But God, don't stop."

"Are you sure?"

Her eyes widened. "Rafe, we're just getting warmed up here." She climbed off me, and I missed her immediately. Bella stretched out on the bed beside me and tugged on my arm. "Get your giant dick over here."

As I rolled to brace myself over her waiting body, all my restraint fled under Bella's door and down the old stairwell. There was something primal about that position — pressing down into her curves — that reached the core of me. "*Jesus Dios*," I whispered, my hips already twitching with anticipation.

"Do it," she begged.

So I did.

Hours ago, I'd been worried about my inexperience. What an *idiota* I'd been. There was nothing more natural than this. Sliding inside Bella felt like something I'd been born to do. My hips set a rhythm that was a lot like the pounding of my heart. "*Tan buena*," I panted. "*Belleza*." *So good. Beautiful.*

Bella lifted her knees, gripping my body with her legs. "Give me that mouth, hottie."

When I dropped my head, our kisses were wild, tangled things. I moaned into her mouth, and she dragged her fingernails down my back.

I have no idea how much time passed. A minute? A half hour?

There was only the feeling of her skin against mine and the ridiculously sexy noises she made while I fucked her. She gripped me with her knees, and then began to moan my *name*.

All of a sudden, everything began to feel just too good. So fucking good. I was *drowning* in lust. Someone was groaning like crazy, and I'm pretty sure it was me. Bella seemed to like that. A lot. She arched her back and gasped. I felt her body pulse around me, and then it was all over for me. I drove my head down into the pillow to muffle the shout I made when I erupted.

"Jesus," Bella panted as silence descended. The only sound was our ragged breathing. It was all I could do to take enough oxygen into my lungs. Her hands skimmed down my sweaty sides, and then she rubbed circles around my hips. "Mmm," she said.

I agreed, but was still unable to say so.

We lay there while my heart rate tried to decide whether or not it would ever slow down again. My thoughts were a swirl of delight and satisfaction and not much else.

"Rafe, you're going to have to pull your sexy self out eventually." Bella gave my ass a playful slap.

That woke me from my stupor fast. It figured my inexperience would crop up somewhere. "Sorry," I choked out, embarrassed now. I began to lift myself off her.

Wait. I couldn't mess up this part. I reached down to secure the top of the condom, just like they told us to in health class. Self-conscious now, I planted a foot on the floor and practically ran to the door of what had to be her bathroom. I opened it, finding a tiny little room tiled in black and white, with a slanted ceiling.

Feeling almost lightheaded, I stumbled over to the wastepaper basket. When I looked down to unroll the condom, my heart practically stopped.

The bottom of it was split open.

For a long moment I stared, just hoping I was wrong. But that flap of latex and my exposed skin stared right back up at me.

I put a hand onto the wall to steady myself. "Bella," I ground out. *Jesus Dios*, I didn't want to say this.

"Yeah," came her breathy murmur.

I'm going to ruin everything now. "The condom broke."

Saying it aloud shook me up even more. I shucked off the useless thing and threw it away.

"Ahem," came another female voice. I whipped my head around. "The whole neighborhood can hear you."

The other voice had come from behind a little wooden door on the opposite wall of the bathroom.

Madre de Dios. I stumbled out of the bathroom and closed the door behind me.

Bella had gotten under the covers, where she now lazed, her head on one curled arm. The lazy expression on her face did not match mine. Why was she not freaking out? "Rafe, relax. It's okay."

"How is it okay?" There was *nothing* about this that was okay.

"Come here." Bella pulled the covers back and beckoned to me. Reluctantly I got into bed beside her. She put a hand on my nervous chest. "I have an IUD. That's a device that protects against pregnancy, and it's more effective than any condom or any pill. So as long as you're clean..."

"Of *course* I'm clean," I sputtered.

"Of course you are," Bella said softly, patting my chest. "I'm just saying. You don't have to worry. I'm as careful as they come."

I put a hand over my eyes, still mortified. A few hours ago, I was an upstanding guy who was taking his girlfriend out for her birthday. And now? I was some asshole who'd had a one-night stand.

And *the condom broke*. I thought I might throw up.

"Please don't freak out." Gently, Bella removed the hand from my eyes. "Because what we just did? That was ten different kinds of hot."

She smiled at me then, and it was hard not to feel just a little calmer. A guy could get pretty lost in that smile if he wasn't careful. "Yeah," I whispered back to her. "Okay." I still felt a little lightheaded. The fact that I'd had no dinner and more than half a bottle of wine probably explained it.

Bella propped herself up on one elbow to reach the lamp. She clicked it off and her room dropped into darkness. "Don't go anywhere," she said, getting comfortable on her pillow. "Because we might have to do that again in the morning. I need to know whether that much hot can be duplicated. For science."

"For science," I repeated in the dark, my head woozy.

I felt her lean in close, and she kissed me on the shoulder. Then she lifted one smooth knee up, dropping it down over my outstretched leg. A few minutes after that, I heard her breathing lengthen into sleep.

That's when I really began to feel alone.

In the pitch dark of Bella's room, I no longer had her smiling eyes to tell me everything was all right. The sleeping girl beside me became a stranger again.

The stillness pressed in on me, and tonight's events began to play back in my mind. And what I saw there made me feel pretty damned *loco*. My plan had been to make love to my girlfriend of many months — a girl I thought I knew.

I'd thought wrong. So wrong.

And before the day was even over, I'd stripped off my clothes for sex with Bella, who I barely knew. It had been amazing, of course. I enjoyed every minute of it.

But what if the night had happened differently? If I'd gotten naked with Alison instead, and the condom broke? What then? A hasty trip to the health center, to get that pill you can take if you're quick enough. The one that doesn't always work.

Jesucristo.

There was a reason I hadn't slept around like a lot of other guys. There were several reasons, but guilt was the main one. If my mother had any idea what I'd done tonight, she would lose her mind. Pregnant at nineteen, Ma's life had never been the same.

After my father disappeared, Ma waited two years to find out what happened to him, saving up to hire a private investigator. The P.I. found my father within the month. He lives in Mexico City now, where he has another family.

We never even got a note.

"Not everyone is as selfish as your father," Ma always said. "But I don't want you putting yourself in the position of having to do the right thing. And you can't put a teenage girl in the position of having to *figure out* what the right thing is. Don't do it at all until you're ready to become somebody's father."

My mother doesn't mince words.

I never planned to take her advice literally. But her story weighed on me. It made me respectful of my high school girl-friends, who liked to make out but rarely let me touch them. And it made me feel guilty for wanting sex from Alison, who did not want to have sex. (With me.)

And now? It made me feel like a tool for sleeping with Bella.

Beside me, Bella breathed deeply, sleeping the sleep of the shameless. I envied her that. My churning thoughts kept me awake until, eventually, even those wore me out.

And I slept.

Chapter Six

SIX

RAFE

At eight in the morning, I rolled over. Or rather, I tried to. My eyes snapped open at the shock of finding another body in the bed. I came to wakefulness against Bella, her bare ass snugged against my thighs. And since it was morning — and I was a guy — my morning wood was basically stabbing her in the back.

Holy...

Holding my breath, I eased away from her body. Bella sighed, but did not wake up. Inch by quiet inch, I extracted myself from the bed, carefully drawing the covers up over her as far as I dared. Her creamy breast lay there exposed, the nipple rosy in the morning light. I averted my eyes, feeling like a creeper for admiring her body.

I realized I was *still* holding my breath. Because it's not every day you wake up naked with your neighbor after losing your virginity in a one-night stand. I exhaled as quietly as possible.

It was time to get the hell out of there.

I put my clothes on as fast as near silence would allow. Picking up my shoes and the stupid gift bag with Alison's earrings inside, I tiptoed to the door, opening it like a thief in the night.

I didn't breathe until the door was closed behind me. Setting my shoes down, I jammed my feet inside.

It was almost a clean getaway.

Abruptly, the neighboring door swung open to reveal a young woman in gym clothes. We were both caught off guard, startling each other right there on the tiny landing.

My surprise only grew when I realized who I was looking at. Lianne Chalice was only the most famous member of the freshman class — and an actual movie star. She'd played Princess Vindi in the film adaptations of all the *Sorceress* books. (My high school girlfriends had dragged me to every one of them. So I'd watched Lianne Chalice duel many a Hollywood actor.) I'd read in the *New York Times* that she was a freshman here this year, but I'd never run into her before. And certainly not in my own stairwell.

"You're staring," she hissed.

"Sorry," I whispered automatically.

She gave me the most dismissive look I have ever seen on a girl in my life, and then stepped around me, heading down the stairs.

My heart thumping with embarrassment, I finished shoving my shoes onto my feet, and then quietly followed her down the stairs. I was only on the third step or so when I realized that the star of several major motion pictures had been the one to hear me announce that the condom broke.

Shoot me.

At least the walk of shame was only two flights of stairs. I took a moment in our hallway bathroom. When I washed my hands, I caught my reflection in the mirror. I don't know what I was expecting, but the face I saw there was the same one I'd seen yesterday. The non-virgin Rafe looked the same as the other one. Only slightly less happy.

Looking myself square in the eyes, I mouthed the word I was thinking. "*Idiota.*"

It was one thing to get taken in by Alison's deception. That had been dumb enough. But then I'd gone and compounded it by sleeping with Bella. I'd practically *inflicted* myself on that girl. It didn't excuse a thing that she'd wanted me, too. I knew better than to take that risk.

Yesterday morning? I was a stand-up guy, trying to do right by his girlfriend. Twenty-four hours later I was just some jerk who'd taken off his clothes for the first person who smiled at him. I let out a long, shaky sigh and tried to compose myself.

Leaving the bathroom, I braced myself for questions from Bickley. He was probably sitting around in the common room, wondering whether or not to go running without me.

When I opened the door to our suite I found Mat instead of Bickley. He was perched on our window seat, smoking a cigarette. At eight in the morning. His eyes flicked toward mine before dropping again. I shut the door, waving my hand in front of my face. The room already smelled of smoke. *Dios.* "Could you at least open the window?"

"Don't ride me, bitch."

"Nice," I grunted, taking two steps forward and face-planting onto the sofa. Everything was just so wrong. My head was pounding, and my mouth was dry. I had an empty feeling in my gut. Lying there, I sucked down a lung full of cigarette smoke along with my own shame.

At least I didn't have to explain myself. Mat was too prickly to bother asking personal questions. Bickley and I hadn't met him until move-in day. With his big frame and excessive tattoos, Mat resembled a TV commando. The first day we'd walked into our assigned room, Bickley and I had found Mat sitting on a camo duffel bag that looked far too authentic to come from a store. When we greeted him, he'd barely looked up from the course schedule in his hands. And were those dog tags around his neck?

Yes, they were. Mat was a naval vet, and although he was a sophomore like Bickley and I, he was three years older.

We'd gotten off on the wrong foot because Bickley started in right away, trying to gain advantage. "So, we've got a single and a double," my roommate had begun.

"The single is mine," Mat said without a glance. "Says so right on the room assignment."

He wasn't wrong. The sheet we'd gotten in the mail had read: *Room A: Mat Douglas. Room B: Rafael Santiago, William Gilchrist Bickley.*

"We should trade off," Bickley had argued. "Everyone will receive one *third* of the year in the single. That's how my brother and his mates did it when they were here."

"That's not going to work," Mat had said.

"Why not?" Bickley had pressed. "You'd have the single for three months. Then I'd have a turn. And then Rafe."

Mat shook his head. "In the first place, I just spent three years on a submarine sharing a room that size with five other guys. So I'm due for some space. But trust me. You don't want me as a roommate during those three months when it would have been your man Rafe's turn."

"Says who?"

A smirk crept across Mat's angular face. "My boyfriend is stationed in Groton, about an hour away. He visits. We get naked. I'm just assuming you don't want to watch."

Bickley maintained a half-decent poker face, but he paled beneath his freckles. "So you're..."

"I'm what?" Mat grinned, enjoying the discomfort he'd created. "Never mind. I'll say it for you. I like dick. I'm a butt pirate. In the navy, they called me the Rear Admiral."

At that, I'd thrown back my head and laughed.

"You think I'm kidding?"

"Not at all. I just never heard that nickname before."

"You got a problem with it?"

"*Dios.*" I shook my head. "I'm from New York City. We don't have a problem with much. Except rats and tourists."

Mat's eyes crinkled for a second, the first sliver of actual humor he'd shown.

But Bickley had been stony. "If you wanted to keep the single without a fuss, that would be a pretty good way to play us."

Mat's jaw hardened. "I don't have to *play* you, asshole. The single is mine already. I figure they gave it to me because I'm three years older than y'all. Nice try, though." He picked up his duffel and disappeared into the single.

"Do you *believe* that guy?" Bickley had muttered.

And so it began. He and Mat had been at each other's throats ever since. I tried to stay out of it, but the jousting never stopped.

"You can tell Bickley it's safe to come home now," Mat said eventually. "He won't walk in on any queer action."

"You flatter yourself," I replied from the couch cushions. "When I came home last night, you were both here. And both getting action."

From the window seat Mat gave a bitter laugh. "Seriously? I didn't hear him."

"I heard the both of you."

Mat snorted. "Bickley was out on the prowl last night, too? That's something I don't need to see. 'Hey baby, come for a ride in my Mercedes.'"

"For once would you just shut it?" I snapped. "And open the fucking window."

I rarely told Mat where to get off, so apparently it made an impression. The next sound I heard was the creak of the window opening. "What crawled up your ass and died?" he asked.

I sighed into the leather of the sofa. "I got dumped last night."

Mat actually *laughed*.

Pissed now, my head shot up off the couch, which unfortunately made the room spin. Ouch. "That's funny to you?"

His lip curled. "It is, actually. Because I got dumped last night, too."

I gave my head a shake. "No lie?"

He shook his head slowly. "I only wish I was lying."

That explained the bags under his eyes and the early morning cigarette. "Sorry."

"Yeah. So am I."

Who knew I'd have something in common with my orneriest roommate? "I don't know about you, but I didn't see it coming."

Mat flicked the ash from his cigarette out the window. "Can't say that I did, either."

"I thought we were doing pretty good. But she cheated on me with some rich guy she met in Ecuador."

"Yeah? Well he cheated on me with a *woman*." He pronounced the word the way some people would say "cockroach."

I pushed my face into Bickley's designer throw pillow. It was a relief to think about someone else's problems for a minute. "I'll bet it won't last, though," I said, my words muffled by cashmere and down feathers.

"Why do you say that?"

"I dunno. Being a gay dude in the military sounds like a whole lot of trouble, no? Why do that if you're not sure?" I was talking out of my ass. "But what the hell do I know?"

Mat heaved a sigh. "Good point. Twenty-four hours ago, I would have agreed with you. But he said he wants kids and all that shit. The picket fence. The dog."

Dios. "I want that stuff, too. And so does Alison. It's just that she wants it with some dick who wears a Rolex."

Mat gave me another grunt. I'm pretty sure it was supposed to sound empathetic.

"At least I didn't spend two hundred bucks on dinner," I added. "The night blew up about two minutes after I walked out of here."

Mat said nothing. With him, that counted as a reply.

"Are you pissed at Devon?" I asked.

"I *wish* I was angry," Mat admitted. "I'm only depressed."

"Yeah? Well I'm both depressed and pissed." I was so tweaked by the whole thing that I'd gone and done something *colossally* stupid. Ugh. I felt ill again just thinking about it.

And then the freaking condom broke — a memory that beat like a drum beat in my aching brain. But that's what you get when you think with your *pito*.

"I *should* be pissed," Mat said. "Pissed would feel better than this. I thought we were *happy*." He put his head in his hands, and for the first time all year I felt sorry for the guy.

"I thought we were happy, too," I commiserated. But even as I said it, I thought about all the times Alison had pushed me away. I should have been paying better attention.

"Maybe it wasn't meant to be." Mat chuckled darkly. "Christ. Listen to me. I'm a fucking greeting card. At least I got laid before I got dumped."

That wasn't a subject I wished to talk about, so I was quiet.

A knock at the door interrupted our silence.

As if by some prior arrangement, Mat and I were both stealthily silent, meeting each other's eyes.

The knock repeated, but neither of us spoke up. There was nobody I wanted to see right now. No one at all.

"Rafe? You must be in there. Open up." It was Alison's voice.

Mat's eyebrows lifted, and I shook my head. Mat lifted a thumb toward his bedroom. Silently, I tiptoed past him and into the little single. Once I'd cleared the doorway, I was hidden from view.

I heard Mat go to the door and answer it. "He's not home," he said.

"Oh," Alison said softly. "Can you give this to him? I want him to have it. In fact, even if he tries to give it back, I won't take it."

"Uh, okay. I'll tell him."

"Thank you," she said, her voice dropping.

I started back into the common room after the outer door closed, only to leap back again when it reopened. This time, it was Bickley at the door. I heard him utter a cheerful greeting to the departing Alison before the door finally closed once again.

"It's safe now," Mat said. "Come and open your present."

"Why is Rafe hiding in your bedroom?" Bickley asked as I emerged.

Mat held up a little gift bag. "The birthday boy does not want to see the girl who dumped him last night."

"Come again?" There was shock on Bickley's face. "Alison cut you loose?"

"Pretty much," I said, not wanting to go into details.

"For the love of God, tell me that you're not still a virgin."

"*What?*" Mat yelped. "He's twenty years old, for fuck's sake. He's *not* a virgin."

I felt a wave of nausea. They were both staring at me.

"Well? Are you or aren't you?" Mat demanded.

"No," I said slowly. "Not that it's any of your business."

Bickley held up two slim hands. "Step back a moment. Something does not add up. Alison let you shag her before she dumped you?"

I shook my head while Bickley did the math. I could practically hear his gears turning. "So... Alison dumped you. And then you had sex with someone *else?*"

Hearing it out loud only made me feel worse. *Yes, that's exactly what a cheap asshole I've been.* Instead of answering, I hung my head.

"Blow me down!" Bickley gasped. "Who?"

I gave my head one more shake. I'd said too much already. And poor Bella. What sort of asshole has a one-night stand, and then tells his roommate ten seconds later?

"Come on." Bickley dropped his coat onto the couch and perched on the armrest. "This is a big development. Uncle Bickley is going to need the details."

Bickley had never heard the term "none of your business." Part of the reason we were roommates was that nobody else on the soccer team could tolerate him.

"Out with it," my stubborn roommate prodded.

"It's private," I muttered, the ache in my temples kicking up a notch.

"That's too good to be private," Bickley argued.

Mat spoke up, baiting Bickley like he always did. "You want to hear about your roommate fucking somebody? Why do you want those details, dude? Maybe you have a boner for Rafe? If you want a little man-on-man action, you can always come to me."

"Fuck you, Mat."

"I was thinking I'd rather fuck you." Mat smirked.

Bickley turned sharply toward our bedroom, stomped inside and slammed the door.

Another soothing day at home. "Why do you do that to him?"

"I got him off your back, didn't I?" Mat's grin was evil. "Besides, he makes it so easy for me."

"Isn't that the definition of a bully?"

He shrugged. "If I held his face in toilet water while I said it, then yeah." He gave me a concerned frown. "You know, man. If you need to get laid again, I'm single now. You don't have to hit the bars. I'm here for you."

I punched him in the shoulder.

"Ow!" He whimpered with such girlish exaggeration that I couldn't help but laugh. Then he grabbed my soccer ball off the floor. "If sex is off the table, let's kick this thing around the court-yard for twenty minutes until brunch opens."

The offer caught me off guard. Mat rarely invited me to do anything except bet on football games. But what better offer did I have? "Sounds like a plan. Just let me change my clothes."

That afternoon, I retreated to my bedroom to sulk. In the bag that Alison had given me, I found a brand new iPod.

Dear Rafe, the note read. *I don't expect you to understand. But I never meant to hurt you. This gift was meant to make it easier for us to communicate. And isn't that ironic? I did a terrible thing, and I'm so sorry. More sorry than you'll ever know. Love you always, Alison.*

I snorted. There was so much wrong with this note it was hard to tally it all up. Alison loved me enough to buy me a fancy toy. And yet she was sleeping with another guy.

Her choice of a gift was another red flag. Alison had always found it weird that I didn't have a texting plan for my cheap-ass phone. "It would be so much easier if I could text you," she'd said more than once. In the first place, I didn't text because I'd rather speak in person, or at least hear her voice on the phone. I'd said that. Many times. I hated that everyone on campus was always bent over, tapping on apps with their thumbs instead of watching where they were walking.

I liked my gadgets vintage. I carried a pocket watch from the forties, for God's sake. My cufflinks were made from old subway tokens.

Alison had obviously not paid attention. Which only served to remind me that I hadn't, either. I only saw the bits of her that fit the image I liked best.

How utterly depressing.

Still, playing with the first iPod I'd ever owned was fun, for about a half hour. It occurred to me that I would like to listen to music on my longer runs. And fiddling with the music library made for a good distraction for my misery, at least until I realized how tricky it was going to be to rip all my CDs on my laptop.

Yay, technology. It saves you time, except when it doesn't.

Bickley wandered in after a while. "How's the iPod?"

"It's apptastic. Hey, where'd you get that arm-band thing that holds your phone when you run?"

Bickley shrugged. "At the bookstore, I think? For twenty quid or so."

Ouch. Maybe I could find one cheaper in the city.

"So who was she, anyway?"

"Not talking about it." I kept my eyes on the little screen.

"Well, are you going to see the mystery woman again?"

That was the real question, wasn't it? But I had a feeling it wasn't up to me. "To be honest, I don't know what to expect." Bella was something of a mystery. I knew she worked with the hockey team as a manager, hence the team jacket. And I knew many of the players were her friends.

I'd once heard a guy say that sleeping with her was part of being initiated onto the team. But that was just jocktarded smack talk, probably started by someone who *couldn't* catch her eye.

"But do you like her?" Bickley pried. He was desperate to trick me into saying who it was. But it wasn't going to work.

"Of course I do," I admitted. Bella was the best kind of girl. Smart, sexy and fun. But spending more time with her was a terrible idea. Because I did not trust myself with her. *Dios.* I'd been like the Incredible Hulk videos I used to watch as a kid. With very little provocation I'd come busting out of all my clothes and *unleashed* myself on that girl.

My neck got hot just thinking about it.

"Are you going to call her?" Bickley pressed.

"Yeah." Of course I would do that. We were neighbors, after all. I couldn't just duck her for the next eight months, even if I wanted to. But I didn't want to duck her at all. So after I calmed down a little, the best plan of action would be to knock on her door and at least say...

I had no idea what.

～

I didn't see Bella on Monday. But on Tuesdays we shared a class. Intro to Urban Studies had about sixty people in it, though, and was held in a lecture hall. The spot was not exactly conducive to a private discussion.

To make matters worse, Alison took that course, too. So now Urban Studies was fast becoming Awkward Studies.

Bella ran in at the last minute, parking herself in a seat by the door. Her cheeks were flushed, as if she'd been hurrying.

My traitorous body heated immediately. Just one look at her and I was transported back to Saturday night. Bella reached into her backpack on the floor for a pen, and the graceful line of her neck made me remember how I'd kissed every inch of that creamy skin.

Looking up then, Bella caught me watching her. And whatever she saw on my face made her frown.

Dios. I snapped my gaze away, staring down at the notebook on my desktop. What an ass I was. I felt guilty about what I'd done with Bella. But here I sat practically frothing at the mouth.

Not cool.

When the professor began speaking, I did my best to listen. I loved this class, actually. The prof was a long-time New York City planner, and often the examples he gave in his lectures were places I knew. Greenwich Village. Lincoln Center. Central Park. I'd passed those spots my whole life without knowing much about how they'd come to be. Professor Giulios knew, though. Soaking up his stories and theories was effortless for me. In this class I felt at least as well equipped to learn the material as anyone else in the room.

That was rare for me at Harkness. I'd gone to a decent New York City public high school. But it wasn't even forty-eight hours into my first semester as a freshman when I'd realized how outclassed I was. My freshman roommate went to Andover where he'd played first violin in the orchestra. The guy across the hall had gone to Exeter, where he'd built rockets in a physics lab and memorized two thousand Chinese characters.

This year, I roomed with Bickley, who had attended Eton, a school I'd only heard about in old books. Even Mat seemed to have gotten a top-notch education at his public school in Virginia.

At Harkness, I worked my ass off for B's and C's. Bickley, on the other hand, often slept through class and pulled A's without seeming to try.

I felt someone's eyes on me and turned to look.

Alison sat a few rows away. Her ivory skin appeared even paler than usual, and there were dark circles under her eyes. When she saw me looking, her face filled with regret.

Oh, just save it, I thought. Bitterness crawled into my throat, and I swallowed it down. She'd been so callous. And *now* she felt bad about it?

Giving the professor my full attention, I took careful notes on the lecture. This is what I'd come to Harkness to do, after all. This, and soccer. Everything else was just a distraction.

When class ended, I zipped my backpack and moved toward the door. As luck would have it, I arrived at the exit just as Bella did. "So you do still exist," she said as we exited the building.

We stopped in a spot where there weren't as many people around. "Look, about Sunday morning..." I began.

She rolled her eyes. "It's no big thing, Rafe. Sneaking out is a time-honored element of the one-night stand."

I studied her for a moment. The look in her eyes didn't match the flippant statement she'd just made. *Dios.* I'd offended her. But what should I say about it now? Bella was awesome, but I didn't know how to tell her I thought so. I rubbed the back of my neck. "I never, um..." And now I was starting to sweat. "I really didn't mean for things to..."

"Rafe?"

I froze at the sound of Alison's voice.

"Rafe? Can I talk to you?"

Bella's eyes danced. "Aw, she wants to apologize. Are you going to let her?"

"No," I said, loudly enough for Alison to hear. "I'm supposed to be at work in five minutes."

"After your shift, then?" Alison asked.

Bella gave me a wink, hitched her backpack onto a shoulder and walked away, which was frustrating because I hadn't apologized to her properly yet.

Alison stepped into my space. "We need to talk."

"No, we really don't," I said.

"Yes we do. There's something I need to explain."

Seriously? "Did you cheat?" I asked. "Because that's really the only relevant fact."

Her eyes filled with tears, and she did not deny it.

"I thought so." Stepping around her, I headed to the dining hall.

That evening my soccer practice ran late. The dining hall was closed by the time I made it out of the locker room, so I bought a sandwich with eight bucks that I didn't really have.

Eating at my desk, I spent some time trying to compose a suitable apology speech for Bella. *I really didn't mean for things to go so far*, I'd tell her. *But I think you're great, and I hope we can hang out some time.*

It all sounded really awkward. Because the situation *was* really awkward. And there was just no getting around it. Anything nice I said to her now was going to sound suspicious. Like a blatant plea to strip her naked and do it again.

That's what you get for shooting first and asking questions later. So to speak. But there were things I needed to say, and I'd need to say them in private.

While I pondered this problem, it got late. I didn't want to knock on Bella's door after ten o'clock. So I waited until the next evening, but she didn't answer my knock. And her neighbor's door was ajar. I felt myself start to sweat just thinking about Saturday night when Lianne Chalice had heard me speaking to Bella from the bathroom.

I turned tail and went back downstairs again.

On Thursday I didn't get a chance to speak to Bella after Urban Studies, because she answered her phone right after class. And anyway, I had to run off for another shift at work.

My work-study job was in the dining hall kitchen. Usually I worked prep in the back — chopping vegetables, cutting up chickens — it was the same work I'd been doing in my family's restaurant since I was old enough to hold a knife. But at Harkness I got paid really well for it.

Thursday, though, they had me serving behind the counter. The serving line wasn't my first choice of jobs, but you can't always have what you want. Unfortunately, some of the guys who came through the line hadn't learned that yet.

"Can't you just give me *two* of those?" a big guy in a football jacket demanded from his side of the counter. "And save me the trip?"

The plate I handed him had *one* hot roast beef sandwich on it. "You can come back through for a second one," I told him. That was the dining hall rule, because they didn't want people to waste the expensive stuff. It was the same rule *every freaking day*, although some guys asked anyway. And I always said no, because I didn't want to be fired.

"Thanks for nothing." The ham-necked guy stalked off, as if I'd offended him.

"You're so welcome," I muttered to myself.

Good times.

Still irritated, I plucked the next plate off the stack. It was still warm from the dishwasher. "What can I get you?" I asked the next person in line. I raised my eyes and then froze.

Bella stared back at me from across the busy counter, one eyebrow cocked. "Hello again," she said.

"Hi." My neck caught fire just at the sight of her cool green-eyed stare. It was impossible not to remember where last I'd seen that level gaze, or hear an echo of all the crazy things we'd said to each other. I felt sweat break out on my back. But I wasn't going to act like a chump this time. "I knocked on your door last night."

"Why? Were you feeling lonely?" She winked at me.

Dios. My gaze swept over the waiting diners, and I wondered if anyone was listening in.

When I brought my eyes back to Bella's, she looked unhappy. "It was just a little joke, Rafe. But if you want to pretend you don't know me when other people are around, I get it. Could I please have the chicken fried rice?"

I reached for the scoop, tongue-tied again. I made Bella's plate, trying to figure out what to say. This wasn't the time or the place to give my little apology speech. "Will that be all?" I said quietly.

"Obviously," Bella said. She took her plate and walked off.

I spent the rest of my shift feeling steamed at myself. *Look, I never had a one-night stand before*. That's all I needed to confess. *I feel like an ass, and I'm sorry. Can we be friends? Because I like you a lot.*

Simple words, right? I could manage that. Except maybe I should go even further. I wanted to do something nice for Bella. But what? Flowers? That was a cliché. No, I would invite her to lunch. A new Thai restaurant had opened off campus, and since I ate every meal in the dining hall, I was kind of craving Asian food. Hopefully she was too.

The more I thought about it, the better the idea sounded. Lunch was a casual meal. Friends did lunch together. It sent the right message. *I want to spend time with you, but I don't expect anything.*

Perfecto. I'd knock on her door and ask her tonight. And if she wasn't home, I'd just have to keep trying. In fact, I made a little promise to myself. The next time I saw Bella, no matter where it was, I would ask her to lunch.

SEVEN

BELLA

The next weekend I found myself at a fraternity party.

At Harkness frats weren't a very big deal. The student body was already divided into twelve "houses," so most people didn't see the point of dividing into further factions. I loved that about Harkness, actually. That frats didn't rule the place.

But there were a few frat parties every year I'd always considered to be worth the effort. Casino Night at Beta Rho was one of them. The brothers rented a bunch of gambling equipment. They set up poker tables in the basement, and craps tables in the living room. There was roulette on the porch and blackjack in the dining room. All the pledges were made to wear tuxedos and funny little 1920s gangster hats.

Every year I went for the spectacle, played a few rounds of cards and watched some high-stakes poker. A fraternity party wasn't half bad when dice and cards were involved.

Blackjack was my Casino Night game because it was simpler than poker but not as brainless as roulette. I was playing at a small table with Big-D, who was not exactly my favorite hockey teammate. (Though I was currently *beating* him, which made it more fun.)

My attention wavered a bit when Rafe walked through the front door with a couple of soccer players. And wouldn't you know? He looked devastating tonight in a tight pair of jeans and another button-down shirt rolled up on his taut forearms.

Crap. I was *not* going to stare at him.

"Hit me," I said to Whittaker, the football player who was acting as our dealer.

"You want a hit on seventeen?" he asked incredulously.

One of the rules I lived by was to never bet what you can't afford to lose. But in this case, that was no problem. "We're playing with Monopoly money, sport," I reminded him. "Also, I feel lucky." Furthermore, the Rangers game was on in the next room, and I'd promised my friend Pepe that I'd watch it with him. Going bust right now would not be the end of the world.

Whittaker turned over a three, and everyone gasped. "You *are* lucky," Whittaker said with a smile. "The dealer takes a hit on thirteen and..." He flipped over a queen. "Bella is the luckiest girl alive." He swept all my winnings, including a substantial portion of Big-D's remaining bills, into a pile and handed them to me.

"She *gets* lucky often enough," Big-D muttered from across the table. A tiny girl with shiny hair hung on his every word. At Big-D's not-so-subtle attempt to impugn my character, she gave a loud giggle.

Only a dumbass like Big-D would have to put me down just because I won some fake money off him. *Sigh.* "That bugged the shit out of you, didn't it?" I asked. "Losing to a *girl*. Is that why your date isn't playing?" I studied the sweet young thing on his arm. Her Casino Night getup included a shimmering, spangled top, an up-do that must have taken an hour and a half and gleaming red lipstick. I decided she was a freshman, because she was trying *way* too hard for Saturday night in a skeevy frat house.

I looked her right in the eye. "There's room at the table if you want to play."

Pursing those shiny lips, she shook her head and smirked. "Suit yourself."

Whittaker shuffled the deck. I placed a new bet and waited for Whittaker to deal. This time he dealt me an ace. And when I asked for a hit, I got ten and won. "Gotcha again, Big-D," I said a little too cheerfully.

There was a roar from the TV room. Truthfully, I was starting to care more about the hockey game than blackjack.

I lifted my eyes over Big-D's shoulder and found Rafe staring at me. In fact, he looked as if he was about to head in my direction. Not going to happen. If he had something to say to me, I did not want it said in front of Big-D, his simpering date and Whittaker.

"I think I'm done for the night," I said suddenly, passing my fat wad of Casino Night money over to Big-D.

"What? Why?" he asked. "I'm just getting warmed up."

"I'm sure you can find another girl to warm you up," I quipped. "And now you have a thousand extra dollars to play with."

"You're just *giving* this to me?"

"I'm so promiscuous like that," I said, patting him on the shoulder.

When I turned away toward the TV room, Whittaker followed me. "Hey, you need a beer?"

I could, in fact, use a beer. But I didn't want Whittaker to get any ideas. "If you're getting one for yourself, I'd love a refill," I said, meeting his eyes. There was absolutely interest there. Too bad I wasn't big on football players. And I *really* wasn't big on fraternity houses. This wasn't going to turn out the way Whittaker hoped.

"It's no trouble," he said, touching my elbow.

"Thanks. I'm going to see how the Rangers are doing," I said, pointing into the TV room.

"I'll find you," he said, his eyes scanning the room.

I'll bet you will.

"Hey, pledge!" he called out to some poor schmo whose lot in life was to be Whittaker's minion. "Deal this table for me. I'm taking a break."

Turning my back on him, I went in search of the Rangers' score.

The TV room was pretty small — it was more of an alcove than a room. But since TV was the lifeblood of the pack of athletes who lived here, it was probably the most popular room in the house.

There were five guys in there already, and I evaluated my seating options. There was a small wedge of sofa available between two frat guys, but I didn't feel like jamming myself between them. There was a tattered footstool, but... Eew. Fraternity house furniture was a dicey proposition, even when it didn't look as if it had been recently chewed by rats.

Luckily, one of the chairs had been taken by Pepe, an enormous French Canadian defensive hockey player and one of my on-again-off-again fuck buddies. "Belluh!" he crowed in his thick French accent. "Zhere is no score yet! But your Rangers look like poo poo tonight."

I walked over and sat down in his lap. He stuck his big feet out onto the coffee table, making both of us more comfortable. And just like that, my seating problem was solved. "Twenty bucks says the Rangers win tonight," I challenged him.

"Noh," he said, his accent thick even on the one syllable word. "I cannot take money from a friend."

I snorted at his overconfidence. He and I had a longstanding Rangers-vs.-Canadiens rivalry, because those were *our* teams. Pepe and I were the same age, although he was only a freshman. He'd spent two years after high school playing semi-pro on a farm team for — wait for it — the Canadiens. So for him, this game was personal.

Unfortunately, he was right that things didn't look so good for my Rangers. The score was still zip-zip, but the Canadiens had already taken twice as many shots on goal as the New York team had.

Behind me, Pepe got excited about the on-screen action. "*Oui! Oui oui oui!*" he yelled at the screen as his team's forward drove the puck towards the goal again.

"Stop him," I yelled. But it was no use. The lamp lit before I could even get the words out.

Pepe threw his scruffy head back on his broad shoulders and whooped.

There is nothing cuter than watching a giant man-child get delirious over his team's goal. Pepe's hands wandered down my sides, and he gave my hips a squeeze. I felt his erection begin to poke me in the lower back.

Turning to whisper into his ear, I asked, "Pepe, did you seriously just pop a boner because the Canadiens scored?"

"Noh," he said. "I have *zee bonnaire* because now we are *weening*."

I giggled, while his hand found its way onto my boob, which he gave a single squeeze. Sports, food and sex. Those were the things which made the men in my life tick. It was really that simple.

"I theenk we need a different bet," he said. "Not money. *Les vêtements*. Clothing. I score a goal, I choose a piece of yours."

I turned my head so I could see him. "You want to play strip hockey?"

"*Oui*. Keep it interesting."

What a goofball. "Fine. But we'll have to watch the game in my room if you want to get naked."

"Not naked. Just take off zee sweater." Carefully, he lifted it over my head, tossing it aside. "It is itching me."

"Sorry," I laughed. It *was* an itchy sweater. Wearing only a tank top now, I settled back against Pepe's broad chest. He was excellent furniture, as long as you didn't mind the sensation of his dick poking at the bottom of your spine.

And I didn't.

I thought of Pepe as the human equivalent of a black Labrador puppy. He had a clumsy, happy attitude, big feet and a lot of dark hair all over his body. (*All* over his body.)

He wasn't the deepest man I'd ever met, but he was a good friend. And tonight I didn't mind soaking up some of his light-hearted affection. Nothing would happen between us, because Pepe had gotten back together with his high school girlfriend over the summer. So a few risqué jokes were the only sex Pepe and I would be having.

Whittaker didn't know that, though. When he came into the TV room with two beers, his eyes narrowed as he found me sitting in Pepe's lap. With a frown, he handed me a glass.

"Thank you," I told him.

His response was a grunt. Whittaker took his own beer and sat on the skeevy ottoman.

The Canadiens, unfortunately, picked that moment to secure a breakaway. Behind me, Pepe sat up a little straighter as his team chased the puck down the ice.

Uh-oh.

"*C'est magnifique!*" Pepe roared in my ear. "*Formidable!*"

Pepe was a very enthusiastic guy, and all that enthusiasm translated well during sex. We'd shared some very energetic sessions, usually with me bent over some piece of furniture while he panted French words of encouragement into my ear. (*C'est bon! C'est bon! Magnifique!*)

"*Exceptionnel!*" Pepe screamed now as they scored for the second time.

"Come *on*, guys!" I hollered at the screen. "This is Montreal you're playing! You're not supposed to lose."

Behind me, Pepe laughed like a little kid. "Eef we were playing for keeps, now I would win this little blouse." He tugged on the fabric of my tank top.

"Sure." I shrugged. "But if you can pretend-win my top, I can pretend to put on my rally cap. You guys are going down."

"*Non, mon amour.* You will watch and see." Pepe took the beer out of my hand and stole a sip.

I took it back, giving his thigh a little pinch. "Pay attention, babe. The Rangers are getting a power play. Your D-man got called for slashing."

The next half hour of the game was intense. My Rangers pulled it together enough to score once. I pretend-demanded Pepe's pants. But then Montreal scored an ugly goal in front of the net. *Again.* And Pepe pretend-claimed my jeans.

In the grand tradition of inside jokes everywhere, we thought our game was hysterical. "If we were playing for real, you'd be sitting here in those teeny tiny purple briefs, right?" I teased Pepe. Because the man did have peculiar taste in underwear.

"*C'est possible.*" He chuckled. "And you — a pair of panties with no...?"

"Crotch?" I guessed. Pepe was in fantasyland now. Sexy lingerie was not my style, and he knew it.

"*Oui.*"

"Sounds tacky. What color are they?"

"Striped. Like zee hide of a zebra. And the brassiere has the same."

I laughed, because you had to give him credit for imagination, and Pepe gave me a wet kiss on the cheek. (Come to think of it, his kisses were all really pretty slobbery. That too reminded me of an enthusiastic puppy.)

We both turned back to face the screen. "Third period, *mon amie.* We find out who ends up naked."

Too bad it was only a *pretend* naked. I'd rather not go home alone tonight.

Both teams skated well during the third period, and Pepe and I were glued to the screen. Whittaker started rooting hard for the Rangers, probably because I was a fan, and hope springs eternal.

The clock ticked down. Several times the Rangers almost tied up the game.

Almost, but not quite.

The game paused for a media time-out. And since I'd had a few beers tonight, I really needed to pee. "Whittaker? Any chance there's a bathroom somewhere without a line in front of it?"

"Pledge!" he bellowed. A few seconds later a freshman — dressed as a twenties casino operator — came skidding around the corner. "Unlock the bathroom off the kitchen for Bella."

Remind me never to pledge a fraternity, I thought as I followed the poor plebe to the secret bathroom. "Thanks, dude," I told the freshman. "You don't have to wait."

The kid tipped his rented bowler hat at me and disappeared.

If the game weren't on, I would just get the heck out of here. Beta Rho had always left a bad taste in my mouth. They were famous among women for their nasty little habit of awarding the Skank of the Week trophy to whichever brother had managed the most unsavory hookup.

I'd seen the trophy once. It was shaped like a pig.

After I did my business in the frat's least disgusting bathroom, I slipped back through the crowd to watch the last few minutes of the Rangers' game.

Or rather, I tried to.

"Um, Bella?" Rafe stopped me at the doorway to the TV alcove with a hand to my elbow.

"Yeah?"

"Could I, uh, speak to you a sec?" he asked. He ran a hand through his dark hair. His eyes traveled down, briefly landing on my skimpy tank top before guiltily snapping back to my face again.

I tilted my chin toward the TV. "Well, it's the last couple minutes of the Rangers game and I was hoping..."

Inside, Pepe started yelling. "*Le chasser! Le tuer! Merci! Merci!*" And then there was a victorious yodel of: "*Ouiiii!*"

I was definitely losing this game. Ah, well. I lifted my chin to get a better look at Rafe. And when his big dark eyes looked down at me, I fought off a shiver. Damn him. Why did he have to be so sexy? It was hard to pull off the indifferent vibe that I needed to show him. "What's up?" I checked my watch, as if I had someplace to be. Subtle, right? I felt like slapping myself.

If I was honest, my encounter with Rafe had unsettled me, and I couldn't figure out why. If there was anyone who understood the fickle nature of a hook-up, it was me. The fact that he'd been so awkward afterward was a letdown, though. Apparently Rafe was a shamer. Shamers felt guilty after having sex, sometimes even apologizing for it, the same way they'd apologize for bumping into you with a dining hall tray. *Sorry. I didn't mean to do that. I'll try not to be so clumsy next time.*

It didn't matter that they were sincere, because shame flowed in both directions. If a shamer had impulsive sex, which he considered a misdeed, then by definition he thought I'd done something wrong, too.

And I was sick of people judging me. Really, really sick of it.

"Bella," Rafe began. "I wanted to invite you out for lunch next week."

That wasn't what I'd expected him to say. He wanted to take me out for lunch? Why?

I didn't get to answer, though, because Pepe began bellowing from the other room. "Belluh! I win the lingerie, cherie! Take everything off!"

Aw, hell. "Pepe, just give me..."

Then he was standing behind me all of a sudden, his giant body pressing against my back. "Show me the boobies! Zee score is four-one."

Dear lord, just shoot me already. I gave Pepe a backward shove. "Just a second, okay?" But it was really too late for Rafe not to get the wrong impression.

When I risked a look at Rafe's face, I saw it turning quite a dark shade of red. "We'll talk another time," he stuttered.

"Rafe, wait. It's just a..." I stopped myself before explaining. Even if Pepe wasn't kidding, I didn't have to apologize for myself.

But Rafe was backing away from me, a pained expression on his face. He held up two hands. "I'm sorry."

"God, why?"

"For... I feel like the world's biggest jackass."

"Because of... two weeks ago?"

He made a guilty face.

I couldn't help but roll my eyes. "The fifties are over, okay? It was just *sex*, Rafe. And you're a bigger jackass for not getting past it than for doing it in the first place."

He swallowed. "Well. Whichever kind of jackass I am, I'm sorry."

He still didn't understand. "Nobody took advantage of me, Rafe. I'm not fragile like that."

"Okay."

"You can't rape the willing," I whispered.

At the word "rape" Rafe's eyes bugged out.

"It's just an expression," I qualified.

"BELLA!" Pepe howled from inside the room. "I am going to have the panties! Montreal has power play!"

I wanted the ground to open up and swallow me.

Rafe's expression shuttered. "I'll see you in class," he mumbled. As Rafe backed away, I could practically hear him making a list of my sins in his head.

"Good night," I called after him anyway.

He raised a hand in a half-hearted wave before disappearing into the crowd.

Lovely. He couldn't even look me in the eye.

I turned around and marched into the TV room.

"Two minutes left," Pepe announced. "Zee power play did not go as planned."

I didn't care about the game anymore. The disappointment on Rafe's face was seared on my brain. He'd looked horrified when he thought that Pepe and I were talking about actually stripping down. Although he'd done the same thing in my room not so long ago.

Where's the sense in that? Even though I hadn't done anything wrong, it still smarted to know Rafe was disappointed in me.

That was the trouble with shamers. They got under your skin.

The Canadiens won, of course. After the buzzer, Pepe gave me another wet kiss on the forehead and got up. "You want me to walk you home?"

"I think I'll stay a little longer," I heard myself say. I don't know why, but I really didn't want to walk out the door under Pepe's arm while Rafe looked on. I shouldn't care what he thought. But I did care. And that bugged the shit out of me.

"Good night, *cherie*," he said.

"Night, honey."

On the footstool, Whittaker perked up. "Another drink?" he asked.

I sat back down on the chair and wondered what I was doing. "Maybe."

"How do you feel about a gin and tonic?" he asked.

"That would be great," I lied.

"Be right back," he said.

Like a fool, I stayed there, waiting to drink a gin and tonic with Whittaker. Knowing that it was a terrible idea.

It was, too. Although it would take me weeks to learn just how terrible.

Chapter Eight

EIGHT

October

RAFE

October was rainy and cold, and my team was on a four game losing streak. Not fun.

When I wasn't chasing down the soccer ball, I took to jogging around campus listening to bachata tunes on my iPod. Alison hadn't liked the Dominican music I listened to, so it was kind of funny that I now used her gift to play it constantly.

Ear buds firmly in place, I headed for an Urban Studies lecture. The class had remained an uncomfortable place in my life. Alison still shot me remorseful looks whenever I happened to glance at her. In contrast, Bella studiously ignored me. The longest conversation we'd had in the past two weeks occurred when I held our entryway door open for her, and she'd said "thank you."

The lecture hall was nearly full when I slipped in, nabbing a seat against the back wall. "Let's get started," Professor Giulios called. "We have a lot to cover today. I'm handing out the final projects. This is for all the marbles, kids."

At that, everyone got quiet.

"At the end of my course, I always hold a contest. The details change from year to year, but the rules remain the same." He began to tick them off on one hand. "In teams, you will compete to redesign and redevelop half of a New York City block. The winning team will come up with the best concepts both economically and spatially. Without building a giant eyesore, you will maximize the square footage of your construction for the benefit of both the tenants and the neighborhood. But *paying* for your development is also part of the assignment. And twenty-five percent of the square footage must be set aside for affordable housing."

I scribbled notes furiously as he spoke. This was going to be fun. I'd seen dozens of redevelopment projects rise over New York in my lifetime, right? I ought to be able to come up with something interesting.

"Last year I put my students to work on a block on the Lower East Side. This year? West 165th Street."

I dropped my pencil. That was really close to my neighborhood.

The professor projected a photo on the screen at the head of the room, and a familiar facade came into view. It was a sketchy low-slung commercial building, with a parking lot beside it. I was pretty sure people often slept on the sidewalk there, because that side of the street didn't have much foot traffic. At night, it was pretty dark and more than a little dodgy.

"Here we are," Professor Giulio said. "This structure has been condemned, and you've got that parking lot beside it to play with, too." He gave rough dimensions for the developable area, and I scribbled them down.

Someone raised his hand in front. "Do we need to include parking in our design?"

The professor shook his head. "This parking lot is too impractical to worry about. Any other questions? Don't you want to hear about the prize?" He grinned. "Every year I have someone in the city government judge the teams with me. This time it's going to be Mr. Jimmy Chan, the commissioner of city restaurant development. He's also the guy who licenses food trucks in New York." The professor rubbed his hands together. "The winning team will take the train down the Friday night before exams to have a food-truck dinner with Jimmy and his favorite vendors. You can even bring a date."

At that, I sat up straighter in my chair. I'd been trying to convince my mother that Tipico, our family restaurant, should have a food truck, too. Food trucks charged higher prices than we could get in Washington Heights. Parking that sucker on Wall Street at noon? We could double our take.

But Ma listened to my uncles, who said that getting paperwork for a food truck was hard. And then there was the truck itself...

I was going to have to win this contest and *meet* the dude who knew all there was to know about how food trucks worked.

Professor Giulios was still talking about the rules. "Twelve teams, one for each house," he was saying, "unless the houses are represented wildly unevenly."

That got my attention.

"So, I'll leave the last five minutes of our time today for breaking into our house groups."

The teams were by *house?* As the professor continued his lecture, I eyed the room. From Beaumont House there was me, Bella and Alison. And also a junior woman I recognized from Alison's entryway.

There had to be more, right? Oh, *Dios.* Let there be too many Beaumonters in the class, so I could join another team. I squinted at all the heads in the room, hoping for more familiar faces.

But I found *nada.*

At the end of class, my fears were confirmed. When the professor asked students from Beaumont House to gather in the front of the room, there was only me, my ex-girlfriend, the hook-up who now hated me and a single stranger.

Jesucristo. My chickens had come home to roost.

Alison cleared her throat. "I propose that we break up further."

We did that already, girl.

"There should be two groups — one pair who looks at the design element and another that does the economics. I'm really more of a design person than a numbers person."

"I'll do numbers," I said quickly.

"Fine," Alison sighed.

The junior who I didn't know looked at Bella. "I'd rather have design. But if you really wanted it, I'd take the economic stuff."

Bella shrugged. "Okay. I'm not afraid of numbers."

Uh-oh.

"I'm Dani by the way," she said. "Short for Danielle."

Bella smiled. "I know you are. I'm Bella, short for a name I don't like. And this is Rafe," she jutted a thumb at me, "and that's Alison."

"I guess we're done for now," Alison said stiffly. She hefted her backpack on one shoulder, taking care not to look at me. "Dani, let's exchange numbers."

Dani followed her toward the door, which left me alone with Bella.

"So," she said.

"So." I swallowed. "Can we walk and talk? I have a shift in the dining hall."

"Sure," Bella said. We walked outside together, and an awkward silence descended. "So," Bella said once more. "We're doing this project."

"Yeah," I said, my voice low. "I need to win it, too."

Bella turned to me with the first smile I'd seen directed at me in weeks. "Well, that's the spirit. Are you sure you want to work with me?"

"Of course," I said with more conviction than I felt.

"All right," she said, hiking her bag higher on her shoulder. "That's good news. Because I hope you're not the type of guy who can't look me in the eye after he's seen me naked."

My throat tightened. "Bella..." *Dios*. It was *me* I couldn't look in the eye. Not her.

"That's the worst kind of sexism, anyway. It's not fair to have a one-night stand with someone, and then act like she's trash because she had one, too. *That* would be hypocritical."

"Um," I said, helplessly. Once again, she had me at a complete loss for words. "It's just... I think we got it backwards. I wanted to start over."

Bella walked silently beside me for a second. "That's still some misplaced guilt, though. If we went out on a date, then you could feel better about what happened."

That shut me up for a second. Because there was a little bit of truth in there. But it wasn't the whole truth. "I just wanted to have some Thai food. You can call it whatever you want."

Bella swallowed. "I'm not a relationship kind of girl."

I put my hands up in submission. "Okay. Thanks for telling me." Wait. Did I just get rejected? Yes, yes I did. My neck began to heat uncomfortably. "Are you the kind of girl who can't eat lunch with her Urban Studies partner, either?"

"No," she said quickly. "We could do that sometime, I guess."

She *guessed*. *Dios*. I always wanted to have lunch with a girl whose arm I had to twist to make it happen.

"Can't we just talk about the project now?" Bella asked.

"Sounds good," I said, my voice tight.

Bella sighed. "We're going to have to work together for eight weeks. Can you do that?"

"Of course," I snapped, proving the exact opposite.

"Right. Did I ever tell you that my father made his billions in commercial real estate?"

We climbed the staircase to the Beaumont dining hall before I worked out just what she was trying to tell me. "So... you know a thing or two about how to develop something in New York?"

"Yep," she said as we stepped into the dining room, with its soaring ceilings. "Twenty-one years of boring dinner table discussion are about to come in handy."

Finally — a little good news. "Well okay then." I held out a hand to her. "This is going to work great. Let's shake on it."

She gave me an eye roll, but she also shook my hand. Hers was soft, and I didn't really want to let go of it. "See you Thursday," she said.

"Thursday," I agreed. And before I could think better of it, I leaned down and gave Bella a quick kiss on the cheek. She smelled of fruity shampoo and soft skin.

Then I got the hell out of there.

NINE

BELLA

For a moment I just stood there in the doorway of the dining hall, watching Rafe's very fine ass disappear into the kitchen. My fingertips found their way onto my cheekbone, to the place where Rafe had put the sneaky kiss that short-circuited my brain.

Rafe was the most confusing boy I'd ever met. A month had gone by since we'd hooked up — it was ancient history. But I still felt too aware of him, and I didn't know why. On our walk over here, I'd given him a freaking lecture on morality, because I couldn't figure out how to shut up.

And then he *kissed* me? Who did that?

"Um, Bella?"

I turned to find Graham and two other friends — Corey and Scarlet — staring up at me from the table just inside the door. "Hi," I said, dropping my hand from my cheek, and feeling self-conscious.

"Hi yourself," Corey said with a grin. In fact, they were all smirking at me.

That unstuck me. I walked over to the empty seat beside Graham and dropped my backpack onto the floor. Sitting down, I stole one of Graham's little dining hall glasses of Coke and drank it down.

"Who's your friend?" Graham asked, turning his head to look pointedly at the kitchen door.

"Neighbor," I corrected. "We have a class together."

"Huh," he said. "Did you notice that your neighbor was smokin' hot?"

Was I ever going to get used to him saying things like that? *Doubtful.* "I did notice," I mumbled, wondering how quickly I could change the subject. "Got any plans for the weekend, guys?" I tried.

"Not really," Corey said. "Then again, it's *Tuesday.*"

Right. "Good point." I looked over at Graham's tray and went in for another glass of Coke.

He blocked my hand. "You know, they'll give you a tray of your own."

"Where is the love?" I complained. I stood up anyway and went over to the beverage counter. The truth was that I didn't feel all that well, and I was strangely thirsty. So I put three glasses on my tray and filled them with ice and soda. Food didn't sound all that appealing, but I made myself a small plate at the salad bar, then went to sit down with my hockey friends again.

While I ate, Scarlet, a goalie on the women's team, asked Corey questions about their upcoming tournament in Boston. "I haven't played in that arena before."

"It's a dump," I said at exactly the same time Corey said the same thing.

"Jinx!" Corey cried. "But it's true. They need a renovation. Badly." She was the manager of the women's team, so she traveled all the same places with her team that I did.

My stomach ached, so I pushed my plate away. Hopefully I wasn't coming down with anything. Strains of "When the Saints Go Marching In" began to rise up from my backpack.

"Whose ringtone is that?" Scarlet asked.

"My mom's," I said, reaching down to decline the call.

"That's hysterical."

"Yeah, I crack myself up."

Unfortunately, the darned song played twice more before lunch was over. When I finally stepped into the empty stairwell, I called her back. "What is it, Mom?"

"Bella! I have good news. Your sister just found out that she got the grant she was so excited about. Now she can open her immunization clinic."

Well at least someone in the family knew what she wanted. "That's great, Mom. Julie must be psyched." My big sister was a public health crusader. She was the *good* daughter, the one who had always done as she was told. And now she spent all her time doing nice, important things for other people from dawn until dusk. Sometimes even on weekends.

"She's over the moon. Be sure to call her to give her your congratulations."

I tried to keep the irritation out of my tone. "Of course I will." *Jesus*. My mother's opinion of me could not be any clearer.

"She'll be delighted to hear from you," my mother said a little too firmly. "Also, I need you to come into the city on the night of Saturday, November seventh."

"Why?" I asked, feeling wary. "I'll have to look at the hockey schedule," I lied. The regular season did not start until the following weekend. Lucky me.

"There's an awards banquet. It's a big deal for her. The whole family should be there together."

Shit. The whole family included one person I tried always to avoid. "Things get pretty busy here," I hedged.

"This is nonnegotiable," my mother said. "You'll want to wear a dress."

"To a banquet? You think?" Annnnnd now I was snapping at my mother like a teenager. Awesome.

"I *do* think." My mother sighed. "Cocktails at six-thirty. Dancing and dinner at seven-thirty."

Dancing! *Ugh*. Well at least I could blow off the cocktail hour without anyone getting tetchy. "Wait. I can bring a date to this thing, right?" A human buffer would make this whole idea far more palatable. My parents were too polite to chew me out in front of strangers.

My mother hesitated. "This will be a family evening."

That was ridiculous, because there would be four hundred people at a charity banquet. "Mom, those tables always seat ten. And I *know* you bought a table for this thing." That was how my mother worked. She loved her charitable causes. "And you can bet that Julie will bring a date."

"Your sister has a *husband*, Bella. That's hardly the same thing."

In a remarkable show of restraint, I did not reply in any of the first dozen ways that leapt to mind. I didn't have any words for Julie's husband that wouldn't set my mother's temper aflame. "I want to bring someone, too," I argued. "It's only fair." *Fair* being a stupid, meaningless word that I only used because I couldn't think of anything better.

"Fine," my mother capitulated. "I'll put you down as plus one."

"That would be lovely," I said as graciously as possible.

"Saturday the seventh."

"Got it."

"And call Julie today."

"*Okay.*" *Jeez*.

After we disconnected, I ducked into the women's bathroom at the bottom of the stairs. All day I'd felt a little... off. My stomach was achy, for starters. But just to make things extra fun, I seemed to be coming down with a yeast infection.

And as long as I was tallying up all the worst things about today, I now owed my sister a phone call — my sister who could not stand me. Furthermore, I needed to find a date to suffer through a few hours of a stuffy banquet in Manhattan in a couple weeks.

Awesome.

In ten minutes I was due to the psych seminar that I took on Tuesday afternoons. But first, a quick pit stop.

After ten seconds in the bathroom stall, I was sorry I'd ever gone in there. "Jesus Fuck!" I shrieked. Because *oh my freaking God* it hurt when I peed. I was alone in that bathroom, thank goodness. Because... damn. I felt tears spring into my eyes.

After an excruciating thirty seconds, I zipped up, washed up and got the hell out of there.

Two hours later, and feeling no better, I dragged myself through the front door of the Student Health Services building and up to the second floor gynecology department. When I asked at the desk if my favorite nurse practitioner could squeeze me in, the receptionist shook her little freckled nose. "Ms. Ogden is off this week. But if you're having an emergency, I can get you in to see Dr. Peterson."

That was a bummer, because Ms. Ogden was amazing. The first time I came in for a pelvic exam, she'd held a hand mirror out to me. "Would you like to see your cervix?" she asked, with the same happy tone as if she were offering to show me a funny cat video. It was hard to feel awkward with Ms. Ogden in the room. Even naked from the waist down, with my feet in the stirrups.

I waited with an outdated copy of *Sports Illustrated* until my name was called. I followed a nurse down the little hallway and into an exam room. "Please undress from the waist down, then hop up on the table. I'll leave a sheet right here."

When she disappeared, I stripped off my jeans and underwear. Out of a misplaced sense of modesty, I folded the panties into a neat square, then tucked them underneath my jeans. It really made no sense to hide my undies when the doctor was about to look at my vag under bright lights. But I did it anyway.

I got onto the table and pulled the sheet across my lap. A double knock sounded on the door.

"Come in," I said, pointlessly.

The doctor who entered the room was older than I expected, with wispy gray hair and an ornery expression on his wrinkled face. But as he cleared the doorway, someone else followed on his heels. In walked a young man. He was tall — probably six foot two — and *so* freaking handsome. Under less awkward circumstances, I would have taken a good long look at him.

Instead, I stared at my knees.

"Hello Miss..." The older doctor stared down at my chart in his hands. "Isabelle Hall. This is Mr. Gaines. He's a medical student following me on rotation today. Is it all right with you if he observes our examination?"

Seriously? What was I supposed to say? *Yeah, let's make a fucking party out of looking at my vag.*

"Okay," I mumbled.

"Now what is your complaint?" the doctor asked, folding his arms.

At that moment, I would have done anything to see Ms. Ogden's blue-eyed gaze blinking calmly at me from behind her spectacles. "It, uh..." *Just spit it out, Bella.* "I have pain in the, um, vulva region. I thought it was a yeast infection. But now it hurts when I pee."

The old doctor nodded. "Let's have a look, then." He pulled some latex gloves from a box on the wall. "Scoot down on the table, please. Feet in the stirrups."

I knew the drill. Still, it was uncomfortable. The little exam room seemed overcrowded. Cold air hit my girly parts when the doctor folded back the sheet.

Both men angled in for a view, and I pretty much wanted to die of embarrassment. The doctor's gloved hand probed me in a way that was not overly rough. But I had to fight to keep the wince off my face when he touched a sensitive area.

"Mr. Gaines," the doctor prompted. "What do you see?"

My gaze shot up to see the young man's face color. He met my eyes for a second before turning to his teacher. "An infection. Probably bacterial."

"What is the likely pathogen?" the old doctor pressed.

The younger man did not look me in the eye this time. "Gonorrhea or Chlamydia."

"What?" I gasped, hoping that I'd somehow misheard.

The doctor nodded. "Glove up and prepare a test. Also, check for other signs of infection."

As the younger man put on a pair of gloves, a trickle of sweat rolled down my back. "What does this mean?"

Dr. Peterson's expression was chilly. "We see signs of infection, which are almost certainly caused by a sexually transmitted infection. Have you ever been diagnosed with one before?"

"No," I gasped, my face prickling with heat. "But I don't understand. I use condoms."

"We hear that a lot," the doctor said, stepping back to give his student some room. "But if you have skin-to-skin contact before the condom is applied, it can happen."

Oh my God.

Oh my God.

Oh. My. God.

My heart began to beat like a drum, and I tasted bile in the back of my throat. The young medical student loomed over me now. My pulse was racing, and there just wasn't enough air. My eyes got hot.

Dr. Peterson shoved a tissue box in my direction suddenly.

"What's that for?" I asked in a voice which was less than polite. My attitude was suddenly the only thing standing between me and a breakdown.

"For when you cry," he said simply.

I pushed the box back toward him. "Keep it then," I ground out, determined not to cry.

Above me, the younger man hesitated. I forced myself to look up at him, finding a pair of empathetic hazel eyes waiting for me. "Do you need a minute?" he asked quietly.

Angrily, I shook my head.

He hesitated anyway. "May I touch your stomach? I'd like to know if any of your lymph nodes are swollen."

I nodded.

He moved around my bent knee to stand next to me. Patient hands pressed gently into my pelvic region. "Please tell me if anything hurts."

He probed lower, and within seconds I was hissing in a breath.

"Sorry," he said quickly, reaching to check the other side. "How about here?"

"Yeah," I said through clenched teeth. I was *really* sore there.

He patted my hip twice, in a way that should have seemed weird but somehow wasn't. "Your lymph nodes are swollen because they're working to fight the infection. Now I only need a quick swab, okay?" the young man said. "Then we'll be all done."

Again, I spoke through gritted teeth. "Do your worst."

The swabbing stung. But not nearly as much as the anguish of hearing the words *sexually transmitted disease*.

"Now you can get dressed," the old coot said when it was done. "Meet me in my office in ten minutes, and I'll give you a prescription and some information."

At that, he turned and left, followed only slightly more graciously by the med student.

I clamped my thighs together, heart pounding.

With shaking hands, I stumbled into my clothes. *STD*. The ugly letters sloshed around in my mind. This wasn't supposed to happen. I practiced safe sex. I'd thought I did, anyway. Why me?

My stomach gave a lurch, which had nothing to do with the infection. This time the pain was from *shame*.

So much for being a sex-positive feminist in control of her own body. Just then I felt exactly like the slut people had claimed I was. People like Lianne across the hall. And the hockey girlfriends.

And my mother.

Ugh. My mother couldn't know this. I was *never* going to tell her.

Still quaking, I wandered down the hallway, wondering which door was Dr. Peterson's office. I stopped when I saw the med student sitting in a chair, then double-checked that the name plate outside the door said "Peterson."

I went into the little room, sitting in the obvious patient chair.

"So, Isabelle," the young man said.

"Bella," I snapped, keeping up the bitch front.

"Bella," he said gently. "I just wanted you to know that this happens all the time. Your test results will probably show that it's easily curable."

I knew what he was trying to do. He was trying to give me some perspective. *Jesus.* I probably should have thanked him for trying, but instead I only swallowed hard.

Dr. Peterson breezed into the room, seating himself on his desk chair. "Miss Hall, I have a prescription here." He slid a little square of paper toward me. "Take the *full* course of antibiotics. That's really important."

Silently, I took the paper.

"Your symptoms should start to disappear immediately, but finish the medicine anyway. Meanwhile, you should have no sexual contact with your boyfriend during this time."

That was easy, of course, since I didn't have a boyfriend. But my stomach filled with dread. "I need to ask a question."

"Of course."

My eyes went to the wood-grain desktop and stayed there. "What's the incubation period?"

The doctor cleared his throat. "Do you mean to ask how long ago were you infected?"

I nodded. Shame and silence descended together, like a mushroom cloud. Depending on his answer, there were two or three people who might have infected me.

And, likewise, there were two or three people who I might have infected.

"Within the last two weeks," the doctor said. "Probably ten days."

"Okay," I whispered. I was going to have to go home and scrutinize my calendar to figure out what I'd done when and with whom.

"Naturally, you're going to have to follow up with your partner," the doctor said. "He or she will need to know that an infection was transmitted."

Every time he said the word "infection" I just wanted to *die*.

"Your test will come back within a few days, and a doctor will call with the results. Then you'll have something more precise to communicate to your partner."

He kept talking, but I'd stopped listening. Because I was realizing just how awful this was going to be. I knew a hundred ways to ask a guy to come home with me. But I couldn't imagine telling someone I may have given him a disease.

"Bella?"

I looked up fast. The medical student was trying to hand me a glossy brochure. I snatched it from his hand.

"There's a lot of information in there. But if you have any questions, call us here. Or ask whomever calls with your results."

I swung my gaze over to Dr. Peterson. "Can I make a request?"

He frowned. "Yes?"

"Would you ask Ms. Ogden to call with my results?"

The doctor's frown deepened. "I'll make a note of it. But no guarantees," he said, scribbling on my file.

"Thanks, I'd really appreciate it," I said. My gaze wandered over to the med student, and he gave me the world's quickest smile. Apparently I wasn't Ms. Ogden's only fan.

"If you have no more questions for now, I'll see the next patient."

"I'm good," I said, lying through my teeth. I was so very far from good.

The doctor rose and strode out, his white coat flapping behind him.

"Gaines," he grumbled, summoning the med student.

Gaines stood up to follow him, but lingered just for a second in the doorway. "I know it's a lot to take in," he whispered. "But once the shock wears off and you do a little reading, it will all seem less awful."

"Thanks," I clipped.

He gave me another quick smile. "Call Helena Ogden with your questions."

"You can bet on it."

He disappeared then, leaving me alone with a prescription in one hand and a glossy brochure in the other. *Taking Your Sexual Health In Hand*, it read.

I folded it up into a tiny square and jammed it into my pocket. Then I got the hell out of there.

An hour later, I'd collected a small prescription bottle from the pharmacy as well as a take-out salad from the student center. The walk home was slow going, though, because the riff of irritation I'd felt down there earlier in the day had blossomed into full-on pain. So I walked carefully, wishing I could just beam myself up into my dorm room.

I needed to be completely alone. To regroup. To furtively Google search terms I never thought I'd type into my browser window. To throw darts at Dr. Peterson's picture. But *not* to cry.

Fuck that guy.

I'd almost made it to my entryway door when someone jogged into the courtyard from the other direction. When he got to our door, he spread his sculpted legs and bent forward, hands on his knees, stretching before tackling the stairs.

Rafe. Even panting and sweat-coated, he was beautiful.

He was also the *last* person I wanted to talk to right now.

Shit.

Noticing me, he stood up straighter. "Hi," he said on the exhale, reaching for the ID he'd clipped to his pocket. He swiped it past the scanner, then opened the door like a perfect gentleman.

Choking on my own discomfort, I gave him a self-conscious little wave.

His expression flickered with uncertainty. "Something wrong?"

Not a thing. And, by the way, do you suppose you gave me a disease? God. How was I ever going to discuss it? How did people do that? Rafe was frowning now, waiting for an answer. *Pull it together, Bella.* "I'm fine," I said grumpily. "You?"

His eyes widened at my rude tone. "Never better" he said, pressing his lips together.

I was somehow *destined* to offend this guy. But that was the least of my problems right now. "Great. Have a good night." I passed him, heading for the stairs. Unfortunately, climbing them was even less comfortable for me than walking had been. I powered up the first half flight anyway, feeling his eyes on me.

The sting made me want to scream.

Running out of ideas, I set my bag down and knelt down to re-tie my perfectly tied shoe. Slow footsteps moved up the stairs behind me. I felt Rafe pass me carefully on the landing. Then he trudged up ahead of me.

When he disappeared around the next curve, I picked up my bag and began again, slower this time. Gripping the railing, I pulled myself up, stair after painful stair.

On the next landing, Rafe waited, his head cocked to the side. "Are you sure you're okay?"

"Yes, thank you," I snapped. "Sore ankle, that's all."

"Oh." His face softened. "You need...?"

"Nope, I'm good."

His face fell again. "Okay. Later, then."

This time he turned and jogged up the next flight as if he couldn't get away fast enough. And I didn't resume my climb until I heard the door to his suite open and close again.

Finally alone, I finished my agonizing journey home. The first thing I did was to take one of the tablets I'd gotten at the pharmacy. I wasn't sure where to keep the bottle. *Not* the bathroom. I could only imagine Lianne's smugness at finding out what had happened to me. Or anyone's smugness, for that matter.

I hid the bottle in my desk drawer.

Then I called Trevi, the hockey captain, and told him I had flu symptoms and couldn't make it to practice. "Could you tell Coach Canning that I'm sorry?" I asked.

"Sure. And feel better," he said.

If only. "Thanks man. See you tomorrow or Thursday."

"Ciao."

Finally, I was alone. I switched on the lamp beside my bed, which cast a homey glow on the slanting ceiling. Flopping down on the bed, I curled into an ornery, achy, frightened little ball.

But I did not cry.

Chapter Ten

BELLA

If there was anything lucky about my debacle, it was that hockey season was not yet in full swing. It would be hard for a girl to hide in her room when weekends meant back-to-back away games.

On Saturday, while sulking after brunch, I got a call from Student Health Services. And when I answered, it was Ms. Ogden on the line.

Thank God.

"Bella? Do you have a minute to talk?"

"Of course. I didn't know you worked Saturdays, though."

"I work whenever the vaginas need me," she said, which made me burst out laughing. "Do you have time for a cup of coffee?"

I hesitated. "Sure. Is it that bad?"

"No!" she said. "Not at all. I just want to see your face. We're not supposed to have favorite patients, but..."

"I'm sure you say that to all the girls."

She laughed. "Meet me at Java Tree in ten?"

~

I bought myself a cup of peppermint tea, and went to sit down across from Ms. Ogden. She'd nabbed a very private table in back. "Hi," I said, feeling calmer than I had in days. There was something about her level gaze that banished panicky thoughts.

She reached across the table to give my hand a quick squeeze. "Bella, dear. I'm sorry I wasn't around when you came in last week."

"Please tell me that you were someplace wonderful. Because Dr. Peterson is an evil troll."

She grinned. "My wife and I went to Bermuda."

"Nice."

"And I know he's a grouch. But he's also a very sharp clinician. Unfortunately, you don't have to be a nice person to get a medical degree."

"I noticed."

"It helps to remember that he's saved lives."

"Pish," I said with a wave of my hand, and she smiled again.

"I have some lab results here." She passed me a sealed envelope. "But I just wanted to make sure — are you doing okay? I'm sorry you got difficult news."

"I'm okay," I lied. *Actually, I'm hiding in my room most of the time. Is that normal?*

"Are your symptoms subsiding?"

"They are, thanks." *But not my shame.*

"Well, I have a small bit of good news," Dr. Ogden said, dropping her voice. "Your test came back positive only for chlamydia, which will easily be killed off by one course of antibiotics."

Well, *yippee.* It isn't every day you find out you've got the *good* kind of STD. "That's... something." I tried not to sound too grim.

She tilted her head, studying me. "Bella, would you be feeling the same way if you'd caught the flu from a partner?"

"God no," I answered immediately.

"Generally, my role is to beat the drum for safer sex. But I want to say something else to you." Her warm eyes studied me. "This isn't a message from God. There's no reason to panic or feel any shame. You're still the same beautiful girl you were the last time I saw you."

Hearing her say that made my throat burn. I took a gulp of tea to hide my reaction.

"Oh, sweetie," she whispered. "You're going to be fine."

I knew that was technically true, but I didn't feel anything like *fine*. "It's hard," I said, my voice cracking. "There's a difficult conversation I need to have, and I haven't done it yet." I'd taken a close look at my calendar. Luckily, only my lackluster night at the Beta Rho house with Whittaker fell within the transmission window.

Just *looking* at my calendar to figure it out had made me feel physically ill. There had been times during the past two years when my number of partners would have been higher than one. That made me cringe — as if the people who judged me for my sex life had pulled off a secret victory.

Ms. Ogden stirred her drink with a straw. "Now, it's not easy to tell someone that he gave you a disease. He may not believe you, because over half the people who carry it don't have any symptoms."

"None?"

She shook her head. "But I can make the conversation a little easier."

"How?"

Ms. Ogden took a card out of her pocket. "Give him my number. If he calls me, I'll ask him a couple of screening questions — to make sure he's not allergic to the antibiotics — and then I'll prescribe over the phone. He doesn't even have to be tested."

"Really?"

She nodded. "It's called expedited partner therapy. If you're pretty sure who gave it to you, then we do it this way. Otherwise, he's just going to keep spreading it around."

"I know," I whispered.

Reaching across the table, she patted my hand. "Hang in

there, Bella. And feel free to call my cell phone if you have any questions. It's on my voicemail message if you call my office phone."

"Thank you," I told her.

"Keep in touch, okay? Because my gut says that you're taking this hard."

"I'll be all right," I said. Convincing no one.

Now that I had a proper diagnosis, I couldn't put off telling Whittaker the bad news.

That night, for the first time all week, I took a long look at the clothes in my closet. If I was going to march into the Beta Rho house and ask to speak to the star running back, I wanted to look good doing it. One of the charities my mother supported gave designer clothes and makeup to cancer patients, with the theory that they'd heal faster if they felt they looked better.

Thinking of those poor women reminded me that it could always be worse.

"It could always be worse," I said to myself as I picked out a little denim skirt, a pretty tank top and a cardigan.

"It could always be worse," I whispered into the mirror while applying a slick of lip gloss. (For me, that was going *all out*.)

"It could always be worse," I repeated as I trotted down the stairs and out into the evening air.

The walk to Beta Rho didn't take nearly long enough for me to compose a suitable speech. When I climbed the wooden steps onto their porch, I noticed how quiet the house was for a Saturday night. For a moment I was thrilled by the prospect that Whittaker and all his pals were out. But as soon as I rang the doorbell, footsteps approached.

The guy who opened the door was a sophomore they called Dash. "'Zup," he said, giving me the generic frat-boy greeting.

"Hey," I returned. "Is Whittaker home by any chance?"

"I'm pretty sure he is. Come on in, and I'll find him for you."

Dash trotted off like a good little newbie. Until tap night in a couple weeks, he was still a low man on the totem pole. When the new crop of pledges showed up, Dash would be the one doling out the orders and ordering someone else to watch the door.

I'm sure he could hardly wait.

I stepped all the way into the living room. On a giant sectional couch, three brothers — all of them football players — held game controllers in their hands. "S'up, Bella," somebody said without removing his eyes from the screen.

"Not much. Pretty quiet here tonight, isn't it?"

"Game tomorrow," came the answer.

Ah. "Coach ordered you to get some Z's?"

Apparently something crucial happened on screen, because I did not get an answer. And anyway, Whittaker appeared, wearing Harkness sweats and flip flops. "Hey, girl," he said, giving me half a smile. "What's shakin'?"

I didn't blame him for looking a little confused. We'd only hooked up that one time after Casino Night.

Now, I stood here regretting it. The sex had been pretty darned average. And afterward, of course I'd had to put myself back together and descend the very public staircase toward the front door, while his frat brothers smirked at me.

And now here I was *again* in this creaky house with sticky floors. *Stupid girl.*

"Can we talk for a minute?" I asked him, trying my best to sound casual.

I saw a flicker of fear cross his face. "Is this the kind of talk I'll need tequila for?"

"Sure, but only because tequila is for every day," I replied.

He gave me a wry grin. "Yo! Dash!" When the younger guy came into view, he asked for two shots. Then he steered me into a breakfast nook off the kitchen, away from everyone else.

Dash carried in our two drinks, lime wedges and salt. After the guy disappeared, Whittaker turned to me with a question in his eyes. "What's up?"

I cleared my throat. There would be no more stalling now. "It's not a big deal," I lied. Because it was to me. "But I found out that I recently acquired chlamydia."

His eyes widened. "No way."

"That was my reaction too."

He drained his shot glass, then set it down with a thunk. "You think I gave it to you."

"It appears that way. But if you didn't give it to me, then you could have caught it from me. So you need to take the pills anyway." I put Ms. Ogden's card on the table and told him what she'd said about prescribing over the phone.

It was hard to say whether he was even listening to me anymore. "Do your shot, Bella."

Right. With nervous fingers, I tossed it back. The wedge of lime had a sharp, sour flavor that seemed to go perfectly with the sharp, sour day I was having.

"Dash!" Whittaker called again. The guy came skidding into the little room like a well-trained dog. "Can you make us tonight's special?"

The guy hesitated for a second, and I decided that he was being tested in some way. There was probably a stupid frat rule about it — forget the drink special, and do two hundred naked push-ups in the middle of Fresh Court. Or something.

"Sure," Dash said after a beat. "I'll be right back."

"I didn't give it to you," Whittaker said when we were alone again. "It wasn't me."

"Okayyy..." I was officially at the end of my script. What was the appropriate response to outright denial? Because if he didn't give it to me, that meant that the shame could only flow in one direction. I'd brought this ugliness to *his* doorstep. "The, uh, doctor said that most people never see symptoms."

"Whatever," he muttered.

Welp, (awkward) mission accomplished. Now I really wanted to get the hell out of there, never to return. I was about to thank him for the drink and make my excuses when Whittaker surprised me by changing the topic to a less loaded one. "How does the hockey team look this year?"

"Pretty good," I said numbly. "We'll miss Hartley a lot, but there's a lot of other talent on the lines."

"Who's the captain? Don't tell me it's that gay dude."

My blood pressure kicked up another notch. I wasn't the kind of girl to let that bit of assholery go unchallenged. But this really wasn't the day to get into an argument with Whittaker over his homophobia. "Trevi is captain," I said quietly. "He's a smart guy."

Dash strode into the room again. He set two drinks on the table, and I looked down to try to identify the drink special. Hmm. It was a rocks drink with a blush color.

One had an umbrella in it. "Aw, mine is accessorized," I said, smiling up at Dash.

He gave an uncomfortable shrug and left the room. Dash was never going to win awards for his conversational skills, that was for sure. I picked up my drink and had a taste. "It's... a madras?" I asked.

Whittaker clinked his glass into mine. "Smart girl," he said, taking a gulp. "Drink up."

I wasn't really in the mood to get drunk, but it seemed rude not to sit a minute longer. I still couldn't tell what Whittaker was thinking. Either he wasn't that worried about what I'd told him, or else he put up a pretty good front. I took a gulp.

"What classes are you taking?" he asked me a minute later, sipping his own drink.

"Um... I'm in that Urban Studies lecture," I said. "And I've got two psych courses..." My head felt a little swimmy now. I hadn't eaten very well since my awful doctor's appointment. Usually, I wasn't such a lightweight.

Across the table, Whittaker asked me another question, but I couldn't quite catch it. "What?" I asked. The glass in my hand felt too heavy, actually. I set it on the table roughly.

The last thing I registered was Whittaker's beady stare.

Chapter Eleven

ELEVEN

RAFE

It was only seven-thirty on a Sunday morning and barely daybreak. I'd already run more than five miles, but a new blister on my heel was giving me trouble. My running shoes needed to be replaced.

That would set me back another hundred dollars. Which I did not have.

I stopped running when I reached the outskirts of campus, slowing to a walk to cool myself down. I loved being alone so early in the morning, when the sun made slanting lines against the limestone facades. Thanks to my fancy new iPod and an over-priced arm band, bachata tunes pulsed in my ears. I walked slowly down the sleepy fraternity row. It was still cold enough outside that my breath made visible puffs in the morning air.

At that hour, I fully expected to be alone. It surprised me to hear a door slam on one of the wooden porches. My eyes traced the row of houses, but it was not a fraternity member who stumbled into view. A girl, her head bent down, made an awkward descent from the last porch in the row. As I watched, she grabbed the railing to steady herself. In spite of the chill, she had on skimpy clothing. And I couldn't help notice that her arms and legs were strangely tattooed.

The drooping girl seemed to gather herself with a deep breath, and then shove off into the morning. But her feet weren't willing to play along. She stumbled after a few steps, and then fell awkwardly to the sidewalk.

Shit.

Yanking my ear buds out, I draped them around my neck. Then I jogged forward as the skin of my heel yelped in protest. By the time I reached her, the girl was attempting to pull herself to her feet.

It was *Bella.*

For a moment I just froze there, my brain too startled to react. But her knees buckled again, and my reflexes came back online. I lunged forward, clamping one hand on either hip to steady her.

Bella let fly with a hoarse shriek of terror.

Shit!

"Bella, *sorry.* It's just me. Rafe. Sorry." I was babbling, but she was trembling in my arms, and it was freaky. I stepped around her body so she could see me. "Are you okay?"

As I waited for an answer, I took in more strange details and began to understand that she was not okay. Not at all. What I'd mistaken for tattoos on her limbs were actually words inked in *marker.* Some person — or people — had *written* on Bella.

FILTHY BITCH had been scrawled on her upper arm in black ink.

And on her leg? If I used any of those words, my Ma would slap me. My chest clenched just to see it. Acting on instinct, I stepped closer to Bella, leaning her against my chest. Then I looked up at the frat house I'd just seen her leave.

Beta Rho.

The house was completely still. And except for the slow creaking of a birch tree moving in the breeze, there was no noise at all. There were no faces in the doorway or at the windows.

What the hell went on in there?

My neck tingled, and I fought off a shiver. Bella was silent. The whole situation was creepy as hell.

I really needed to get Bella home before she fell over again. "Come on. Let's go." I repositioned her in the crook of my arm, my hand pressed against her hip.

Moving down the sidewalk, I was practically frog-marching her. Not that it was easy. Every few steps she stumbled. With my free hand, I grasped Bella's other elbow. Her skin was cold to the touch.

Thankfully, it was only a few minutes' walk from fraternity row to Beaumont. "Can you tell me what happened?" I asked once.

"No," Bella whispered. The glassy look in her eyes gave nothing away.

When we reached our entryway, I hip-checked the laser reader, hoping for enough contact to unlock the door. I heard a reassuring click, and stepped up to open the door. Bella stumbled over the marble threshold, and there was an awkward moment when I thought one or both of us was going to end up on the tile floor.

"Whoa," I said, steadying us. I peered up the stairs. "Come on, now," I whispered. "Almost there." With Bella still tucked under my arm, we reached the first stair step.

With a hand on the railing, she dragged herself up the first five or six steps. Then she stopped. "Just leave me here," she said, her voice low.

"No can do," I replied.

She actually gave me a little shove with her hip. "Go."

There was no way in hell I would walk away from her. Maybe I hadn't known what to say or do since our crazy night together. I'd probably handled things pretty badly. But I knew *exactly* what to do right now.

Instead of arguing with Bella, I stepped into her space. I bent my knees and wrapped my arms around her hips, lifting her into the air.

For one shocked second, she said nothing. I slung her over my shoulder, grabbing the railing with my free hand. Then I began to climb.

"Down," she insisted to my back. "Put me *down*."

"Nope," I exhaled.

She gave my back a thump with her arm, but I only held her more tightly. I powered up the stairs. I didn't want someone sticking his head out to catch us this way. It would look as though I was overpowering a drunk girl.

And I was, if you wanted to get all technical about it.

About a minute later, I was sliding Bella down my body and onto her feet in front of her fourth-floor door.

Her face had pinked up, and her eyes narrowed. I was glad to see it. An ornery Bella was much better than a stony-eyed one. She patted the pocket of her skirt, drew out a set of keys and then dropped them.

Before she could react, I snatched them off the floor and stuck the room key in the lock.

"Hey," Bella argued. But I wanted her inside her room and off her feet. She still looked as if the slightest breeze might knock her down.

Behind us I heard the squeak of a door. Turning my head, I caught a glimpse of her famous neighbor's face peeking out. Lianne's eyes grew wide before she shut her door again.

Bella pushed her own door open, yanking the knob from my hand. She crashed into the room, stumbled over to the bed and fell onto it.

I shut the door behind me, then went over to kneel beside the bed. "Bella," I whispered. "Are you hurt anywhere?" She seemed so weak and that was odd. I didn't have much experience with alcohol poisoning, though.

In answer, Bella only closed her eyes.

I took the opportunity to examine the words marked on her

limbs. Two or three different pens had been used. The lines weren't all the same width, and some of the handwriting was different.

The only consistent feature was how *awful* it was. DANGER someone had written. And that was just about the only word in the bunch you could say in church. A lot of it wasn't coherent, which may have been a blessing. But even misspelled, FILTY PUSSY was unfortunately legible.

As I looked her over, the creepy tingle returned to my spine. Someone had done this to Bella. No — several someones. It was almost impossible to picture. They must have stood around her passed-out body, egging each other on.

I tasted bile imagining it. And I couldn't help wondering what else they might have done to her.

Shit. I'd gotten Bella home safely. But it occurred to me that the job wasn't over. "Bella," I whispered. "Do you need to go to the police? Or the hospital?"

Her eyes flew open again. "No," she ground out. "They didn't... It wasn't about that."

"Then..." I grasped for the right question. "What was it about?"

"EMBARRASSING me!" She sat up. "It worked. You're *staring!*"

I sat back on my heels and took a deep breath. It wouldn't be right to just let this go. "I don't know what happened to you, but this is disgusting, and you need to tell someone." I slipped my iPod out of its sports sleeve. I opened up the camera app and aimed my device at Bella's leg.

"What are you doing?" she gasped, swatting at my iPod.

I held it out for her to take. "When you're ready to talk, you're going to want proof."

For the first time since I'd found her on fraternity row, she squared her shoulders. Then, before I even knew what was happening, she grabbed my iPod and threw it across the room. I heard a sickening crack as it crashed into the plaster wall.

Sections of my fancy toy flung themselves in opposite directions on Bella's floor.

"OUT!" Bella yelled. She dragged herself onto her feet and pointed her body toward the little bathroom.

I stood up to follow because she still looked unsteady.

She gripped the door frame and swung an angry face toward mine. "Don't you *dare* follow me into the *bathroom*."

I heard the sound of another door opening. I looked past Bella into the bathroom and saw the neighbor's face peering at me again, this time with shocked, wide-open eyes.

Fantastico. I took a step back, hoping to look nonthreatening. "Listen. If you don't want me here, that's fine. But who can I call for you? I don't think you should be alone right now."

Bella gave her head a single shake. "Just GO!" Bella's head swiveled to take in Lianne's curious gaze. "What are *you* staring at?"

The other girl's bathroom door closed quickly. That was a shame, because now was really the perfect time for a girlfriend to step in.

"I'm *showering*," Bella said, her hand on the bathroom door. The expression on her face was fierce.

I took a couple steps backward, still unsure what to do.

"Get *out* of here," Bella slurred. Then she shut the bathroom door in my face.

Standing there, staring at the wooden panels, I didn't know what to do. After a moment, I heard the sound of the shower. Still, I was not going to leave her alone here. Not in her condition.

I left Bella's room, as she'd asked me to, but I didn't go downstairs. Instead, I knocked on the neighbor's door.

She opened it warily. "Hi," she said through the narrow opening.

"Hi. I'm Rafe. I'm your downstairs neighbor."

"I know," she whispered.

Fair enough. "So... Bella is not doing so well, and she won't tell me why. Are the two of you close?"

Slowly, the girl shook her head, a look of regret in her eyes.

"Okay." I cleared my throat. "That makes two of us. She's in the shower now I think."

Lianne tipped her head toward her own bathroom door, and nodded.

"Can you just... check on her in a few minutes?"

"Okay," she whispered. "What's the deal with...?" She gestured toward her arms and legs.

"I really don't know. I was out running when I found her. And she won't talk about it."

Lianne cringed.

"Just check on her, okay? Are you going to be home for a while? I'll come back upstairs later to see how she is."

I waited for Lianne's nod before I turned away.

Still in my sweaty running clothes, I went downstairs to my own bathroom. I showered and dressed. Bickley was still passed out in his bed where I'd left him a couple of hours before.

This morning I'd almost slept in too, skipping the run. If I hadn't gone, Bella might still be sprawled on the sidewalk somewhere. The idea made me feel sick.

I was hunting for a pair of clean socks when there was a tentative knock on our outer door. When I opened it, Lianne stood there, looking uncomfortable. "She's still in the shower," she said.

"Okay." A long shower wasn't the end of the world.

Lianne bit her lip. "She sounds really upset. But when I tried to ask her if she needed help, she just screamed at me. She doesn't want me in there."

Dios. "Do you want me to try to talk to her?"

Lianne nodded.

"All right." I headed up the stairs followed by Lianne. On the landing, I caught her elbow. "Hey. Can you tell me who Bella *does* talk to? Does she have a girlfriend I could call? Someone she trusts?"

Lianne looked thoughtful. "Bella doesn't have girlfriends. She hangs around with the hockey team."

"Well..." I couldn't exactly start dialing from the top of the team roster. "Anyone special?"

"I don't know their names. One of them speaks a lot of French."

I remembered that guy from Casino Night, but had no idea who he was. And for all I knew, he was the one who hurt her. "Can you let me into the bathroom?"

Lianne led me through her room. When I entered the bathroom, the shower curtain was only partially closed, and I could see movement. Bella was seated on the shower floor, furiously scraping at her skin with a bar of soap. "Damn it, damn, damn," she chanted. I took one step closer. The skin on her leg was raw-looking and red.

"Bella," I said. I think I startled her. She dropped the soap and folded over herself. "Come on out of there now," I said as gently as I could. She didn't answer me. She only hugged her bent knee more tightly, her face turned away from mine.

Jesucristo. Someone needed to help Bella get a grip. Since there was nobody else handy, seemed like that someone was going to be me.

I stuck my arm into the shower, turning off the water. Towels hung from hooks on the opposite wall. I grabbed the largest one and draped it over Bella's dripping back and shoulders. "Come on now. Stand up."

She didn't move.

"Get up, *princesita*." I spoke to her the way I might address one of my cranky little cousins who needed a nap. "Come on now. Get up or I'm going to pick you up." I didn't really want to make good on that threat. Luckily, Bella didn't want me too, either. She gathered the edges of the towel together and rose, her back to me.

I gave her some space. Bella stepped out of the shower, avoiding my eyes. I followed her into her room, averting my gaze while she wrapped the towel properly across her chest and under her arms.

When she sat down on the bed, I noticed that although the skin on her legs was rubbed raw, I could still see the faded outlines of the words written there. The marks were still quite dark on her shoulders and upper arms, too.

Bella saw me looking and clamped her arms across her chest, hands over her shoulders. "I want you to leave me alone." She spared me a single glance, and it was full of pain.

Instead of obeying, I sat down beside her on the bed, but not too close. "I'll go if you call someone else to be here with you."

She made an irritated noise. "I don't want company, Rafe."

"That's too bad," I said as gently as possible. "But it's me or a friend. Because honestly, I feel like I should go get the house dean."

Bella's blue eyes widened with horror. "Don't you fucking *dare*. I don't need the dean. I don't need you. I just need to..." She broke off, rubbing at a spot on her upper arm with her thumb. The ink was particularly dark there. She scraped at it with her thumbnail — the letter "D" in *DIRTY BITCH*. Still pink from the hot water, Bella's skin looked tender.

While I watched, Bella made an angry red scratch across her velvet skin.

I wasn't even thinking when I reached out, but I couldn't stand to see her hurt herself any more than I could stand the words on her skin. I covered up the scratch with my hand, knocking her clawing finger out of the way.

She froze solid under my touch.

"Don't hurt yourself. *Please*," I begged.

Her face got tight, and her eyes began to redden. When she spoke again, her voice had an edge of hysteria. "But I can't get it *off*."

"I'll help you get it off," I promised. "Just don't do that."

She inhaled through her nose. I saw her fighting for control, and my throat got tight. I'd been operating on pure adrenaline up until this moment. But now it felt as if all the air had been sucked out of the room and replaced by sadness.

Bella dropped her head. Then she let out a sob so raw my gut clenched at the sound. And I wanted to *maim* whoever caused her to make that awful noise. She hunched forward, her towel slipping. Her back rose and fell with sobs.

I lunged for the blanket at the foot of her bed, which I wrapped around her body. Only then did I reach for her. Grabbing her shoulders, I leaned her against me.

She didn't fight me, but her shoulders continued to shake. I wrapped my arms around her, pulling her close to me. I just wanted to make the shaking stop. "Shh, *cariño*. You're going to be okay." *Dios*, what meaningless words. But I didn't know any better ones.

She didn't acknowledge me. She turned her face away from mine and I could still feel every silent sob wracking her.

That would not do.

I swept her wet hair off her face and wiped the tears away with my thumb. "Shhh."

Bella had always struck me as a tough cookie. There was just something so buoyant in the way she held herself. Even now, I watched her slow down her breathing, forcing herself to get calm. She lifted her eyes to the ceiling, blinking back unshed tears. "Sorry," she whispered.

I gave her shoulder a squeeze. "Do you have any rubbing alcohol?"

She shook her head.

"Okay. What about nail-polish remover?"

Bella gave me the side eye. Then she shook her head again. "Not my style."

I tucked the blanket around her and then slid out from under her. "I'm going to go get us some breakfast and coffee. And find something to get that ink off."

Bella looked up at me, measuring me with her gaze. "You don't have to."

"Back in a jif."

It took me thirty minutes to visit the pharmacy and the dining hall. Soon enough I was trotting back up the entryway stairs, passing my own door to climb to Bella's.

"Knock knock," I said outside. My hands were full.

She opened the door wearing sweatpants and a long-sleeved T-shirt. "You didn't have to do this."

I ignored that comment and walked in, setting all the booty down on her desk. "Do you want the bagel with smoked salmon, or the egg burrito? Or we could go halfsies."

Bella cleared her throat. "The bagel?"

I passed her a cardboard clamshell container and a coffee cup. Then I moved a stack of books off her desk chair and sat in it, opening my own coffee.

There were a couple minutes of silence while we ate. I'd run something like six miles that morning, then carried Bella up the stairs. I was desperately hungry.

Across from me, Bella nibbled at her breakfast and snuck looks at me. "Nice work getting take-out from the dining hall," she said eventually. The Beaumont House dining room was eat-in only, except for coffee.

"I work there." I shrugged. "I know where the takeout containers are hiding."

"That's handy. And I guess you can't beat the commute."

"Sure. But it's really all about the paycheck. The dining halls are unionized, so I get fifteen bucks an hour."

"Not bad," Bella said. "That's more than I get as the hockey manager."

I doubted that Bella actually needed the money. "It's almost twice what an office or library job pays. And the weird thing is that very few students take dining-hall jobs. I guess people don't want to be the guy in the paper hat, serving their friends."

"But for twice the pay..." Bella took a sip of her coffee. She was looking more and more like herself now.

"The money is good. I'm not usually on the serving line anyway. I'm a prep cook, which means I chop vegetables, mostly. It's the same job I've been doing in my family's restaurant since I was ten. But now I get paid."

"I don't know how to cook," Bella admitted. "But it's on my to-do list."

"Yeah?" I finished my egg burrito and got up to put the empty carton in her trash bin. Then I plucked the pharmacy bag off the floor and took out a bottle of nail-polish remover and a bag of cotton balls. I punctured the bag and tried to remove a couple of them, but a bunch more came along for the ride, scattering in my lap and onto the floor.

Bella raised an eyebrow. "I appreciate this. But I can take it from here."

I shook my head. "Let me see your shoulder. You can't see that spot."

She stayed put. "There's this thing called a mirror."

"Bella." We had a stare-down. "Just let me see if this stuff works. Then I'll leave you to it."

"Fine," she huffed. Then, in one smooth motion, she whipped off her Harkness Hockey T-shirt.

I practically jumped to stand behind her, so that my eyes wouldn't drift down to her chest. A few seconds later the room was invaded by the smell of the acetone — the scent I associated with the nail salons that I passed on New York City streets. The dampened cotton ball that I rubbed against her skin began to turn a bluish-purple color as it weakened the marker.

"This is working." I showed her the cotton ball. Then I worked to get the word SLUTTY off her perfect, creamy shoulder. Seeing the word there made me so angry I had to take a long breath in through my nose, just to try to calm down.

"Is the scent getting to you?" she asked.

"Yeah," I muttered, my voice like gravel. *Dios. Who would do this?* "Bella. Would you tell me what happened?"

"No," she said quickly.

I considered her answer for a minute. "Would you please tell somebody else, then?"

Silence was her only answer.

Meanwhile, I'd faded the word SLUTTY to the point where it was not quite legible. I tossed the cotton ball into Bella's garbage can and dunked another one, going to work on the word CUNT next. Getting these words off Bella's skin wasn't that difficult. But I was worried something worse than marks on her skin had happened to her. And if it had, I was basically involved in a cover-up job at the moment. Some sicko was going to get away with this shit, and I was helping him.

"Bella," I whispered. We were so close to one another that my nearly inaudible words were delivered right to her ear. "If something *else* happened to you last night, would you tell someone? It's important."

"There's nothing to tell." Her voice was flat.

"What do you remember?" I pressed.

She took a step forward and turned around. "Enough to know that it isn't what you're thinking."

"Okay," I said, holding a smelly cotton ball in the air like a moron. I could only hope she was telling me the truth.

"I'm sorry I broke your iPod." Her eyes darted to the remains in the corner.

"Easy come, easy go," I said. "Never really needed that thing."

"I'll get you another one anyway."

"Don't bother. Really." I put the cap on the bottle of remover. It seemed that Bella was herding me toward the exit. And even if I still felt unsure about leaving her, I couldn't force her to let me help.

"I can take it from here," she said.

"Okay." I picked up our empty coffee cups and shoved them in the bag. "I'm right downstairs if you need anything."

"Thanks," she said stiffly.

Feeling as though I hadn't really done much to help, I left Bella alone.

That evening I spent hours in the library. At Harkness you couldn't really say "the library" without qualifying your location. There were *forty* libraries, and everyone had a couple of favorite spots. Some libraries were good for people watching, some were close to the better coffee shops.

I didn't go to the library to socialize. There weren't enough hours in the day. So I favored the basement of the Central Campus Library with my business. Down there, a guy could snag a private study carrel. They were nothing but a built-in desk, a chair, three walls and a sliding glass door. We called them weenie bins, and that night I spread out my books and went to it.

Eventually, I fell asleep on a book for Urban Studies. I didn't wake up until the midnight announcement that the library was closing. Shoving books into my bag, I staggered outside to walk home.

Harkness was breathtaking at this hour, with its old fashioned glass lamps making long shadows on the brick pathways. There was nobody else out on the street, and I could almost imagine that a horse-drawn carriage was about to round the corner from Chapel Street.

The iron gate creaked as I let myself into Beaumont gate. As I approached the entryway door, I tipped my head back to look up at the building. A single light burned on the fourth floor in Bella's room.

I wondered why she wasn't sleeping.

TWELVE

BELLA

Even though I was exhausted, I didn't want to turn off my light.

I wasn't a girl who scared easily — not at all. But the last time I'd fallen asleep had been against my will. Many hours later, I'd woken up on a dirty wooden floor. It's not that I thought it would happen again. But I had a lingering smudge of dread in my gut. I couldn't relax.

So I sat there in my bed, a book abandoned on my lap, just waiting to feel drowsy. Instead, felt only wired and jumpy.

When I heard footsteps on the landing outside my door, all the hair on my neck stood up.

The tap on my door was so gentle, I found my voice. "Yeah?"

"It's Rafe."

When I opened the door, he stood there in a T-shirt and flannel pants, a book in his hand. "Hey." His big brown eyes studied me, as if performing an assessment.

"Hey," I echoed. I turned to get away from his stare, heading back to the bed and climbing in.

"Did you eat dinner?"

"Yes, Mom." *As long as granola bars count.* I shouldn't be sassing Rafe. He was just trying to be nice.

"Okay," he said slowly, as if he didn't think he should believe me. An uncomfortable beat passed, and I was sure he was about to open his mouth and ask me again what happened last night.

I was never going to tell him.

"I did the Urban Studies reading," he said instead. He walked right over to sit on the edge of the bed. "Move over," he demanded.

Seriously? "You want to talk about Urban Studies at one in the morning?" I moved over, though.

"Urban renewal is older than I thought," he said, as if I cared. "The renovation of Paris was in 1853." He flipped open the book in his hands and read a paragraph.

I yawned. Then I rolled toward the wall to get away from the facts of nineteenth-century urban renewal.

Rafe stretched out on top of the quilt beside me, trapping me under my covers. He rolled, too, putting the book on my hip. "It says here that the streets were widened for military maneuvers. Have you seen Paris?" He gave me a little nudge when I didn't answer right away.

"Mm-hmm," I said, suddenly sleepy. It was easy to finally let my guard down now that my neighbor was trying to bore me to death.

"I haven't been there," he said quietly. "But now I want to go. Listen to this..."

Rafe's voice droned on behind me. The warmth of his body seeped through my covers and heated my back. He was like a big sturdy wall between me and the rest of the world. I began to relax, muscle by muscle. I drifted on the sound of his voice.

Sometime later I heard the click of my lamp shutting off, but the solid heat of Rafe's body did not disappear. At some point I became aware of his slow breathing, and the faint thud of a book dropping to the floor.

I slept on.

Chapter Thirteen

THIRTEEN

RAFE

For the second time, I woke up in Bella's bed.

When I opened my eyes, I saw her slanted ceiling. She was lying on her side, her butt tucked against me, the soles of her feet against my calf. Carefully, I turned my head to see her more clearly. Her back rose and fell slowly as she slept. Relaxed in her sleep, she looked sweet and so vulnerable. I had a strong urge to roll onto my side and curl up around her body.

Not going to happen. I'd had that chance once, and I'd handled it very poorly.

Quietly, I got out of bed. She didn't wake at all, not even when I fumbled into my shoes.

Grabbing my book off the floor, I tiptoed out, leaving her to rest.

I didn't speak to her on Monday at all, though I did get a glimpse of her when she came through the lunch line. She wore a long-sleeve T-shirt and jeans, and a tight expression on her face. Since she was up and around, I counted it as a win.

Monday night her light was out when I got back from the

library. So I left her alone. Tuesday morning we had Urban Studies together.

She didn't show.

I sat through the lecture, worried about her. The only thing that kept me from ditching class to check on her was the fact that Professor Giulio was lecturing about the affordable housing movement, which Bella and I would need to understand to complete our part of the project. So I did my best to take notes.

The minute class was over, I got up and headed back to Beaumont House. Thankfully I wasn't on the lunch schedule today. Knocking on Bella's door got me nowhere. "It's Rafe," I called, as if that would make a difference. "Are you in there?"

Silence.

After a moment, Lianne's door opened behind me, and I spun around. She beckoned, and I followed her into her room, letting the door fall closed behind me.

"I have to show you something," Lianne whispered. She waved me toward a seriously grand computer setup — the girl had several monitors lit at once.

As I stood behind her, the computer screen in the middle loaded a web page called *Brodacious*. I'd seen this website once before. It was a catalog of fraternity boasts and pranks. Bickley had forwarded a link last year when some frat managed to hang a fifteen-foot banner off the top of Harkness Chapel illustrating the relative size difference between a Harkness guy's dick and a Princeton guy's.

Classy, right?

This time what I saw on the screen was much worse. It was a photo of Bella sprawled on a floor somewhere. Her face was mostly obscured by one arm thrown over her eyes. But anyone who knew her could identify her. She'd been wearing the same clothes as in the picture when I'd carried her up the stairs, but I'd know her distinctive curls anywhere.

"PUBLIC SERVICE ANNOUNCEMENT. STEER CLEAR

OF THE HOCKEY MASCOT," the text screamed. "DIRTY PUSSY ALERT."

Jesucristo.

FOURTEEN

BELLA

I knew the *exact* moment when Rafe saw that fucking picture, because I heard the strangled sound he let out. The noise he made crept under my bathroom door, stole across the room and curled around me on the bed. It squeezed my soul into a tight little knot in the center of my chest.

I *burned* with shame.

For almost twenty-four hours I'd been lying here imagining what would happen when my friends saw that photo. Everyone I'd ever been close to was destined to see it, if they hadn't already. Pepe. Graham. Rikker. Trevi.

The hockey girlfriends who already hated me.

Coach Canning, who thought I was a nuisance.

Nobody was *ever* going look at me the same way again. I had fucked up too badly this time to recover.

From Lianne's room Rafe's voice demanded, "Who the fuck did this?"

"I don't know, but the web host is a saas-based content management company. The editor used off-campus internet connections."

Hell. No wonder she'd gotten miffed about sex noises from my room. It was easy to hear every word. Our bathroom was an echo chamber, apparently.

"I'm going to... FUCK! What language are you speaking?" Rafe demanded.

I could even hear Lianne's sigh. "*Nerd* language. I was able to learn quite a bit about the website itself but not about who owns it. I think it's Beta Rho, though, because Brodacious is a play on their name."

Lianne was pretty clever for a girl who never left her room.

"Did Bella see this?" he asked her.

"I showed it to her yesterday afternoon."

"What did she say?"

"Nothing. But she hasn't come out since."

Shit. I braced for impact, turning toward the wall and curling into a protective ball. Aside from closing my eyes, there was no way I could hide from Rafe. I'd left the door to the bathroom unlocked, and now I could hear it opening. The next thing I heard were his feet crossing the floor toward me.

The mattress dipped under his weight. Then a warm hand covered my elbow. "Bella," he whispered.

I rolled my face into the pillow, imagining what he saw. It was stuffy in my room, and the place reeked of acetone. Cotton balls littered the floor. The skin on my arms looked chafed and red, and faint outlines of the marker remained.

"Bella, you're scaring me."

"So," I said, the word muffled by the pillow.

"Get up, okay?"

"No." I knew he was being nice, but I couldn't find it in me to care. For every Rafe, there were ten Whittakers. And I didn't want to face any of them.

"Lianne showed me the picture," he said.

I said nothing.

"Are you going to report it?"

"No."

He made an angry sound. "Why the hell not?"

Damn him. Couldn't a girl be left alone to suffer her indignities in peace? I lifted my head from the pillow to glower at him. "God, do you *get* that I don't want to talk about it? With anyone? Or *see* anyone?"

That shut him up.

"I know you're being nice," I whispered. "But I just can't..." I dropped my head back onto the pillow, facing the wall. Maybe if I just ignored him, he'd go away.

For a long moment Rafe was silent. "Fine," he said eventually. "We don't have to talk. But you still have to get up."

"No."

"Yes. We're going running."

"What?" I was confused enough to turn my head again so I could see his face.

"Running," he repeated. "That's when you put shoes on and move your feet real fast, transporting yourself from one spot to another."

"I don't run," I said, turning back to the wall.

"Today you do," I said. "Or else."

"Or else what?"

"I'm going to Dean Darling to tell him you're having a break-down and won't get out of bed."

My chin whipped around at this latest indignity. "No you will *not*."

He pushed a limp curl out of my eyes. "Yeah, I will. Try me."

I shoved his hand away. I'd had enough of his bullshit. "Get out of my face, Rafe. None of this has anything to do with you."

"That's not the point," he said, those big chocolate eyes watching me closely.

"What *is* the point?"

"You're not okay. And I'm the one who noticed."

Great. Rafe was some kind of do-gooder. I sure knew how to pick 'em. "It's none of your business," I whispered.

He stood. "I'm going downstairs to change. That takes about

five minutes. You're already wearing sweats. Put on running shoes while I'm gone."

"I'll get right on that," I lied.

He left. When he was on his way out of my room, I heard the telltale click the lock makes when it's toggled from locked to unlocked.

I got off the bed for the first time in hours and flipped it locked again. My stomach made an angry growl when I crawled back onto the bed. I hadn't eaten because that required leaving my room.

Whatever. I lay down again. When the knock came five minutes later, I ignored it. When Rafe tried to turn the knob, it did not budge.

"Fine," he said from the hallway. "I'm going to knock on the house dean's door next."

I leapt off the bed and yanked the door open. "You can't just *order* me!"

He raised one dark eyebrow. "When I'm in a major funk, exercise helps."

"Thanks for the tip." There was no way to stop the bitchy things that fell from my mouth. But I wasn't sure I cared.

"Come running," he demanded.

"Fuck no! I can't even *do* that."

"Sure you can." He stared me down. "Either we run or we have lunch together in the dining hall."

I felt heat on my neck just imagining it. When my eyes flicked in the direction of the dining hall, I knew I'd given myself away. But fuck it. I did *not* want to see a hundred pairs of on me. "I'm not going anywhere near that place."

"Put your running shoes on," said the most bull-headed neighbor that ever was.

For a few seconds, I wavered. But Rafe was exactly the sort of guy who would go to the dean, imagining he'd done me a favor. I did not have time for *that*.

Damn. It.

"I don't even own running shoes," I said as a last ditch effort to avoid this.

"You can borrow mine!" Lianne's voice piped up.

I yelled toward the bathroom. "Your feet are probably a size five."

"Nope!" she said cheerfully. "Seven and a half. Same as you."

Fuck.

A few minutes later, I found myself stepping outside into a crisp October day. I kept my head down as I grudgingly followed Rafe out of the Beaumont courtyard.

He pointed up the street. "Come on. You set the pace."

"I don't run."

"Everybody runs."

"No, Rafe, they really don't."

"Really? If they were giving out free cones at Scoops to the first hundred takers, you'd just mosey over there?"

I rolled my eyes at the flagstone pathway.

"Then follow me." He began to jog at an easy pace down the block.

This was ridiculous, but I still jogged after him. At least at this hour, most everyone was in class. I only had to swerve around a few students on the sidewalk.

The people around me were oblivious — tapping on their phones or talking to friends. What I wouldn't give to go back in time just a few days. I wanted to be oblivious too — to walk around campus like I owned the place. But now I didn't know what to do with my eyes whenever we approached someone. Harkness was a small school, and even the people I didn't know looked familiar.

Every time we passed someone, I looked down at my shoes. And I couldn't help but wonder, *Have you seen the picture? Have you read the caption?*

Harkness College had turned on me, and I was never going to feel the same way about it again.

Rafe didn't try to talk as we ran, thank God. And I was grateful when he steered us toward the old Harkness graveyard, because we wouldn't have to dodge pedestrians there.

"Never came through here before," I panted when we ran through the gate.

"It's cool," he said. "On the way home I'll show you my favorite grave."

"Bet you say that to all the girls," I puffed.

He chuckled, but he didn't slow down, damn him. At the other end of the cemetery, he ran us up Science Hill, where the pedestrian traffic was also minimal. But my pace had slowed to a crawl, so he took a hint and stopped at a drinking fountain in the tiny park at the top.

"Dying here," I groaned, bending over to lean on my knees. "Why do people do this?"

He took a drink before answering. "Just to prove they can."

"But I don't care if I can."

"You'd care if you couldn't," he pointed out.

"That's deep," I scoffed.

While I took my turn at the fountain, I saw Rafe giving me the once-over. "We'll turn back now," he promised.

I must have looked as tired as I felt. "You go ahead. I'm walking back."

"No way," he said immediately. "You're going to do this right."

"God, why? I'm not an athlete."

He shook his head. "An athlete isn't a special kind of person. Anyone can be an athlete. You just do it, and then you can call yourself one."

"Just do it, huh? Are you on Nike's payroll?" My stream of bitchiness was on autopilot now.

"Move your ass, Bella." He pointed back toward campus. "It's downhill, for God's sake. My grandma could run that."

Was there anyone bossier in all of Harkness College? I doubted it. "You're not my favorite person today."

He stretched his quads. "Eh. It's been awhile since I was your favorite person. What's one more day in the doghouse?"

I gave him one more ornery look, then I took off down the hill.

He was startled, I think. I swear he had to hustle to catch up.

If it hadn't been downhill, I wouldn't have been able to make it.

When I'd told Rafe I didn't run, I wasn't kidding. By the time the gates of the graveyard loomed, my lungs were burning and I had a painful stitch in my side. My body was clearly stunned at this sudden demand for locomotion. *What the fuck*, it seemed to say as I pounded out the last hundred yards, drawing up short in the cemetery.

"We're not back yet," Rafe said, stopping alongside me. And that bastard wasn't even breathing hard.

"You think?" I growled. "Where's your favorite grave?"

He took off running, heading to the right. After twenty paces or so I saw him turn.

Crap.

With my chest burning on each inhale, I chased after him.

He didn't go far. Half way down the row of headstones, Rafe stood just off the path, waiting for me. I'd assumed he would bring me to one of the gaudy mausoleums I had glimpsed many times from the street. But he waited in front of a simple slate stone that was rounded at the top. "This is your favorite?" I gasped, sounding like an emphysemic octogenarian.

"Yeah, because it tells a story."

I knelt in front of the stone, both to see it better and also as a cheap way of resting. "Here lies Daniel Webber, age 14, killed by a log he made." *Yikes.* "That's your favorite? Why?"

Rafe shrugged. "I'm not sure why they bothered to put that

on here. Most of the other stones just give the dates and maybe the spouse's name."

I shivered. "He cut down a tree, and it fell on him. It was a revenge killing."

Rafe's lips twitched. "That must have happened all the time back then. Or other shit like it."

"Are you trying to say that I don't have it so bad?"

"Nah. I just like old things. And this is one of them." He turned to walk down the row, and I followed, grateful he wasn't running anymore.

"How far did we go, anyway?"

He glanced over his shoulder, then down at his watch. "Probably... a mile and a half?"

"*Really?*" I ran a mile and a half?" That couldn't be right.

He grinned, the way you smile at a kitten that's done something stupid. "That's nothing, Bella. You probably walk twice that far every day."

"Still," I said. He wouldn't understand. I spent a lot of time looking after athletes who benched three hundred in the weight room and squatted six hundred. But it was never me who wore the tired, satisfied look of someone who'd just completed a workout.

"You know," Rafe said, "the running path around the reservoir in Central Park is just a mile and a half."

"Really?" I squeaked. "I could do that."

"No kidding," he said, smiling again. "My grandma could do that."

For that he deserved the poke in the ribs I gave him. I was so bowled over by my newfound athletic prowess that I let Rafe walk me into the deli on Broad Street before I thought better of it. The place was crowded with students. "Let's go home," I begged. "I don't have my wallet."

"I do," he said.

Great. And who said chivalry was dead?

"What's good here?" He eyed the menu board.

"Everything." Besides one last granola bar from my stash, I hadn't eaten anything since yesterday. And it was probably almost two o'clock. "I like the Greek chicken wrap."

Rafe pulled out his wallet and ordered two of them.

My stomach began to growl in earnest while we waited for our food. But it didn't growl loud enough to cover the sounds of male laughter coming from the back of the room.

The sweat on my neck instantly cooled. *Don't look*, I ordered myself. There was another swell of laughter. Goosebumps rose on my arms. What if *he* was back there? I gave a full body shiver. And then I couldn't help myself. I turned to scan a group of thick-necked guys at the table in back.

One of them made eye contact with me. And his smile widened.

My knees felt trembly all of a sudden, and I reached out to grip the deli's counter.

"You okay?" Rafe asked.

"Yeah," I said, my voice thick. Somewhere in the depths of my suddenly spinning head I knew they could be laughing about anything. But it didn't even matter. Because if it wasn't those particular assholes having a chuckle at my expense, then it was another group somewhere nearby.

Another wave of laughter came from the table in back, and I just wanted to *die*. Rafe was so proud of himself for distracting me for an hour. But what was the point? Those fuckers at Beta Rho had framed my troubles for the whole world, and everyone at Harkness was going to see it.

And *know*.

My distress must have shown on my face, because now I saw Rafe eyeing the table in the corner, too. "Do you know them?" he asked softly.

I shook my head.

His dark brown eyes studied me warily. "You want to wait outside? I'll get the food."

He really didn't understand. Outside wasn't any better. There was *no place* to hide. "I'm good," I lied. But then another guffaw burst forth from the dudes in the corner, and I must have stiffened. Because Rafe moved a little, changing the angle of his body, shielding me from view.

With a cold sweat breaking out on my back, I was counting the seconds until we could get away from here. In my whole life, I didn't remember ever feeling this way — like I'd rather erase myself than hear another peal of laughter.

We'd discussed embarrassment in one of my psych classes. Embarrassment is just a construct you build for yourself. Nobody can *make* you feel embarrassed. Intellectually, I knew this to be true. But standing there in the deli sweating all over myself, it didn't really matter.

My stomach was churning now. I didn't even *want* a sandwich.

"So," Rafe said, trying to distract me. "Your neighbor is a movie star. What's up with that? I never see her coming in or out of the entryway."

I looked up into Rafe's calm brown eyes, and they steadied me. A little. "Lianne barely leaves her room. And she gets tetchy if I have music playing." *Or loud men in my room.* Lucky for Lianne, there weren't going to be any of *those* anymore. Probably forever. "Honestly, she's a piece of work. I tried to be friendly, but it didn't take."

"Huh," Rafe said. "Why doesn't she live on Fresh Court with the other first years?"

"I think it's a security thing. Anyone can walk into Fresh Court, but Beaumont has an extra set of locked gates, right?" I watched a guy behind the counter put two wrap sandwiches into a bag, praying that it was ours.

"That makes sense." The man slid the bag across the stainless steel counter and Rafe took it. I turned on my heel and made for the door.

If Rafe was surprised I would be willing to *run* back to Beaumont, he didn't say so. I even ran up the stairs, relaxing only when I'd made it back to the safety of my room.

Inside, Rafe opened the bag, handing me one of the sandwiches. "Drink some water while you eat this, okay?"

"Sure," I said. I guess he wasn't staying for lunch. I was disappointed, too, which was weird. Because I hadn't wanted to see him at all in the first place.

"I've got a study session now," he said by way of explanation. "But I'll see you tonight?"

"Why?"

"We have to do some work on our project."

"The one that's due six weeks from now?" My tone practically dripped with attitude. Nobody had been nicer to me this past week than Rafe. But I couldn't help mouthing off. Because I didn't want his babysitting. And it bugged the shit out of me to even *look* like I needed help.

"I don't do things at the last minute," he said, his face serious. "That isn't my style."

I didn't think before I spoke. "Rafe, I have proof that you sometimes act *very* impulsively."

His face shut down, making me sorry I'd said it. "See you later. Maybe seven." He left, pulling the door closed behind him.

Rafe left me alone with my sandwich and a thudding heart. He was gone so fast I didn't get a chance to say thank you for making me go running. Or for making sure I didn't starve to death in this room.

God, I was *such* a bitch.

After eating lunch I took a shower. I'd spent more time in the shower these past forty-eight hours than anywhere else. The ink markings were *almost* gone from my skin. But almost wasn't good enough.

I toweled off, then dressed in a turtleneck and jeans. Not that anyone would see me. I didn't plan on leaving my room again. I'd missed two classes already today, and the third was beginning without me.

But classes weren't my real problem. In two hours, I was due to arrive at hockey practice, where the Brodacious photo would have already made the rounds. My friends were going to see that picture. Then they would wonder about the caption.

And *talk* about it.

There was no fucking way I was walking into that locker room today. Or tomorrow. Or the day after that.

I sat on the edge of my bed and pressed my fingertips into the corners of my too-hot eyes.

FIFTEEN

RAFE

Soccer practice was brutal that afternoon.

Coach ran us like greyhounds. And just before practice there'd been a little cloudburst, so the grass was damp and slippery. My knees were screaming by the time it was done, exhausted by the constant stop-start torque required to change direction as I dribbled the ball.

By the time the whistle blew, it was too dark to see the ball.

Bickley clapped a hand on my sweaty shoulder as we walked into the locker room. "What a lovely little stroll we've had this afternoon," he said. "I feel so refreshed."

"Coach was in a mood, wasn't he?"

"That he was."

My roommate and I went straight to dinner after showering, just barely making it into the Beaumont dining hall before closing time. When we got back to our room, Bickley threw himself on the sofa. But I gathered my Urban Studies stuff and headed for our door again.

"Where are you headed?" my roommate asked.

"Uh, upstairs. Bella and I are paired up on a project."

"Reeeally." He grinned. "That could be *just* what you require. She's quite the slapper, I've heard."

My blood pressure kicked up several notches on Bella's behalf. "What's that supposed to mean?"

Bickley spread his hands. "It's a shame that she prefers hockey players, though. Maybe she'd make an exception for a soccer player. It's a similar enough game — we're all trying to get the round thing into the goal. Maybe she'll let you put your round thing into her goal."

"Shut your mouth," I growled, walking out and letting the door slam. If I'd stood there a minute longer, I can't say what I would have done to him.

Fucking Bickley.

I headed upstairs and knocked on Bella's door. I was more than a little surprised to hear her say "come in." Pushing the door open, I saw Bella on the bed. She looked a hell of a lot better than when I'd walked in here a few hours ago. Wearing clean clothes and a slick of lip gloss, she looked more like the Bella that I used to see. "Hey," she said, her eyes flickering up into mine.

"Hey yourself."

"I just need to tell you something quickly, and then I never want to speak of it again."

"Um, okay?" I chuckled.

She swung her legs over the side of the bed and braced her elbows on her knees. "The reason I went into that frat house last Saturday night was that I needed to tell one of the guys something." Bella took a sudden interest in her fingernails. "My doctor told me that I'd caught an, um, infection. Not a serious one. But contagious." She looked up to meet my eyes for a fractional second. "I got it within a short time frame, though. So that means I didn't have it when we, uh..." She crossed her arms.

"I'm sorry," I said quietly.

Bella opened her mouth and then closed it again, as if she hadn't expected me to say that. "I'm just telling you because you

might hear all sorts of shit about me. But you don't have anything
to worry about."

"I understand."

She clapped her hands. "Moving on. Now let's talk about West
165th Street."

I opened my notebook and sifted through the pages. My brain
was still trying to catch up with what she'd just said — and what
she *hadn't*. If Bella had walked into that house on fraternity row to
deliver some very unpleasant news, she sure stayed there a while.
It was after seven in the morning when I'd seen her
stumbling out.

With insults inked all over her body.

What the hell happened during all that time? It didn't take
nine hours to tell a guy that kind of news.

Bella misinterpreted my silence. "I'm sure you're clean."

"I wasn't worried, Bella."

Her face showed very clearly that she didn't believe me.
"Urban Studies," she clipped.

"Yes ma'am." I took a seat in her desk chair, which was free of
debris. "I took good notes yesterday because he was talking about
affordable housing. So we have to decide whether we want to use
a voucher system, or whatever."

"Okay." She twirled a strand of her hair between her fingers.

I knew exactly how soft her hair was, and how it felt in my
hands. Her happy smile was another perfectly formed memory.
After everything that had happened to her, I wondered when I
might see that happy smile again, and whether there was anything
I could do to bring it back.

Whatever it was, I would do it.

"Vouchers are the simplest," Bella was saying. "If we wanted to
get fancy, we could do something with sweat equity. Or even
better — a rent-to-own setup. How complicated do you want to
make this?"

"I'm not afraid of the work," I told her. "I really need to win
this thing."

"Why?"

"The prize."

She quirked an eyebrow. "Can't you visit food trucks any old time? I mean, you can't swing a pair of chopsticks without hitting one."

"That's not the point. I need to meet that guy in charge — the food truck guru. Our family restaurant could really rock one of those things. And I need to convince my mom that it's a good idea. So if we win, I'd bring her as my date."

Bella's expression softened. "You're like a walking chick flick."

"Whatever. Just tell me what sweat equity is. And that other thing."

Bella crossed her legs on the bed and began to explain. And for a little while, peace reigned in the kingdom. She looked like the old Bella, too, talking with her hands, her green eyes flashing. And I took notes so I could remember all the things she was telling me.

"Where'd you learn all of this?" I asked, scribbling furiously before I forgot what she'd said.

"I told you. Dinner table conversation. One-sided conference calls. Buildings are all my father ever talks about."

There was a knock at the door. "Bella!" came a male voice.

Across from me, Bella flinched. She raised a finger to her lips, asking me to stay silent.

The knock persisted. "Bells, open up. Come *on*. I'm freaking out, here."

With a sigh, Bella stood and crossed to the door. When she opened it, two men loomed in the doorway. When she backed away, they came inside.

The energy in the room changed in a way I did not like. The first guy in the door — a big blond guy — stared down at Bella, tension radiating off him. "Rikker said you weren't at practice."

Two pink spots appeared on Bella's cheeks. She looked past her blond friend at the other guy. I recognized him — he was in about a hundred newspaper articles last year. *The First Out Gay*

Player In Division One Hockey, etc. "You ratted me out?" Bella asked.

Rikker rolled his eyes. "We're just worried about you, Bells."

"That does not even *begin* to cover it," the blond guy said. His jacket said GRAHAM on it. "What the hell happened? Who took that picture?"

Great. "Not the question," I muttered, wishing he would just stand down. A minute ago, Bella had been relaxed for the first time in days. Now she sat down heavily, looking for all the world like she'd rather crawl under the bed than sit on it.

"And who are *you?*" Graham demanded, his attention swinging to me.

"A friend," I said testily. "The downstairs neighbor. The guy who *isn't* talking about that freaking picture."

Graham's glance dismissed me. He sat down on Bella's bed right beside her, putting an arm around her. "Seriously. Who did that? And what's with..." He picked up her arm and pushed up the sleeve of her T-shirt to expose a few inches of her wrist.

Bella yanked her arm away. "I'm fine."

"There is nothing fine about—"

"I'm FINE!" she yelled. Her face was a bright shade of pink, and her eyes glittered.

"Come on," he pressed. "I need to know."

"Not true," she clipped, turning her face away from him.

Rikker sat down on the other side of her, so Bella ended up burying her nose in his shoulder. Rikker put his palm on her cheek and pulled her close. "Bella," he whispered, and I watched her back rise and fall as she tried to hold herself together.

"I am *done* with guys," she croaked. "Men suck."

The two guys on the bed turned in toward Bella, gathering her in their arms. "No," Graham crooned. "Some guys are awesome. We love you."

Bella gave her head a single shake. "I just... The whole *team* saw it, didn't they?" she gasped. "I'm *never* going back to practice."

Rikker made an unhappy noise. "But then the asshole wins."

"I don't *care*."

"Yeah, you do," Graham said, rubbing her back. "We don't let the assholes win."

"I just can't..." Her back heaved. "*Stand* this."

My throat got tight, and the other two men held her even closer. They murmured soothing things while Bella began to sniff.

I don't know how long it took me to realize I was no longer needed. It was hard to just walk out of the room, but I'd done what I could, even if it did not feel like nearly enough.

When I slipped out, she did not even look up.

SIXTEEN

BELLA

How mortifying to end up crying in Graham's arms.

I pulled myself together after a few minutes, wiping my face on my sleeve. "I'll be okay," I promised.

"Yeah, you will be," Rikker said softly. "But we have to get that picture taken down. Who's the asshole? We want to help you with that."

"Absolutely not," I said. There was no *way* I would contact him. Ever, ever again. And I wasn't going to turn Graham and Rikker on him, either. How ugly would that get? My two gay friends, beating down the door of the football fraternity? That was the worst idea I'd ever heard.

"What they did must be against a whole lot of rules," Graham said.

"Don't be so sure," I argued. "It isn't a Harkness website. It isn't even an official..." I almost said "Beta Rho website," but caught myself just in case they hadn't already made the connection. "It's just a random spot on the web, where no names are given. Including mine."

"So you're just going to *ignore* it?" Graham yelped.

I pressed my hands against my hot face, trying to stay calm. "In a few days they'll humiliate someone else, right? My picture will sink down on the page."

"That is so fucked," Rikker complained.

"What would be *so fucked*," I said icily, "is making a complaint that doesn't stick." I'd thought about this for many hours already, and I was positive there was nothing to be gained by reporting Whittaker. "Humiliation is not against the law. And if marking up a drunk person was illegal, every frat in North America would be shut down. If I make a big stink, then anyone who hasn't seen the picture *will* see it."

"Sexual harassment is not okay," Rikker said quietly. "The college is obligated to put a stop to it. I could have won a judgment against St. B's if I'd gone after them. And I don't see how this is different."

"You're right," I said brightly. "It *is* the same thing. And you *didn't* go after them in court, did you?"

"No, but..."

"But *nothing*. I've seen what happens when someone like me goes up against someone like him."

"Like who?" Graham asked.

God, did he think I was that stupid? "Nice try, Graham. But I'm not exactly Snow White. Nobody cares if somebody says a few shitty things about me. Right now, my name is not on the front page of that newspaper you write for. If I report him, tomorrow it will be. How is that better?"

Graham's eyes squeezed shut, probably because he knew I was right. His arms tightened around me once again. "I can't make you turn him in. But I really need to know one thing. Was the ink the worst thing that happened to you that night?"

"No!" I spat, and his whole body stiffened. "The fucking *picture* was the worst thing that happened. Duh."

He let out a breath, and I felt just *steeped* in misery and drama. As a rule, I didn't do drama. I didn't manufacture it or traffic in it. But now it was all around me.

What I *didn't* tell Graham — or Rafe — was that I knew those assholes had put something more than alcohol in my drink. But that's not what Graham had been asking. He'd wanted to know if I'd been assaulted, just like Rafe had tried to ask, too. In their minds, it was the worst thing that could've happened to me. And maybe they were right. It's not like I had any experience with that.

But I'd had enough experience with other kinds of assholery to know public humiliation was no trip to Hollywood, either. I wasn't about to make my own life worse by making a complaint against the fraternity, because there was no way I'd prevail. The Beta Rho national chapter probably *wrote* their own slut-shaming tactical handbook.

"A lot of guys would want to help you." Rikker gave my lower back a supportive rub.

I disentangled myself from the two of them. "I know." I cleared my throat. "Thanks."

"The hockey team knows you always have our backs. So we're going to have yours."

Now *that* was naive. Because it didn't matter how many clean jerseys I'd handed out before practice, or how quickly I could organize fifteen hotel room reservations. If I walked into that locker room right now, those guys were still going to wonder: *What did she catch? I wonder who gave it to her?*

I was *tainted*. And nobody was ever going to let me forget it.

"I'll be fine," I fibbed, rubbing the drying tears off my face. "Seriously. And I have a whole lot of homework tonight."

Graham and Rikker exchanged a loaded glance. "Will I see you at practice tomorrow night?" Rikker asked.

"Sure," I lied.

Graham kissed me on the eyebrow. "Will you come to Capri's Pizza tomorrow night?"

Fat chance. "Maybe."

"All right." Rikker stood up. "Call us if you need us."

"I will," I promised, just to shut them up. What I needed was for everyone to stop talking about it.

They left, and my room was silent again.

Before my life went to hell, I used to sleep like a baby. Now? Not so much.

At four in the morning, I found myself tangled up in the sheets, trying to find a way out of my misery. Sometimes my mind would drift, and I'd end up thinking about normal things — the next Rangers game, or a psych essay that I'd read. But then a glimpse of the faded ink on my arm, or the memory of picking up that drink that I'd been served at the Beta Rho house... *Shudder*.

I lay there, working it through my mind, like a logical puzzle that might be solved if I could only find a way. But short of time travel, there was no solution at all.

If I'd only said no to the drink.

If I'd only told Whittaker over the phone...

A girl could go crazy this way. And whenever my brain veered any further down this path, I had to force myself to turn back toward the light. The memory of waking up on the floor of Beta Rho that morning was not a place in my mind I could visit without becoming fearful. So I tucked that away to think about sometime later.

Much later.

After tossing and turning for hours, I finally fell asleep again when the first light was in the sky.

Whatevs. I wasn't going to class, anyway.

Unfortunately, it's not easy to hide from the world when you have nosy neighbors.

Lianne walked into the bathroom while I was brushing my

teeth around ten in the morning. "Don't you have class?" she asked.

I did, as a matter of fact. The seminar was an upper-level psych class with only a dozen or so people in it. But I would have had to cross the entire campus to get there, and I just didn't feel up to it.

"Did you eat breakfast?" Lianne tried, even though I'd never answered her first question.

"Who eats breakfast?" I countered.

"Did you get coffee?"

Seriously? "What's it to you?"

"Want to hit the coffee shop with me?"

I couldn't help but sneak a look at her in the mirror. Since when did Lianne make friendly overtures? Rafe probably put her up to it. "I'm good," I said. "But thanks."

She gave me a single, frustrated frown. Then she darted into her room and shut the door again.

If Lianne had picked any other day this year to be nice to me, I would have responded differently. But it was going to take a little more than coffee to extract me from the privacy of my room.

I wrote an apologetic email to the grad student who led my psych seminar and stayed home.

As soon as I settled on my bed again, my phone rang to the tune of "The Saints Go Marching In." And as soon as I heard that little tune, I realized I'd made an error of epic proportions.

"Oh shit," I said to the walls of my room. I answered the phone anyway, because ducking my own fuck-ups wasn't my style. "Hi Mom," I said.

"Bella, your sister—"

"I *know*. I'm sorry. I've been frantic, and it totally slipped my mind." That was sure true. "I'll call her immediately."

My mother's sigh was loud. "You've offended her, sweetie. The grant and the award are very important to her. How busy could you be?"

Well, the total implosion of my life has been surprisingly consuming.
"I'll call right now. But you have to let me hang up with you."

"Don't you dare forget the banquet."

Shit! The fucking banquet. "I won't forget."

"I'll see you then, sweetie."

"Yes, you will."

"Call your sister," she couldn't resist saying once more.

"Doing it now!" I hung up and inspected my ceiling again. But the task could not be avoided, so I dialed my sister.

And, lo! God smiled down and gave me her voicemail, which meant I could say my piece without groveling in real time. I opened with, "I'm so sorry," and then I followed up with enthusiastic congratulations, followed by more apologies.

"That should do it," I said to nobody, throwing the phone down and rolling toward the wall. I recommenced my hibernation.

But the world would not be ignored.

Rafe showed up next, and he was not so easily shaken off as Lianne. "Bella," he said, knocking. "Open up."

I decided opening the door would be the quicker method of ducking him. Seeing as I'd brushed my hair and made my bed, he might not call the authorities.

When I opened the door, he walked in wearing running clothes. He had a pair of those spandex compression shorts sticking out from underneath his running shorts, which somehow managed to highlight how muscular his thighs were. *Rawr*. The boy was practically edible.

Or rather, he would be, *if* I were still into men. Which I wasn't.

"It's time for our run," he said, as if we were running buddies.

"I don't run," I reminded him.

"Sure you do. I've seen you. First we run, then we go to class."

Lovely. He thought he had me all schooled up. "And what if I don't?"

"Same threat applies today."

God! You bossy...! I wanted to scream. "Look. I'm *fine*. And you can't keep blackmailing me like this."

"Funny." He chuckled. "Hanging out with you is not the effortless payoff that blackmail implies. But I *will* tell someone if I think you're not okay. And if you leave the building with me, then I know you're all right."

"You could just take my word for it."

"Not happening, *chica*."

With a curse, I got up to find some running clothes.

We jogged a little farther than last time. By the time we arrived panting at our entryway door again, I was tremendously impressed with myself. But I sure wasn't about to admit it to Rafe.

He looked at his watch. "You've got twenty minutes to get cleaned up for class. I'll knock on your door."

"I'll just meet you there," I tried, climbing the stairs slowly. My legs were shaky from exertion.

Rafe just shook his head. "We go together, Bella. I'm not falling for that."

Christ.

I took the world's fastest shower and then hopped into my nicest jeans and a fancier sweater than I'd usually wear to class. As if that mattered. As if anyone in the lecture hall would look at me and decide I wasn't actually a filthy slut because I was wearing a cashmere sweater from Bergdorf's that matched my eyes.

Rafe was maddeningly prompt, of course. When he knocked on my door, I followed him downstairs and outside. The closer we got to the lecture hall, though, the more my feet dragged on the flagstones. Urban Studies was a big lecture with at least sixty people in it. I did not want to sit there and wonder how many of them had seen my picture.

My feet stopped altogether.

Rafe drew up behind me. "By all means, move at a glacial pace."

I whirled on him. "You're quoting *The Devil Wears Prada* while I'm about to lose my shit?" *Whoa. Too much truth-telling.*

His big brown eyes went wide. "What's the matter?"

I looked up into his handsome face and felt like punching him in the teeth. "What's the *matter?* Just *everything.* And your only concern is a project that's not due for an aeon."

His face softened. "That is *not* my only concern. Let's just go sit down inside."

"No! I'm *not* going in there."

I tried to duck around him, but he caught me around the waist. "Bella," he whispered into my ear. "What's the alternative?"

"Transferring." The word popped out as if it had been waiting there all along. I needed to be somewhere else — a college where I wasn't that mess of a girl in that picture. Graham had said I shouldn't let the assholes win. But right now I was willing to hand over the trophy without a fight.

"Bella," he said again, his voice low and steady. The sound of it cut through the clatter of the hamster wheel in my brain, the one that was running scared. He put his arms around me, and I hid my face against his soccer jacket. "We'll sit in the last row. Nobody will even know we're there."

I doubted that was true. But, as he'd pointed out, what was the alternative? I didn't really have a Plan B. There were seven months left of my college career. I used to think of myself as a person who could survive anything for seven months.

Obviously I'd thought wrong.

My heart thumped spastically against my ribs as I considered leaving school. But where would I go? If I showed up on my parents' doorstep, they'd want to know why. That would be a fun conversation. This problem wasn't going away, even if I ran.

All these thoughts battered around in my brain while I stood pressing my nose into my neighbor's shoulder. Because that wasn't weird or anything.

I took a tiny step back, even though I didn't want to. "All right. Let's go."

With his hand at the small of my back, Rafe walked me into the lecture room. He didn't let go until the second we took our seats in the last row. When class was over, I was up and out of there faster than you can say *later, suckers*.

"Going to lunch?" Rafe asked, practically jogging after me.

"Not yet," I said, hoping he wouldn't slow down my getaway.

"I have to work. I'll see you later?"

I gave him a salute, then jogged toward Beaumont as fast as my legs could carry me.

Who knew running was so useful? Obviously I'd never been mortified enough before to understand its charms.

SEVENTEEN

RAFE

During the lunch shift, I chopped a lot of vegetables, washed a lot of pans and worried about Bella. I was in way over my head. Maybe a smarter man would have already gone to the dean and explained the situation. But some of what Bella had said rang true. What could they do, anyway? If Bella named the guy who'd brutalized her reputation, they could make him take the picture down. But that could take weeks, and the damage was already done.

Also, if I went to the dean she'd never speak to me again.

That was the wrong reason to keep her secret, though. I worried that my judgment was completely obliterated by all the complicated feelings I had for her. Every time I saw her square her shoulders against the latest indignity, I wanted to scoop her up and hold her close. Nice, right? Just what she needed—another guy to ogle her.

My job was just to be the best friend I could be. For right now, that meant watching and waiting. If Bella went to class, ate meals and went to work at the rink, then maybe I didn't have to take any drastic action.

Before lunch was almost over, I went out to the salad bar with one last pan of lettuce.

"Hey," someone said. "I didn't catch your name the other day."

I looked up to see Bella's friend Graham. "It's Rafe," I told him.

"Can I ask you a question?"

"Kinda working here," I said, more annoyed with him than I ought to have been. But I was pretty sure this was the guy Bella had fallen for, and so I disliked him just on principle.

"It will just take a second."

"All right." I led him over to the door to the kitchen, where nobody else could hear. "What's up?" I asked, noticing that Graham's boyfriend had also joined us.

Graham got right to the point. "Who's fucking with Bella?"

"I have no idea," I said truthfully.

"It was someone from Beta Rho, though," Graham said. "That website is theirs."

"Sure," I agreed. "But that's... forty guys?"

Graham flushed. "Seriously, if you have *any* idea..."

Rikker put a hand on Graham's shoulder. "He hears you, babe. Message received."

Graham's shoulders slumped. "I just... I hate that some asshole is getting away with this."

"No kidding," I grunted. "It's all I think about."

Rikker lifted his eyebrows. "Is it?"

Now they were both staring at me. "How do you know Bella, anyway?" Graham asked.

Smooth, Rafe. "We're neighbors," I said. There was a beat of silence during which both guys seemed to debate whether to ask me more questions. "Look. If you want to help Bella, make sure she eats dinner tonight. I'll be at a team meal."

Rikker's eyebrows shot up again. "She's not eating?"

"She's avoiding public places," I said. "Or maybe she isn't anymore. But it would be great if you could check."

"Done," Graham said. "I'll bring her some dinner."

"I have to get back to work," I said.

"Hey, thanks!" Rikker called after me.

I walked back into the kitchen, wondering why he was thanking me. Had I helped Bella at all?

I really had no idea.

The soccer schedule swallowed up my next few days. I cajoled Bella into running with me once more, and she came to Urban Studies class again. But for several days in a row, I didn't see much of her.

My team made a road trip, where we beat Harvard and lost to Dartmouth. Bickley chattered in my ear all the way home from New Hampshire, when really all I wanted to do was sleep.

Bickley could afford to squander his time on gossip. But the second I stepped off that bus, I had to hustle to make a Sunday night dining hall shift.

Fighting exhaustion, I cut up chickens for three hours straight, and then chopped vegetables for tomorrow's omelets.

Dinner service was almost over when I saw Bella slip into the dining hall. Good news. She got herself a plate and carried it over to sit by Graham and Rikker. I gave her a wave when I went out to pull trays off the salad bar.

"Hey, Graham?" I heard her ask. An edge in her voice made me linger nearby. "Do you have anything going on next Saturday night? I have a thing in New York that I have to go to, and I need a date. It's an open bar."

"What about my needs?" Rikker joked, his arms spread wide. "I like free drinks. And you're stealing my date."

Graham cleared his throat. "Um, guys? That's the night of Skate with Harkness Hockey. I have to cover it, because a couple of Bruins players are supposed to show up, too."

"Oh," she said slowly. "The charity thing?"

"Yeah."

"Fuck," Bella said. "The game schedule made that look like a night off."

Rikker frowned. "Wait. I could come down with the flu, or something," he suggested. "I don't see why they need two dozen players out there." He gave a faux cough into his hand. "I think I feel it coming on."

Bella shook her head. "Yeah, and nobody would notice if the most famous Harkness teammate wasn't there."

Rikker grabbed her hand and stuck it on his forehead. "That's a fever, right? Don't I feel hot to you?"

She gave him a sad smile. "Don't worry about it, Rik. It's not a big deal."

"I would totally blow it off, Bells."

Bella stood. "Really, I'm good. Thanks anyway, guys." She trotted over to the conveyor belt to bus her tray.

I caught up to her on the rebound. "Hey, Bella?"

She looked up, startled. "Yeah?"

"I can go to your thing in New York."

Bella hesitated, which bummed me out a little bit. Maybe I wasn't Upper East Side enough to be her date. "Are you sure?" she asked after a long pause.

"Well, I don't have a game until Sunday night. So my mother decided that I should make an appearance at my little cousin's christening on Sunday morning. I was supposed to take the train down anyway."

"Huh." She raised her eyes to mine. "The reason I asked Graham to go was because he already knows the story of my crazy family."

Oh. "Well... how bad could they really be? You said there'd be drinks."

She seemed to consider the question. "Drinks will help. I just hope we won't need them too badly. With my family, you never know." She bit her lip, and even though it was inappropriate of me to think this way, I kind of wanted to bite it, too. "If you're *sure* it's not a big inconvenience, I could really use the company."

Holding up a hand for a high five, I said, "No problem. But first, we make some headway on the Urban Studies project."

She slapped my hand. "Okay, slave driver."

EIGHTEEN

November

BELLA

As a favor to Rafe, I wrote a spreadsheet to help tally up all the different business loans we were considering for our Urban Studies project. Truthfully, I'd never been so caught up on homework as I was this semester. Since I was still calling in sick to hockey, I had a lot of time on my hands.

"Damn," Rafe said the next night when I showed him the spreadsheet. "We are going to *win* this thing."

"We so are." It's really astonishing what you can accomplish when you barely leave your room. I was quite pleased with myself.

Rafe threw his soccer jacket on the desk chair and sat down on my bed, pulling my computer into his lap. "Are these interest rates accurate? They look high."

"Of *course* they're right. What do you take me for?" I gave him a nudge with my elbow. "Commercial rates are higher than regular mortgage rates. And the terms aren't as good."

Rafe's dark eyes looked up at me in alarm. "What if another team doesn't know that? We could lose the contest and all because you're smarter."

"Huh. Well that's a depressing idea. It's usually the opposite —

being stupid is what bites me in the ass."

"Me too," Rafe mumbled.

"Although, under the right circumstances, ass biting can be awfully fun."

His eyes got wide, and I laughed. "Don't worry about the interest rate thing. I'll put a range of interest rates in the write-up."

"Good idea." He handed my laptop back on a yawn.

"Tough practice today?"

"Always. We're playing Princeton on Sunday night, and coach is all fired up." He unzipped the book bag at his feet and took out his Urban Studies notebook.

"If you're tired, we can work on this tomorrow."

He shook his head. "I'm good. Let's make a list of all the businesses in the neighborhood, so we can see what's missing."

We worked on that for awhile, with me manning the search engine on my computer while he made detailed notes in the nicest handwriting I'd ever seen from a guy.

"You're very methodical," I said, trying to pay him a compliment. I was trying to act like less of a bitch when Rafe was around. It made me self-conscious to know he'd seen me at my absolute worst.

"Eh," he sighed. "Methodical is what keeps me afloat. The Harkness workload has been a real shock to my system."

"Lots of people say that," I said quickly.

"Do they?" he grumbled, turning the page in his notebook. "I haven't met any of them."

There was a knock on my door. I glanced at the clock. It was ten already, so I didn't know who it might be. "Come in?"

Trevi opened the door. "Hey, Bella. You feeling any better?"

"Uh, sure. Trevi, this is my neighbor Rafe."

"Hey man." He shook hands with Rafe and then perched on my desk chair. "Bella, I have some shitty news."

"Oh, goody," I said, my voice light. But inside, I trembled. *More* shitty news? Really?

"Coach Canning made the brilliant decision to hire his son as the student manager."

"What?" I gasped. "He gave my *job* away?" Even as I said the words aloud, I wished I could take them back. Because I sounded so pathetic.

Across from me, Trevi rubbed the back of his neck with one hand. "Yeah. The guys are pretty pissed off. In fact, I was thinking I'd get a bunch of them together and we'd write a letter to coach. If there's a dozen signatures on it, maybe he'll listen."

"No," I said quickly. "He won't fire his own *kid*. And Coach warned me. His email said that if I didn't come back to practice he was going to have to look around for someone else. I just didn't think he'd do it so fast. I thought I had a little time."

"You didn't go back to practice?" Rafe asked softly.

I shot him a look. See? Rafe was destined to think I was a bitch. Because when shit went bad in my life, he always happened to be around.

Trevi looked uncomfortable. "It's just not *right*, though. His kid isn't even a Harkness student."

I laughed. "I'd bet any amount of money that he will be next year. This is going to look so good on his application."

Trevi pulled a face. "As if the kid even needed to fill one out. I hate nepotism."

"That's like saying you hate gravity, Trevi. It's here to stay."

"That is craptastic." Trevi stood. "Let me know if you change your mind about fighting it. It's more fun with you around, Bella."

My heart broke a little bit when he said that. Because I wanted to believe him. But I did not want to walk into that locker room, either. And now I didn't have to.

"Come to Capri's on Saturday night?" Trevi said, his hand on my doorknob.

"I can't. I have a family thing in New York."

"Sunday then," he insisted.

"Maybe."

"I'm not above throwing you over my shoulder and dragging

you there," Trevi teased.

"Great idea," I deadpanned. "Chicks really dig that."

I heard Trevi snicker as the door fell shut. When I turned back to Rafe, he was studying me with those big brown eyes that didn't miss much. "What?" I asked, testily.

"You haven't been going to practice?"

Ugh. Now he was going to go all bossy on me again. "Nope."

"So you're just going to let the job *go?*"

I closed my computer, hoping Rafe would take the hint that study time was over. "It's not like I need the money, right? That's lucky." In a strange way, Trevi's shitty news was a relief. Because now I could stop worrying about missing practice and letting people down.

"It was never about the money, I think."

So true. "The new coach was never my biggest fan, okay? Maybe this is the best way for him to say it without having to say it. The man can hire whomever he wants."

Rafe made an irritated sound in the back of his throat. Then he closed his notebook and shoved it into his book bag. "It sucks, though." He stood. "I won't see you tomorrow. Are we still on for Saturday night?"

I was going to have to give myself a *major* pep talk before I faced my family. "Saturday night is unavoidable for me. But if you don't feel like dressing up to eat fussy food in a room full of philanthropists, I wouldn't blame you."

He shrugged. "It's no trouble. How dressy are we talking about?"

"Coat and tie."

"That's easy," he said, pausing beside the bed. He put one warm hand on my head for a second, and it was all I could do to keep from leaning into it. Then he took it away again. "Take care of yourself."

"You too," I said, as if it was something friends just said to one another. As if I weren't the one who was quite obviously self-destructing.

NINETEEN

RAFE

Bella and I rode into the city on the Metro North train in a comfortable silence. As the buildings began to get taller, I asked, "What's the goal for tonight?"

She looked up from the book she was reading on her phone. "The goal?"

If tonight weren't complicated for some reason, then Bella wouldn't have needed a date. "Who needs to be impressed, and who needs to be avoided? Just give me the lay of the land."

She stashed her phone. "Well, I invited you as a buffer. My family will be nicer to me if you're there."

"Why wouldn't they be nice?" I asked.

She looked out the window. "We had a blow-up a couple of years ago. There isn't a lot of trust between us. But my parents are civil people to the core. They'll be nice. They're very good at it. My sister is more of a wild card. And if there's anyone I'm avoiding, it's her snake of a husband."

"Okay," I said. I could work with that.

When the train pulled into the 125th Street station, I found it odd not to get off. My whole life I'd lived in the northernmost part of the city, where Bella and her friends never bothered to tread.

The doors shut again after a minute, and the train barreled downtown, entering the tunnel at 97th Street. When the train stopped at Grand Central, we got out to head for the 42nd Street exit. "Can't beat this commute," I said. Cipriani was right across the street.

"That's the only thing tonight has going for it," Bella said, her face stony.

I patted my chest. "The only thing? What about your fabulous fake boyfriend who's here to meet the parents?"

Bella's eyes crinkled with the first humor that I'd seen on her in a week. "You don't have to be the fake boyfriend. You can just be the date. They wouldn't believe that we were really together, anyway. They know me."

They wouldn't believe her? *That's fucked*, I felt like saying. "I like a challenge," I said instead.

"Whatever floats your paddleboat," Bella said as we approached the door. "I appreciate you coming with me tonight."

I hustled past Bella so I could open the door for my fake girlfriend. "This is really such a chore," I told her, holding it open. "A night without dining hall food."

"The food won't be *that* good," Bella warned.

"Yeah, but I'm not cooking it. Big difference."

"And there's free wine," she added.

"That's my favorite kind." Although I couldn't help remembering what had happened the last time Bella and I drank wine together. *Dios.* I needed to stop thinking about that. But Bella was wearing a sleek red dress that drew my eyes down her body to her long legs. Even though I rarely saw Bella in anything dressier than a pair of jeans and a hockey T-shirt, she had the kind of curves loose clothing couldn't hide. And tonight they were all on display.

It was going to be a long evening.

Bella led me toward the main ballroom. Cipriani was an old

New York mainstay of the banquet set. It was the sort of place that was built to impress, with high columns stretching up to a soaring ceiling. "What a dump," I joked as Bella declined the coat check.

"I'll keep my wrap in case we need to make a quick getaway," she said.

Tonight I'd let Bickley lend me one of his designer jackets. Looking at the crowd in this room, I was glad I had. The men wore sleek dark suits and European ties. The women wore dresses, many of which were far more elaborate than Bella's simple design.

None of them were half as beautiful as Bella.

"Drinks before family," she said, grabbing my hand in order to lead me toward a bar.

I closed my fingers around her slim palm. When we reached the bartender, Bella tried to let go, but I wasn't having it. "I always hold my fake girlfriend's hand in a crowd," I explained.

She shifted her handbag around her body. "Just don't get between me and my alcoholic beverage, or your fake girlfriend is going to get ornery."

After the bartender passed two glasses of red wine to us, Bella began to look around the room. "This boondoggle is for a public health nonprofit. But it's all Wall Street types. Because that's who can afford a thousand dollars a plate."

I nearly dropped my glass. "A *grand?* Are you telling me that your parents spent a thousand dollars to have your fake boyfriend attend this thing?"

"Not really." Bella gave her head a single shake. "They bought a table because my sister works for this charity. The organization is giving her an award tonight, which is why my presence was requested. But it's just a scam, anyway. When Mommy and Daddy are one of your biggest contributors, who else are they going to hand that award to?"

Huh. The politics of Bella's family were different than the politics of my family. But just as complicated.

"There they are," she said suddenly, gesturing toward a round table up front.

Hand in hand, we walked over to the front corner of the room, where Bella's parents sat. Even if she hadn't pointed them out, I would have had no trouble identifying Bella's mother. She was beautiful like her daughter, though her hair was swept up in a severe style Bella would never have tolerated. Her father looked much older than his wife. While Bella's mom looked to be in her forties, Bella's dad was sixty-five if he was a day.

Bella's mom jumped up to kiss her when we arrived. "You look lovely, sweetheart," she said, and I relaxed a little bit. After our conversation on the way in, I'd half expected Bella's parents to have horns and a tail.

"This is Rafe," Bella said, squeezing my hand. "Rafe, this is Lydia and Jack."

I had to drop Bella's hand in order to shake. "It's a pleasure to finally meet you, ma'am," I said. "And you too, sir."

Bella gave my finger a pinch, as if to suggest I was laying it on a little too thick.

"Likewise." Bella's mother beamed at me. "Did you two just get off the train?"

The question put me on my guard, because it made me wonder if she was trying to figure out whether or not I was a Harkness student. Maybe I'm paranoid, but the only other Hispanic dudes in this room were pouring water into the drinking glasses. It was hard not to get a chip on your shoulder sometimes.

"Rafe lives in my entryway," Bella said, perhaps reading the same thing into the question. "And we have a class together. Urban Studies."

"Lovely," Lydia said, seating herself again.

"Here, *belleza*," I said, using a Spanish word for "beautiful" which had the same root as Bella's name. If she were my real girlfriend, that's what I'd call her. I pulled out Bella's chair with a small flourish.

She gave me the wide eyes as she sat down. "Thank you."

Bella's mother — Lydia — asked us a couple more polite questions about school, while Jack nodded along blandly. A band started up in the opposite corner of the room, and we all turned to look. It was a nine-piece band and when they began to play, Bella's mother reached for her husband's hand. "You'll dance with me, won't you Jack?"

He held up his empty scotch glass. "I was going to make a trip to the bar."

She stood and smiled at him. "You can do that after we foxtrot."

With a weary chuckle, he stood. "It's a deal."

I watched them move toward the dance floor, Mr. Hall taking his wife's hand gamely enough. He had it pretty good, I thought. When I was sixty-five, with two grown kids, I hoped my wife would still want to dance with me.

Bella took a big gulp of her wine. "Brace yourself. Here comes my sister."

I turned to see another beauty approaching. Bella's sister was too thin, though. She looked angular in places where Bella was soft. Her smile wasn't as genuine as her sister's, either. And it was hard to get a fix on her age. She probably wasn't that much older than Bella, but she carried herself stiffly, like somebody's uptight auntie.

"Hi, Isabelle," she said, leaning in for a kiss on the cheek. She went for both sides, too, which caught Bella off guard.

"What, are we European now?" she asked.

Her sister's mouth got tight. "I haven't seen you in forever, that's all." She looked to me as I rose from my chair to shake her hand. "I'm Julie," she offered.

"Rafe. It's a pleasure."

"The pleasure is mine," Julie insisted, picking out a seat and tossing her little purse on the table. "I never meet Bella's friends anymore. She's never around."

Beside me, Bella seemed to grit her teeth. Her wine glass was empty, and that wouldn't do. I stood. "Julie, you don't have a drink, yet. Can I make a run to the bar for you?"

Julie tilted her head to the side and smiled at me. "Aren't *you* sweet. I'd love a glass of chardonnay."

"One chardonnay and..." I put a hand on the back of Bella's neck. "Another cab?" I picked up Bella's empty glass.

She looked up at me, and there was a glimmer of hesitation in her expression. "Don't be a stranger."

I leaned down and kissed her forehead. "I'll be right back," I whispered in my best (fake) boyfriend voice. It was an easy role for me, because when given the chance, I was a good boyfriend. The kind people weren't afraid to bring home to mom.

Five minutes later I returned to find that Bella and her sister were still the only two at the table. Bella's sister was giving Bella chapter and verse on some point of public health policy, while Bella listened with a half-interested gaze. Maybe a rescue was in order.

"So, are we going to dance?" I asked.

"I'm not much of a dancer," Bella said, picking up her fresh glass of wine.

"Bella doesn't like activities that you have to stand up for," her sister said.

I actually choked on a sip of my wine. Either Julie had just made a blatant attack on Bella's character, or else she had no sense for innuendo.

But Bella looked unfazed. "Actually, Julie, upright fucking is pretty awesome, especially against a wall. And I know Tucker likes it."

Her sister gasped. "For *one night* can you not act like a crazy bitch? When will you stop?"

"When someone listens," Bella said, her voice flat.

Whoa. I practically had whiplash from the sudden turn this conversation had taken. And then it changed again, because Mrs. Hall returned to the table alone, a fresh glass of wine in her hand.

She sat down between her two daughters, seeming not to notice the fact that they were staring daggers at each other.

A moment later, an elderly stranger in a tuxedo approached the table. I expected him to greet the family, but he had a different agenda. "The band is taking requests," he said. "Would anyone like a request card?" He held up a fountain pen in his hand.

"No thank you," Bella said quickly.

"I would," I said, raising my hand.

The old man beamed. "Here you are." He handed me a thick card. "Write down as many songs as you like."

I quickly jotted the word MERENGUE and handed it back.

He palmed the card, squinting at it. "That's not terribly specific," he said. "Do you care to elaborate?"

"Any one will do," I said.

The old man grinned. "All right, then. I believe I will take your request over right away. It would be worth it to get some young blood on that floor." He winked and walked toward the band.

"What did you just do?" asked a wary Bella.

"I made a request. Hope you're wearing comfortable shoes."

Her eyes widened. "I told you I don't dance."

I sipped my wine so I wouldn't laugh. "It's just like running, Bella. Anyone with two feet can do it. And I'm pretty sure that some of those people over there are making do with barely that."

She crossed her arms. "It's not my thing."

"Try anything once, right?"

Bella's mother and sister were hanging on every word. At least Bella and Julie weren't fighting anymore.

It was only two minutes later when I heard it starting up — that classic one-two merengue rhythm. It was the soundtrack of my whole life. "Here we go," I said, standing up. I offered Bella my hand.

She shook her head. Even worse, she scooted her chair toward the wall. On the dance floor, the energy picked up as the geezers began to move to the faster beat. "Don't leave me hanging," I said, my hand still hanging there in the air. "Come on now. Nobody puts Bella in a corner."

On the other side of the table, Bella's sister snorted into her white wine, then began to laugh.

Bella rolled her eyes. Hard. "You did *not* just quote *Dirty Dancing.*"

I leaned down near Bella's ear. "I did. Now get your ass out of that chair like the girl in the movie or I'll have to put you in a fireman's hold."

Her mouth tight, Bella stood. Not one to waste an opportunity, I clasped her hand, tugging her onto the dance floor. When we reached the center, I put one hand onto Bella's waist and took her opposite hand in mine. She was as stiff as a piece of wood. "Shake it off, *chica.* This is supposed to be fun."

"Your job tonight was to make my life *less* embarrassing. Not more."

"I am. Because we're going to be the best looking dancers on this floor, and everyone in this mausoleum is going to wonder how I got so lucky as to be here with you. Now listen to this rhythm, okay? Just *step* to the beat. And let your hips absorb the motion." I began to step in place, moving to the music. The merengue is a Dominican dance and every kid in my neighborhood can merengue before his fifth birthday. It's just not that complicated.

With nervous eyes, Bella began to move.

"Use the hips," I prompted, tapping a finger to the silky fabric of her dress. As I watched, she loosened up a tiny fraction. I leaned in to whisper in her ear. "You look amazing in this dress. Now move those hips a little more and you're there."

Biting her lip, Bella moved with me.

"See? Nothing to it. Now here's the final touch — step forward towards me, then back again." I guided her close to my body. "See? Now you like me..." I let her fall back. "Now you don't. Just like in real life."

And, just like that, we had a proper merengue going on. "There. I knew you could move."

Bella pouted. "We've *seen* each other's moves, Rafe."

She lifted her eyes, and the heat in them went straight to my dick. *Jesucristo*. That was the trouble with getting too close to Bella. I was always going to be susceptible to her. Anything she did to remind me of that night was always going to knock me right over.

"Ha," she said. "I finally found a way to shut you up." Bella put a little more effort into her merengue, looking smug.

"Just for that, I'm going to spin you now."

Her eyes popped wide. "No, don't."

I shook my head. "This isn't the tango. Merengue is an easygoing dance. I'm raising your right arm, and you're going to turn around under it without breaking the beat. Nice and slow. Now *turn*. To your right." I lifted our hands above her head.

Bella rotated right on schedule, facing me again after four beats. If I wasn't mistaken, she looked rather pleased with herself.

"See? You can stop acting like this is torture. I've kept you away from your family for at least three minutes." I returned my hand to Bella's sleek waist, trying not to notice how good it felt to hold her there.

"Good point," she murmured.

The dance floor was more crowded than it had been a few minutes ago. And I could tell when Bella relaxed, because she smiled at me the next time I turned her.

This was worth a weird-ass night with her family. Because I'd finally made Bella smile.

Unfortunately, all good merengues come to an end. And even though the crowd applauded more enthusiastically for my dance than for any other, the band segued into a slow song. I heard the opening strains of Louis Armstrong's "A Kiss to Build a Dream On."

"Okay," Bella said, stepping back. "I danced. Can I have more wine now?"

"Almost," I said, stepping close again, putting my hand on the small of her back. "One more. Because it just doesn't make sense for your fake boyfriend to skip the slow dance."

"This is your game, not mine." But Bella put her hand on my shoulder anyway, and let me lead her slowly around the floor.

I was born in the wrong decade, I swear it. Because dancing to live music with a beautiful girl was absolutely my idea of a good time. "Turn, *belleza*," I said, lifting my hand to gently spin her.

When she came back around to face me, she had a startled look on her face.

"It just means *beautiful*," I said. "A good fake boyfriend would use that word."

"I get that," she said, putting her head on my shoulder. "It's just that the first time you called me that, I was riding your dick."

"What?" I sputtered.

Her mouth was just beside my ear, so she whispered. "You heard me. All those things you whispered to me in Spanish when we were naked. That was hot as fuck."

Annnd now I was hard. *Do not think about that night*, I ordered myself. But my body heated anyway.

"Damn, that was fun," Bella sighed, her hand on my chest. "It's really too bad I've given up men."

All the awkwardness of the moment bubbled up then, and I laughed. "Maybe you should have brought a fake *girlfriend* as your date. That would shake up the family."

Bella giggled, and her hair tickled my chin. "You're a freaking *genius*. Next time I'm doing that."

Does it make me an idiot that I hated to hear her agree with me? I was really enjoying my role tonight. Maybe too much. I held her a little closer as we danced. The band had no vocalist, but I could hear Louis Armstrong's voice in my head. *Give me... a kiss to build a dream on.* "I've always loved this song," I confessed.

"Wait, really?" Bella stood up taller so she could look me in the eye. "Have you listened to the lyrics? The guy gets a single kiss, and he basically says that it's enough — he's just going to fantasize about it for the rest of his life. I mean... what a *rip*."

I bit back a smile. "It's romantic."

"It's *unsatisfying*," she countered. "Here, I'll show you." Before I knew what was happening, Bella came closer. Her silky thumb stroked once across my cheekbone. Then she stood up on her toes and kissed me.

The first press of her sweet lips against mine stopped my breathing. Though you couldn't have paid me to resist her. Sheer instinct made me lean into that kiss with my entire being.

Bella's mouth melted onto mine, and a needy little sound issued from the back of her throat. *Heaven*. I deepened the kiss, and our tongues touched once. She tasted of red wine and desire. An electric pulse traveled the length of my body. Unbidden, my hands pulled her closer, my fingers in her hair...

The sound of applause brought me back to earth with a thunk. The song had ended, and the band segued into some kind of swing tune. Bella and I broke apart on a gasp. For a second we just stared at each other. "See?" she said eventually.

But I didn't have the faintest recollection of the point she'd been trying to make. "What?"

Amusement tickled her features. "Never mind. I hear my wine glass calling me." She tugged on my hand.

I got a hold of myself as we walked toward the table. There was nobody on the planet like Bella. And no matter how fucked up things were, she was never boring. Smiling to myself, I gave her a single kiss on the temple as we walked. "Thanks for the dance."

"Wow, they are totally buying it," she said.

"What?"

"The fake boyfriend thing. Look at them."

I lifted my eyes to the table, and found Bella's family watching us. To be more accurate, they were staring at us in fascination.

"You underestimated me," I said as we approached the table.

"Eh," Bella said, pinching me on the wrist. "They can be super gullible. You have no idea."

I laughed, but our private moment was over. I pulled out Bella's chair again, and she gave me a slight eyebrow lift that seemed to say: *now you're overselling it*.

"I do hope that Tucker sits down before the meal," Julie said, scanning the crowd.

"Where *is* Prince Charming, anyway?" Bella asked, gulping her wine.

"He saw some of his associates across the way," Julie replied. "You know how he is, always working."

"Oh, I know how he is," Bella muttered. "Always working *something*."

"You two looked lovely out there," their mother said, changing the subject. "Where did you learn to dance, Rafe?"

"In my mama's kitchen," I said. "Every good Dominican boy can merengue." I let the Spanish roll off my tongue, the way it's supposed to. "But I can do all the ballroom dances. I learned them at my public elementary school in Washington Heights."

"Really," Lydia enthused. "That is so charming."

"That's just Rafe," Bella put in. "He's the charming one in this relationship."

A salad plate landed on the table in front of me then, and I realized how hungry I was.

"Is someone seated here?" the waiter asked, indicating the empty place next to Julie.

"Yes," she said.

"Here I am!" a man's voice boomed. He yanked back the chair beside Julie and kissed her before he sat down. "So sorry! But I saw the boys from State Street over there. You *know*..." He dropped his voice and turned to face Bella's father. "They're still sitting on that vacant piece of land in Red Hook. I think we can pry it away from them after the new year."

Bella's father, who hadn't said ten words all night, nodded sagely. "Can we now? That sounds promising."

The newcomer jerked his napkin off the table with a snap and dropped it in his lap. He had a way of moving which drew attention to everything he did.

I hated him on sight.

Julie gave her husband's shoulder an affectionate rub. "Maybe you can spend some time with your family now? We're almost never together like this."

Beside me, Bella stabbed her lettuce with unnecessary force. She did not spare a glance at her brother-in-law, even though he was right across the table from her.

"You haven't met Rafe," Julie continued. "Bella's boyfriend."

I gave Bella a gentle kick under the table. *See? It worked*, I telegraphed.

She didn't even look up.

"I'm Tucker Fanning," Julie's husband said. "Nice to meet you." He gave me a salute in lieu of a handshake, since the table was so wide.

"Pleasure," I said, reminding myself of Bickley. I wondered what he'd make of this party.

Julie carried the conversation after that. She did a lot of gushing about the night's keynote speaker, but I was watching Bella eat her salad. I could feel waves of stress rolling off her, and I didn't like it.

Tucker Fanning must have been indifferent to them, because eventually he asked her a direct question. "So, Bella. What do the undergraduates do for fun these days?"

Bella set down her fork. "Well, Tucker. We do whatever we can to broaden our little horizons. It isn't all keg stands and bong hits anymore."

If I wasn't mistaken, Bella's sister practically braced herself against whatever Bella was about to say.

"Truthfully, I've gotten a bit bored with my usual."

"Is that so?" Tucker asked, holding his wine glass in a way that somehow managed to look pompous.

"Vanilla sex just doesn't do it for me anymore. I've been

dabbling in some kink and fetish play. Just the sort of thing you'd enjoy, actually."

Her father dropped his fork onto his plate with a loud clatter. "Jesus, Isabelle!"

At that, Lydia laid a hand on his arm. "She's just saying it to get a rise out of us. *Must* you always fall for it?"

Without a word, he rose from his chair. Taking his scotch glass in hand, he drained it, then marched off toward one of the bars.

"I'll just..." Tucker got up and took off after him. If I didn't know better, I'd think that it was Tucker and Mr. Hall who were married.

"*Why?*" squealed Julie. "Why must you do this? Now Daddy will be all upset, and on the night when I'm getting my award!"

Bella gave her sister a laser stare. "Your award was bought and paid for, Julie. The ceremony doesn't matter, does it?"

"*That* is a wicked thing to say," her sister argued, pointing her salad fork at Bella like a spear. "Couldn't you just give Tucker the benefit of the doubt? For just a couple of hours?"

Bella rolled her eyes. "I keep *telling* you. He got plenty of *benefits* from me."

Their mother put her face in her hands. "Why? Why must we always end up here?"

"Because he is still here," Bella said. She threw her napkin on the table and stood. "And that means I can't be." Bella picked her wrap up off the back of her chair and tucked her little handbag under one arm.

"Bella!" her mother called.

Stunned, it took me a second to react. But Bella wasn't coming back. "Excuse me," I said. Then I left the table too, jogging to catch up with the sexy red streak who was aiming for the exit.

Note to self: Bella is a darned good runner, whether she knows it or not.

TWENTY

BELLA

Fuck!

Fuck, fuck, fuck, fuckity fuck.

I hightailed it out of Cipriani, making poor Rafe chase after me.

By the time we hit the sidewalk on 42nd Street, I was breathing hard and trying not to cry.

Rafe steered me down the block, across the street, and down into the subway entrance. He swiped a Metrocard through the turnstile then pointed at me to go through. When he joined me on the other side, I had the presence of mind to ask, "Where are we going?"

"Uptown," he said, steering me toward the shuttle track.

"I'm sorry," I said. "I thought I could get through tonight without wigging out."

"What's the deal with that guy?"

I *really* didn't want to tell him the story. On the other hand, I'd dragged him to a dinner he did not get to eat. And then dragged him out again. Meanwhile, he got a glimpse of both me and my family at its worst. "He works for my father."

"So I gathered."

"Three years ago, I spent the summer before my freshman year at Harkness in South Hampton. We have a beach house there. My father was staying out there, too."

"Okay."

"Well, Dad never comes out of his office. And I was working at a kids' camp, but mostly just goofing off."

"Okay." He chuckled.

"Tucker Fanning — who I shall henceforth only refer to as Fucker Tanning — used to take the train out during the week to meet with my father. And he stayed in our guest house."

"Sounds pretty grand."

"Oh, it was. He and I had a fling. And by 'fling' I mean we had lots and lots of sex. I was eighteen, and he was twenty-six."

Rafe flinched. "Whoa. Was he married to your sister then?"

"Oh, *God* no." What a question! Even at eighteen I'd never screw a married man. And I'd never do that to my sister. Because I'd assumed she had my back.

I was wrong.

"In fact," I told Rafe, "he'd just broken up with the Norwegian model he'd been dating. I was flattered. And quite obviously an idiot."

The train came then, the doors opening right in front of us. We stepped inside and sat down on the bench. "He shouldn't have taken advantage of you like that," Rafe said, his face stony.

I touched his elbow. "That's not really the problem. I had it bad for him. I thought the sun shone out of his ass. Really, I did." Rafe gave me a sad little smile, and it gave me the courage to plunge ahead. "I served myself up to him on a silver platter, Rafe. It's not like I was some innocent virgin before him, either."

Rafe flinched. "But he broke it off?"

With a groan, I shook my head. "He didn't break it off. That's the weird thing. He made all these crazy promises to stupid eighteen-year-old me. We were going to meet up in Europe during one of my school vacations. We were going to keep our affair secret, because it was too big to tell the world." I rolled my eyes for emphasis. "I don't know what came over me, honestly. But the sex was really good. It wasn't like fumbling around with the teenagers at my high school, you know?"

He gave me an awkward shrug.

"We carried on like this, stolen hours on the beach, etc. At the beginning of freshman year, there were a lot of texts, and a lot of dirty Skype calls. Then Christmas comes around, and we have a house full of people. And I'm wondering which bathroom we'll end up screwing in. But Fucker Tanning gets down on one knee in front of God and everybody and proposes to my sister."

Rafe's eyebrows shot toward the sky. "Say what?"

"That's right. He'd been seeing her the whole time. They kept it on the D.L. though, and he said it was because he didn't want people to gossip about how he was dating the boss's daughter."

"*Jesucristo.* What did you do?"

"I did what any self-respecting girl does. I cried my eyes out in my bedroom for all of Christmas break. Then I went back to college. They set a wedding date for a year later."

"You didn't *tell* her?" Rafe asked.

I crossed my arms, indignant. "Of *course* I told her. *Eventually.* It took me a pretty long time to just get over the shock. I kept waiting for someone to call me up and say that it was a joke. I mean... the things he used to say to me. So many promises, so many lies. It took me a few months just to wrap my head around it. But when summer came, I had to look my sister in the eye again. And *he* was always around. And I just couldn't stand it anymore. So one night when my sister was over for dinner, and it was just the family, I told them the whole sordid tale."

Rafe was watching me so closely then. I could see wheels turning behind his chocolate eyes. And when he figured out what had happened, he suddenly looked sad. "They didn't believe you."

Slowly, I shook my head.

"Seriously? They thought you *invented* that?"

"Well." I had to clear my throat. "At first, they listened. My sister freaked out. She confronted him. And for one whole day I thought logic would prevail. But of course he lied through his teeth. The guy is *slick*."

Rafe made an angry sound in his throat. "That's... incredible, Bella. Your parents ought to believe family first."

Maybe. But Rafe didn't know me all that well. "My family already thought of me as the crazy one. 'There goes poor, slutty Bella, looking for attention.' I wasn't an easy kid. They set rules, and I broke them. I was always lying about where I was going, and who I was with."

Rafe did not look convinced, and I loved him for it. "Skirting your curfew is not the same as making up a story about your sister's fiancé."

True. "They didn't take the trouble to make the distinction, I guess. To my father, Fucker Tanning had been part of the family for a few years already. They thought of him as the good son they never had. And he said he wanted to take care of their perfect daughter. Meanwhile, they had this *other* daughter that was always giving them heart attacks. My parents walked in on me once with a boy from high school. We were screwing in their bed."

Rafe laughed into his hand.

"I know. It's hysterical. I was always *that* kid. When my sister was eighteen and I was fourteen, my mother took us out for a girls' brunch at the Russian Tea Room. My sister said, 'Mom, I think I need birth control.' And then I said, 'Oh, that's easy. You can just buy condoms at the drugstore. That's what I do.' My mother choked on her caviar."

"*Dios.*"

"*Dios* shakes his head whenever I get a big idea."

At least I had Rafe smiling now. And I loved his smile. "Someday," he said, "you might have a daughter..."

"People keep warning me that karma is a bitch."

He shook his head. "That's not what I mean at *all*. You'll have a daughter, and she'll be able to tell you whatever is in her head. And you won't hit the roof — you'll just deal with it, you know?

The girls in my neighborhood, they hit high school and all the aunties start heaping on the guilt. 'Don't wear short skirts, because the boys will think you're easy. Don't let him kiss you. Don't let him touch you. Go to confession.' It's crazy."

"I wouldn't last an hour."

His smile fell. "I'm sorry your family got it so wrong, though. That's not fair. Even if he is slick, they should listen to you."

"I've had a long time to think about it now, though. I think my mother actually believes me. But she doesn't know what to do. And the more psych classes I take, the easier it is to see that Fucker Tanning is pretty cracked."

"He has to wreck it some time, right? Nobody can lie so much and get away with it."

I'd thought that, too. But three years later... "I have to assume that he's still cheating on her." Even though I was pissed at my sister, this bothered me. I'd just discovered the horrors of having a doctor tell me I'd caught something. I hope my sister didn't eventually figure it out *that* way. *God.* "He's held it together until now. Besides, my sister also thinks that the sun shines out of his ass. I've tried to warn her. But it's not like anyone wants to hear what I say."

The shuttle docked underneath Times Square, and Rafe and I walked out. I followed him to the uptown number two and three train platform. "Where exactly are we going?" I suddenly thought to ask.

"To get some dinner in Washington Heights," Rafe answered immediately. "I'm starved."

"Sorry," I said again.

He reached over and squeezed my hand. "Don't be."

An express pulled up, and we got on. After the sing-song warning tone, the doors clattered shut. Rafe pointed at a single empty seat, and I dropped into it. He took up a position right in front of me, holding the bar over my head.

Looking up at him, I said, "I got really drunk at their wedding."

"I'll bet." Rafe chuckled.

"Julie claims that I ruined her special day by puking onto the topiary after the cake was cut. But that shit was tainted long before I threw up."

Rafe snickered. "I *almost* feel sorry for her. Almost."

When the doors opened at 72nd, quite a bit of the crowd got off. So Rafe dropped into the seat next to mine.

"Tell me where you're taking me," I said, hoping to lighten up the evening again. For a few minutes there, I'd actually had fun. Dancing with Rafe had been the high point of the last few weeks. Not that I was about to tell him that.

"To my family's restaurant," he said. "Is there anything you don't eat?"

I grabbed my chest in mock horror. "Dude, I'm from New York. You can't scare me even if you try."

Rafe grinned.

Many subway stops later, we emerged in Washington Heights. I'd never been to this neighborhood before. It was past Columbia University, where my high school friends and I used to go to drink in the bars that served college students without ID. It was north of the hospital and north of pretty much everything. The only time I'd set foot up here was on a school trip to The Cloisters museum.

I didn't like to think of myself as an Upper East Side snob. But there it was.

"Are you freezing?" Rafe asked.

"No, I'm fine." Truly, I was getting cold. But after that scene I'd put Rafe through earlier, I wasn't going to complain about *anything* else tonight.

"I wanted to walk past the site." Rafe pointed down the block.

"Oh! For our project?" What a lousy teammate I was. It hadn't even occurred to me that we were only blocks away from our

Urban Studies assignment. I followed him to West 165th Street. And there it was, the ugly building from the photograph. "Can't imagine why we'd tear this down," I teased.

"Right? But we don't need to look at the building so much as what surrounds it." He put his hands on my shoulders and turned me. "Across the intersection, there's an apartment building. That looks like a nice place."

It did, too. It was six stories high, a pre-war brick building. One of thousands in the city.

"But those are some pretty gritty retailers over there." Rafe indicated a check-cashing joint and a pawn shop. There was also a skeevy little bodega and a shoe repair store.

"This spot has good foot traffic, though," I said. "We could put something better here. A grocery, or a restaurant." I took out my phone and began to turn in a circle, snapping photographs of everything.

"The judge is a food guy, remember. If we did something with food, he might like it."

I gave Rafe a little poke in the ribs. "Look at you, Mr. Tactical! I like it."

He put a hand on my back. "Speaking of food, let's go eat."

A few minutes later he led me under a striped awning into a brightly lit hive of activity. The restaurant wasn't fancy. The interior looked like it had been there since the seventies, if I had to guess. There were Formica tables with metal edges, and the walls were painted in colors which were just a little too bright to be stylish.

But the place was *jammed*. I couldn't even see it properly, because there was a knot of people between the door and the dining room.

"*Dios*," Rafe said under his breath. A small missile hurtled into his knees. When I looked down, I saw a toddler-sized person with gorgeous brown skin and curly black hair. Rafe leaned over and scooped the child off the floor.

"Wafe," it said.

"Hey, Gael," Rafe said. "Where is your *mami*? There are a lot of people who are trying to pay."

"*No sé*," the child said.

Rafe carried him around the end of the counter to where the cash register was. "Sorry for the wait," he said to the couple who was first in line. "Did you need to check out?"

The couple handed him their check and a credit card, and Rafe handled the transaction, while his very small relative poked him in the cheekbone.

"None of that," Rafe said, grabbing one little arm in his hand and tucking the kid farther back onto his hip. "Your hands are sticky, little man. Did you get into the *dulce de leche?*"

Rafe cashed out three couples before he was even able to mouth "I'm sorry" in my direction.

A young woman came skidding on high heels to the front of the restaurant. "Rafael!" she cried. "*Lo siento*. I got caught up helping untangle a delivery order." She grabbed the child out of his arms.

"His hands are sticky," Rafe warned. He skirted the woman to come back to my side.

"You look handsome tonight, *señor*." She grinned. I saw her eyes flick toward me. "And aren't you going to introduce me?"

"Cara, this is Bella, who has not had dinner yet. Bella, this is my aunt Cara. Now we're grabbing that two top before somebody else does." Rafe put a hand on my lower back and guided me towards a little table by the window.

I sat down, but then Rafe made an irritated noise. "*Ay*, the table." He disappeared for a moment, reappearing with a cloth to wipe it off. Then he put two rolls of silverware down before finally collapsing into the seat across from me. "Nothing is easy tonight."

"So true," I agreed. But privately, I was soaking it all in. The music playing in the restaurant had a sexy Latin beat. Tipico had a relaxed, neighborly vibe that was a hell of a lot less stressful than the other place we'd been tonight.

And watching Rafe step behind the counter of his family's business with a toddler on his hip had a strange effect on me. He'd looked so comfortable there. I'm sure Rafe wasn't intending to use his Harkness degree to make change for restaurant customers. But he already had a place in the world where he knew exactly what he was doing. Where he fit in. Where he was needed. I'd never had that. And with each passing month, it seemed increasingly likely that I never would.

A teenage girl bounced over to our table and let out a little squeal. "Rafael! What are *you* doing sitting in my section?"

"*Florecita*, what do people usually want when they sit in your section? We're hungry."

She put her hands on her hips, her eyes sparkling back and forth between us. "Is this your *girlfriend?*"

"Subtle, Flori. This is my *friend* Bella. Bella, this is Flori, my nosy cousin."

"Hi," I said, trying not to smile.

"She must be your girlfriend," Flori declared. "You're all dressed up."

"If I lied and said she was, could we get some food?"

"You are no fun at all, you know that?" But her expression said the opposite. She looked at Rafe with hero worship in her eyes.

"Flori, bring us a couple of beers, and leave your order pad." To make his point, Rafe grabbed the pad out of her apron pocket and then gave her a little shove toward the back.

She sighed, taking the pencil from behind her ear and dropping it on the table. "Fine. But I'm telling everyone in the kitchen that you're here with your girlfriend." Then she flounced away.

Rafe looked at me wearily. "I thought this would be a quick way to score some food. But I may have miscalculated."

"I think she's hysterical."

"That's one word for it." He took the pencil and began scribbling on the pad. "I'm going to get a little of everything, okay? You can pick out the dishes that appeal to you."

"You're going to tip me, right?" Flori had reappeared. She held on to the beers for collateral, waiting for Rafe's answer.

He raised one dark eyebrow. "You think I'd stiff you? Really?"

She put the bottles down. "You never sit at a table, so how do I know? Papi says he'll comp your food but not the beer."

Rafe shrugged. "I'd pass out face down in the mangu if your Papi ever bought me a beer, Florecita. I'm half expecting him to come out here and remind me to wash my own dishes."

She patted his shoulder. "Since you brought company, he probably won't do that. I should try that sometime."

Rafe handed her the pad and the pencil. "You bring a boy in here, he's going to chase him off with a chef's knife."

Her smile faded. "That is probably true."

When she went away with our order, he folded his arms on the table and smiled at me. "Hungry? I ordered a lot of food."

"Sure." I was, too. "What should I expect?"

"Dominican food is sort of like Cuban. Lots of fried things. It's not health food."

I picked up my beer bottle and touched it to his. "Fuck health food. We've earned a few fried plantains tonight."

"Damn straight," he said, then lifted the bottle to his beautiful mouth.

"You work here during the summer?"

"Yeah. And every holiday. And all the years in high school. They didn't even pay me minimum wage until last summer. My uncles are slave drivers. They think blood relatives should work for almost nothing."

"But you get tips?"

He shook his head. "I've been working in that kitchen since I could hold a knife. I wrote my Harkness essay about learning to keep my cool in a crowded kitchen."

"That's awesome, Rafe. I'm not like you."

He gave me a lazy grin. Slouched back in his chair across from me holding his beer, rocking a five o'clock shadow on his jaw, Rafe was easy on the eyes. "What am I *like*, then?"

"You're good at everything." Honest to God, the sight of Rafe dancing the merengue as easily as he walked was the sexiest thing I'd ever seen. The boy could *move*. It made me want to gobble him down and ask for seconds.

He set the bottle down with a snort. "Right. I wish that was true. School isn't easy for me."

"No? You seem like you've got it all together."

His eyes took a tour of the room. "My family thinks I live a cushy life, going to school and working a few shifts in the dining hall. They think it's like a four-year vacation. And I'm sweating buckets just to keep my grades at a B- average. My mother wanted me to pick a school in the City so I could live with her across the street from this place and work five nights a week."

"She doesn't understand, though. You're going to have the word 'Harkness' on your resume in two and a half years. That sticker is going to be worth a pile of money to you, if you want it to be."

He leaned that handsome face into one of his hands. "What about you, Bella? What are you going to do with your Harkness sticker?"

That was the question, wasn't it? "I really wish I knew. And the fact that I don't is starting to freak me out. I mean... it's not like I'm going to starve. But I really don't want to move back into my bedroom on East 78th Street with nothing but a diploma to show for my effort."

"But hey, the diploma will be in *Latin*," Rafe said. He touched his bottle to mine and then drained his beer. "Where is that cousin of mine. Flori?" he called as she ran past. "Where's our food?"

"Some of it is up, I think," she said over her shoulder. "Why don't you check?"

"What is the deal with this joint?" he asked, and I laughed. He swept our empty beer bottles off the table and went into the kitchen.

Two minutes later I saw him reappear through the swinging doors, a tray in his hands. I was so busy admiring the sexy sway of his shoulders that I almost missed the gorgeous woman hot on his heels. She had exquisite cheekbones, dark skin and wavy hair which had been captured into a clip on the top of her head.

"Rafael! *Adónde vas? Espera a tu madre.*"

He answered her in rapid-fire Spanish. Setting the edge of the tray down on the table, he began removing dishes. Each one he put in front of me looked better than the last. And the smell! I was salivating in seconds.

Behind him, the beautiful woman put her hands on her hips. I couldn't understand what she was saying, but from her tone it was obvious that a) she was his mother, though she looked almost too young to have a college-age son and b) she wasn't entirely happy with him.

"Ma, stop yelling," Rafe commanded. "This is my friend Bella. She has never had Dominican food, and we did not have any dinner. So be nice and let us eat."

Rafe's mother peered around his shoulder, taking in our dressy clothes. Her face softened just a little. She offered her hand. "It is so nice to meet you, Bella. And Rafael! Why do you not have water glasses? And extra plates, if you're going to share?"

"That would be a question for Flori, I think."

But Rafe's mom had already turned on her heel, running off presumably to get them.

Rafe rubbed his hands together. "Food, at last! Okay. The dish in front of you is called La Bandera."

"That just means 'flag,' right?" I couldn't resist showing off that I knew a Spanish word.

"Exactly. It's supposed to look like the colors of the flag. But every Dominican kid is like, 'What the hell?' Rice is white. Fine. And the sauce on the meat is reddish. But beans aren't *blue*. It doesn't make a lot of sense."

I picked up my fork and popped a flake of the stewed pork into my mouth. "It's really good, though. I don't think it would be better if it were actually blue."

"This is mofongo." He pointed at the weirdest looking thing on the table. "Mashed plantains, fried, with a meat sauce on top. But they're even better like this." He pointed at gorgeously crispy pieces of plantain on another plate.

"What's that?" I asked, aiming my fork at another fried thing. It was square, about the size of a playing card. And when I sank my fork into the corner, it squished.

"Fried cheese. Another health food. The only lighter thing is this bulgur salad." He picked up the bowl and showed me the contents. On top of the grains sat tomatoes, avocados and parsley, with a few grilled shrimp on top.

A clean plate landed on the table in front of me. In a blur of motion, Rafe's mother tucked a serving spoon on to each of our dishes. Then she set a glass of water down in front of me. "Enjoy!" she said before stomping off.

"Your mother is a whirlwind," I said.

Rafe grinned at me as he scooped food onto his plate. "The kitchen boys call her *la tormenta*. The storm."

"Are you going to be in the doghouse for coming in here tonight?"

Rafe looked surprised. "Not a chance. They'd like to have me working in back. But they'd rather I show my face than stay away. We bitch at each other a lot, I guess. That's just how we talk." He ate a piece of plantain with a thoughtful expression on his face. "You know, coming back here after I've been away for a while, this place looks shabby to me. I want to give it a facelift. I tried to say that this summer and the uncles didn't want to hear it."

"It's comfortable, though," I supplied. "Not every restaurant needs to be fancy."

"I know. But I think we could update it a little, then raise the menu prices about thirty percent. But they're afraid to change anything."

"My dad is the opposite. There's no building in New York that he's afraid to bulldoze. If people actually knew what he looked like, he'd need a bodyguard in certain neighborhoods."

"Seriously?"

"Yeah. I don't mean that he's knocking down historical treasures or anything. But most people are resistant to change. That's normal."

"I don't know if 'normal' and '*mi familia*' belong together in the same sentence." He stabbed a bite of mofongo with his fork.

"Mmm," I said, stuffing my face. The food was incredibly good. The stewed meats were tender and flavorful; the rice was fluffy. "You're going to have to roll me out of here after this."

A skinny teenage boy was shuffling toward us, wiping his hands on a chef's apron. "*Hola, primo.*" He put a hand on Rafe's shoulder. "You know Flori is in the kitchen, texting all her sisters that you're here with your girlfriend." The boy smiled, and his eyes crinkled up in the corners. "I tell her that your girlfriend's name is Alison, but she say maybe you have more than one."

"Well, that's me," Rafe said, putting his fork down. "The Don Juan of Harkness College."

"Wherever Rafe goes," I teased, "the girls follow in little packs, hoping he'll notice them. I had to follow him all the way to Manhattan just to get this close."

The boy laughed, and Rafe rolled his eyes. Kidding aside, Rafe probably could have girls hanging off of him if he wanted it that way.

Rafe's mother snuck up behind the kid and asked him a pointed question in Spanish. With a sigh, he headed back into the kitchen.

"He was only here for a second," Rafe protested. "Just saying hello."

"We do not stand around in the dining room wearing kitchen clothes." She sniffed. "It looks unprofessional."

"Relax, Ma," he said, his head tilting back to look at her. "Since when do you work Saturday night?"

"There was a party to cater. Nobody else was free. And you saw — Cara was here late with her little one. This is our busy season."

"It's always our busy season." He began to stack our finished plates. Rafe and I had demolished all that food in an almost embarrassingly short amount of time. "Flori!" he called, and his cute little cousin came bounding over. "Can you scare up a check?" He handed a stack of plates to her, too.

His mother lunged for the remaining dishes, practically clucking over him. "There is no *check*, Rafael."

"We had a couple of beers."

"Eh. Pablo will live. Do not run out yet. I'll bring you *dulce de leche en table*." She turned to me. "Would you like coffee?"

"Oh! No thank you. Everything was wonderful."

She smiled and darted away. Rafe's mother reminded me of a little bird, flitting from one place to another in an instant.

Rafe rubbed his stomach. "I needed that. Putting up with the crazy family was almost worth it."

I gave a little groan. "Sorry, but your crazy is not nearly as crazy as our crazy."

Rafe measured me with his chocolate eyes. "You only win this contest because of the creepy brother-in-law. Otherwise I think I'd have you beat."

Gazing at him from across the very small table, my neck heated. Not only was it a beautiful view, but I was remembering the last time we had a contest to figure out which of us had it worse. The crazy night we'd shared was still special to me, even if I'd never figured out why Rafe had been so miserable afterward.

His mother reappeared with a plate holding four little sugary-looking squares and several slices of star fruit. "It was lovely to meet you," she said, giving me another smile. "I am going upstairs now. You'll be along soon?" she asked her son.

"I'm going to take Bella home, but then I'll be right back," he said quickly.

"You don't have to do that," I protested. "I'll just catch a cab to the train station. Or Uber."

Rafe's eyebrows lifted. "You're going back to Harkness? Tonight?"

I locked eyes with him, wondering why he'd assume I wanted to go home to my parents' house after that awful scene at dinner.

We had a mini stare-down, but he caved first, looking at his watch. "When's the last train?"

"Eleven-fifteen. I'll make it."

He stood. "I'll take you."

"Grand Central is perfectly safe," I argued, embarrassed that he'd go all that way. After everything I'd already put him through tonight.

"125th is closer," his mother pointed out. "And pretty girls don't go there alone at night."

The path of least resistance was clearly to let Rafe accompany me to the train station. "All right," I murmured. I thanked his mother one more time for the lovely meal, and then I let Rafe lead me out of the restaurant, his hand at my back. I caught his cousin Flori smirking as we passed by. Her eyes were full of romantic theories about us.

Oh, honey. If she only knew the strange truth, she wouldn't smile like that.

Outside, it was chilly. I pulled my wrap as tightly around me as I could. Without even a thought, Rafe put an arm around me and pulled me closer to his warm body. There was nothing sexual about it. Rafe was so... *sturdy*. The way I used to be, too.

I leaned in, if only for tonight.

TWENTY-ONE

BELLA

Sunday evening, Lianne came through my bathroom door unannounced. "Hey!" she said breathlessly. "I have news."

"It's dangerous to barge in here, you know," I said, tossing a book off my lap. "Might have been an orgy in progress."

"Uh-huh," she said, dismissing my 'tude with a flip of her hand. "This is worth interrupting an orgy, anyway."

That got my attention. "What is?"

"Come here." She beckoned, then turned on her heel and headed back through the bathroom toward her own room.

Curious, I followed her into her tiny single, which was illuminated only by the blue light emitted by three computer monitors. "Jesus. What's all this? You could run NASA from here."

"I got into their site," Lianne announced without a preamble. "But I need to know how you want to play this."

"Whose site?" I asked. I found my answer on Lianne's monitors. *Brodacious.com* was displayed on one screen beside another filled with long scripts in computereze. "What do you mean, you *got into it?*"

"I cracked it open. Which means we can pull down that photo

if you want to."

My heart skipped a beat. "*Seriously?* Just like that?"

"Yes and no," Lianne warned, her face serious. "If I take the picture down, they'll notice. It's right at the top of the page."

"Still?" I gasped. I hadn't looked at Brodacious since that first awful day. I'd been imagining my picture had already been buried under whatever other stupid things Beta Rho had to say.

"Yeah," she sighed.

"So..." I tried to do the math. "If you take it down, they might just put it up again."

"Or worse," Lianne said grimly. Her flawless face was tinted blue by the light from the computer screen. "If they think you were responsible for tampering with their website, I have no clue what they'd do to get even."

I shivered. "I didn't think of that. Men can be assholes."

"Most men are *certified* assholes," she agreed quietly.

I sat down on Lianne's bed. "Shit. Do I have to decide right this second?"

"Probably not. There's only a *small* chance that their web host will notice my invasion." She crossed her tiny arms. "I was pretty sneaky, though."

Wow. I let that sink in for a second. I'd been so bowled over by this reversal of fortune that I hadn't given enough thought to the fact that Lianne was capable of such a thing. *Lianne.* The neighborhood movie star and... hacker? *Really?* "Buddy?" I asked. "Could you get in trouble for doing this?"

"I committed a federal crime just by breaking in." She gave me the same evil smile her sorceress princess character made on the big screen. "But I break the law every day, Bella. And nobody would prosecute this. *Ever.* No state's attorney wants to slap the cuffs on an eighteen year-old college student for taking down a humiliating photo of a friend. Or *neighbor*," she added quickly.

"What about school rules?" I worried. "Aren't you on their network right now?"

"Nope." Lianne smiled. "I'm using my cell phone hotspot and

a VPN."

"A what?"

She waved a hand. "It's like wearing an invisibility cloak."

"Cool. I had no idea you were a computer genius."

Lianne shrugged. "I didn't go to a regular high school. I don't have friends. That leaves a lot of hours for playing with my computer."

Yikes. "I see."

"Do me a favor, though? Don't tell anyone. The tabloids would be all over this."

"All over what?" came a voice from the bathroom doorway.

We both looked up to see Rafe standing there. For the second time in ten minutes, my heart gave a little jump. He was just so fucking handsome. And I didn't really expect to see him tonight. I was pretty sure that after the family freak show I'd treated him to yesterday, he'd steer clear of me.

"Is this, like, girl talk?" Rafe grinned. "Should I go back in the other room?"

"No, it's okay," Lianne said. "You wouldn't tell anyone if I asked you not to."

His eyes widened. "Of course I won't. What's the matter?"

"Nothing." I beckoned to him. "You have to see this. Lianne has been totally holding out on us."

"Oh my God." Rafe chuckled. "Are you going to tell me that she's *actually* a sorceress?"

"That would explain a lot, I'm sure," Lianne muttered.

"It's so much cooler than that." I moved out of the way so Rafe could see the screen. "Lianne is a hacker."

"Huh," Rafe said, peering at the long script on the screen. "I'm not sure you and I have the same definition of cool. What's the punchline?"

"She hacked *Brodacious*."

"*Oh.*" I saw the understanding bloom on his face. "You're right. That *is* cool. But where does that leave you?"

That was the problem, wasn't it? "I have no idea."

TWENTY-TWO

RAFE

Bella thanked Lianne. "My mind is blown, okay? I need to think."

Lianne smiled like a cat. "You know where to find me."

We went back into Bella's room, where she threw my notebook on the floor and lay down on the bed on her stomach. I'd come up here to work on our Urban Studies project, but now there were more important things to discuss.

"Are you going to have her take the picture down?"

"I'm not sure," she said, hugging a pillow under her arms.

Moving a stack of books off her desk chair, I made room for my ass. Bella looked far too sexy on that bed for me to get anywhere near her.

"I want that picture down, but I need to think it over."

"Because you're worried about retaliation?"

She shook her head. "Not really. I'm pretty sure that the boys of Beta Rho have short little attention spans. They'll probably just move on to the next victim. But that bothers me, too."

"Are you thinking about reporting them?" I tried not to sound too eager, but I wanted that fucker to *pay*. Whoever he was.

"Nope. But that doesn't mean I'm going to let it go. I definitely want revenge."

That didn't sound good. "What kind? You told me that you were a fan of revenge. It was the night that I found out Alison…" I cleared my throat instead of finishing that sentence. *The night that I found out Alison cheated, and then we stripped each other and went at it like horny rabbits.*

Nice. I had to go and dredge that up. "What kind of revenge?" I asked again, moving the conversation along.

"That's the thing," she said slowly. "I haven't hit on the right solution yet. I want to *humiliate* him."

I would have asked "who?" if I thought she'd fall for it. "Humiliation, huh? You could ask Lianne to redirect the Brodacious website. Instead of their web content, you'd end up…" I thought about it for a second. "…on a porno, with frat boys getting spanked by a dominatrix."

Bella began to chuckle. "'*Please, mistress. May I have another?*' I *knew* I liked you, Rafe. And you know why that's a great idea? Because there'd be no way to know which of their many enemies pulled it off. There must be plenty of girls who hate Beta Rho."

"And rival frats."

She turned one cheek to the pillow and looked up at me. "The thing is, I want my revenge to be more personal. I want *them* to look ridiculous, and not just because the website didn't go where it was supposed to. I've been trying to figure out how to catch them in the act of doing something stupid."

"That sounds tricky."

"Yes and no. The number of stupid things they do in a week probably helps my odds." She stretched, arching her back, and I found myself admiring her butt. Which was not what I'd come upstairs to do. "I have a couple ideas. I've been doing some thinking."

"Feel like sharing?"

Bella grinned. "Nope. You'd just try to talk me out of them."

Fantástico. "So." I cleared my throat. "Have you thought about what foodie business we want in our new commercial development?"

"Nope!" Bella said cheerfully. "I've been working on a paper for this women's studies course I'm taking. It's kicking my ass."

Women's studies. That sounded like what lonely guys do on freshman on move-in day. "Can't say that I know what those classes are about. Though the topic sounds like something I'd like." Yeah. I should really just shut up now.

"It's politics and culture, from the feminist perspective. And I thought I'd really love it, you know? I'm interested in empowering females."

"Sure. But you don't like the class?"

Bella bent her knees, lifting her toes into the air — a move that immediately yanked her long legs into the center of my consciousness. My stupid brain decided to flash back to the time when I was lying on top of her in that bed, with those legs wrapped around me...

I mentally slapped myself and tried to focus on what Bella was saying. "Have you been going to class?" I asked, wondering if she'd give me a straight answer.

"That one, yeah. I figure even if I'm having trouble looking half the campus in the eye, a women's studies lecture should be no problem, right? Since the basic premise is that men have been fucking up the world for women since the beginning of time."

"Um..." I chuckled. "Not *all* of them."

Bella waved a dismissive hand. "Fine. But we're reading about institutionalized sexism, and wage inequality. That kind of thing."

"Fair enough."

"Some of it makes sense. But the professor's big theory is that our culture defines a woman's body as a void which needs filling. She thinks that idea is responsible for all kinds of evils: the wage gap, underrepresentation in seats of power..." Bella dropped her legs to the bed and pushed her cheek into the pillow. The girl had no idea what it did to me to see her all splayed out like that — her curvy body like a landscape on the bed.

"But you don't think that sounds right?" I asked, still trying to stay on topic.

"I'm sure she's right about a lot of things. But every time I lay down on this bed lately, I'm feeling a lot of sympathy for the void which needs filling." Her eyes cut over to me. "Celibacy isn't easy. I'm supposed to be writing a paper about female subjugation. But all I want is for someone to give me a good pounding."

Jesucristo. I let out the world's most strangled laugh. The picture she'd just put into my head was not very academic.

"I'm a failed feminist," Bella complained.

"Nah. You're your own brand of feminist. And there's your paper topic."

She grinned. "I'm pretty sure the professor would flunk me if she could see inside my brain. Today it's like ninety percent sexual positions, nine percent food and one percent homework."

Was it hot in here? I was going to have to go back downstairs to study if we didn't talk about something else. "Let's see if we can get that homework percentage up a little bit. Urban Studies, for example."

Bella sat up. "Fine. Let's talk Urban Studies. I really need to get out of my head."

And I needed to cool off. I yanked my backpack into my lap, practically ducking for cover. I pretended to search for something inside, though all I really needed was a way to disguise the tent I was pitching in my pants.

"Your notebook is here," Bella said, lifting it off the floor.

"Ah, right." I grabbed it as if that had been my goal the whole time.

"Name all the food businesses you can think of. Go."

"Dominican restaurant."

Bella giggled. "How *ever* did you come up with that one?"

"Everyone's a critic. Okay — grocery store. Wine shop. Sushi place. Bella, this isn't going to get us anywhere. Except now I'm starving."

She looked up from her own notebook. "Didn't you eat dinner?"

"Of course I did. But that was hours ago."

"Boys." She shook her head. "They're always hungry."

"Pretty much," I sighed. Though there were several kinds of hunger. And I was feeling more than one of them at the moment.

Bella smiled at me right then, and it broke my heart a little bit. Because I wanted to see her smile. And it felt really damned selfish to want other things, too.

"Is there another wine shop in that neighborhood?" she asked. "That sounds like a high-margin business. And it doesn't need as much floor space as a grocery store."

"I'll look it up," I said, reaching for my laptop.

On Monday, Alison emailed the rest of the tiny Beaumont Urban Studies team, informing us that it was time to hold a meeting. I let Bella and Dani reply to the email first, and both of them agreed to meet. So I grudgingly agreed, too.

Bella had chosen the location — the creaky little Beaumont library. So at least the commute was short. Bella knocked on my door a few minutes before the meeting. "Your girlfriend's message said that she wanted to outline the tasks at hand and ready herself for the challenge," Bella said. "Does she always sound that constipated?"

"Ex-girlfriend," I corrected. Alison had always been a little formal. I didn't really trust myself to give an opinion right now, because there was probably nothing Alison could say today that *wouldn't* irritate me.

My anger at her was still fresh. Whenever I saw her across the dining hall or the Urban Studies lecture hall, it always took me back to that awful moment when Mr. Rolex appeared. I got all kinds of angry when I thought of that night — and not just at Alison. I was pissed off at myself, too. Because I *knew* things hadn't been quite right with her. There had been so many little signs, and I'd ignored them all.

Next time, I'd be more careful with my trust.

"Earth to Rafe." We were standing in front of the library, but I'd been too deep inside my head to notice. Bella put both hands on my shoulders. "Are you okay? Do you want me to tell her that you were too busy to come to her little planning session?"

"Nah," I grumbled. "Lead on."

Bella grabbed my elbow to tug me inside, but she happened to hit me a little too high up under my arm. And I'm very ticklish. "Shit." I laughed, twisting away from her.

"What the fuck?" She dug her fingers into my inner bicep again. "Who's ticklish *there?*"

"*Dios.*" I grabbed her arm. "You are such a pain in the ass."

"Uh-oh!" Bella sang. "Somebody looks jealous!"

I looked through the window to see Alison staring at us.

"Eh. I doubt it." I let go of Bella, anyway.

Luckily, when we reached the table Alison had saved for our meeting, Dani was just arriving, too. So I didn't have to make small talk. For the next fifteen minutes, I let Bella speak for both of us.

"Jeez, you guys are doing great," Dani said. "That's a lot of progress."

Bella nudged me with her elbow. "I told you we started too early."

"I like to get a jump on things," I mumbled.

"He always does that," Alison said, crossing her arms. "It's a thing with him."

Ack. I did not want to be a topic of discussion. "So what about the, uh, design part?"

Alison and Dani rambled on for a few minutes about their ideas, while I pretended to listen.

"I don't know about that green roof idea," Bella argued. "That sounds expensive."

"It's excellent for the environment," Alison argued.

"As long as we can *pay* for it," Bella said. "Are we done for now?"

I grabbed my book bag in the hopes of making a quick getaway.

"Wait," Alison said. "Rafe, I really need to talk to you for a minute."

Uh-oh. "Is it about the project?"

She shook her head. I opened my mouth to argue, but she held up a hand. "Please, it will just take a second. *Please.*" She beckoned to me, then walked outside, where I assumed she was waiting for me.

"*Dios,*" I muttered.

Bella picked up her backpack. "Do you want me to rescue you in a minute? I could tell her that we're late to a thing."

"A thing?"

"Work with me, here."

"Okay. Yeah. Come and get me for the *thing.* In three minutes." That should be plenty of time. Because what was there to say?

I marched myself outside, stopping in front of Alison.

"How have you been?" she asked.

"Peachy." *Let's get to the point, here.*

"Look, I owe you an apology."

"You think?"

Alison gave me a bit of an eye roll. "Can you just let me do this? I wasn't honest with you."

"I *got* that."

She threw her arms out to the sides. "Just *give* me a second, okay? This isn't easy for me to tell you." The crystalline blue eyes that I'd always loved filled.

That pretty much crushed my asshole 'tude, because I never could stand to see a girl cry. "Okay," I said softly. "I'm listening."

"Rafe, I'm..." She swallowed. "I'm asexual."

I replayed those words in my mind and came up blank. "You're... what?"

"Asexual. I can't... I don't experience sexual desire. Ever. Not for *anyone*."

That was the craziest thing I'd ever heard. And I'd already spent a couple of months choking on the message that she didn't want me like that. Why make a weird excuse? "Then why did you sleep with Mr. Rolex? And don't try to tell me you didn't. *Something* happened with him."

She took a deep breath in through her perfect nose. "I slept with him because I wanted to know if I could do it. It was an *experiment*. If I could live through it with him, then I thought I could handle sex with you."

At that moment, you could have pushed me over with a feather. "*Dios*. I always hoped you could *tolerate* sex with me. Do you even hear yourself?"

Her face got red. "I *know*, okay? It's taken me a bunch of counseling sessions to even admit that it was a stupid idea. But I loved you, and I just wanted what so many other people have. A normal relationship."

Again, the fact that she was getting upset checked my anger. "But I just don't understand. Not at all. Because everybody wants *someone*."

Slowly, she shook her head. "Not necessarily. Not me. I'd been wondering about myself for years, honestly. My boarding school roommates were always talking about how so and so has lickable abs. I've never wanted to *lick* anyone in my life."

I managed to crack a smile, even as I realized that she wasn't joking. "Maybe you like girls?"

She shook her head. "If I did, that would be easier. I'd never even heard the term 'asexual' until a year ago. I started Googling right away, but reading about it only depressed me. Because I suspected that was me. And then we started dating, and I *tried*. I really did."

"So..." I cleared my throat. "It's not just you. This is a... thing."

Alison gave me a tiny eye roll. "Yes, it's a *thing*. There are support groups and the whole nine yards."

It was at that moment when Bella decided to stage her rescue. She came wandering over to me with a comical smile. "I need to steal you." She put her hands on my chest and rubbed my pecs. "There's a half an hour until class, and I'm feeling so *tense*. I was hoping you could help me relax."

I kept a straight face, but just barely. "Just give me a minute, Bells. I need one more minute here."

Bella made a sad, pouty face that was entirely out of character. "I'll be waiting, lover." She sauntered off, hips swaying. I admired the view, because it was important to stay in character.

When I looked at Alison again, her eyes were hard. "Wait. You asked her to *rescue* you from this conversation? Is it really that hard to talk to me?"

That's when I lost it a little. "*Cristo.* Is it really so hard to believe that someone would ever want to have sex with me?" Too bad I didn't keep my voice down. A couple of freshman girls walking past us looked up quickly.

"Of course not," Alison whispered. Her face went soft. "My counselor was right."

"What about?"

"That sex was tied up with most people's self-esteem. And that I almost certainly hurt your feelings because I didn't want you that way. I'm sorry I've been so dense."

"It's..." *Argh.* "Can we just move on?"

"I was hoping that we could be friends."

"Isn't that all we ever were?"

Alison let out a shaky sigh. "I loved you, Rafe, and then I did something really stupid because I couldn't figure out how to make it work. And I'm sorry."

"Okay," I whispered. Was I supposed to tell her now that all was forgiven? I just couldn't make myself say the words. Although I didn't like the idea that my pride had been wounded at least as badly as my feelings. "Thank you for telling me," I added, hoping that it would be enough.

Alison gave me a watery smile. "You'd better go. Your friend is waiting for you. Actually, she's looking like she'd like to kill me. You probably told her I was a monster."

Yeah, I probably did. "See you around, Alison." Trying to be generous, I leaned forward and gave her a peck on the cheek. Then I spun around and caught up with Bella, who was waiting by the door. She did, in fact, look ornery. "Sorry," I said. "I didn't mean for that to take so long."

"Let me guess. She's sorry, and she wants you back."

"Eh," I said. "She's sorry, at least."

"Would you take her back if she asked?"

"No," I said quickly. "We weren't... a good fit." I was still trying to understand what Alison had told me. If she was right about not wanting sex with anyone, that meant most relationships were off the table. She'd told me once that she wanted kids, too. So that wouldn't be easy.

It was pretty damned depressing, really.

"I have an idea," Bella said. "About Beta Rho."

"What?" That got my attention. "What kind of idea?"

"I read in *The Harkness* that they're having a centennial celebration next month. 'One Hundred Years of Beta Rho.'"

"Ugh. Just what we all need — a hundred years of assholes."

"I know. But I figure that a bunch of their alumni will be in town for it. They're having a big tailgate party for the last football game."

"Are they now?" I sure hoped Bella wasn't planning to go. I didn't want her anywhere near a couple hundred drunk frat boys.

"The article said that they bought out a big block of tickets to the game."

"So?"

"So, my wheels are turning."

I opened our entryway door. "Bella, I can't think of a single good thing that could come of you mingling at the Beta Rho centennial."

"I don't want to be *good*, Rafe. I want to be bad. Very bad."

Dios. "I don't even want to know," I said, and we began walking again.

Yes you do, a little voice nagged. *You absolutely want to know.*

TWENTY-THREE

BELLA

It was Saturday, and I'd been to all my classes this week. Maybe it's not much of an achievement, but every time I stepped outside the Beaumont gates, I still felt eyes on me. That freaking picture was still up on *Brodacious*, although Lianne had informed me that a set of photos of the new pledges dressed in drag had replaced me at the top of the page.

So that was something. You had to hand it to an organization which attempted to embarrass its own members almost as badly as the women they were finished with. They were equal-opportunity assholes.

At any rate I wasn't going to flunk out of school. But my social life was *over*. My hockey friends had twenty hours of practice a week and a full game schedule on the weekends. Not that they'd forgotten about me. The week I'd staged my vanishing act, my phone lit up with texts from Pepe, Graham, Rikker and Trevi. They invited me to Capri's. They sent me funny videos.

They tried.

But all I sent back were excuses. And when they didn't give up, I started ignoring them altogether. They were busy, anyway, and I wanted them focused on hockey, like they should be. Last year, the hockey team was my whole world. Lately, my world was confined to entryway B.

And I had a dangerous case of cabin fever.

Grabbing the book that I was supposed to be reading, I stuck my feet in my Chuck T's and headed down two flights of stairs. I knocked on Rafe's common room door.

"Yeah!" The sound of his voice sent a happy little shiver up my back.

I opened the door to find him sprawled out on a generous leather sofa. "Hi," I said, feeling shy all of a sudden.

He sat up. "Hi. You okay?"

"Sure." I came in and shut the door. "Except there's a small spider on the ceiling over my bed, and it's staring at me."

He smiled, and I felt a little flutter down below. Damn that smile. "You want me to kill it?"

"What?" I asked, swaying under the effects of his sexy mouth.

"The spider? Should I kill it?"

Focus, Bella. "No. But could I, uh, read down here for a little while? I just need a change of scenery."

Something warm flickered through those big brown eyes. "Sure. Come on over." He bent his knees to make room for me.

I sat down, noticing that all the furniture was fancy. "Nice place you got here."

"It's Lord Bickley's."

"Ah." The seat was so wide that when I stretched my legs out there was still plenty of room for Rafe's.

He did the same, then picked up his French book again.

I turned my attention to my own reading. But after ten minutes or so, I got in trouble for tickling the arch of Rafe's foot, which lay within arm's reach.

"Not fair," he said, jerking his foot way. "I have enough trouble with irregular French verbs without your help."

"Sorry." Even though his ticklish foot was still *right there*, I didn't want to make a nuisance of myself. Rafe had become my best friend during what was otherwise the worst semester of my life. He was more important to me than I was capable of expressing.

At my end of the sofa, I struggled to read another essay for Women's Studies. College coursework was all about theories, and after four years I was a little sick of them. On the other hand, my real life this year had been about as pleasant as walking repeatedly into various stone walls. So maybe the theories were the way to go.

Rafe's suitemate Mat emerged from his room. "There's a game tomorrow," he said. "I was thinking of giving you the spread plus one..."

"No thanks," Rafe said quickly.

I poked him in the thigh. "You didn't even hear what game he's talking about."

"Doesn't matter," Rafe said from behind his book.

Mat snickered. "Fine. Later, guys," he said, grabbing a knapsack off the floor. "I'm going to lock myself into a study carrel until my physics homework starts to make sense."

Rafe gave his roommate a salute as he left the room. And the two of us on the sofa went back to our reading. At least Rafe did. My book wasn't nearly as interesting as the warm weight of Rafe's leg against mine. Instead of plowing through the next feminist theory, I indulged in a private fantasy. In my dirty little mind, I crawled onto Rafe's body and tossed his book on the floor. Then I put my hand in the center of those fine abs, rubbing him gently, feeling all that muscle beneath my palm.

When he began to squirm, I'd slide that naughty hand down... down...

This lovely picture was interrupted by Rafe's roommate Bickley stomping through the room again, looking for his "trainers." "Ah," he said, grabbing his shoes out of the corner and sitting on the coffee table to put them on. "I think I need to run some sprints. Care to join me?"

"Negative," Rafe said. "Too much homework."

Bickley snorted. "Bella, see what you can do to lighten this one up. He thinks he's here to be a *scholar*."

At the other end of the couch, Rafe made a grumpy noise.

His roommate did not notice, of course. Bickley wasn't the sort of guy who understood how the words falling from his mouth affected other people. "Looks like you two kids have the place to yourself for a bit. Try *not* to behave yourselves." He gave me a salacious wink.

Rafe dropped his book on his chest and looked at me. "Bella, it's impossible to imagine why you gave up men."

"Gave *up* on us?" Bickley grasped his chest in mock horror. "That sounds like a poor plan. Maybe she meant to *climb* up men."

Rafe glared at Bickley. "Oh fuck *off* now."

"Fine, fine. Ta ta for now." When he left, the door closed with a bang.

"I'm sorry he's such an ass," Rafe said. The smile he flashed me was so beautiful I felt another shimmy in my stomach. The boy could melt granite with that smile.

"He didn't mean anything by it. Bickley is a nervous talker."

"What?"

"Some of that verbal diarrhea is because he doesn't know what to say. Listen to your neighborhood psych major."

Rafe made an irritated noise. "Is there a cure? Please say yes."

"Duct tape?" I suggested.

"Great idea."

We went back to our books for a moment, but I was still distracted by the warmth of his body against mine. Tucked into a sofa with Rafe was a really good place to be. It wasn't enough for me, though. There were things besides reading that I'd rather do with him on this fine piece of furniture. I took a second to admire the way his Manchester United T-shirt hugged his chest, and the smooth skin on his hands as he turned the page.

"Rafe," I whispered.

"Hmm?" He did not look up from the page.

"How come we're not friends with benefits?"

Well, *that* got his attention. His eyes flew up to meet mine, and I saw a flicker of something hot pass through them before he schooled his features into a thoughtful frown. "What?"

"You know." I gave his knee a nudge. "Studying is easier after you work off a little tension."

He watched me for a long moment. "I can't tell if you're serious or not. But it doesn't really matter. Friends with benefits is not my style. I don't do casual."

Seriously? "Sure you do. I'm a witness. I can place you at the scene of the crime."

Slowly, he shook his head. "You're forgetting what happened afterward. You told me yourself that I was a jackass."

Fuck me, I did. "That was just because the timing was so bad. We could do better."

He let out a breath. "Nope. I don't think I can."

Holy crap. I was losing my touch. I'd just been *rejected*, which rarely happened. And here's the real kicker — I actually felt bad about it. Really bad. All the way to awful, even.

"Shit," I whispered as an unfamiliar heat rose up in my eyes. I felt tears forming. *Actual tears.* I raised my book in front of my face, creating a rather dubious curtain of shame. If I had any luck at all left in the universe, maybe Rafe wouldn't notice.

"Bella?" he whispered.

Yep. No luck left. Not even a speck.

"*Cristo*, Bella. It's not you."

I would never again believe those words. From anyone. *Thank you, Whittaker. And thank you, medical diagnosis.* I threw the book down, pressing my fingers into the corners of my eyes.

Rafe sighed, throwing his book on the floor, too. Which I'd fantasized about not a half hour ago. But in my fantasy he'd done it so we could have sex, and not because I'd become a weepy *girl*.

"Come here," he said, reaching forward, closing his big hands around my legs just above the knee. With a good tug, I slid across the leather until I was closer to him. Then he took my hands and pulled. "Over here," he coaxed.

Bending my knees, I ended up in his lap. He wrapped both arms around me, and I tucked my chin onto his shoulder, so he wouldn't see me looking teary.

Rafe held me tightly, making it even harder not to cry. Because the feel of those strong arms around me was exquisite. He smelled like clean man and laundry detergent. So I burrowed even further into him, with no plans to ever leave.

Welp. Sorry, Rafe. I'm never coming out of here. I was going to live out my life right here, hiding in Rafe's neck. He would have to have me surgically removed. Not only was I comforted, but I was enjoying the delicious scrape of his Saturday whiskers against my cheek.

"Didn't mean to offend you," he said, running a hand down the back of my head. "It's not that I don't want to."

Ugh. "You don't have to lie to me. I know it's *icky*, all right? I already *know*."

His hand came to a stop on my back. "What's icky?"

"Me," I gasped. "I get it. It's *gross*... that I had..." I couldn't even say it out loud. To Rafe, who already knew! I was never getting my mojo back. Never ever.

"*That's* what you think?" he whispered. "Really?"

I pulled my head back and looked into those chocolate eyes. The intensity I found there made my heart stutter. "Isn't it?"

"No, baby. You could never be gross." He frowned. "You really don't believe me, do you?"

Slowly, I shook my head.

He sighed, his shoulders sagging. Then he muttered, "*Dios*, forgive me for what I am about to do."

I didn't see it coming until Rafe cupped his hand under my jaw. He brushed my cheekbone with his thumb, and I swear to God I developed an extra set of nerve endings right then and there. He leaned in and brushed his mouth over the corner of mine, sweeping up my cheek and over my ear.

"You," he whispered, pausing to touch his tongue to my earlobe, "will *always* be the sexiest girl I have ever known."

It was the classiest, swooniest thing anyone had ever said to me. And my poor, long-ignored body lit up like a sparkler on the Fourth of July. While I quivered, Rafe left gentle kisses up the side of my neck. I had to tip my head back to give him better access, and I found myself squeezing my legs together against the electric current suddenly sizzling through my fun zone.

Later I would realize he almost certainly meant to stop there. The hot sigh that Rafe gave off next sounded like a capitulation. "*Belleza*," he growled. "Give me that mouth."

I wasted no time. Leaning in, I pushed my aching breasts against his chest and I dipped my head for the hot kiss that was waiting for me. Rafe groaned at the contact. Two hands slid down, grasping my hips, straightening my body out until I was spread out like a blanket on his beautiful body. Arching his neck, he nibbled my lips, as if reacquainting himself with the shape of my mouth.

Every touch seemed to shoot waves of heat through my entire being. I'd been *starving* for this. Then he parted his lips. A bossy tongue invaded my mouth. And... *holy fuck*. I practically burst into flames. Even as our tongues met and tangled, I felt myself get wet for him. That had to be a personal record. Either I got this boy's clothes off immediately, or we were going to need one of the fire extinguishers hanging out in the stairwell.

It didn't matter that I was on top of him. Each kiss I received was like a command. There was something *fierce* about the way Rafe kissed. About the way he did *everything*. He reminded me of the lion at the Bronx Zoo — often quiet and still. But when he roared, the effect was earthshaking.

And I wanted to be shaken.

I nuzzled his neck, stretching the collar of his T-shirt to reveal more skin, kissing and sucking every inch I uncovered. He made a desperate noise, and planted his hands on my ass, holding me tightly.

Yes! Yesyesyesyes. There was a very hard dick pressing against me, and I shifted against it. The closer we got, the happier I felt.

But there were too many clothes in the way. I reared up to kiss him again, and our tongues tangled. "Rafe," I moaned into his mouth.

"Mmm," he answered, giving my ass such a dirty, sexy squeeze that I thought I might lose my mind.

I flopped to the side so I could touch him. Sliding a hand down his body, I let my fingers wander over his waistband and onto the hard bulge at his crotch. "I want to play with the nicest cock in the neighborhood." I flipped the button on his jeans.

That's when everything stopped.

First, his hand reached down to catch mine, pushing me off his fly. Then, he turned his face away, taking a big breath of air.

Oh no, my heart murmured. I knew immediately that I had wrecked everything. It's just that my lust-muddled brain was too scrambled to process the reason.

"Bella," he whispered. "I'm sorry. I can't... we can't go through with this."

"What?" I became fixated on the fact that he wasn't looking me in the eye. Whatever the problem was, it was so bad he couldn't even face me.

"I want to," he said quickly. "But it can't be like this."

I began to panic. "God, why not?"

He turned his chin to finally look at me, and it was almost worse. Because I saw real regret there. "Like I said. I don't do casual."

"What does that even mean?" There wasn't enough oxygen here on the sofa. Nothing made any sense.

"It means..." He winced. "I don't do casual, because I don't want to feel like the most convenient dick in the neighborhood."

Oh, crap. Me and my dirty mouth. What the hell was wrong with me? The back of my throat began to sting. Again! I was not going to cry, though. This was already embarrassing enough. After extracting myself from Rafe, I slid from the couch and onto the floor where I began fumbling for my book.

"Bella," he said softly. "Nobody tempts me like you do. We'd be great. *Again*. I know we would. But then I'll feel shitty after-wards, just like last time. And I like you too much for that."

"You *like me* too much to have sex with me," I said, chasing my book under the sofa. I was suddenly furious with myself. Or him. One or the other. "That's so *logical*."

He sighed. "Don't be dense. I care about you. A lot, okay? You are someone I could *love*."

"Right. I hear that a lot right after a guy rejects me." My face was on fire now. My humiliation shone brightly, and I could not wait to get out of his room. Abandoning my book under the stupid couch, I stood and went for the door.

"Bella! Don't do a runner," Rafe argued. "That isn't like you."

"Thought you were trying to teach me to run," I muttered. He was right. I was more of a stay-and-fight kind of girl. But I needed a time-out before I dug the hole any deeper. Without a glance at him, I flung open his door and jogged down the stairs.

It felt good to be moving. So I kept doing it. I jogged across the courtyard. But I had to stop at the gate because Bickley was stretching in front of it. "Excuse me," I prompted.

"Bella!" he yodeled. "When are you going to shag my room-mate, already? The tension is killing me."

Lovely. I knew I was right about Bickley being a nervous talker, but he was also annoying as fuck. "Sorry to dash your hopes. But the shagging only happened that once."

Bickley swung around, his eyebrows flying up into his unruly hair. "What? You *do* know what that word means?"

I snorted. "Oh, honey. That word and I are very well acquainted. Now *move*, would you?"

He didn't. He stared at me instead. "So *you're* the one? From that night in September? You popped Rafe's cherry?"

It was one of those moments in life that might have been punctuated by the sound of screeching brakes. I inwardly yelped, *SAY WHAT?*

Bickley and I stared at each other while I tried to decide if he was serious. "I..." *Really?* "He didn't say."

The Brit misinterpreted me. "No, he would never wag his chin to me. Rafe is a vault. But the mystery has been killing me. I've been wondering who it was for ages!" He cackled. "Can't believe I missed that. It's so obvious now."

I gave Bickley an impatient nudge, slipping past him, hiding my face. Because I did not trust myself to look calm. "Gotta go," I mumbled, opening the gate at last.

"Nicely done, by the way," Bickley called after me.

He was lucky I wasn't carrying any sharp objects.

On the street outside Beaumont House, I began jogging toward the graveyard. I barely registered this plan, however, since my brain was busy reeling through every encounter I'd ever had with Rafe.

Especially the first one.

That night in September, he had been sitting in the stairwell looking forlorn. He'd caught his girlfriend cheating...

He'd had condoms in his bag.

I jogged faster, growing more horrified by the second. Rafe had been planning to give it up that night to his long-term girl-friend! He'd been *saving* it for her. But then she cheated, making a fool of him at the same time.

A couple of hours later, I'd stripped him naked and sat on his cock.

Jesus Christ. No wonder he'd been weird afterward. "Casual sex isn't my thing," he'd said. And now he'd said it again, only ten minutes ago.

The dude wasn't lying. He'd done it *once*.

The condom broke, too.

I let out a groan of pure horror, because I'd been so callous with him. I hadn't meant to, of course. But he would have processed our night together a lot differently than I had.

What the hell kind of shitty psych major was I? Perspective was *everything*. And I hadn't allowed for the possibility that his perspective was different than mine.

Oh. My. God. What had I done?

I kept running. It wasn't as easy in jeans and Chuck Ts, but I soon found myself in the graveyard in front of Rafe's favorite headstone. If you needed a little perspective in your life, a cemetery was as good a place as any to find it. I hadn't done or said anything right since September. But at least I was still breathing.

Breathing hard, actually. I was not an impressive runner. I stood there a while, listening to the thump of my own heartbeat, rereading the headstone of a teenager who'd been flattened by a tree.

Killed by a log he made.

I stood there a long time, wondering which would be the best way to apologize.

Maybe it had been a long, crappy year so far. But the time had come to get over myself.

Chapter Twenty-Four

TWENTY-FOUR

RAFE

That night, I worked the dinner shift. Thankfully, I was on prep duty, dicing onions and garlic in a corner of the kitchen where I didn't have to talk to anyone. Because I was in no mood.

Somehow I'd managed to make Bella *cry* when that was just about the last thing I wanted to do. Ever.

Even more boggling, I'd turned down sex with the one person who made me feel hot just by smiling at me. I'd actually said no.

What I'd done seemed ridiculous. But I'd had a very good reason — what would have been awesome today would have made me feel like dirt tomorrow.

Bella was a *friend*. (I hoped she still was, anyway.) And I had it pretty bad for her. If I declared us friends with bennies, or fuck buddies, or whatever, that would be dishonest. There was just no way I could have sex with Bella, and then walk away like it didn't matter.

It *would* matter. A great deal.

My brain chased this impasse around and around for several hours. Bella wasn't just a girl I wanted. She was *the* girl I wanted.

There was only one solution, but I didn't like my chances. She and I could have lots of sex if she'd be with me for real.

Be my girlfriend.

I leaned over the garlic again, shaking my head. A girl like Bella could have *anyone*. Even if she did decide to break her rule against relationships, I was two years younger. I played the wrong sport. I was too conservative, apparently.

And my hands smelled of onions and garlic after every shift.

Also, I wore a paper hat.

Dios. The odds were terrible. They were worse than winning money off Mat on the Patriots game.

I groaned over the cutting board. If I was honest with myself, a relationship with Bella was exactly what I wanted. I hadn't tried to go there, because she'd sworn off men.

Or so I'd thought.

When she'd propositioned me, I'd been caught off guard. *Way* off guard. I'd ended up giving her a speech about how I'd only have sex in a relationship. (As if I knew a *thing* about that.) The problem was I'd stopped short of telling her I wanted a relationship with *her*. I'd hinted at it. Sort of. But I hadn't manned up and said so.

Which meant I'd rejected her twice inside of half an hour. Rejected the very person I wanted in my life. And in my bed.

I'd pushed her away, when I really wanted to do the opposite.

Classy, Rafe.

After work, I went back to our suite. For a whole blissful minute I believed I was home alone. But when I walked into our bedroom, I found Bickley lying on his bed. He rolled onto an elbow and shot me a shit-eating grin.

"What?"

He chuckled. "Nothing."

Today that was all it took to get me steaming mad. "If you have something to say, just say it."

"Why? And ruin my fun?"

I was just *done* with him. "I'm not in the mood for your superior bullshit, *Dick*ley."

If I wasn't mistaken, my roommate paled. "*What* did you just call me?"

The stupid nickname had just come rolling off my tongue. It wasn't even clever. A sixth-grader could probably do better. "I just need you to mind your own business for once in your sorry life, okay?"

He lifted his aristocratic nose in the air, then turned away from me.

Great. Now my roommate and I weren't speaking, either. The day wasn't over yet, though. I wondered who else I might piss off before I went to bed.

A quick inspection of my cell phone revealed five missed calls from Bella, and a voice message. I touched *play*.

"Rafe," she'd said in her message. "I need to talk to you. And I want to apologize. I didn't... I wasn't looking at things the same way you were. So..." I'd never heard Bella at a loss for words. "Please can I apologize? Would you stop over? Pretty please?"

I wanted to. But I hadn't yet figured out what I would say to her. Asking a girl out was like a tough soccer practice. You had to warm up before you ran onto the field.

In the common room, I threw myself down on the sofa and tried to think what to say.

TWENTY-FIVE

BELLA

I was never meant to lead a solitary life. That much was obvious.

But there I was, bumping around my room *again*. After my impulsive run, I'd bought some coffee and headed back to my room, where I proceeded to brood over everything I'd done wrong.

Or I tried to. Brooding didn't come naturally to me, and I'd swear it made my dorm room feel even smaller.

Just when I was feeling truly desperate, someone knocked on the door.

Rafe.

I sat up fast, running my fingers through my hair. Vanity didn't come naturally to me, either, but Rafe looked delicious 24/7, and I'd humiliated myself in front of him twice already today. Also, the boy should be made to remember what he was missing.

"Just a sec!" I called out.

Looking down, I took a quick inventory. The jeans were fine, of course. But I was wearing a baggy Bruins shirt, so I whipped that over my head and tossed it on the desk chair. A pink oxford shirt I'd abandoned at some point hung on my closet door's hook.

I grabbed it, shoving my arms into the sleeves, and buttoning it up *most* of the way.

Perfect.

The knock came again, and my heart did an unfamiliar shimmy. I braced myself and went to the door.

It opened to reveal Graham, of all people.

"Oh," I said, probably failing to hide my disappointment. "Hi."

He cocked his head to the side and began to smile. I saw his gaze come to a halt on my unusually generous cleavage. "Maybe I'm not who you were expecting?"

"I wasn't expecting anyone," I argued, holding the door open for him. And that was strictly true. I hadn't heard from Rafe since leaving him a voicemail, which he seemed to have ignored.

"Good. Because I've come to escort you to Capri's."

My stomach twisted at the idea of stepping into my favorite pizza and beer joint in the world. I practically used to *live* at Capri's. That's where the hockey team went about four nights a week to blow off steam.

But I did not. Not anymore.

"I can't make it tonight," I lied. "Sorry."

Graham's face fell. "Bella, please? Just because you don't work for the team anymore doesn't mean they don't miss you. And I miss you. If I can walk in there, so can you."

I sat down on the bed to give myself a little distance from Graham's blue-eyed stare. It *was* pretty impressive that Graham often went out drinking with the hockey team. For months he and Rikker had kept their relationship a secret, and coming out of the closet had been really hard on him. He'd quit the team after his concussion, but he hadn't quit his circle of friends. There were some curious stares last spring as everyone figured out how things were between Graham and their star right wing. But Graham pushed through all that, and kept most of his friendships on the team.

He was obviously a whole lot braver than I was.

Without another word, he came over and sat down beside me, putting an arm around my back.

Damn him. I wanted to lean against his shoulder and tell him everything in my heart, the way I used to. I still missed Graham. It wasn't about lust anymore. I'd had enough time to realize that the sex part of our relationship hadn't been the best part. But I still felt an ache when he was nearby. I missed his company, and I missed the idea that we were two peas in a pod. Both slightly jaded, but probably redeemable.

Fast forward one year, and Graham was having the happiest year of his life. Me? Total disaster.

"Come on, Bells." He gave me a little squeeze. "You're hiding in your room, because you're embarrassed about something that you didn't even do wrong."

I groaned. "You're right. It wasn't *something* I did wrong. It was *someone*." And then that someone let the whole world know just how stupid I really was. "I'm not ready."

"You look ready to me," he quipped. "Come out with me."

For the hundredth time today, my throat was hot. There had been so many nights last winter when all I wanted was for Graham to show up at my door and say, "You're important to me." Now he'd done that. But not in the way that I'd once hoped for.

"You know," I said, clearing my throat. "You used to hide too, okay? So it's not like you can really give me a hard time about this."

I expected him to get irritated that I'd poke his old wound. But he didn't. Instead, I received an even tighter hug. "Aw, Bella. I *know* that. And it sucked. I wasted so much time worrying about what other people thought. *Years*, okay? But you're smarter than that."

"I used to be," I mumbled.

Graham cleared his throat. "Well, I had Rikker to show me how it's done. Who's going to do that for you?"

Well, ouch. Because I had no clue. "I need a little more time, Graham. Right now, I'm still everyone's gossip nugget."

"You aren't," he argued. "And the new manager is a pain in the ass. I heard he ordered shin guard tape instead of hockey tape."

"What?" I yelped. "Who could mix that up?"

Graham chuckled. "See? The team misses you. Come and show your face."

"Another time," I said firmly. I stood, putting myself out of the orbit of Graham's hugs. Because those were potent.

Sensing defeat, Graham stood too. "All right. If you change your mind, you know where to find me. And aren't you going to eat dinner?"

"Of course I am. I was waiting for my neighbor," I lied, pointing in the direction of Lianne's room.

"Promise?" Graham's icy blue eyes regarded me seriously.

I held up a hand, like an oath-taker on the witness stand. "Promise."

He stepped in to kiss me on the cheek. Then he headed for the door. "Good night, Bells."

"G'night Graham." I used to say that when we were both naked in his bed.

Then he was gone, and I was — wait for it — alone in my room again. And since he'd mentioned dinner, now I *was* hungry. I went into the bathroom and tapped on Lianne's door.

"Yeah?"

I opened it, finding Lianne seated in front of her massive computer cockpit. "Feel like ordering a pizza?"

She blinked at me for a moment, probably because it was not a usual thing for me to make a friendly overture. "Does it have to be pizza?" she asked finally. "That's too carby for me."

I sat down on her bed. "What, then? Salads?"

She swiveled around to face me. "Thai? The Orchid Garden has some things I can eat."

"Okay. Let me get my wallet." I stood up.

She waved me off. "You get the next one. I already have my credit card in their system."

I sat down again. "You do?"

"Yup." She turned to her keyboard, and I saw her pull up the restaurant's website. "It's funny. My manager made me live at Beaumont instead of on Fresh Court where I might actually meet First Years. He said it was a security risk. But now every deliveryman in the greater Harkness area knows exactly where I live."

I laughed, even though that was too sad to be funny. "You don't like the dining hall food?"

Lianne only shrugged, which made me wonder whether she ever went in there. She was waiting for my order.

"I'll have the chicken pad Thai, extra peanuts."

Lianne typed furiously for a moment, fingers flying over the keyboard. "All set. They say it will be twenty-five minutes. But they're usually slower than they say." She turned around to face me.

"So," I said. I wasn't used to making conversation with Lianne. "Did I interrupt anything important? Now that I know you're a computer genius, I just assume you're over here hacking into the Federal Reserve Bank or something."

"Right," Lianne scoffed, kicking her tiny feet up onto the bed beside me. "I only break into government networks on the weekend. Just now I was ordering my favorite lip gloss." She grabbed something off the desk and thrust it out for my inspection. "Have you tried this? It's tinted in a warm berry color, and I love the packaging."

"Can't say that I have. Sorry." Over the years, I'd heard people whisper about the fact that I never had female friends. People have told me to my face that I can't stand competition from other girls. Not true. The real reason I lacked female friends was that I don't speak lip gloss.

"What's up with you, anyway?" she asked. "You look kind of... strung out."

"Well..." Was I going to share with Lianne? What a weird idea. "It hasn't been the best day. I sort of threw myself at Rafe, and he turned me down."

Her famously expressive eyes widened. "Really? Are you sure?"

"Of *course* I'm sure. I'm not a subtle girl. No eyelashes were batted. I stuck my tongue down his throat. He definitely noticed."

She tapped the fingers of each hand together thoughtfully. "Sorry, but that does not compute. I was starting to think that the two of you were just inevitable."

That made me grin. "If anyone can ruin a sure thing, it's me."

She frowned. "Speaking of ruining things, I looked at *Brodacious* again today. They haven't changed the password. If you want me to take down the photo, it's still easy to do that."

"That's cool. But I had a different idea, actually." Doing laps in my room this morning, I'd had a bit of a brainstorm. Lianne was probably the wrong person to share it with. Then again, who else would want to hear about this plan? Not Rafe, because apparently we weren't speaking. Not Graham, because he'd tell me it was too crazy. And there were several reasons why I couldn't ask my hockey friends for help.

I clapped my hands. "Okay. Let me bounce something off you. It's really a non-technical solution. But, say, ten days from now I might have a *new* picture to post up there. Do you think you could make that happen?"

Lianne frowned. "Posting a picture on *Brodacious* is a snap. But they could just delete it. Even if I changed the password to Bite-My-Feminist-Ass, they could just call up their web host and take the whole site down. Within minutes, probably."

"I've thought of that," I admitted. "But if I play my cards right, the whole school will have the same picture on their phones, even if it doesn't stay up on the website."

She blinked at me. "What exactly is this low-tech idea of yours?"

"I'm going to try to humiliate Beta Rho using nothing but a couple of reams of colored paper. It will either be the best use of ten dollars ever or a complete failure."

Lianne sat back in her chair. "I'm listening."

I continued to outline my big idea, while Lianne's eyes got

bigger and bigger. When I stopped speaking, she just stared at me silently.

"Well?" I finally prompted her. "What do you think?" I braced myself to hear that she thought I was insane. And I probably was.

"That is GENIUS!" she shrieked. "Where do we start?"

～

After our Thai food showed up, we continued to scheme.

"You know," Lianne said, pausing to chew a bite of chicken, "your odds of success are greater if we can find you a little more manpower."

"That is true." I offered her the pad Thai. "Want some noodles?"

She shook her head. "I can't eat carbs. If I gain an ounce, my manager nags me."

I lowered the carton to my lap. "Seriously? Can't you just tell him to fuck off?"

"It's complicated." She got up to throw her empty carton in the trash. "Now, where are we going to find some extra sets of hands? I'm sure there are a lot more girls who want to get even with Beta Rho."

"Sure..." This was something I'd thought about, too. "But if they all show up at the football game together, that will look really suspicious. Even drunk frat boys can recognize their former hook-ups. And if I bring in outsiders, that would be a big red flag."

Lianne tapped a pencil on her knee. "Who would a bunch of drunk frat boys listen to?"

I laughed, because there was one obvious answer. "The Rock-ettes or the Laker Girls. The Swedish Bikini Team?"

Across from me, Lianne gasped. "That's it!" She spun her chair to face her computers, grabbed the keyboard and commenced typing.

"What are you doing?"

"I know a casting agent in New York. We need *models*. Not the famous, catwalk kind. But the ones they call when there's an automotive convention. The girls who get paid thirty bucks an hour to drape themselves over next year's Porsche Carrera."

"That's going to blow my ten-dollar budget," I pointed out.

"Honey, I'm from Hollywood," she said, grabbing her phone. "Blowing the budget is what we do."

Huh. "How much do you think this will cost?"

Lianne spoke into her phone, leaving a message. "Harvey, it's Lianne. I have a little job that needs doing. Let's say six or eight models, for three hours next Saturday. Call me." She hung up. "I don't mind paying for it."

"No, I can," I said quickly. Money was one problem I did not have.

Lianne waved a hand as if this detail was beneath our concern. "Now we need to generate a diagram of the bleachers. Tomorrow we can go over to the stadium and count the number of rows. But estimating the density is still kind of tricky. Even with a spreadsheet."

Jesus Christ. I'd underestimated this girl *again*. "I'll ask my friend Graham for a photograph of the stands during a game. The newspaper must have that in a file somewhere. We can count the heads in the picture."

"That's a great idea."

This brainstorm was interrupted by the sound of a distant knock on my door.

Lianne and I both silenced our planning immediately. "To be continued?" I whispered.

Is that Rafe? she mouthed.

"Probably."

"I'm going to need you to report back," she whispered.

Saluting her, I slipped into my room, closing the bathroom door. The knock came again. "Bella?" Rafe called. "I have your book."

I opened the door. "Did you think I wasn't going to answer unless I got *Essays on the Feminist Perspective* back?"

He came into the room warily, handing me the book. For several seconds we just stared at each other. We both decided to speak at once.

"I'm sorry," we said in unison.

"Aw," Lianne said from behind the door.

"I have to talk to you," Rafe said. He slipped past me and went to sit on the bed. "Sit down," he said, patting the spot next to him. His dark eyes flicked up, locking on mine. Then they darted away again.

"Can I go first?" I asked.

He shook his head and smiled. "Nope. There's something I need to say."

"But my thing came first," I argued.

"It doesn't matter, Bella! I'm trying to..."

I cut him off, by virtue of hollering. "*I'm* trying to apologize for stealing your virginity!"

There was a sharp intake of breath from the other side of the bathroom door.

"Lianne!" I hollered. "Take your skinny butt over to that fancy stereo and find yourself some tunes."

There was a grumble and the sound of feet moving away from the door.

Rafe's shoulders sagged. "Freaking Bickley."

"I know," I sympathized. "But I had no idea—"

He held a hand up to silence me. "Just *stop*, okay? I don't want to talk about this."

"But we have to, because—"

"*No,*" he said forcefully. "We really don't. That's ridiculous."

"No it *isn't,*" I said, dropping my voice. "I was so hard on you..."

He held up that hand again.

"Fine!" I yelped. "But I feel like an ass. You've been really good to me. Always really good to me. Since that first day you carried a box up to my room, okay? I just wanted to say thank you. I haven't been... my best self this year."

Those brown eyes softened. "You had reasons."

I let out a breath. "I had a few here and there. But you're just about the only *good* thing that's happened to me this year. And I want you to know I appreciate it."

That may have caught him off guard. I saw him swallow roughly. "Thank you."

"That night in September..."

He made an impatient noise. "Don't go there."

"Hey! I'm not going to embarrass you. I promise. But you... I couldn't *tell*, Rafe. I would have never guessed."

He rolled his eyes at me. "Uh... thanks?"

"You've been really patient with me when I had a shitty time, and I wasn't so patient with you. I wish I had been."

"It's *okay*, Bella. I'm done with this topic."

Ugh. Well, I tried. "Okay then. What was your thing?"

"My thing," he repeated.

"Yeah. I cede the floor to the gentleman from Washington Heights." I sat beside him.

Rafe put a hand on the small of my back, and the heat seeping through my T-shirt felt divine. "Okay," he said, rubbing small circles on my back. "When I said today that I don't do casual, I wasn't kidding."

"Yep. I believe you now."

He groaned. "Right. So. What I didn't say, but wanted to, is that I think we should be together. For real." He looked me right in the eye with a gaze so warm that I got a little lump in my throat.

"For real," I echoed stupidly. "You mean...?" I couldn't finish the sentence, because I was afraid of what he meant. Rafe wanted to be my... boyfriend? I'd never had one of those.

He curled his arm around my back to give me a squeeze, and dropped mouth to my ear. "You make me crazy in a good way, Bella. We'd be great together."

They were lovely words, but I was already panicking. The fact that Rafe wanted me to be his girlfriend was tricky to process. No sane man would want a relationship with me. I choked on my reply, just wondering what to say.

"*Belleza*, you don't look as excited about this idea as I am."

"But..." I was still at a loss. "Why does it have to be some kind of pact? We're already friends. Who have a hell of a lot of chemistry. I don't do relationships."

"Why?" he challenged.

"Because that's when it all goes to hell! Everybody gets big expectations the the other person can't live up to. Then they get sick of each other and break up."

He tipped his handsome face toward the ceiling. "That's obscenely pessimistic, even for you. Some of your friends are very happy together. You told me so yourself."

"For now," I pointed out. "And maybe you haven't done the math yet, but in May I'm graduating. Who knows where I'd be next year? Probably at a graduate school somewhere."

The dusty stack of graduate school brochures laughed at me from the back corner of my desk.

Rafe eased away from my body and leaned forward, chin in hand. "You have a long list of objections. I could keep arguing with you. Except I don't think you want me to."

"We don't have to argue at all. That's my point. We could just have sex and skip all the philosophizing. My way is easier."

"No," he said quietly. "It's not. Because suppose you and I fool around right now..."

"Let's call it what it is," I suggested. "I could have you naked about sixty seconds from now. At which point we would have hot, sweaty sex." How could he not think that was a good idea? I was feeling hot just saying the words.

"Fine," he said. "Hot, mind-bending sex. I have a very active imagination, Bella. It would take us a week just to get through my most recent ideas." He glanced up at me then with heat in his eyes, and my fun zone gave a shimmy. "But next week, if I pass you on the stairs with one of your hockey player friends, that will kill me."

"You'd be jealous?"

His dark eyes bored into mine. "*Ridiculously* jealous."

"That's so... possessive."

He threw his hands in the air. "Call it whatever you want, I guess. But I care about you. A lot. If we have sex, it's not just... exercise. If that's what possessive means, I guess I'm it." He stood.

"Hang on." Rafe was half-way to the door, so I hurried to finish my thought. "So let's say we *don't* have sex right now. And two weeks from now I do pass you on the stairs and I'm with a guy. You're saying it's *better* that way?"

He turned around, wearing a look on his face like I'd just kicked his puppy. "That will suck, too. But it will suck just a little bit less."

Seriously? "Not from my perspective. Because we would have missed out on the mind-bending sex part. You're just not comfortable with my sex life. You're *shaming* me."

"*No!*" he protested immediately. The anger in his eyes startled me. "I think you're *amazing*, and I've said so every chance I get. Don't put words in my mouth. I *never* said your way was wrong. It's just wrong for *me*." Then, as I watched, all the fight went out of him. His shoulders dropped, and he leaned his head against the door. "Let's, uh, take the night off from Urban Studies," he said.

My heart lurched. When Rafe put his hand on the doorknob, I had an irrational urge to stop him. "Rafe?"

He turned back, his expression guarded. "Yeah?"

"Maybe you didn't mean it to happen, but I'm a lucky girl to have been your first."

For a split second, his eyes closed with something like grief. But when they flew open again, he was all business. "I'll see you tomorrow."

"Okay."

A moment later I was alone. *Again!* I threw myself down on the bed, trying to figure out what had just happened. Rafe wanted a relationship? I tried to picture it, but that was hard for me because I'd never had a boyfriend. There'd been Fucker Tanning, whom I'd thought of as my boyfriend. But that was just a myth he'd built for his stupid teenage fling. Then there was Graham, whom I hadn't been dating, but in my heart I'd felt there was a future there.

Yeah. A perfect record for disaster.

Even if I told Rafe yes, it would be a temporary arrangement. In May we'd both be sad. And for what?

RAFE! my traitorous body screamed. Whenever he got near me, I felt him like a gravitational pull. Even in my lowest moments, I'd leaned into Rafe. That day in the deli — when he'd moved to block me from the view of those frat boys in the corner — the solid wall of his chest was something that I wanted to lay my head upon. And watching him teach me to merengue would make any girl dampen her panties.

He was the whole package. Sexy. Fun. Sexy. Kind. Loving. Sexy.

Did I mention sexy?

I groaned aloud. If he weren't hung up about dating, we could be undressing each other right now. And so much more. The brief but combustible makeout session we'd had on his sofa only proved that our chemistry was a real. I definitely wanted more of that.

But Rafe wanted a *commitment*, followed by a break up at graduation.

And he thought I was the impulsive one?

I flopped over to bury my face in the pillow. If you wanted to be really philosophical about it, *life* was a temporary arrangement. So why get hung-up on relationships at all?

An angry knock sounded on the bathroom door.

"What?"

Lianne walked in. "Did I just hear Rafe leave?"

"Yep."

"God, why?"

"He wants us to be a *couple*."

Lianne clapped her hands. "Really? He's *delicious*."

"He is," I agreed. "But I don't think I can date him. I don't do relationships. And I'm not sure I want to break my rule."

Her forehead furrowed. "What does your heart say?"

"My heart is a traitorous bitch and a horrible judge of character."

Lianne closed her eyes, then knocked her forehead three times into the bathroom door. "I swear to God, Bella."

"What?"

She pinned me with a stare. "Here's what we know about Rafe." She ticked off the points on her tiny fingers. "He's hot, he's polite, he carried you up a flight of stairs, then stood guard over you like a video game dragon until you were back on your feet. He looks at you like you're his own personal angel, and he does all of this without ever taking a *shred of credit*. If you weren't attracted to him, that would be fine. But you are! So your heart had better get with the program."

For a second I just blinked at her. It was easily the longest speech I'd ever heard Lianne make. "You make a few good points," I said eventually.

She had the strangest look in her eye. It was a little wild and a little fierce. "Good guys like that are as rare as vampires on a sunny day, Bella. I'm not kidding."

"I know," I said quietly. It was true. And I *was* attracted to Rafe. So much. But it was hard for me to go there. The second I decided I loved someone, they always let me down.

She came all the way into the room and sat on the bed. "You sound *afraid* to be with him. And that's not like you."

"Yeah? If you're so brave, what are you doing up here in Lonelyville with me?"

Lianne gave me the side eye. "I didn't say *I* was brave. I'm a total chicken. But you're with guys all the time..."

I snorted. Lianne still thought I was the biggest slut in the world.

She held up a hand. "Okay, that came out wrong. I just mean that you're not intimidated. You know what to say to a guy. And Rafe's the best one! So how is that tricky?"

"Because…" Lianne was not going to understand. "In order to be with him, it's like I have to *reform*. I have to be the girl that everyone always told me to be."

"Do you think Rafe is trying to reform you?" Lianne asked.

"No," I said immediately. In my gut I knew it was true. He wanted what he wanted, and he wasn't afraid to say so. "But the rest of the world would like to."

Her young brow furrowed. "I get that. But it just comes down to the question of who matters more? If you want to be with Rafe, nobody else's opinion should count."

"Lianne, if this acting thing doesn't work out, you should consider litigation."

We sat there quietly together for a moment. "We're still going to prank the football game, right?" Lianne asked eventually.

"Absofuckinglutely."

TWENTY-SIX

BELLA

For several nights in a row, Lianne and I plotted like Churchill and FDR. Focusing on my little revenge plot was just what I needed. Even though our Urban Studies project was due soon, Rafe and I were avoiding each other. And I was still ducking the rest of the world. But Lianne enjoyed planning with me, and I sure did appreciate it.

We'd just finished our dinner — sushi this time — when Lianne's phone rang. "I gotta take this before we talk about transportation," she said. Startling me, she answered the phone, "God! What do you want?" She listened for a moment, her eyes darting around like an angry pinball. "Yeah, I haven't decided where I'm going for Thanksgiving. Bermuda sounds nice, but I might fly out to Palm Springs to be with Mom. Or I might go home with a friend." She rolled her eyes. "It's a *he*. And he lives in Massachusetts."

I was eavesdropping like mad, of course. Lianne never said much about her life. And come to think of it, I'd never heard her phone ring before.

"Bob, I haven't been able to make up my mind. Cross me off

your guest list, if you need clarity. I'll go elsewhere." She smiled to herself, as if she'd scored a point in some game that only she knew how to play. "Don't nag me okay? It's so unattractive. Later." She disconnected the call.

Damn. And here I'd begun the year thinking Lianne was meek.

"What?" she asked, and I realized I was staring.

"Who just got a beat-down?" I asked.

She wrinkled her world-famous nose. "My manager is a pain in the ass. And I talk tough, but somehow I always end up doing whatever he wants."

"Do you not have plans for Thanksgiving?"

She waved a dismissive hand. "I'll probably go to Palm Springs, where my bitch of a mother lives. But I can't tell *him* in advance because then he'll show up there. And he'll drum up some parties or appearances or some other crap that I don't want to do. So I need to keep him guessing."

Ouch. "I'd vote for going home with the guy from Massachusetts. Sounds like fun."

Lianne picked up her clipboard again. "Bella, if he were real, he'd be at the top of the list."

"Oh." *Oops.* "You were very convincing."

She sighed. "That's why they pay me the big bucks. Now, back to our plan. The models can take the train up from the city, and we'll pick them up in the rental van."

I sat down next to her and looked over her shoulder at the notes. "Don't forget that we're going to need an excellent parking spot — between the tailgate tent and the stadium, with quick access to the road," I argued. "The van has to be in position well before the train comes."

"Good point." She scribbled a note on her clipboard.

"The girls will have to take taxis to campus. It's better if they don't arrive until the game is underway. I want them to attract attention, but not until go time."

"Gotcha."

"Hi," said a voice behind me.

Whipping my head around, I found Rafe leaning against the frame of the bathroom door. "Where did you come from?"

He raised his eyebrows. "We still need to finish our project. You want me to go back downstairs?"

A somewhat awkward silence followed, during which Lianne looked from me to Rafe and back again.

"No," I said slowly. "It's just that we were plotting something, and you startled me."

"Plotting what?" he asked, crossing his arms in front of his beautiful chest. I got a little lost for a second staring at the way his T-shirt stretched across his lickable abs. And by the fact that I knew if I stood up and went to him, he'd wrap those long arms around me.

I checked that urge, though. Because that way lay the abyss.

"What are you plotting?" he asked again.

Lianne beat me to it. "The best thing *ever!* I can't wait to see the looks on their faces."

Rafe lifted an eyebrow at me.

"Maybe we should talk," I said.

We went into my room for a little privacy. Rafe listened to my plan with a serious expression in his dark brown eyes. "What if you get into trouble for this?" was his first question.

There was a very real chance that I'd end up in a dean's office trying to explain myself. "I've thought of that. And I think I'd just come clean. I'd show them the photo on *Brodacious*. And..." This was not going to make Rafe happy. "I'd tell them that I was roofied that night at the Beta Rho house."

Rafe stood up so fast that I jumped. He went over to the window. As I watched, he took a long, slow breath and then let it out. When he spoke again, his voice was tight. "Did I just hear that correctly? They *drugged* you?"

"I think so," I whispered.

"*Jesucristo.* How did I miss that?"

"I think you were busy carrying me up the stairs. And I purposefully didn't say anything, because I didn't want you to go to the cops."

"But *why*, Bella? That fucker should be in *jail*."

"I was *mortified*, Rafe. I was *ashamed*, okay? I finally understand why girls who are sexually assaulted don't report it."

His fists clenched on the window frame. "Were *you* assaulted?"

"No sir," I shook my head. "But I'm still ashamed."

He dropped his head, blowing out another gust of air. "Please report him. I'm begging you."

"First I want to do this thing at the football game. I want to make a point."

"He'll get the *point* when his ass is in jail."

"But it's *all* of them!" I yelped. "They do what they're told! And I can prove it with two reams of colored paper and a dozen rent-a-babes. It's *poetry*, Rafe. Their ugly prank begets mine. It's just like that gravestone you showed me. 'Killed by a log he made.'"

Rafe scrubbed a hand across his forehead. "Your plan is brilliant. You're the cleverest girl I know. But it's also *risky*."

"All good things are risky," I countered.

Slowly, Rafe lifted his eyes to mine. Our gazes locked. Rafe lifted an eyebrow in that maddening way he had.

Shit. *All good things are risky*, I'd said. And yet I wouldn't even take a risk on him. I was such a shit.

"I don't expect you to be there," I said quietly. I'd been such a shitty friend.

"Oh, I will be. You don't have a choice."

"Why?"

His eyes practically bugged out. "You think I can just go about my Saturday business, take in a movie or whatever, all the while wondering if you and Lianne are going to end up *roofied* in some closet at a frat house?" In a rare fit of temper, Rafe delivered a swift kick to the foot of my desk chair. Then he put his hands on his head and stared up at the ceiling. "Sorry," he managed.

"I promise to be careful."

He dropped his arms, looking grumpier than I'd ever seen him. "Yeah? Well I'll just be watching to make sure that you are."

I wondered what Lianne would have to say about that. Rafe stood in front of me, looking ten different kinds of hot. He had a sort of maddening alpha-male scowl on his face. I wanted to launch myself at him. I could kiss that frown off his face. I could scale him like a tree until I had him muttering Spanish curses in my ear. I could strip him down, and finish what we'd started the other day. And when we were done, I could lay my head upon his chest — my *boyfriend's* chest — and go to sleep.

The urge was strong. But I didn't give in to it.

"Do you happen to have any graph paper?" I asked instead.

TWENTY-SEVEN

RAFE

I aged about twenty-seven years on the day of the football game.

Bella and Lianne had begun their day by renting a van and parking it at the edge of the tailgate lot. As far as I could tell from their plan, they wouldn't be in any danger until halftime. But I showed up about two hours before game time anyway, because I wanted to be present if any assholes arrived on the scene.

When I found the girls, Lianne was busy signing autographs for all the models they'd hired, and Bella was handing out matching V-neck Beta Rho sweatshirts.

I could see how this would go down. Those assholes in the Beta Rho section were going to take one look at those models' tatas and do anything they asked. And then when they discovered they'd been tricked, they were going to be *pissed*. At Bella.

Que desastre.

Marching over to the van, I saw Bella look up in surprise. "Hi," she said. "You know this game doesn't start for a while, right?"

"Then you have plenty of time to listen to me."

Bella gave me a look. But then she followed me around to the back of the van. "What's the deal?" she asked, folding her arms. Her cheeks were flushed in typical Bella style, her eyes flashing with mischief. There wasn't anything I wouldn't do for this girl. But apparently I hadn't convinced her. Or worse — she didn't care.

"Please don't do this," I said, my voice low. "It's not a good idea."

Her eyes flared. "It's an amazing idea. You said so yourself."

I closed my eyes for a moment, trying to be calm. "It's just not *safe*. I know you want to make your point, but anything could happen."

Bella squared her shoulders. "I'm doing this my way, and I'm going to say what I came here to say. But thank you for your input." With one more irritated glance, she disappeared around the nose of the van.

Dios. I'd been dismissed. How utterly familiar.

So of course I spent the next three hours standing at a distance, watching for trouble and thinking of all the ways it could all go wrong.

Over at Bella's mission control center, the crowd of models around the van had swelled considerably. Each of them was taller and more stunning than the last. They were all wearing the type of full-on makeup that a guy didn't usually see at a Harkness football game. If only my stomach would stop churning, I might be able to enjoy the show.

Bella sat inside the rental van, aiming a pair of binoculars into the Beta Rho tent where the anniversary party was held. When the football game started, partiers began streaming into the stadium. I watched them walk past me, faces red from the November chill and from drinking a few too many beers.

The Beta Rho guys were the drunkest of the lot. I wasn't sure whether that made things easier or more perilous for Bella's big plan.

Please let this work, I kept saying to myself. Because bargaining with God was always an effective strategy for success. And if things went bad, the phone jammed into my pocket was the only weapon I had.

There was only one saving grace — Beta Rho was a football frat. And since Bella intended to pull off her stunt during half-time, that meant that a good portion of the current membership would be in the locker rooms when it went down.

So that was something.

After the Beta Rho tent had emptied and I'd heard the crowd in the stadium roar quite a few times, Bella and Lianne got busy. They lined up the tall women they'd hired to help them and spent a good long time explaining their plan. Lianne kept checking her phone, probably keeping an eye on the game clock. Announcements echoing from inside the stadium let me know that the second quarter of the game had already begun.

Bella and Lianne pulled two long rolls of fabric from the back of the van. Each roll was mounted on poles. They were obviously banners of some kind, though I couldn't see their design. Each banner was assigned to a pair of models. The tricky part came next. Bella handed out burgundy-colored file folders to each of the remaining girls. With animated hand motions, she explained what to do. And then she explained it again.

I couldn't decide if I was more worried that Bella's plan would fail, or more worried that it would succeed. If it failed, she'd be crushed. If it succeeded, she'd be in danger. My stomach was in knots now.

After the pep talk, the tall girls shed their sweatpants, revealing tiny little shorts underneath. Then Lianne passed out Beta Rho baseball caps, which they donned. Finally, all the women picked up a shopping bag from the back of the van and began walking toward the stadium entrance. I waited for them to pass me, and then I jogged to reach Bella. "Hey," I said. "Good luck in there."

When she turned her face to mine, there was a soft expression on it. "Thank you."

I couldn't help myself. I leaned in and kissed her cheek.

"Please don't take any chances. If this goes bad, just get the hell away."

"Okay." Her eyes dipped, then met mine again. "I promise."

"Go get 'em."

Bella held up a hand. "Hold up. I need to make a call." She yanked her phone out of her pocket and dialed. "Graham? You're in the press box, right? I need you to get yourself somewhere you have a good view of sections six and seven. That's where all the Beta Rho guys are sitting together. And bring a video camera." There was a pause. "I can't tell you why. But the minute you see people passing out papers over there, start filming right away. This is important." She listened again. "I *know* I'm a pain in the ass, Graham. But get over there, okay? You'll get a great story out of it. And if anything goes wrong, I need that on video, too."

My stomach gave another lurch.

She stowed her phone and clapped her hands. "Okay. Let's go!"

I followed fourteen of the most attractive women in the zip code through the stadium arches. An usher ripped my ticket, and I was inside. But where to stand?

I settled on a spot beside the end-zone bleachers. I could see the stands from there yet was also quite mobile. Half time had just begun, and the Harkness band was marching onto the field.

When the models first approached the regular student section I was confused. They dipped into their shopping bags and began handing out empty plastic cups — the kind that were often sold as souvenirs at a sporting event. They were burgundy, though, which probably meant they were Beta Rho swag.

After passing out all the cups, the models took places in front and along the sides of the Beta Rho sections.

Meanwhile, Bella had tucked herself onto the end of a bench in the student section, while Lianne did the same a few rows up.

Then Lianne put a coach's whistle to her lips and blew.

Immediately, the models bent over whichever guy was seated on the end of the nearest stadium row. With animated hands, they explained what they wanted, and then they passed a stack of cards

into each man's willing hands. After only a small amount of prod-
ding, I saw those cards begin to travel down the row, some
burgandy and some white...

My heart thumped like crazy.

On the ground level, two models had recruited a couple of
people to hold the ends of a banner which read, SINCE 1915. And
at the very top of the stands, a similar banner was unfurled, this
one reading, BETA RHO FRATERNITY.

Now came the tricky part of the operation that would only
work if Bella and Lianne had executed their graph-paper design
perfectly, and if most everyone sitting in those twenty rows of
seats held up his card as he'd been told to.

When all the cards had made it across all the rows of seats I
heard Lianne give another blast on her whistle. That's when the
models began lifting their folders into the air, pantomiming the
action they wanted to see down the row. They did this with come-
hither smiles on their faces. It was quite a sight—and one that
several decades worth of frat boys did not fail to notice.

As my breath stuck in my chest, several hundred white and
burgandy sheets of cardstock were raised into the air.

For a heart-stopping second, I couldn't decipher a pattern. But
as two hundred fraternity members and their dates raised their
arms into position, it became obvious that the card mosaic
formed letters. Bella's message was unmistakable. Together with
the banners, the frat boys had unwittingly spelled out:

>*Beta Rho Fraternity*
>*THINKING w/*
>*OUR DICKS*
>*Since 1915*

Several things happened at once.

There was a roar of surprise and laughter from the opposite
side of the stadium and a scramble as everyone reached for his or

her phone. In the student section, people were holding up the souvenir cups and passing them around for inspection.

Lianne's models began their speedy getaway, jogging quickly down the stairs. But their progress was slowed by all the other people crowding those steps, coming and going from the bathrooms and concession stands. Bella and Lianne stayed put, watching their girls retreat, like captains willing to go down with the ship.

"Come on," I whispered to myself. The sooner Bella was out of there, the better. I saw her rise to follow the last model down the steps, and I tracked her progress as she wove through the crowd. I found myself walking slowly toward the staircase, as if to meet her at the bottom.

That's when I saw him — a guy I recognized from the Casino Night party at Beta Rho. He was wearing his football jacket slung over his shoulders because one of his arms was in a sling. The jacket had "Whittaker" printed on the arm. In his good hand he held a molded tray with three drinks on it.

His face broke open in shock as he took in the sight of his fraternity's declaration. And then his features morphed into rage. "What the FUCK?" I heard him yell. "Guys! Put those down!"

Now I was moving faster, weaving between people, trying to get to Bella.

"Hey, watch it!" somebody said as I swerved past.

There was no time to apologize because Whittaker was sweeping the stands with his eyes, his mouth still open from shock. He was turning... toward Bella, who had almost made it down to ground level.

I ran the last few paces, deciding not to slow down as I approached him. Instead? I collided with his drink tray, smacking right into him. The result was an instant curse, followed by the splash of soda all over my upper body.

"You asshole!" Whittaker yelled. "What the..."

"Oops," I said quickly. I righted what was left of the tray in his hands. "Hey, I'm sorry about that. Can I buy you another one?"

As I apologized, I braced myself for a punch. I'd gotten him all wet, too.

But the dude couldn't decide where to put his eyes or his temper. His baffled gaze kept jumping between the soda running down his arm and the horrors of his fraternity's unfortunate public statement. "Hey!" he yelled toward someone in the stands. "Who did this?"

He tried to step around me, but I blocked him, because I couldn't see whether Bella was clear of the place yet.

"Look," I said, taking a ten out of my pocket. "Take this, I'm sorry about the drinks."

"Whatever, asshole. Just *move it*."

I tucked the ten in his shirt pocket and then cut around him, heading for the exits.

Neither Bella nor Lianne was anywhere in sight. By the time I made it out to the tailgate lot again, the van's engine had started, its taillights glowing cheerily in the evening light.

Feeling the first whiff of relief, I watched it drive away.

TWENTY-EIGHT

BELLA

I drove the van through the streets of Harkness while laughing like a maniac.

Apparently the body's physiological response to getting away with pranking a fraternity was an epic attack of the giggles. I hadn't giggled so much since the ninth grade, but here I was, losing my shit in the driver's seat, while Lianne lost hers beside me. And in the seats behind us, a dozen models laughed and chattered among themselves.

"Oh God, these shots are perfect," Lianne said between laughing jags. "Your friend Graham sent photos *and* a video. I can't wait to see these in high-res. There's a bunch of texts from him, too."

"What do they say?"

"There's... 'Oh my God, Oh my God. You are a genius. Best idea since fortune cookies.'"

That one made me laugh.

"And the last one says 'marry me.'"

I snorted. "There was a time when I would have."

"Really? I need to meet this guy."

"I'm sure you will. And his boyfriend."

"Oh."

"Yup." I stopped at the last traffic light before the train station. My heart was still thumping with adrenaline, even though the fun part of our mission was over. It was just dawning on me that maybe I was about to get into *so* much trouble. Anyone from Beta Rho could have spotted me in the van with the models, or sitting across the aisle at the game. "Hey, Lianne? Can you see us in the pictures Graham sent?"

She manipulated my phone, squinting down at the screen. "Yeah, but just barely. And we're off to the side. And so what?"

"I'm not letting you take the fall for this," I said, already bracing for the consequences.

Lianne reached across the gear box and put a hand on my arm. "You do *not* need to worry about me. I'm serious. If this gets out, my manager will be pissed, but my publicist will do a happy dance."

"Why?"

"Because I'm her most boring client. I mean, it's not like she wants to see me land in rehab. But it's hard to get media attention for someone who never leaves her room."

I swung the van into the train station drop-off circle and killed the engine. Lianne turned around in her seat. "Thank you for your service, ladies. It's been a pleasure. Paychecks are coming from your agency."

One of the models opened the sliding door and another called out a question. "Can we keep the sweatshirts?"

"Sure!" I called. "But I wouldn't wear them on the train. It's unlikely, but there could be Beta Rho guys onboard, and they might give you a hard time."

"Oh, I'm wearing mine," said a statuesque redhead named Amber. "Fuck it."

That set us off on another round of laughing, and the models climbed out of the van. Lianne shut the door behind them and I drove off again.

The final steps in our plan took another hour and also made me feel like a criminal.

In a dumpster behind the van rental place, we threw away the extra Beta Rho shirts and the instructions we'd printed out for the models. Then, after checking the van for incriminating evidence, we turned it in. Finally, we called a taxi to take us back to campus.

"I'm starving," Lianne admitted while we rode back in the cab. "Let's order something the minute we get home."

"But the dining hall is serving for another fifteen minutes," I pointed out. "We can just run in there right now."

"Well, okay," Lianne said quietly.

When we walked into the dining hall entryway, Lianne went straight instead of climbing the stairs. "Um, where are you going?" I asked.

She spun around, looking sheepish. "Lead the way."

"How have you never been to the dining hall?" I demanded. "It's *November*."

Her face closed down. "I just order in. It's easier."

"March." I pointed at the granite steps. "You just need your ID. It doesn't get any easier than that." I showed her where to swipe in at the doorway, then herded her into the kitchen for a tray. "And don't forget silverware," I said. "That's a rookie mistake."

An older woman behind the serving counter lifted a plate off the stack. "What'll it be?"

"Spaghetti and meatballs." Since a look of horror was dawning on Lianne's face, I pointed toward the doorway. "Don't panic. There's a salad bar out in the dining room. And the soup is right there." I nodded at the self-serve pot.

"Hold up," the serving-line lady said, her spoon halting above the meatballs. "You look *just* like that girl in those movies. The magic princess."

"Mmm," Lianne said noncommittally. Then she put her head down and wandered toward the soups.

When my plate was handed over, I thanked the server and turned to find Lianne waiting for me. She had a bowl of Mexican chicken soup and an anxious frown. "Come on," I said.

In the dining room, I spotted Graham at a table with Rikker and Corey Callahan. There was only space for one, but I stopped for a second anyway. "Hey, guys!"

Corey slipped her tray to the edge of the table and then stood. "Hey! I'm on my way out," she said. "Take this spot..." her voice trailed off when she realized who was standing next to me. "Oh, um, hi," she said, recovering quickly. "I'm Corey."

"Hi," Lianne said softly.

I put my tray down. "Corey, Graham, Rikker, this is Lianne."

"Hey," the guys said. But Corey was still staring.

"Do you need help with that?" I asked, pointing at her tray. She walked with a cane, and once in a while she needed an assist if there were too many things to balance on the tray.

But she seemed to snap out of it. "Nope. No problem. And congratulations!" She gave me a big smile. "Graham was just telling me about..."

I gave my head a quick shake. "I wouldn't know a thing about it."

Her eyebrows shot up. "Oh. Of *course* you wouldn't. How ridiculous." With another big smile, she hefted her tray in one hand and carefully moved toward the exit.

"That was..." Graham was grinning at me, too. He whispered the last word. "*Spectacular.*"

Rikker leaned in close to me. "Would it have killed you to *warn* a few people? I never go to football games. And I'm pissed that I missed it."

Graham squeezed his wrist. "But I got excellent pictures. After dinner I'm going over to the newspaper to file my story. Front page, of course."

My stomach gave a nervous flutter. "We are in such deep shit." I yanked the other chair out for Lianne. "Sit down already. Wait — I promised you rabbit food. The salad bar is right there."

Lianne set her tray down and walked toward the salad bar in the center of the room.

Then the weirdest thing happened. At the table nearest to the salad bar, I saw a couple of people nudge each other. The whole table went quiet. The same thing happened at the next table. Thirty seconds later, everyone who sat lingering over the last half hour of Sunday dinner was staring at Lianne.

"Wait," Graham said, following my gaze. "She looks really familiar. Isn't she that...?"

"Yeah," I said. "She's my neighbor on the fourth floor."

He sat back in his chair. "She's in *Beaumont* House? I've never seen her before."

I reached across the table and gave his hand a warning stab with my fork. "Don't stare."

Lianne returned a minute later, sitting down with her salad. After a few beats, the ambient sound of conversation returned to the room.

"That was trippy," I said.

She sighed, lifting her soup spoon. "I had this weird idea that I could just blend in here. It took me about an hour on move-in day to figure out that wasn't true."

"I think it is," I insisted. "But you have to actually *blend* if you want to blend. If you came in here every night, it wouldn't be interesting."

"I have no idea how to blend," Lianne admitted. "I've never gone to school before."

"*What?*" Rikker sputtered. "That's impossible."

Lianne shook her head. "I finished kindergarten in a regular school. After that, my mother dragged me to whichever continent she thought would amuse her most. I had private tutors. And then I *worked* all the way through high school. The only people I saw every day wore capes."

"Wow. I thought my high school years were fucked," Rikker muttered.

Lianne waved a hand, as if brushing the whole conversation aside. "Thanks for sending us the pictures, Graham," she said.

He grinned. "You were in on it, too?"

"She was my partner in crime," I said. "The models were her idea."

"And the sweatshirts," she added.

"The *cleavage*," I agreed.

"Remind me never to piss you two off," Rikker said. "Can I tell the team that you're my new idol?"

"I wish," I said. "But please don't. I have to be careful."

Graham's face got serious. "Shit, you're right." He tapped my hand. "There's your hot neighbor."

Out of the corner of my eye I saw Rafe remove a couple of pans from the salad bar. How anyone could look that good doing kitchen work was really a mystery.

"He stood guard today," Lianne said. "I saw him."

"*Did* he now?" Rikker asked, smiling at me.

"Yep," Lianne said even as I kicked her under the table. "He'd like to help Bella with some other things, too. But she turned him down."

"Lianne," I warned. "What do you care?"

"Because," she said, with a toss of her shiny hair. "The tension is *killing* me. You two look at each other like you wished clothing was never invented. When we're all in the same room, I feel like I'm intruding."

"Well you're *not*," I insisted.

"Uh-huh." Lianne stabbed an olive on her plate.

"New topic," I suggested. "What is your newspaper article going to say?"

Graham chuckled. "Let's see. We lost the game, because our quarterback threw three interceptions. Also, two hundred Beta Rho brothers proclaimed themselves to be idiots. And nobody argued."

"I dare you to write that, babe," Rikker said.

"Oh, I'm going to. I need a good headline, though. 'Frat Gets Bitchslapped' probably won't make it past the editorial board."

"That's missing the point, anyway," I argued. "'Frat Bitchslaps *Itself* While Ogling Models' Boobs.' Nobody made them do it."

"True, but that's too many characters for the headline typeface," Graham said. "I'll think of something, though."

"I'm sure you will." I cut a meatball with my fork. "Hey, Lianne? I signed for a FedEx package for you yesterday. I forgot to tell you, but I left it in the bathroom so that you'd see it."

"Cool. It's a script."

"Yeah? A new film?"

She shook her head. "A play. Romeo and Juliet. Isn't it funny that they FedExed me a copy for Saturday delivery? As if I couldn't find a copy in Harkness, Connecticut."

"You're playing Juliet? Do you have to stab yourself in the heart with a dagger?"

"Yep!" She jabbed her salad with glee. "That's the best part."

"Can I watch? When is this happening?"

"Over Christmas. And you *can* watch, because it's at the Public Theater."

I dropped my napkin. "You're doing Juliet at the Public Theater? You *are* fancy."

"It's a good gig," she admitted. "I'm doing it because there's a part I want in a new film adaptation of Shakespeare. But it sure kills Christmas break. I'll have ten days of rehearsal and then fifteen performances."

"Wow."

"Yeah. It'll be a grind. But, hey! New and different take-out foods."

"And New York," Rikker offered. "You can't beat that."

She shrugged again. "New York is fine. But I'm not looking forward to staying in a hotel for three weeks."

"Why not?" Graham asked. "Sounds like easy living."

My neighbor looked uncomfortable. "It's not enough privacy.

My manager is, like, Hitler. And he can just walk through the front door anytime he wants."

Her manager must be a serious piece of work She almost sounded afraid of him. "Lianne? Do you need a place to stay? I have a guest room. You'd have to share a bathroom with me. It would be just like we have it now."

She gave me the side eye. "For three weeks? Your parents would freak."

"No they wouldn't," Graham said, crumpling up his napkin. "Bella's got the whole second floor of this sick townhouse to herself since her bitch of a sister moved out."

Rikker nudged my foot under the table. "I want to stay at Hotel Bella sometime. Where's my invite?"

"Come. Seriously. If you visit over Christmas, we can see a Rangers game. You too, Lianne. If you don't want to be in a hotel, stay with me. Your manager can kiss my ass."

She stared at me, her face coloring. "Wow. I'm liking this plan. Now finish your carbs. We need to get home and see how many pictures of this got tweeted already. And I want to edit Graham's video."

"We can't post it under our own names," I said quickly.

"You think?" She rolled her eyes. "I want it for posterity. The music will be a tricky choice, though. I can't think of any songs about stupid frat boys."

"'Who Let the Dogs Out?'" Graham suggested.

"Huh." My neighbor looked thoughtful. "I'll try it on."

When we got up to leave, the dining hall was almost empty. The four of us deposited our trays on the conveyor belt then headed for the door.

"Wait up."

I turned to find Rafe walking towards me. Everyone stopped, which meant there were four pairs of eyes watching him approach. And I probably wasn't the only one who noticed how perfectly his faded jeans clung to his hips or how taut all that muscle looked underneath his Harkness T-shirt. "Hi," I said, feeling self-conscious.

"Hey." He hesitated, those dark eyes studying me. It was going to be awkward between us for a while. There was no getting around it. "I, uh, just wanted to suggest that you don't go anywhere alone for the next couple of days," he said.

I held Rafe's gaze, but I swear I could feel my three friends nudging each other behind me. "I'm not, um, alone," I pointed out.

"Good," he said, wiping his hands on the towel he held. "Just be careful, okay? We don't know how pissed off they are. I'm stuck here another half hour, but..."

"We'll walk her all the way to her door," Graham said.

"Which is a hundred yards from here," I pointed out. I was done with being looked after. Really very *done*.

"Then it won't take us long," Rikker said, putting a hand on my shoulder. "Come on."

"Thanks," Rafe said, as if he'd handed over the baton at one of his races. But then he smiled at me. "Goodnight, *belleza*. Congratulations."

Christ, that smile. And when he called me beautiful in Spanish, my insides melted into a puddle. "Goodnight."

We left, and my friends were quiet for about fifteen seconds.

"Well, I wouldn't kick him out of bed," Graham said.

"Me neither," Lianne agreed.

"*Quiet!*" I hissed, and they all laughed.

TWENTY-NINE

RAFE

After my shift at the dining hall, I took all my books to the library.

Hunkered down in a weenie bin, I tried to study. But it was impossible to concentrate. I kept picturing Bella's victory in my mind. So I sat there refreshing the school newspaper's website, waiting for the story.

Finally, after I'd clicked the button about a thousand times, it came up — a big picture showing the frat's messy but legible declaration of inadequacy. And the headline? FOOTBALL TEAM AND FRAT BOTH FUMBLE DURING RAUCOUS LOSS TO TIGERS.

Damn, I liked seeing that.

I read the article written by Bella's friend Michael Graham. It was a straightforward account of the game and about the half-time shenanigans. Graham wrote: "No one has claimed responsibility for the performance art in the Beta Rho section."

There was a quote from an alum who was pretty pissed off. "This is libel. We will get to the bottom of this prank, and we will take legal action."

That made me cringe. I didn't think Bella's prank was legally actionable. But what the hell did I know?

My eye was drawn a sidebar article. CUPS AND CUPS OF QUESTIONS.

"Several hundred plastic tumblers with the Beta Rho crest were passed out in the student section during half-time," it read.

I'd assumed the cups were just cover for the models' presence, but I'd been wrong. A photo of the back of a cup showed another message:

Beta Rho: 100 Years of Misogyny
First frat to incorporate at Harkness College.
1974: First frat to protest the admission of women to the
college
1981: Site of the first sexual assault of a female student
Reprimands and/or probation 7 times in the last 16 years

Side Effects of Drinking at Beta Rho Include
Your photo on the Brodacious website
Winning Skank of the Week
Getting roofied
If a brother hands you "tonight's special" DO NOT
drink it
If you suspect a friend has been drugged, call 911

"*Jesucristo,*" I whispered to myself. Bella had been wrong when she called herself a failed feminist. She ought to be teaching the class.

The article went on to quote several women on the subject of Beta Rho. "*Everybody thinks that Skank of the Week thing is awful,*" said a female volleyball player who asked for her name to be withheld. "*But nobody speaks out, because no one wants to admit winning it.*" The article went on to quote an RA on fresh court who said she always cautioned her First Year charges against getting drunk at a fraternity. *"They egg each other on,"* she said. *"So it's not a safe place."*

There in the weenie bin, I sat grinning at my computer screen. If Bella was trying to warn women away from Beta Rho, she'd done an excellent job. Front page. And her name was nowhere in the article.

I'd told her not to go through with it. She probably thought I was a jackass. Maybe she was right.

I still didn't know what to do with my feelings for Bella. Standing around outside today I'd had several hours alone with my thoughts. We were still at an impasse. Several times today I'd considered just giving in — agreeing to be friends with benefits if that's what she really wanted.

But... *Dios*, it would never work. The point of arranging a casual hook-up was the *casual* part. And I'd be carrying all sorts of extra yearning into that bedroom, whether I meant to or not. I could agree to shed my clothes, but I couldn't agree to shed my feelings. They were permanent. Like an invisible tattoo. It wouldn't be fair to either of us.

So I had two choices. I could either slink away and hide how bummed out I was about the whole thing. Or I could try again. I could wait a week and press my case. And if she said no, I could ask again sometime.

There was an old Wayne Gretzky quote that my soccer coach liked to use, even though it was supposed to refer to hockey. "You miss one hundred percent of the shots you don't take."

It was an easy decision, really.

I pulled my French book closer to me, but then ended up tossing it away again. It occurred to me that I hadn't been as forthright with Alison as I planned to be with Bella. Which meant that my troubles with Alison weren't all her fault...

Jesucristo.

I fired up my laptop one more time and composed an email message:

Dear Alison,

Hi. I just wanted to tell you that what happened between us wasn't all your fault.

It cost me something to write that. Because my inner cave man wanted to protest. But I soldiered on.

It always bothered me when you pushed me away. But instead of trying to figure out what was wrong, I just brooded about it. I made up a dozen reasons in my mind, and all of them were wrong. If I'd been able to speak up earlier, we might have avoided all the drama on our birthday. And so for that, I am sorry.

See you at Urban Studies on Tuesday,

—Rafe

Feeling satisfied, and suddenly exhausted, I snapped the computer shut and picked up my French book. At least I had a plan now. It might not be much. But it was something.

Chapter Thirty

THIRTY

BELLA

After dinner, Lianne and I had retreated to our rabbit warren under the eaves.

My crazy neighbor blasted celebratory dance music in her room. Every three minutes she popped through the bathroom door to update me on how many people had uploaded pictures of Beta Rho's humiliation to various social networking sites. "It has its own hashtag!" she shrieked from her room. "They're calling it BroDoh! God, this is so cool."

It was amusing how pumped up Lianne was. This was a girl whose Oscar-night dress was tweeted by tens of thousands — a girl who showed up in *People Magazine* on a monthly basis. And she was all riled up about a little football game mayhem.

As for me, I just felt... unsettled. I'd scored every point I'd gone for today. But here I was, pacing my room again, monitoring my phone for threatening calls.

There weren't any. Not a one.

"There's a funny thread on Yik Yak!" Lianne announced from her room. "People are rewriting our message. Like, 'Fucktards since 1915 would have worked just as well, with fewer characters.'"

She let out a gleeful laugh. "And on Twitter the women's soccer team would like to throw a party for whoever was responsible."

"Cool." It was pretty great to hear my efforts were appreciated. But at the end of the day, what had I really accomplished? I wrecked their self-aggrandizing party, and I proved they were morons. I probably made two hundred new enemies in the process.

Oh, the drama. In my heart, I wasn't cut out for drama. I just wanted to be close to my friends again and feel comfortable with myself.

There had been precious little comfort and happiness this year, and all of it had come from one man. My heart gave a creaky little squeeze when I thought of Rafe. If I was lucky, he'd come barreling in here in the next half hour demanding that we finish our Urban Studies project.

Wait, what? My brain did a slow replay of that strange little desire. But there it was. I'd become accustomed to seeing one particular devilishly handsome face every day. And except for that glimpse in the dining hall, I hadn't gotten my daily fix.

He'd probably turn up soon. And if he decided to work on something else tonight, I'd see him tomorrow. That was soon enough, right?

Of course it was.

But ten minutes later, I was eyeing the clock again, calculating how long ago Rafe's shift had ended. Maybe he'd gone out with his teammates?

Maybe he was chatting up some cute Alison lookalike and asking for her phone number.

"Shit!" I yelled. Why the *hell* did that idea bother me so much?

"What is it?" Lianne yelped, dashing into my room. "Did anyone call?" Her blue eyes were round with worry.

"No," I said quickly. "Just, um, stubbed my toe."

Her shoulders relaxed. "Don't scare me like that. By the way, I've counted twenty-seven uploads to YouTube."

"Awesome," I said.

"This is the best day of my life," Lianne said from over my shoulder. "Who else needs to be pranked?" she asked. "I'm ready to do it all again."

It was official. I'd created a monster. A very small one, with flawless skin.

By midnight, I was a twitchy basket case. While the interwebs continued to erupt with glee over my victory, my own phone was utterly silent.

And Rafe had never showed.

The urge to see him had reached painful proportions. Why hadn't it occurred to me that when I'd sent him away he might actually stay there?

I was lonely tonight. Sure, I could have called a few of my hockey friends. Pepe or Trevi would have been surprised to hear from me, but they probably would have been happy to see me.

But Pepe and Trevi weren't who I wanted to see.

Rafe was probably asleep by now. Here I was, having some kind of freaky revelation about how much I cared about him. And he was right downstairs.

"Fuck it," I whispered to myself, shoving my feet into my Converse high-tops. "I'm goin' in."

I was half-way down the stairs when I realized I'd get some strange looks from Rafe's roommates when I showed up in a tiny little tank top and flannel PJ pants. But it was really too late to worry about that.

There was an encouraging stripe of light underneath their common room door. I knocked.

Nothing.

I knocked again. Since I'm not exactly famous for propriety, I tried the door, which opened in my hand.

The common room was empty and both bedroom doors were shut. I thought I heard male voices, but when I tiptoed to Rafe's door, there was only silence. The sound must have been coming from Mat's room.

The right thing to do was to go back upstairs and wait to talk to Rafe in the morning. But... in for a penny, in for a pound. I tapped on the door. "Rafe? It's Bella. Can I come in?" I listened to the silence. Then I opened the door.

Both beds were empty. "Fuck!"

Mat's bedroom door opened, and he stuck his head out. "Can I help you?"

"Where's Rafe?" I probably should have apologized for breaking and entering. But when you're trying to re-enact the romantic ending of a chick flick, there just wasn't time.

"Um." His roommate ran a hand through tousled hair. "The library?" he guessed.

"Which library?" I demanded.

Mat gave me an irritated look. "How would I know? He likes Central Campus."

"Thanks!" I called over my shoulder. I ran out of the room, and down the stairs. I'd forgotten my coat, and it was cold out. Very cold. But the romantic heroines of movies didn't worry about that sort of thing, so neither would I. Beginning a nicely paced jog to Central Campus Library, I had to hold my boobs in crossed arms, because I'd neglected to wear a bra.

Awkward, but I made good time.

Central Campus Library was not a small place. I began on the ground level, searching every carrel, chair and table. It wasn't too crowded, given the hour. But I did not spot Rafe anywhere.

Okay, I was officially off the chick flick script. And people were starting to stare.

On the lower level, it was the same story. I couldn't find him anywhere. The library would close soon. The only place I hadn't searched were the weenie bins, so I began peeking through the little windows of each one. I was discouraged. Maybe Rafe *was* out at a party.

Halfway down the row, I had to stand on my tiptoes to see a

weenie bin's occupant because someone had slumped over on the desk. Peering in, I saw a set of broad shoulders, and a gorgeous masculine face asleep on a book. I opened the door a few inches. "Rafe?"

"Mmm?" he said.

I went into the tiny room and slid the door closed behind me. "Rafe?" I whispered, putting my hand on his shoulder. He felt warm and solid beneath my touch.

He lifted his head from the textbook, and I watched him wake up fast. "Bella? Are you okay?" He turned in his seat, and his eyes swept me from top to toe, as if looking for damage. "What's wrong?"

What's wrong. Here was a boy who had done so much for me, only to have me reject him. And when I woke him from a sound sleep, the first thing he did was try to figure out if I was in need of help.

God, I was such an idiot.

"Nothing's wrong," I whispered. "I just wanted to see you."

His eyes went squinty for a second, as if he was trying to solve a math problem. He propped his head in one hand. "It's late," he said, closing his eyes again.

"I know, Captain Obvious. It's late. But I hope it's not *too* late." I dropped both hands to his shoulders. My thumbs stroked the skin of his neck, while his head tipped forward to land against my stomach.

"I don't know what you're saying," he whispered. "But I like the visit."

"I'm saying..." I began. But I wasn't sure how to proceed. I'd never told a guy that I'd wanted to be with him. Except for Fucker Tanning. And I'd long blocked all the sweet things I'd ever said to him out of my brain. When I was in love with Graham, I'd never told him. I'd never hinted. Not once. Too risky.

Rafe waited. He waited by reaching up to slowly trace the line of my forearm with his thumb. It felt distractingly nice.

Focus, Bella! "I'm saying that I think you were right. We're, um, compatible."

Rafe smiled without opening his eyes. "You think so, huh?"

"Yeah," I said softly.

"All right," he murmured. "What do you want to do about that?"

"Uh." Wasn't it obvious? "We can be together."

"Huh," he said, opening his eyes. "I don't know, Bella. We need to be sure that there aren't any misunderstandings, here. I'm not sure that 'being together' is clear enough. Spell it out for me. You'd be my...?"

"Well..." I cleared my throat. "I'd be your..."

Rafe grinned.

I pinched his shoulder. "You're enjoying this."

"A little bit."

"Do we need labels, though? I'm trying to say that we should be exclusive. I want that. But a *girlfriend* is someone who is always on the phone with her boyfriend, or waiting for him to call. Or always talking about him, or making sure their plans line up for everything. She never says yes to anything without checking with him first..." Yeah, it's really no surprise I'd never signed up for that.

Rafe tipped his handsome chin upward, so he could see me clearly. "There is only one thing you have to do, and that's care."

That was all? "I *do* care."

He smiled again, and it was like the sun coming out. "I know, baby. Now come here." Rafe pulled me onto his lap and wrapped both arms around me.

For a moment I hesitated. I'd been a one-woman show for so long I wasn't sure I was ready to fold myself into a man's embrace. But he was warm and sturdy, and I tucked my head against his shoulder and sighed. I suddenly realized the feeling was really familiar. I'd been leaning on him for months without ever admitting how much.

And this was *really* nice.

His big hand cupped my head and then stroked my hair. His lips found my forehead, and the kiss he placed there was so sweet I felt a lump in my throat.

Remind me why I'd resisted this?

"You feel good right here," Rafe murmured. His hand skated down my spine, leaving tingles in its wake.

"I was lonely for you tonight," I admitted. "I kept wishing you'd show up and demand to work on our spreadsheets."

"You *are* a sexy girl," Rafe whispered, and I laughed into his neck.

I lifted my face to his. "It's true what they say about me. I like big, long *columns* of numbers. I want to make your interest rate spike."

With a chuckle, he kissed my forehead again. "You've got my attention now. But I was never giving up on you, *belleza*. I thought I needed a night to regroup. But I was always coming back for you. To try to win you over."

"I'm sorry I've been so dense."

He shook his head. "Nothing dense about you. You *schooled* those boys today. People are going to talk about it for weeks."

That might be true, but I didn't want to think about it right now. Instead, I put my lips on his jaw. Then I tasted him, enjoying the scrape of his whiskers on my tongue.

His breath hitched. "*Belleza*," he whispered hoarsely, making me shiver. Then he tilted that sexy mouth down to mine and kissed me slowly. His lips were warm and firm, and so very *Rafe*.

"Mmm," I sighed against his lips. I wondered how it would be between us now that we knew each other's secrets. Maybe Rafe would be tentative. I hoped not.

He deepened the kiss. I opened for him, and his bossy tongue tangled with mine. One big hand slipped around my waist to palm my quivering belly, and the gentle pressure sent waves of electricity zinging through my core, lighting up my fun zone.

Not tentative! Nope!

Rafe stoked our kiss, his lips coaxing mine, his hands skimming, teasing...

A loud moan reverberated off the weenie bin walls, and it came from me. The single night we'd shared in September had lived on in my mind, so hot and wild that I'd wondered if my memory had embellished it. But now I knew it hadn't. Inside the thoughtful, quiet Rafe I'd come to know lurked the sensual beast I'd remembered. As he kissed me, those strong arms were in motion, squeezing my hips, pulling me against his sturdy chest.

I turned my whole body to face him, seeking even better contact. Tossing a knee over his lap, I managed to straddle him properly. His arms clamped around me, his hands landing on my ass. He squeezed, and we both groaned.

Our kisses were as deep as the ocean. I hadn't let my guard down like this — truly letting myself go — in so very long. I'd been tied up in knots for so many weeks that it had come to seem normal. But this was glorious. I basked in the circle of Rafe's arms and let him know exactly how happy he made me.

"ATTENTION PLEASE. THE LIBRARY WILL CLOSE IN TEN MINUTES."

The intercom's warning was barely enough to separate us. After several more drugging kisses, we finally broke apart, both of us panting. "We should go," Rafe said.

"Yeah," I agreed. But then I kissed him again, because my mouth overruled my brain.

Rafe chuckled against my lips. "Come on," he said, slapping my backside. "Let's get out of here."

I'd never heard a better idea in my life.

Rafe shoved his books and computer into his backpack then followed me out of the little room. He put an arm around my waist, and together we climbed the stairs and walked out into the night. "Where's your jacket?" he asked, eyeing me. "Wait. Where are your *clothes?*"

"Um," I said as he stopped to shuck off his jacket and drape it over my shoulders. "I was in a hurry to find you."

"You ran over here alone, in your PJs?"

"Rafe, it's *two blocks*."

He put his arm around me again. "Can I remind you that it's important to stay off a certain fraternity's radar right now?"

"Nope," I argued, steering him down the street again. "Think about it. Do you really want your first move as my boyfriend to be an argument? That's going to hold up your trip to pound town."

He laughed. "Hearing you, *belleza*. On the other hand, if we don't keep you safe, it's going to be that much harder to have a whole lot of sex."

"I'm fine, Rafe."

"You are *very* fine," he answered, his voice rough.

The next two minutes were a comical pantomime entitled "Two People Who Want Sex Fumble Through a Gate and Two Doors." Thanks to electronics, the first two locks were easy. We ran up the stairs, passing Rafe's door and finally making it to mine. The key was on a stretchy loop around my wrist, but my need for instant gratification was overpowering. I stopped on the landing and grabbed Rafe.

With an achy groan, he pressed me against the door. "*Bésame*," he demanded.

I forgot everything except for the perfect mold of his lips and the feeling of his hard body against me. When his bossy tongue invaded my mouth, there was no more shame. There was no fraternity, no scandal and no football game. There were only his broad hands coasting possessively down my body and the rumble of longing in his throat.

Until Lianne opened her door.

"Guys? Oh...!" I heard her laugh, but I was too busy to worry about it. "So I guess now is a bad time?" On another snicker, the door closed again.

Rafe had finally noticed we were still outside my room. He swept the keychain off my wrist and opened the door. He steered me inside, then kicked the door shut. I threw his jacket over the desk chair, and a second later we were on the bed. *Finally!* Rafe rolled on top of me immediately, his big body pressing against all my favorite places. And then it was all kissing and moaning and hands wandering everywhere. And I couldn't get enough. Except...

"Rafe?" I whispered.

"*Belleza?*"

"How come you were a virgin until September? Is it because of religion?"

"No, baby." He gave me a series of slow, drugging kisses so good I almost forgot I still had a question.

Somehow I found the will to put a hand on his hard chest and give a little push. "I'm not trying to be nosy. I just need to know. Because if you are going to feel bad again after this..."

He smiled down at me. "That's not nosy. That's just *caring*. See, you're already good at this relationship thing." He bent down, rubbing the tip of his nose under my chin until I squirmed because it tickled.

"Are you going to answer the question?"

"Sure." He pushed a piece of my hair out of my face. "Two reasons. Opportunity, and respect."

"*You* never had the opportunity? A hottie like you?"

He grinned. "Thanks, *belleza*. I had girlfriends in high school, and I was willing to give them the goods, but they weren't ready. I *liked* these girls, and I wasn't going to force the issue. It's not easy being a Catholic, immigrant girl. They hear the whole 'good girls don't do that' from birth. I wasn't going to break up with them just because they wouldn't..."

"Put out," I supplied.

"Yeah." He smiled again, and my knees melted even further. "We fooled around whenever we got the chance. Just never rounded home plate."

"Ah." That explained his impressive kissing skills. Actually, it explained a lot. Rafe was passionate in a controlled way. Like a banked fire that's always hot enough to burst into flames.

He kissed my nose. "And then Alison was a different story. She just didn't like sex." As he said this, he dragged a single finger down my tank top, over the peak of one breast, and down my tummy. I shivered.

"She didn't like it?" I gasped. "I've heard that's possible. But it's so hard to imagine."

"No kidding, right?" He kissed my neck again, making me shudder with desire.

"What were we talking about again?" I mumbled.

"*No recuerdo.*" Rafe kissed a line across the upper edge of my tiny tank top. Then he cupped a hand over my breast and began to nuzzle me, his nose dipping between my breasts. He kissed his way up to the peak, and I wanted that little shirt *gone*. I wanted *all* my clothes gone. Right now.

"Let's take this off," I begged, grabbing the hem of the shirt. "Hurry."

Chuckling, he dropped his lips to my belly button, which I'd just exposed. "Who would rush something like this?"

Lots of people, actually. Including me. If he didn't undress me soon, I was going to burst from impatience. His fine mouth dropped kisses just above the waistline of my pajama pants. Moist, teasing kisses. I shifted my hips around, hoping he'd move lower.

It wasn't every day I decided to have a relationship with someone. I felt like celebrating. Right now.

To make that point, I hustled my tiny tank over my head, and received an appreciative growl, since there was no bra underneath. "Damn, *belleza. Tu me vuelves loco.*"

I put a hand behind his neck and tugged him down, right where I wanted him. He sucked my nipple into his mouth, and the jolt it gave me traveled *everywhere*. And I let him know.

"You like that?" he whispered.

"Ahh," I moaned as he switched, bathing my other nipple. "Anywhere you put your tongue is good with me."

Rafe chuckled. Then he kissed his way down to my hip bone, tugging down the waistband of my pants just an inch or two.

Kissing and nibbling, he crossed my lower belly, his beautiful mouth stopping to worship me *just* a few inches north of the fun zone.

He hovered there, kissing and teasing while I squirmed, wondering what would happen next. I wanted his mouth on my body. But for the first time in my life, I was *nervous*, afraid to ask for what I wanted. A long bout of celibacy meant I hadn't even shaved lately. I was probably rocking a bush worthy of Chewbacca. Maybe Rafe wouldn't find me attractive...

I didn't get to finish that dismal thought because my PJ pants were yanked away. I heard a grunt of satisfaction at the discovery that I wasn't wearing underwear, either. And before I even knew what had happened, a gentle, soft kiss parted my legs. "Oh, *belleza*," he sighed, dragging a thumb through my wetness. "*Tan hermosa*." He tongued me then, and I almost died of happiness. "*Tan sabrosa*."

It was certainly not the first time I'd ever had an enthusiastic mouth between my legs. But those sexy words and soft kisses and *ohhhh*.

I had never felt so beautiful. Rafe had seen every ugly detail of my life this year, and a few from past years, too. Yet here he was, worshipping me like none of that mattered.

Gripping the quilt, I raised myself up on my elbows to watch. And what a view to behold. Smooth, muscular arms braced my pale skin. Rafe's face was flushed, and there was a naughty gleam in his half-closed eyes.

I canted my hips toward his mouth, and Rafe growled. He was nibbling and sucking gently, and I was crazy for it. "Damn," I whispered. Every wet slide of his mouth brought me close to the edge. I'd been *starving* for this. For him. I wanted everything. All of it. *Right now*. "Rafe?" I panted.

"Can't hear you," he said between licks.

"Want you."

"You got me." Strong arms braced my thighs in place, and he lowered his mouth onto my body again.

My entire fun zone quivered with joy. "Ohh," I gasped.

"Mmm," he encouraged. "*Dámelo.*"

Give it to me, he'd said. So I flopped back onto the bed and let myself sink into all that sensation while Rafe worshipped me. It had been a long time since I'd truly let go with someone. But tonight it was as easy as rolling off a log. I reached down to ruffle my fingers through Rafe's hair, and he gave a quiet moan. That was all it took. I lifted my hips off the bed and gasped as waves of sweet release began to roll through me.

In the background I heard some very sexy Spanish curses, followed by the sound of music starting up in Lianne's room. When I floated back down to earth, Rafe was still nuzzling my thighs, planting soft kisses everywhere he could reach.

"Whew," I said, flopping an arm over my head. "Why are you wearing so many clothes?"

He looked up at me and grinned. Then he swung off the bed and lifted his T-shirt over his head.

His rippling abs made my mouth water. "Keep going," I demanded after he'd tossed the T-shirt aside.

He unzipped his jeans, dropping them to the floor. Then he toed off his socks. I could see the shape of a very impressive erection practically bursting out of his black briefs. But to my dismay, he left those on.

When he perched on the edge of the bed, I sat up to meet him. "Rafe?"

"Mmm?" he asked, leaning in to kiss me.

I could taste myself on him, and just the memory gave me a new jolt of longing. "When I attacked you on your sofa, I got in trouble for complimenting your dick."

He laughed against my lips. "Let's forget about that day."

"Fine but..." I kissed him again. "Is it okay to admit that I'm *really* looking forward to playing with it?"

Rafe put a big hand on the back of my neck and drew me close. "Everything is different now." His voice rumbled into my ear. "Take what's yours, *belleza.*"

Oh, hell yes. I dropped my hand into his lap and caressed his hard cock through the cotton.

His abs clenched, and he let out a hiss.

I slid to my knees on the floor, palming him. Then I began kissing those gorgeous abs, moving closer and closer to the waistband of his briefs. Above me, Rafe braced himself on taut arms, his breath hitching as I moved ever closer to the target.

"*Jesucristo*," he muttered. When I ducked my head to trace the hard length of him with my lips, he moaned my name.

Payback was *sweet*.

I tugged his waistband down to reveal the object of my affection. *God.* He was just as gorgeous as I remembered — thick and long, with a bead of precum right on the head. I leaned down to lick it off, and he gasped when I made contact. I could barely wrap my hand around his incredibly hard dick.

It seemed we'd *both* been yearning for this.

Kissing the tip, I teased him some more. Then I bathed him with my tongue, and every muscle in Rafe's body went rigid. Wrapping my hand around the base of him, I realized blowing this boy was not going to be easy. *Welp. I'm just the woman for the job.*

Opening wide, I sucked him down.

The moan Rafe let out could probably be heard all the way to Grand Central Station.

I popped off him and gave his stomach a gentle shove. "Lie back. And let me have these." I tugged on his underwear.

"You don't have to..."

I looked up into his lust-filled eyes. "Do you honestly want me to stop?"

"No." He put a hand on my hair. "But I won't last."

Leaning into his hand, I smiled up at him. "You won't last right *now*. But later tonight, when we're fucking, you'll last even longer."

He blew out a hot breath. "That's a plan I can get behind."

"Mmm," I said. "I *do* like it from behind. But enough talking."

I gave his chest another push and he reclined onto his elbows. Three seconds later I had his briefs off and his thick cock in my mouth.

Heaven.

Rafe was practically levitating off the bed as I tongued him. As he cursed and writhed beneath me, I sure did appreciate his enthusiasm.

Relaxing my throat, I took him deep. Cupping his heavy balls in one hand, I moaned around his dick.

"Fuck, *belleza*," he panted. *"Tan bueno. Demasiado..."*

He torqued his hips in a sexy rhythm, and I was on fire again, too. A turned-on Rafe was just so, so sexy. He didn't try to play it cool. He showed me exactly how much he wanted this. His breath hitched, and his thrusts became short and erratic. I knew the signs — he was close. So I gave him a good, hard suck.

On a groan, Rafe nudged my cheek with his hand — a wordless warning. Damn, my new boyfriend was considerate. But that only made me more eager to finish him. I swirled my tongue around the head of him while he panted. Then I took him all the way to the back of my throat again and moaned.

He came on a shout, his stomach going rigid. I swallowed again and again until finally he collapsed, legs splayed out, one arm over his eyes. *"Dios,"* he mumbled.

For a moment, I rested my cheek on his thigh. Rafe's hand smoothed my hair out of my face. "Are you okay?" I asked him.

He grunted. "Never better. Just don't ask me to get up."

I climbed up on the bed and gave his flank a little slap. "Move your hot self over a little."

"That I can manage." He moved over a foot and then pulled me into his arms. "There aren't words for how good I feel."

That made me surprisingly happy. "Didn't you ever get a blowjob before?" It was none of my business, and probably hypocritical of me to ask.

"Not a *good* one."

That made me laugh. "You've been hanging out with the wrong girls, Rafe."

"Truth." He pulled me closer, pressing his lips to my forehead. "What is that song Lianne's playing?"

I listened, then snickered. "It's Marvin Gaye's 'Let's Get it On.'"

His eyes were closing, but he chuffed out a laugh. "She cracks herself up."

"Yeah," I whispered, running a thumb over his cheekbone. Over my *boyfriend's* cheekbone. I was going to have to repeat that word to myself a whole bunch of times until it didn't seem weird anymore. "Sleepy?" I asked him.

"Mmm. I wish I wasn't." He opened his eyes and stretched. "Just give me a few minutes. I can rally."

I went into the bathroom and brushed my teeth, admiring Rafe's naked form through the doorway. He *did* look tired. And it was almost two in the morning. When I came back to bed, I tugged on my quilt. "Hottie, lift up a second." A minute later, we were tucked under the covers, and I reached up to click off the lamp.

"The more comfortable you make me, the quicker I'm gonna fall asleep," Rafe said.

"I know." I curled up to him. "Thing is, I just realized that we get to do it again tomorrow. And the day after that. And the one after that."

"I like the sound of that," he said.

"Me too. So rest up. You're going to need your strength."

My boyfriend's chuckle made his body undulate beneath my head. I rested my hand on his heart, and Rafe's fingers made loving strokes down my spine. It was glorious. "I'm glad you're here," I whispered.

"No place I'd rather be, *belleza*." His voice was thick with emotion.

His words curled around me like a blanket. They settled over my soul, beginning the work of filling all the dings and scratches I'd sustained these past few weeks.

People say that revenge is sweet. And they're right. But lying naked beside the boy who guards your heart is even sweeter.

I pressed one more kiss onto Rafe's pec, and then let him sleep.

Chapter Thirty-One

THIRTY-ONE

RAFE

Unlike the first time I'd slept in Bella's bed, I crashed hard and slept the sleep of the shameless.

Waking up was a pleasant surprise. I'd fallen asleep with the world's brightest, sexiest, funniest girl in my arms. And I woke up with the world's brightest, sexiest, funniest girl lying curled up against my body. *And still naked.*

Pinch me.

Bella's soft curls spilled across my chest. And don't get me started on the soft feel of her skin on mine, or the swell of her breast against my arm.

For a while I just lay there admiring her. But it was hard to look and not touch. So I dragged a single finger down the silky skin of her arm.

"Mmh," she said as if guarding her sleep. Then she rolled, putting her back to me.

I adjusted my position so that I was spooning her and closed my eyes. But it was no use. My body was well aware that I was in bed with my favorite naked woman. My morning wood poked her bottom. Just that small amount of contact was giving both my dick and my imagination some big ideas. Falling asleep was out of the question, so I tried to just relax and think of other things. Urban Studies, for example. Our project was due in a matter of days.

Right. As if our assignment had any hope of distracting me from the velvet texture of Bella's skin against mine, and the soft sound of her breathing. I knew I should really just get out of bed and let her sleep. But I wasn't about to walk out on her like I'd done the last time.

She shifted against me, making just a whisper of friction against my cock, and I had to bite my lip. *Dios*. Then she did it again, pushing back into my lap. I let out a slow, patient breath and reined myself in.

"Mmm," she said again. Then she wiggled her ass, torturing me.

I couldn't help it that time. I groaned.

Bella said nothing, and her eyes were still closed. She reached for the hand I'd draped on her hip, brought it up to her breast and left it there.

Another groan worked its way out of my throat as the soft swell filled my palm. I brought my lips to the creamy skin on the back of her neck. Bella pressed her body back, fitting it to mine, the invitation unmistakable.

I slipped my other arm under her pillow, which allowed me to cup both of her *tatas* at once. On a quiet whimper, she arched her back, pressing against my crotch. I kissed her nape again and again. "Belleza," I whispered. And when I kissed the soft skin underneath her ear, she shivered in my arms. "Do you want to wake up for me, baby?"

Instead of answering, she lifted her top knee, making a space between her legs. Then she hiked her thigh in order to catch my dick. She lowered her knee again, trapping me between her legs.

When I flexed my hips to tighten our connection, I could feel the wet slide of her *concha* against my erection. "Oh, fuck," I gasped. My whole body was on fire, now. With my heart beginning to pound, I thrust in the space between her legs. I had both her breasts cradled in my hands, and my mouth on her neck. Bella's curves were *everywhere*, and it was exquisite.

With a sexy little moan, Bella ground against my dick. "Okay," she breathed, dropping a hand to the sensitive head of my cock. "Who do I have to blow around here to get this thing inside me?"

The kiss I'd been pressing against her neck suddenly became a snort of laughter. "Love that idea, *belleza*. But I don't have any condoms."

She let go of my dick and pushed herself up on an elbow. "Then you've come to the right place. So to speak."

While Bella opened the drawer in her bedside table and fished around, I tried to slow my breathing.

"I thought I had... here it is. Try this." Bella settled onto her side again, then reached over her shoulder. The packet she handed me read "XL" in big letters. I slit it open and carefully fitted the condom over my cockhead. When I rolled it down, the fit was much more comfortable than the one that had broken on the night we hooked up. "Thanks, *belleza*," I said softly.

She reached a hand over the top of her head and pushed her fingers into my hair. "If that fits, we're going to buy a case of those."

Chuckling, I put my arms around her again. "It does. And you feel so fucking good."

"I could feel even better." She didn't turn over. Instead, she lifted her knee and reached between her legs. When her hand wrapped around me, I stopped breathing. She lined me up, and I pressed forward on an exhale.

Just like that, I was inside my girl and groaning from the feel of her body hugging my cock.

"Yessss." She pushed back against me, taking me deeper. I grabbed her hip and thrust. Then we were both moving and moaning together.

Never had a Sunday begun so perfectly.

After only a few amazing minutes, my motor revved all the way into the red zone again. But I wasn't ready for this to end—not by a long shot. So I wrapped my arm around Bella's chest and rolled onto my back, keeping our connection.

Her head came to rest on my shoulder. "Why'd you stop?" she breathed.

"Don't want to finish yet," I admitted.

She flexed her hips, and the friction was delicious. But I wasn't quite so trigger-happy anymore. I reached a hand down between her legs, my fingertips advancing through the little triangle of hair to the very place where we were connected. *Jesucristo*. That was the sexiest thing I'd ever felt — Bella's softness around my hardness.

"Oh, fuck," she whispered, shivering in my arms. She dug her heels into the bed and arched into my hand.

"You like that?" I began to stroke her.

"So much." She writhed on my chest, responding with a breath or a shiver every time my fingers grazed her. I'd never felt so powerful. "Ohhhh," she sighed. "Don't stop."

But I was afraid that if she came on my dick, she'd take me with her. And I wasn't ready. I didn't want it to happen quite like this.

I withdrew my hand.

She groaned with frustration. "I thought you were a nice person."

"I am," I said, lifting her body so that I could slip out. "The nicest." Dropping Bella to the sheet, I rolled on top of her. With her curls spread out on the pillow, and her eyes made extra green by the morning light, she looked like an angel. "Hi."

"Hi," she whispered, her chest heaving. "Is there a problem?"

I shook my head. Then I dropped my forehead to hers. "I just want to see your pretty face while we're fucking, *belleza*." I kissed her on the nose. "*Eres mi novia. Mi hermosa novia.*"

At that, her eyes went a little glassy, and her mouth opened into an "O." She lifted her hips, and I pushed back inside.

For a long moment, I didn't move at all. I just let myself soak up her warmth and the glory of being as close to someone as it was possible to be. "Thank you, *belleza*." I gave my hips a little shove, and she sighed beneath me. That felt so good I thrust again. And then again. *Dios*. This wasn't going to last long. Staring into her lust-filled eyes was killing me.

"Rafe..." she whispered, and the sound of my name on her lips was intoxicating.

"*Belleza*," I returned, thrusting faster.

"Kiss me, baby."

Sí señorita. Dropping my mouth onto hers, I forced my tongue inside, and she answered with an epic moan. She reached up, then dragged her fingernails down my back. It was so good it almost finished me off. My rhythm stuttered for a second as I grabbed her naughty hands and pinned them down on either side of the mattress. I laced my fingers in hers and held her still beneath me.

"Oh, *fuck*," she cried, meeting me stroke for stroke with her hips. That's when I felt it — her body rippling around my cock. And it was all over then. My balls tightened immediately, and then I was groaning and shooting and delirious with joy.

Collapsing onto Bella's sweet body, I felt strong arms wrap around my back. I tried to lift my hips to avoid crushing her, but she wasn't having it.

"Don't you dare move. *God*, you feel so good."

I smiled into her pillow. We lay there together, just feeling happy. A few minutes went by before I even noticed which uptempo song was coming through the bathroom door. "She's at it again," I whispered.

"Mmm?"

"That song is 'Love Shack.'"

Bella snorted. "There's something I need to ask you. Because I'm a newbie at this girlfriend thing."

"What is it, *chica*?"

"What do couples do on Sunday morning together?"

"Do I need to teach you the secret handshake?"

Bella giggled.

"You got this," I said, nuzzling her cheek. "First we make out some more. Then we drag your lonely neighbor to brunch with us. Then we drink a whole lot of coffee."

Her soft hands began to stroke my chest. "Sounds like a plan."

THIRTY-TWO

BELLA

Life looked a little brighter on Monday than it had in weeks. Maybe it was the revenge. Maybe it was the sex.

Okay, it was probably the sex.

Whatever the reason, I felt more like myself than I had in a long time. I walked all the way to my psych seminar thinking dreamy thoughts about Rafe instead of ducking my head when people passed by.

Twenty-four hours had elapsed since my prank. And then forty-eight. There were still plenty of pics and videos on social media, but I hadn't heard my name in conjunction with any of them. And there were no more scary mentions of Beta Rho alumni taking legal action.

Life was good.

On Tuesday I went for a run with Rafe before Urban Studies. After class he left for a dining hall shift, and I took a moment to call the nurse practitioner on my way back to Beaumont.

Ms. Ogden answered on the first ring. "How are you, Bella?"

"I'm good. Really good. But I have a question."

"Shoot."

"Well, I have a new boyfriend..."

"Congratulations!"

"Thanks. And I wanted to get tested once again, just out of an abundance of caution."

"Right. You don't even need to make an appointment for that. Just come in during business hours."

"That's easy," I said. "So here's one more question — I had a swab test of my fun zone when I was sick. But I'm assuming that this time I just have to pee in a cup?"

"That's right. And it's the same for him if he wants to be tested. If you're starting a new relationship after a non-monogamous time, it's good practice for anyone to get tested."

"Right." Monogamy was treating me really well these days. I'd woken up this morning with a horny Rafe in my bed again. And after we'd scratched that itch, he went out and *brought back coffee*. If I hadn't already seen the point of having a boyfriend, it would have sunk in while I was drinking that latte in bed.

"Remind me, Bella," Ms. Ogden said into my ear. "What's your major?"

"Psych."

"Huh. Have you ever considered nursing school? I think you'd make a great nurse practitioner. Or a midwife. There's definitely some psych involved. You have a great attitude, and you'd get to talk fun zones for a living."

"Wow." What a crazy idea. "I'd never considered anything medical. Because the people who are trying to get into med school are the most stressed-out students at Harkness."

"I'll bet they are. And maybe nursing isn't as glamorous as being a full-fledged doctor. But the grad school piece is so much easier. If your plans for next year aren't firm yet, you should take a peek at the Harkness nursing program. Just to see if it interests you."

"Harkness has a nursing program?"

She laughed. "I suppose the undergrads wouldn't necessarily

notice it because it's hidden inside the med school. I'm on the faculty, actually."

"Wow," I said again. Me, a nurse? Maybe that wasn't as crazy as it sounded. "I'll look it up. Today."

"You do that. And call me if you want to talk more about it."

I walked home in a daze, wondering if I had the right coursework on my transcript to get into a nursing program. For the first time all year, I felt a tug of interest toward life beyond my Harkness degree.

The happy high I was riding lasted an entire week.

Then, inevitably, a certain voicemail message plunged me back to earth. If I'd thought there would be no repercussions for pranking Beta Rho at the football game, I'd been naive. My stomach bottomed out when I listened to the voice on the other end of the line. "This call is from the offices of Wilma Waite, dean of students. Please call us immediately regarding a confidential matter."

Oh, shit. It was time to pay the piper. Wilma Waite wasn't just a dean. She was the top-dog dean.

She wasn't an easy lady, or so I'd heard. Her nickname was Whomping Wilma. My hands were actually sweating as I hit redial. I put the phone to my ear, listening to it ring. Then I gave myself a pep talk. Short of expulsion, whatever punishment they doled out to me would be worth it, right? Getting even with Beta Rho had felt very, very good. I just needed to remember that while they were grilling me in Whomping Wilma's lair.

"Dean Waite's office."

"This is Bella Hall returning your call..."

"Miss Hall." The receptionist's voice was cool. "Thank you for being so prompt. Is there any way that you could come in to Dean Waite's offices right now?"

Yikes. If the dean had *cleared her schedule* to deal with me, that couldn't be good. "Sure," I said, wanting to get this over with.

"I need to ask you not to speak to anyone on your way in."

"Um, okay." Holy crap. Did I need a lawyer? I'd watched plenty of TV. If I didn't like the questions they were asking me, I could always stop the interview and call my father. He'd love *that*. But I knew he'd help me immediately.

The receptionist told me where to find the dean's office, but I already knew where it was and it took me only two minutes of walking to reach Tappanworth Hall. The place was built to intimidate. When I pulled open the giant wooden doors, I found myself in an echoing marble anteroom. Through another set of imposing doors was a double-height office with thick Persian rugs on the floor. There were two assistants seated behind enormous desks. One jumped out of her seat when I came in. "Isabelle?"

"Yes."

"Let me take your coat. The dean is quite grateful you could make it."

Grateful? The rumors must be true, then. Whomping Wilma must *enjoy* punishing undergraduates.

"Can I get you coffee? Tea? Water?"

"Uh, water would be great."

A few minutes later I was ushered through yet another set of carved oak doors into the dean's private office. Dean Waite didn't look like the dominatrix I'd expected, though. She was a rather ordinary looking lady with grey, librarian hair. "Have a seat, Isabelle. And thank you for coming."

"It's Bella," I said, just to make myself feel brave.

"Bella, take a chair," she said.

I did. Nothing happened until the receptionist had left the room and closed the door.

Then Whomping Wilma folded her hands on the desk. "Bella, we have received a complaint against the members of the Beta Rho fraternity."

My heart lurched as I replayed that sentence in my head. She'd said the complaint was *against* the fraternity, not *from* the fraternity. Oh.

Ohhhhh. *Oh no.* I was afraid to hear where this was going.

"Given what the complainant has told us, the school is investigating several of the fraternity members. We have an obligation under Title Nine to maintain a safe and harassment-free atmosphere for all students."

"Okay," I squeaked, trying to do the math on what might have happened and how Whomping Wilma got my name.

"One member of the fraternity is cooperating with this investigation. And this member brought your name to our attention."

Oh. But... who?

"It's really quite unusual to have the testimony of one fraternity brother against the rest of them. So we need to corroborate the things he's telling us." She stared at me with expectation in her eyes.

"I see?" I said. Although I didn't really.

"Bella, do you have anything you'd like to report?" Her gaze was like a laser.

Wow. I didn't want to report anything. But now she had me wondering where the other complaint had come from. If another woman had gotten hurt by Whittaker and his cronies, that changed things. It *had* to. If I told Dean Waite that I had nothing to say, he might get away with it.

And what if they'd done something truly awful to someone else?

I swallowed hard.

"If you're worried about implicating yourself in any wrongdoing, you could speak to a lawyer first."

"I didn't do anything wrong," I said quickly. (Unless we *were* counting the football game stunt.) "It's just that I really don't want attention."

"Bella, this office will not release your name. The investigation is private."

Oh honey, *really?* "Dean Waite, there's no such thing as private. If I tell you my story, and you start asking the fraternity questions, they'll know *exactly* who talked. They have a nasty little website where they air all their grievances."

"Do you mean..." The dean shifted the papers on her desk. "*Brodacious.com?*"

"That's the one."

The dean made a note on her pad. *Shit!* I'd already contributed to the investigation.

She sighed and set down her pen. "A former member of the fraternity has made serious allegations regarding their treatment of you, and I was hoping you could corroborate his story. That's all I can say. Except that if it happened, and you don't help us prove it, it could easily happen again to someone else."

Ugh. She was right, of course. The college didn't want trouble. And I didn't want that on my conscience. It's just that I also didn't want to be targeted for telling the truth.

Coward much? "Okay. Fine. I get it. I'll tell you."

Her eyes lifted. "Can we do this now? I'll need to record our interview."

Oh good God. What had I just agreed to do?

The assistant was called back in to set up a video camera. I just sat there in my chair, sweating. The assistant sat down too, a notepad in her lap.

They both stared at me. "Okay, Bella. Please tell us about your recent interactions with members of the Beta Rho fraternity."

After a big gulp of my water, I tried to think where to start. "Well, in September I went to their Casino Night party..." Jesus Christ. I was going to have to tell a dean, her assistant and a *video camera* that I'd had sex with Whittaker.

So I did.

"It was consensual?" Dean Waite asked.

"Absolutely — no question," I admitted. *Shoot me already.* Nobody at Harkness would ever have sex again if they knew they could end up telling Whomping Wilma about it later.

"What happened afterwards?" the dean prodded.

Marching onward through my tale of woe, I walked them

through my medical diagnosis, eventually arriving at the ugly night in question.

I told my audience that Whittaker had sat me down in the breakfast nook.

I told them that we'd done shots of tequila.

And while my face burned bright red, I told them that Whittaker had *denied* giving me an STI. And in the next breath, he'd asked Dash to mix up "the special."

The fucking *special*. It had leveled me like a tranquilizer dart. I'd spent six weeks trying not to think about that night, but the dean's clarifying questions kept pinning me back inside that awful moment. "How did the drink appear?" Cloudy. "What was in it?" Orange juice, and an umbrella, but *only in mine*.

Jesus God, I was such an idiot. How could I have missed that big red flag? Why did I think guys who bragged about drinking beer out of their jock straps would suddenly decorate a lady's drink, just to be nice?

The whole situation was mortifying. And it was also *really fucking scary*. I'd done a fine job of blocking all this out until today. But now as I described to the dean how tired I'd gotten immediately after drinking it... Saying it out loud brought me right back to the moment.

In spite of the water I'd been gulping, my throat went dry. "The next thing I remember is waking up on the wood floor." The sensations clobbered me all over again. *Freezing. Stiff. Confused.* My missing sweater. Awful words written *all over my skin*.

Weirdly, there were tears dripping down my face, and I'd barely even noticed them. It was all too vivid. I was gripping the armrests of the wingback chair, terrified at the idea that I'd been so defenseless in that house.

They'd put me on the *floor*, and covered my body with taunts while I was unconscious.

Then they'd left me there, like garbage.

"Bella?"

I looked up to see the assistant offering me a box of tissues.

"Th...thanks," I stammered, grabbing it.

"I'm sorry that happened to you," she said, her voice soft.

"Yeah. It, um..." I was reaching the end of my ability to speak. I felt almost as wiped out as I had that morning, when my limbs wouldn't do as I'd asked.

"You're almost through it," the dean said, her voice calm. "Tell us what happened when you left. How did you feel when you left? Physically, I mean."

Now that I was allowed to leave the frat house behind, I started to feel a little better. "I... Weird, I guess. Heavy. Clumsy. I fell down on the sidewalk."

She scribbled furiously on her notepad. "Did anyone witness this?"

Hoo boy. "Yes. One person walked me home."

Her eyebrows lifted. "Who?"

A few minutes later, I was drinking another glass of ice water while the dean's assistant tracked down one Rafael Santiago. And ten minutes after *that*, I heard my boyfriend's voice in the lobby. "What is this about?"

"Can we please be done now?" I asked the dean.

"Yes — for now. But I may need you again for follow-up questions."

"Any time," I offered. I would have promised her my firstborn to get out of that room.

In the outer office, Rafe stood by a window, drumming a pencil against his leg. I'd never been so happy to see anyone in my life.

When he got a look at my face, he crossed the room in three paces. "What's the matter?" He pulled me to his chest without giving me a chance to answer. "Did something happen?"

"Bella," the dean said behind me. "Please don't answer. His testimony has to be unbiased."

"My *testimony?*" His voice rose dangerously. "Forget that. Tell me who made her *cry*. Bella never cries."

This used to be true. "I'm fine," I said from the comfort of his sweater. "They were just asking me—"

"Bella!" the dean interrupted.

I pushed back to look up into Rafe's eyes. "Nothing happened to me *today*," I tried. "This is old news."

His shoulders relaxed. "Oh."

"Mr. Santiago, if you would *please* step into my office."

"I will do that as soon as my girlfriend does not look so freaked out." He led me over to a chair.

"I'm okay," I promised, blinking away my latest batch of tears. "I promise. The sooner you talk to her, the sooner we can go home."

He was still frowning, and I loved that frown. I didn't think I was the sort of girl who wanted a knight in shining armor. But apparently the occasional display of chivalry was pretty fucking sexy. Who knew?

"Don't go *anywhere*," he ordered me in his bossiest tone.

I gave him a salute. He kissed me on the top of my head and went into the dean's office.

THIRTY-THREE

BELLA

After my painful interview with Whomping Wilma, things calmed down again.

For the second time in ten days, Beta Rho made the front page of the Harkness newspaper. According to the latest article, an unnamed football player had made allegations against his own fraternity, and the college had launched an investigation. No further details were given due to the ongoing investigation.

My name was nowhere in the article, either. I read it three times to make sure.

And anyway, there were other things to worry about. Our Urban Studies project was finally due the next day.

So, on a Wednesday night during the first week of December, Rafe and I were putting the finishing touches on our half of the presentation. He sat in my desk chair, and I lay on the bed.

I got the distinct impression he was keeping his distance on purpose, and it made me want to test his will power. I said something really subtle to test the waters. "So, baby, if you just turned that chair a few degrees, I could blow you while you check that spreadsheet."

He dropped his face into one hand. "*Bella.* Maybe we should go to the library. Because this is due *tomorrow.*"

"We can go to the library if you want. I can blow you there, instead. All I'd have to do is crawl underneath one of those study carrels..."

"Nooooo," he groaned. "The library is where I *used* to go to keep my mind on the books. There goes *that.*"

"Not my problem." I stood and put my hands over his strong shoulder muscles, squeezing firmly. "How much more time do you think it needs, anyway? I could leave you alone if you give me some parameters."

He dropped his head back against my belly and looked up. "You know I don't really *want* you to leave me alone."

I kissed his forehead. "I get that. But after we win this thing, we are going to celebrate. We'll have champagne and do it on every piece of furniture in this room."

His forehead crinkled. "There are only two pieces of furniture. Or three, if you count the desk."

I dropped down to put my mouth beside his ear. "I want you to bend me over the desk."

Rafe gave a little grunt of longing.

"And don't forget to count the floor, *all* the walls and perhaps the ceiling."

He began to shake with laughter.

There was a knock on my door. "Bella?" It was Graham's voice.

This was a surprise. I crossed to the door and opened it. "Hey! What's up?"

He stepped into the room, giving Rafe a wave. "Hey, man." He leaned in and kissed my cheek. "Bella, I've come to take you to Capri's, and I won't take no for an answer."

Rafe looked up from his spreadsheet, and I knew I couldn't bail on our project. For once I felt an honest-to-God twinge of disappointment. A few beers with the hockey team sounded awesome right now. Which either meant I was finally feeling better, or just really sick of studying. Or both.

"I'm so sorry," I said. "We have a presentation due tomorrow."

"I'll finish up," Rafe volunteered. "You go."

But that wouldn't be right. "Not fair." I sighed. "I haven't been, um, easy to work with this week."

I saw him bite his lip and lock his eyes on the screen. He was charmingly discreet.

Graham cleared his throat. "Look, Bells. Even if it's for only half an hour. It's time to stop ducking us."

Aw. I threw myself at Graham's chest and hugged him. "I love you, and I love what you're trying to do. And I promise I'll come out soon. But it's not a good time."

"Just come for thirty minutes," he pressed.

"No." I gave him a little shove toward the door. "Soon."

Graham gave me an odd smile. "Soon." He walked out.

"You could go, you know," Rafe said.

"Let's just finish up," I said. "No funny business. Scout's honor."

"You were a girl scout?"

"Nope!"

He laughed.

There was another knock on the door.

"Oh, for God's sake," I said. "Graham..." I opened the door. But it wasn't Graham standing there, it was his boyfriend Rikker. "Hi. Fancy meeting you here."

Rikker grinned. "Bella, please come to Capri's."

"Okay, you are both adorable. And if you want, I'll get out my calendar and we'll choose a date to go out. But tonight isn't good."

"I think it is," Rikker said, grinning like a maniac.

"Um, that's nice. But *no*. Soon, okay?"

"Okay!" Chuckling, he walked out.

When the door closed, Rafe and I looked at each other. "Was that just a little weird?"

The bathroom door opened. "Who keeps knocking?" Lianne wanted to know.

"You know," Rafe said, snapping the laptop shut. "I think *Dios* is trying to say that we'll finish this tomorrow morning."

Someone knocked on the door. *Again.*

"Don't..." I said.

But Lianne opened it. And Trevi stood smiling on the other side. "Evening Bella. And friends. I came to invite you to Capri's."

Rafe started laughing. "Bella, I think they're trying to tell you something."

"Bella!" another voice echoed in the stairwell. Then several voices began to *chant* my name. "Bella! Bella! Bella!"

"Oh my God," Lianne said. She went to the door, peeking around Trevi. I didn't have to follow her to know what she saw. Because I knew those voices.

The entire hockey team was in the stairwell, calling my name.

"Oh, crap," I said. I had to press my fingertips against my tear ducts because they suddenly threatened to leak.

"Come on," Trevi pressed. "Where's your jacket? We're not going to take no for an answer."

"It's right here," Rafe said, standing up to grab my hockey jacket out of the closet. He draped it over my shoulders. "Go already. It's only eight o'clock."

Getting ahold of myself, I grabbed Rafe's elbow. "You're coming, too."

"I am?"

"Yep. And so is Lianne."

"I really don't think so," my neighbor argued, breaking for the bathroom door.

I caught her by the tiny waist. "You are getting out of here for an hour, okay? If it's good for me, it's good for you."

"Bella! Bella! Bella!" was still coming from the stairwell.

I went out onto the landing, where more than a dozen of my friends, in matching jackets, smiled up at me. Tears threatened *again.* "I'm coming! Jeez! Sixty seconds!"

Swallowing hard, I went back into my room and clicked off the lamp. "Let's go, guys. Now."

Lianne shook her head, even as I went past her to get her coat from her room. Returning, I pushed it into her arms. "I'm not trying to drag you to a frat party, okay? It's a pizza joint. For an hour. You'll live."

"Can I at least get my hat?"

"You have fifteen seconds," I said.

Not ten minutes later, I was standing in Capri's, where the scent of stale beer and pizza grease was as welcoming as anything I'd ever smelled. It was Monday night, which meant the place was uncrowded. The hockey team occupied the middle room, and I ended up at the head of the big, central table, with Lianne and Rafe to my right and Graham, Rikker and Pepe to my left.

"Have we met before?" Pepe asked Rafe, offering him a hand to shake.

"Maybe not," I said. "Rafe is my neighbor and..." My throat tightened as I realized what I was about to say. The team was never going to believe this. "My *boyfriend*," I eked out, my voice cracking a little on the word.

Rafe's face lit with amusement at my delivery. I was surely catching hell for this later.

Or now, maybe, because Lianne drained her beer glass and set it down with a thunk. "CUT!" she yelled. "Bella, you blew the line! Say it again. You can do better. Once more, with feeling."

Oh, hell. Rafe was laughing now, while Graham and Pepe exchanged a startled look.

"Fine," I said through gritted teeth. "Rafe is my *boyfriend*," I articulated. "Did everyone hear? Should I repeat it for the back row?"

"Wow," Trevi said from the next table.

"What *le fuck?*" Pepe echoed.

"Really?" Rikker grinned.

Someone poured Lianne another glass of beer, and she took a big gulp. "That's better." She sniffed.

"Just for that, I'm going to make you eat a slice of pizza," I threatened. I'd never seen Lianne drink *anything* before. She would need something in her stomach if she was going to discover beer tonight. Sometimes I forgot she was just a freshman.

"I'll go order a pie," Rikker said, standing up. Before he walked away, he leaned down and whispered in my ear. "Your boyfriend is *hot*."

I pinched his ass. "Don't even *think* about stealing this one, asshole."

Laughing, he pecked my cheek and walked away.

After pizza, we began playing quarters. Lianne didn't join in. Instead, she was leaning against the old-fashioned jukebox, chatting up Trevi's younger brother. We'd taken to calling Trevi-the-younger "DJ," because that was his job — choosing all the music played during face-offs at our hockey games. I'd never spent any time trying to guess what Lianne's type of guy would look like, but I could see that DJ might suit her. I could only hear snippets of their conversation, but the two of them seemed to be trying to out-nerd each other with obscure song titles.

Unfortunately, Lianne seemed to be drinking an awful lot of Capri's beer. Weak as the stuff was, it was working its magic. Lianne looked flushed and glassy-eyed.

"Excuse me, guys," I said. "My little frosh neighbor is looking unsteady. I might have to send her home."

"Bells, you didn't tell us you had Princess Vindi as your floor-mate," Trevi said. "Don't you worry that she'll disappear you in your sleep?"

I slapped him on the back. "I'll bet she's never heard that one before."

"Can you imagine?" Rikker asked, lining up the quarters on the table. "Little kids probably ask to see her wand."

"So? Girls ask to see my wand all the time," Trevi boasted. He was rewarded with several groans.

Making my way over to Lianne, I tried to assess the damage. "How are we doing over here?"

"Awesome!" Lianne yelled. "We are playing makelists," she slurred. "I mean, making playlists."

I gave DJ a glance. He just grinned.

"Maybe you should head home?" I suggested to Lianne.

"Maybe," she conceded, clutching the jukebox for support.

"DJ, could you do the honors?" I would've been happy to take her home myself, but since the entire team had dragged me out, I had planned to stay a little longer. Also, DJ was a good guy, and Lianne deserved to make a new friend, or ten.

But his face shut down when I made the suggestion, and he shook his head. "Can't do that. Sorry. Should I ask Graham?"

"I got it," Rafe said, appearing at my shoulder. "I'll walk Lianne home. You stay a while longer."

"Are you sure?"

He kissed me on the neck. "Perfectly. I'll look over our spreadsheet one more time, and wait for you in your room. Besides, I wouldn't be too shocked if Lianne spent some quality time in your bathroom tonight. If I'm upstairs, I'll be able to make sure she's okay."

I put my arms around his neck. "You really are the best one, you know that?"

"Been trying to tell you that, *belleza*." He grinned down at me. "Glad you're listening now." He kissed me, which elicited whoops and catcalls from the hockey team.

My whole life, I've never been one to blush. But I think my face turned bright red right then.

Rafe released me, then took Lianne by the hand. "Let's go home, okay?" he prodded her. "I think the cold air will do you some good."

"Kay," she said, swaying.

Rafe tucked an arm around her shoulders and steered Lianne toward the door. I watched them go. Maybe some girls would be reluctant to ask their boyfriends to walk a beautiful movie star home, but it didn't faze me. Rafe was solid gold, all the way to the center.

Why had it taken me so long to figure out?

"*Belluh!*" Pepe called out. "One more game?"

"Sure," I agreed. "Just let me hit the girls' room." I maneuvered toward the dark hallway at the back of Capri's. It wasn't the nicest john in the world, that was for damned sure. The men's room door opened up in front of me, and I was suddenly face to face with one of the guys I'd just spent weeks avoiding.

Dash McGibb.

Shit! My stomach dove, and I took a big step backward, crashing into a chair.

"Easy," he said, reaching out to steady the chair.

But I wasn't taking anything easy. I spun around to get away from him.

"Bella." There was something in his voice that slowed me down. I turned to check his face.

"Wait," he said quietly. "There's something I need to say to you."

I waited. But I could hear blood rushing in my ears, and the urge to flee was strong. If the urge to avoid looking afraid wasn't also strong, I would have probably pinballed from one piece of furniture to another, making tracks out of there.

"I'm so sorry. I'm sorry for what happened to you." Dash cleared his throat. "Wait, that's not good enough. I'm sorry I *let* it happen."

"You mixed my drink," I hissed.

Slowly, he nodded. "I told the dean everything. Whittaker told me to make the 'special.' So I did it. But then I regretted it immediately. And when he decided to recruit some help for his—" Dash took a deep breath "—*Artwork*, I said no way."

"You did?"

He ran a hand through his short hair. "Yeah. I stayed, though, because the whole thing was really freaky. And I knew that since I was stupid enough to mix that drink, whatever happened afterward was on me. So I watched to make sure they wouldn't do anything dangerous."

My urge to flee had morphed into something hotter and angrier. Now I wanted to pick up one of the chairs and brain him with it. "They didn't *rape* me, right? So you didn't feel the need to stop them. Carry on, guys. It's only marker."

Dash pushed the heels of both hands against his temples. "I know you hate me, Bella. But I didn't think I could stop them, short of calling the police. And since I'd just committed a *crime*, I didn't do that. That's how Whittaker sets up all his shit — he always makes sure that someone else is more culpable than he is. I didn't understand until then. And I never went back."

"What do you mean?"

"I slept on the sofa that night, in the same room where they left you alone to sleep it off. And after you left in the morning, so did I. And I haven't been back since."

"You haven't?"

He shook his beefy head. "But I was still guilty of mixing your drink, so I didn't say anything. Not until last week. They started harassing me, so I had a chat with my father, and then I went to the dean."

"Why were they harassing you?" I asked, as the hair stood up on the back of my neck.

He chuckled. "There was a certain prank at the football game. They thought I did it."

"*What?*" Beta Rho thought an idiot like *Dash McGibb* had pulled my stunt?

He gave me a wry smile. "Don't look so outraged, Bella. You'll give yourself away."

Shit! Focus! "You must be in a pile of trouble for telling the dean what you helped Whittaker do."

"You bet." He nodded. "I got a year's probation. And I'm off the football team."

My inner bitch gave a snort. What kind of punishment was that? "What about the cops?"

He looked up with a wince. "After the dean finishes her investigation, she'll probably ask you if you want to press charges against me. I asked my dad's lawyer, and he said that's probably what would happen."

"Oh." *Oh.* Jesus Christ. His fate was in my hands. How appropriate, really. And how *strange*.

The moment stretched on. We had a staring contest, which I won when Dash looked at his shoes again. "My dad's lawyer probably wouldn't want me talking about it. But I just wanted to tell you that I'm sorry. G'night." He met my eyes one more time before walking away.

I don't think I even answered him, I was too busy trying to understand what had just happened. How absolutely trippy.

After taking a few minutes in the (gross) Capri's bathroom, I went back to our table. The quarters game had wound down, and all my friends were finishing their beers. Someone had taken my seat, so I took a seat on Graham's lap, the way I used to. And that felt... fine, actually. The old ache was finally lifting. I looked from face to face, each one lit by the soft light of Capri's neon beer signs, and dusty old lamps which hung from the ceiling.

I'd never be able to say that this was an easy year at Harkness. But not everything had gone wrong, and some things had gone very, very right. "What time is it?" I asked suddenly.

Graham lifted his hand to peer at his watch. "Almost eleven."

"Damn. I have a presentation to give tomorrow. Walk me home?"

"Sure." Graham gave me a friendly nudge off his lap. "You coming?" he asked Rikker.

And that was trippy, too. Graham never used to acknowledge Rikker in public. That's why it had taken me so long to figure out they were a couple.

"Think I will," Rikker said, getting up.

"Night, guys!" I called to the hockey players who were still there.

"Bella! Bella!" Trevi chanted.

A couple of other guys picked up the chant, so I held my hands up to silence them. "Stop already. But will you *please* beat Harvard this weekend? Because I'm going to be watching." And not on TV, either. I had the sudden urge to see some hockey games again.

"You bet, lady." Trevi winked at me from across the room. "Then you'll come out with us afterward, right?"

"Sure." This whole being-seen-in-public thing wasn't as hard as I thought it would be.

We made our way outside and walked home to the Beaumont gate. Rikker didn't live in Beaumont, but Graham had a roomy senior single, and it was probably their favorite hook-up spot.

"Goodnight, guys!" I kissed them both on the cheek. I didn't need to fake any cheer, either. Because there was someone waiting for me in my room. Someone I was very happy to see, especially if he'd removed any of his clothing since the last time I'd seen him.

"Night, sweetie," Rikker said, giving me a squeeze. "Good to have you back."

I don't do mushy, so I slapped him on the ass and gave them both one more wave. Then I let myself into my own entryway, trotting up the steps as fast as I could. At the top, I opened my door to find a shirtless Rafe asleep face-down on my bed, his face buried in the crook of his muscular arm. My bathroom door was standing open. So I tiptoed through to peer at Lianne, who was asleep on her own bed in the exact same position.

In her case, though, an empty plastic wastebasket stood beside her bed. Perhaps Lianne and Rafe had a bit of a rough trip home.

Bummer.

I went back through the bathroom, shutting my door with a soft click. For a moment, I just stood there, admiring Rafe. His face was peaceful, and his back muscles rose and fell as he slept. I just had to touch him. I crawled onto the bed beside him and kissed the back of his neck.

Nothing happened.

"Honey, I'm home," I whispered. "I always wanted to say that."

"You did?" he rasped.

"Well, not always. Only now."

He smiled without opening his eyes.

"There's a subtext, you know," I said, peeling off my jacket. "'Honey, I'm home' really means, 'take off your clothes and fuck me.'"

"I never knew that." Rafe rolled over and stretched his arms above his head.

His position gave me access to his fly, which I unzipped.

"Our project is ready," he said, rubbing his eyes.

"What project?" I leaned over him and began to kiss the skin just above the waistband of his briefs.

Rafe propped himself up on his elbows and looked down his body at me. "Did you have fun tonight?"

I tugged on his waistband. "I'm trying to right now."

With a chuckle, Rafe put a warm hand on my hair. "I like what you're doing, *belleza*. Just give me a minute to wake up." He lifted his hips, allowing me to slide his jeans and briefs off.

"Did Lianne puke?" I asked, removing his socks.

"Only twice."

"I'm sorry."

He shrugged, stretching out on the bed, naked now. "No big deal. I didn't have to do anything except hold her hair."

"Aw. You did that for her? I think you deserve a blow job."

"From *you* though, right?" He winked up at me.

I slapped his thigh. "Who else? And you don't even have to be quiet, because she's passed out."

Rafe must have liked that idea, because his dick began to swell. I slipped my hand around him, and he groaned. "Take off your clothes," he ordered.

"Bossy much?" I grasped the hem of my T-shirt and pulled.

"I'm bossy for a reason." He helped me shuck off my shirt.

"Why's that?"

He caught my face in both his hands, and those espresso-colored eyes bored into mine. "Because whenever I tell you to take off your clothes, you get the best look on your face."

"I do?" The proximity of my boyfriend's naked body made it hard for me to listen, though.

"Yeah," he whispered, his gaze dropping appreciatively to my cleavage. "Your face says, 'Do me Rafe. And be quick about it.'"

I closed my eyes and groaned. "That sounds like something my face would say."

"Yeah?" He pulled me down onto the bed and popped the button on my jeans.

"It does." I helped him shuck them off. Then, wearing nothing but my favorite black bra, I stretched out on my back. "Are you awake yet?"

"Oh yeah."

"Good. Because I want you to do me. And be quick about it."

Chuckling, he rolled on top of me and kissed me.

THIRTY-FOUR

RAFE

"Don't forget to mention that there's a sale-ratio trigger on the equity component," Bella prompted me on our way to Urban Studies.

"Yes, ma'am."

"And then flip back to the diagram that shows how the trust is funded after the first wave of sales." She tugged me toward the lecture hall. It was time for our presentation.

Outside the door, I spotted Alison and Dani waiting for us. I grabbed Bella's hand and stopped to give us a second alone. "Hey. I'm happy to give our half of the presentation. And I promise to remember all the nerdy bits."

She grinned at me.

"But I think you should consider doing it instead."

Her smile faded.

I put my hands on both her shoulders. "Nobody knows this stuff better than you do. *Nobody*."

Bella looked down at her shoes. "Maybe it makes me a coward, but I'm just not ready to stand up in front of that room."

"Hold on." I lifted her chin gently. "There is *nothing* you could do to make me think you're a coward. Except about spiders, but I'm just going to let that slide." Her lips twitched. "You've worked hard on this thing, and you sound formidable when you're talking about it. Like, ass-kicking ninja real-estate developer woman. And you look hot in that sweater. If you were ever going to pick a moment to look the whole world in the eye, today's not a bad choice."

"I don't know, Rafe. Maybe you should incentivize me." She lifted an eyebrow. "What do I get if I do the presentation?"

I laughed. "I know!" I leaned over and whispered very closely into her ear. "An A in the class."

She gave me a tiny smirk. "I'd rather you slip me the D."

I leaned in again, brushing the sensitive place right below her ear. "You're going to get the D no matter what happens."

"Okay." She wrapped her arms around me. "I'll do it. I really want to win this for you."

I pulled her tightly to my body. "Relax, baby. It's all good."

"How do you figure?"

I kissed her cheekbone, then whispered. "I *already* won. You're a whole lot more important to me than this contest."

The look of surprise on her face practically broke my heart. "Nobody ever said that to me before."

I curved my hand around the back of her neck. "You know, maybe you didn't plan it this way, but I'm happy to be your first."

She let out a giggle, then rose to her toes to kiss me.

Pulling herself together, Bella did a fabulous job with our half of the presentation. And, if I was honest, so did Alison with hers. But there were *twelve* houses competing. So even though I was certain we'd bested seven or eight of them just with our excellent preparation, it was still a long shot.

After the last team was through, there was a five-minute lull while professor Giulios and his guest — Jimmy Chan, the food truck guy — conferred over the scoring.

Then Giulios took the stage, and Bella grabbed my hand. "Ladies and gentlemen, we saw some very fine work here today. In fact, it breaks my heart to know that a certain block of West 165th Street is not truly poised to go under the wrecking ball." He lifted his clipboard. "We have a second-place winner to announce first. Team Beaumont, you did an excellent job, especially with just four team members."

"*Shit*," Bella cursed under her breath.

"There was some fine attention to detail on your project. And I think you were the only team to actually visit the site and take pictures. But ultimately, your design and your funding strategies were at war, which is why Coleman House will win tonight's competition."

Cheers erupted from team Coleman, and Bella heaved a sigh.

"I'm sorry," Alison said from the other side of Bella. "This is my fault. That damned green roof."

"Not your fault," I argued, meeting Alison's eyes. "We didn't lose the World Cup here. We're going to get an A in this class. And your green roof was cool."

My ex's cheeks pinked up at the compliment, and she gave me a tiny smile.

"The man makes a good point," Dani said, tossing her notebook into her backpack. "I call that a win."

Up front, Giulios was finished complimenting Coleman's strategies, and the lecture was breaking up. "I'll be right back," I said, hopping out of my seat.

I found Mr. Chan at the front of the room, chatting with a student. I planted myself a few feet away, and was eventually rewarded by a glance and a smile when the other student moved off.

"Hi," I said, thrusting out a hand. "I'm Rafe Santiago, and I was on team Beaumont."

"Ah!" the man said, shaking my hand. "You were so close."

"Yeah, that's cool. But I was wondering how I can figure out the food-truck business. My family runs a Dominican restaurant in Washington Heights. We need to think about a food truck, but we don't know the steps."

He nodded. "How's your health department rating?"

"It's awesome because my mom is a slavedriver."

The man laughed while he reached for his pocket. "Take my card. When you're ready to get serious with it, call my secretary and tell her that you were the Harkness kid who wanted to get going on a Dominican food truck. We'll have a meeting."

My fingers closed around the card. "Thank you, sir. I will do that."

"Nice to meet you, Rafe. And feel free to bring some majarete to the meeting." He patted his stomach. "I love that stuff."

"It's a deal."

I walked away, patting the card in my pocket. And just like that I really *did* win everything. I got a good grade and a connection at the City of New York.

And the girl, too.

Pinch me.

THIRTY-FIVE

December

RAFE

On the first day of Christmas vacation, I came down with a nasty cold.

In my family, we called mid-December "catering season" because of all the orders for holiday parties. Naturally, I was helping out in the restaurant kitchen. Because that's what a Santiago did.

But after the third time I had to step out the back door to sneeze and blow my nose, my mother fired me. "Go home," she said. "I don't want sickness in my kitchen. I'll bring you soup later."

On my way out the door, I slipped my phone out of my pocket and found a call from Bella. When I listened to the message, all she'd said was, "I have the most disgusting cold. Damned Lianne! Miss you." *Click*.

I laughed. Lianne had been sick during exams, and the poor girl had been all freaked out that she was going to deliver "Romeo, O Romeo" in a frog voice. Though she'd recovered already, it was no surprise Bella and I had gotten sick next.

I called her. "Me too," I said when she picked up. "The cold and the missing. Can I bring you some fresh-squeezed OJ?"

"Really? I thought you were working today."

"I got the plague too. And Ma doesn't let anyone sick work in the kitchen."

"I knew I liked your mom. Get your cute butt down here and bring orange juice. We are going to have a movie marathon."

"You need anything else?" I asked her. "Tissues? Cold medicine?"

"I've got all that. Get on the train, hot stuff. Lianne went to rehearsal, and I'm bored and lonely." She hung up on me.

Turning around, I stuck my head back into the restaurant kitchen. "Ma? Don't bring me soup later. I'm going to Bella's. She's sick, too."

My mother frowned. "Take that girl some juice." She went to the refrigerator and pulled out a quart of the stuff.

"What are you doing?" my cousin Pablito complained. "Takes me half an hour to juice a quart."

He wasn't wrong. This stuff was like liquid gold. "I'll pay you back later. I'll take one of your shifts." Then I got the heck out of there.

The front of Bella's mansion on East 78th Street was just as grand as I'd expected it to be. It had a limestone facade and arched, leaded-glass windows. I walked up five steps to a paneled oak door that had been buffed to a high sheen. There was a little button beside the door and a small black sign reading: "Please ring the bell."

So I did.

A few seconds later the door was opened by a comfortable-looking, middle-aged Hispanic lady. "You must be Rafe."

"Good morning, ma'am."

She smiled and took a step backwards. "Miss Cranky is upstairs in her room. I will show you up."

"Thank you." I held up the bottle of juice. "I brought her some orange juice. Can I pour her a glass?"

Now she beamed. "Follow me."

We went through a gleaming entryway, and then through a white-paneled sitting room. In the back was the most beautiful kitchen I'd ever seen in a New York City home. "*Aquí están los vasos*," the housekeeper said. She opened a cabinet and brought out two juice glasses.

"*Gracias.*" I opened the bottle on the pristine stone counter-top. "Grab another one, though, because this is really good juice. You should have some. My family makes it for our restaurant in Washington Heights."

For a second the housekeeper just stared at me. Then her face broke open into an enormous smile. "Call me Maria. And I will try your juice." She turned to get another glass, and I heard her mutter something in Spanish under her breath. Something like: *at least one of my girls has good taste in men.*

I filled three glasses. Then I lifted one toward Maria, the housekeeper. "*Salud.*"

She touched another glass to mine and then took a sip. "*Perfecto.*"

Smiling, I picked up Bella's glass. "I'll take this upstairs if you don't mind."

She pointed at a narrow doorway off the kitchen. "The back stairs are closest — just one flight up, and to your right. But I warn you, she is cranky. My Bella — always a happy child, except when she is sick. When she was a little thing, you see a grumpy look on her face? You go looking for the children's Tylenol. That's Bella. Not her sister — that child was unhappy for any number of reasons. But it takes a lot to make Bella miserable."

"I'll keep that in mind." Recently, I'd seen Bella *very* miserable, but I wasn't about to share that. Besides, I was pretty sure that the tide had turned.

"You look sick, too," she said, patting my arm.

"Exams," I explained. "Maybe we worked too hard." *Or maybe we spent a lot of time having sex instead of sleeping.*

"I will bring you both soup later. Now go up to Miss Cranky." She gave me a small shove toward the stairs.

I carried two glasses of juice up the little stairway. At the top, I turned right into a generous bedroom, where I found Bella. She sat surrounded by pillows on a queen-sized upholstered bed. Her nose was red, and she wore an oversized T-shirt that said: *Huck Farvard.* She was still the most beautiful girl I knew.

"Hey!" she said, pausing the TV. "You *did* bring me juice!"

"Of course, *belleza.*" I set the glasses down on the nightstand and kicked off my shoes. "Nice pad you got here." There were gorgeous old windows that looked out over a brick patio, and a thick Oriental rug on the floor. All the upholstery was rose-colored. Comfortable, but a little girlier than I expected from Bella.

She took my hand and tugged me onto the bed. "I missed you." She put her hands on either side of my face, but I only got a tiny peck on the lips. "I probably look disgusting."

"No way." I gave her a bigger kiss. "You look great. We only *feel* disgusting."

"You too, huh?"

"Yeah, but I'll survive." I sat myself up against the headboard next to her. "Is this okay? Can I sit on your bed without breaking any rules?"

Bella snorted. "Oh, honey. They gave up on making rules for me a long time ago. My parents just went out of town anyway — to West Palm for a golf thing. My mother tried to get me to go with her, because she's going to be bored out of her skull by a bunch of real estate people. I played the sick card, and I don't think she blamed me at all."

I handed her a glass of juice. "Drink up, *belleza.* What are we watching?"

"Let's see..." She navigated to the Netflix menu. Then she

turned to me with a little smile. "This is nice." One of her bare feet found its way to mine. "Thank you for coming."

It *was* nice. "Anytime. I feel like I'm getting away with something. The rest of my family is slaving in the kitchen, and you and I are going to watch TV all day."

"And Maria is going to bring us food and tea." She snuggled closer. "And I'm going to man up and check my email at some point."

"For what?"

"Ms. Ogden was going to get back to me today about my application to nursing school. I filled everything out like she said and lined up the recommendations. But I need to get good grades in three biology courses next semester to be truly eligible. She was trying to get them to consider my application as if those classes were a done deal. She said she'd tell me today if it was going to work."

I massaged the sole of her foot with mine. "And if it doesn't?"

"I'll take some post-grad classes at NYU next year and then reapply. It wouldn't be the end of the world, but it would set me back."

"Ah." I drained my glass and set it aside. "Let's watch a movie, and then you can check."

"Okay. Deal." She picked up the remote. "I think I feel a chick flick coming on."

I did my best Joan Cusack. "Coffee? Tea? Me?"

Bella's eyes widened. "I love *Working Girl*. And you've got that Staten Island accent down. Are you sure you're not from there?"

"I *thought* you were a nice person."

Bella laughed, and I pulled her a little closer to me, burying my nose in the clean scent of her hair.

Maria stuck her head in the bedroom door as our movie was ending. "I made pozole. But you have to come downstairs to eat it."

I groaned. "I *love* pozole, especially when I'm not the one making it."

"You cook?" Maria asked.

"Sure. Doesn't everyone?"

The housekeeper sniffed. "Bella, this boy is a keeper."

"I know," she said, sliding off the bed. "He convinced me already."

"Bring your phone," I reminded Bella. "You have to check your email."

She blew out a breath and grabbed it off the nightstand. "I'm goin' in."

Downstairs, Maria fixed us giant bowls of soup, thick with braised pork and hominy. "I have toppings," the housekeeper said. She brought us a tray with chopped onions, diced avocado and a couple bottles of hot sauce.

"Wow," I said, finding Bella's feet under the table. "That's it. I'm never leaving."

But Bella didn't listen. She was staring at her phone, and her eyes got big. "I can't believe it."

"What?"

"This is going to work! Ms. Ogden thinks they'll offer me a conditional acceptance. And if I do okay on the bio coursework, I can start at the nursing school in the fall." She smacked her phone down on the table. "You know what this means, right?"

"You're going to spend all of next semester in a weenie bin?"

She waved a hand, dismissing that problem. "Whatever. I'll come out for hockey games and sex. But next year? I'm at Harkness again." She got up from her chair and moved into my lap. "How do you feel about that?" she whispered.

I slid my hand between her legs and squeezed one of her thighs. "I like that a lot."

She clenched her thighs around my hand. "I was hoping you'd say that."

I found Bella's mouth with my own. The first kiss was slow

and soft. But one wasn't nearly enough. I pressed forward, parting her lips with my tongue. She tasted of orange juice and happiness.

Bella wrapped both arms around me, and the kiss went from "congratulations, honey" to "rip my clothes off" within a minute.

"I *know* you're not letting my soup get cold," came a scolding voice.

Guilty, I pulled back.

But Bella didn't look guilty. She only smiled at me. "More on that later," she promised.

I gave her ass one more good squeeze before she went back to her own seat.

Propped up on cushions on her big pink bed, Bella and I used up a lot of tissues, played some cards, and watched TV. We were beginning to nod off when I heard a sound at the door. I opened my eyes and saw Maria peeking in from the hallway.

She put a finger to her lips. "I didn't mean to disturb you two. But I'm heading out for the night."

"Thank you for lunch," I whispered.

"Anytime, *chiquito*. Will you make sure that my Bella eats something for dinner? There's more soup. Or homemade pizzas in the freezer."

"I will."

She winked at me and then left.

It was dark outside now, and the only light came from Bella's muted TV. I just lay there enjoying the warmth of her body next to mine, until eventually she woke up with a gasp and a cough.

Sitting up, I handed her a glass of water.

"What time is it?" she asked eventually.

"Seven."

"We are so lazy."

"Eh. We're sick. It's allowed." I stretched toward the lamp on her bedside table and clicked it on.

Lianne's voice came up the stairs. "Hi honey I'm home!" She

appeared a moment later. "Hey! It's Rafe, too. Good timing! I got what you asked me for." She lifted the handles of a shopping bag. "I'm going to put it away." Lianne scurried off, toward the guest room I supposed.

"What did she buy for you?" Bella asked.

"Can't tell you."

"Why not?"

"Um, Bella? It's a week until Christmas. Duh."

She poked me in the belly. "What *is* it?"

"Didn't you *just* hear me say I wasn't telling?"

"I can make you talk," Bella insisted.

"No, *belleza*. Nobody can make me talk."

"Okay. No sex until I know what's in the bag."

I laughed. "If that's the way you want it."

She turned to study me. Then she ran a hand from my chest to my crotch. "Goddamn it. What did I just do to myself?"

"Break it up," Lianne said, bouncing into the room. "You two had all day to grope each other whilst I toiled in yonder salt mines."

"You poor thing. We were busy with TV and naps," Bella answered. "Thanks for the plague."

"Sorry."

"You can make it up to me if you tell me what's in the bag."

Lianne rolled her eyes. "I'm not telling."

She tried me again. "Please can I open it? It's almost Christmas."

"It's not wrapped," I argued.

"Actually, it is," Lianne said. "The store offered, so I said yes."

"What store?" Bella asked.

"Nice try." Lianne climbed onto the foot of the bed. "I bought some cocoa on the way home. Can we make hot chocolate?"

"Sure we can." Bella used her toe to poke Lianne's hip. "You know that will have calories, right?"

"Yep. But I've decided to make a few changes. I'm going to eat whatever I want, for starters."

"*Really*." Bella wrapped her arms around her knees and stared. "What else?"

Lianne picked at one of her perfect fingernails. "I'm going to spend time only with people I like. And stop listening to the ones who try to control me."

Bella and I exchanged a glance. "That sounds like a good plan for anyone," I said quietly.

"I need to stop letting people push me around," she said. Then she looked up at Bella. "You wouldn't put up with a quarter of the shit that I do. The next time some Hollywood asshole tries to step on me, I'm going to ask myself, 'What would Bella do?'"

Bella snorted. "I don't want you to take any shit from anybody, Lianne. But maybe we should find you a less notorious role model."

"No." Lianne shook her head. "I never take any risks, and you do. And I know they didn't all work out the way you planned..."

"That's putting it mildly," Bella said.

"But you are *fierce*," Lianne finished. "And I admire you."

Bella's mouth opened and then shut again. Pink spots appeared on each of her cheeks. "Thank you," she said, swallowing. "Let's go have hot chocolate. You can start your bold adventures in my kitchen."

THIRTY-SIX

BELLA

Downstairs, I began opening and shutting cabinets.

"What are you looking for?" Rafe asked.

"A pan."

"You don't know where they *are?*" he yelped.

"Don't judge. Found one!" I yanked a skillet out of a drawer.

Rafe crossed the kitchen and took it out of my hand. "*Belleza*, that's not the right shape. When you stir, it's going to spill." He leaned over to exchange the skillet for a heavy saucepan, then pushed the drawer closed. He put a hand on my hip and gave me a squeeze.

And I freaking loved it.

It should have been a drag to be sick over Christmas vacation. But standing in my kitchen with the two people who'd gotten me through the worst semester *ever* was really lovely.

On a counter stool across the room, Lianne scrutinized the label of the Dutch cocoa she'd bought. "There should be directions on here somewhere."

Rafe leaned his strong arms on the counter and shook his head. "You know I love you girls, but you are helpless in the kitchen. Just hand that over," he said. "Bella, raid your refrigerator for some milk."

You know I love you, he'd said. Even though he'd only been kidding, I really liked the sound of that.

Rafe plucked a whisk out of Maria's utensil jar and lit one of the burners on our range. Cracking open Lianne's cocoa canister, he dumped a heap of cocoa into the pan.

"You didn't measure that," I pointed out.

"Measuring is for sissies." He took the milk out of my hands and poured a dollop onto the chocolate.

"Don't you need more?" I asked.

"You think?" He laughed. "See, if you start this way, making a *paste*, it's easier to get the lumps out."

"Wow," Lianne said. "He cooks, too? When I was trying to talk you into dating him, I didn't even know that."

Rafe grinned into the chocolate pot. "Thank you for your support, *pequeña*. Now find some sugar for me? Check those canisters." He pointed at the ceramic containers on the countertop.

Adding milk and sugar, stirring constantly, Rafe made a lovely pot of sweet-smelling chocolate. I was just about ready to get out the mugs when the house phone rang. I peeked at the caller ID. It was my mother, so I answered it. "Hello?"

"Hi sweetheart. Are you feeling any better?"

"I'm all right. Lianne and Rafe and I are making hot chocolate."

"That sounds cozy."

It really was.

"Your father and I are coming home on an early flight tomorrow morning. I have some difficult news."

Something went wrong in my gut. "What?" I found a barstool and sat down.

"Your sister is leaving Tucker."

I let out a breath of air. I'd been expecting her to say that someone was sick or dying. "Oh. Okay." *Do not express glee*, I ordered myself. Even if glee was justified, my mother wouldn't want to hear it. "Why?"

She sighed into my ear. "Perhaps it won't surprise you to hear that he was cheating with the office intern."

"Well..." I cleared my throat. "You're right. I'm not surprised."

My mother hesitated. "Before this is all over, I think we're going to end up owing you a big apology."

You could have pushed me off that barstool with a feather. "Uh, okay?"

"At the moment, your sister is too shocked to think. And your father is so angry that he can't even form sentences."

"Okay." I could wait for my apology. I'm big like that.

"But in the meantime, I need to give you a few details. Tucker is out of town at a conference in Chicago. So he doesn't know that Julie read all his texts. Instead of confronting him, she's hired an investigator to document everything."

"Wow. That's smart."

"Your father is going to have to audit his business in case Tucker lied about more than just his sex life."

"Ouch."

"It will all turn out okay. But in the meantime, do not take any calls from Tucker."

"He doesn't call me, Mom. Not since Julie's engagement."

"Okay. That's good. Just know that he's in a precarious place. If he were to suddenly reach out to you, don't trust him."

"You can't get me within fifty yards of the man, mom. Don't worry."

"All right, sweetie. Be well. I'll see you tomorrow. I guess it's a good thing that you put Lianne in the guest room. Because it looks like Julie's going to need her old room again."

I felt a stab of sympathy for my poor sister — landing in her childhood bedroom again after discovering her husband was cheating. "I'm just so glad they didn't have kids," I said suddenly.

"Me too, sweetie. Julie can start over someday. And we'll have you screen all the candidates."

Aw. "Don't forget, Mom — he fooled me too for a long time."

"That's big of you to say. Now go drink hot chocolate with your friends, and I'll see you tomorrow."

I hung up the phone, still shocked by this turn of events.

"What?" Rafe asked. "Is your sister in trouble?"

"Quite the opposite," I said. "She's just getting out from under it." I picked up the mug he passed me and took a sip of the best hot chocolate I'd ever tasted.

~

RAFE

"I should go," I said after we all had dinner together.

"Stay," Bella said, rinsing a plate and then putting it in the dishwasher. "It's cold outside. You're still sick. And my parents aren't even here."

"Well, I'm going to bed," Lianne said. "I'm beat. And maybe I can fall asleep before the sex noises start up. You two are as loud as howler monkeys."

"Now there's a sexy image," Bella muttered.

"Goodnight," Rafe said to her.

"Night," she replied. "And I'm leaving our secret in the hall outside my room."

"Please can I open my present?" Bella asked.

I ignored her to pull out my phone and dial home.

"Rafael," my mother said. "*Dónde estás?*"

I felt my neck get hot as I answered her. "I'm at Bella's, and I'll see you tomorrow, okay?"

There was an uncomfortable silence. "That's not right," she said. "You should come home."

As much as I really did not want to have this conversation, I switched to Spanish and persevered. "You have to trust me to handle myself, Ma. I know how it is. I know it as well as anyone. I couldn't grow up in your house and not learn that it's important to be careful."

"I know you're a smart boy, Rafe. But be a good one, too."

"I am, Ma." It was true, too. I may not do things just as she wished I would. But I had nothing to be ashamed of.

"I will see you tomorrow," she said finally. "If you feel better, you can work the lunch shift."

"Fine," I chuckled. "See you then."

Twenty minutes later I found myself on my knees on Bella's bed, giving it to her from behind. My girlfriend had both hands braced against the big padded headboard. She'd turned her head over her shoulder so that I could kiss her while we fucked.

Sexiest thing ever. I wrapped my arm around her ribcage, holding her close enough that I could feel her heart pounding against my hand. I was sure nothing could be better than that. Nothing. Except...

Five minutes after *that*, we cuddled in a sweaty, post-sex haze in her bed. With my eyes slammed shut, I kissed her neck, her chin, her jaw... everything.

"We might have been loud," she murmured. "But for the record, I do *not* sound like a howler monkey."

"Mmm," I said. Because that was all I was capable of saying.

"I feel the best I've felt all day," Bella said, her smooth hand stroking my chest. "I think I'm cured. It's a miracle." Then she turned her head away from me suddenly and sneezed. "Spoke too soon."

"Mmm," I said again, holding her closer.

She tucked one silky knee between mine and sighed. "Can I have my Christmas present now?"

"Nope," I said automatically. Although, it wasn't the worst idea to give it to her early. I wanted her to be able to use it before school started again. "I'd love to hand it over, *belleza*. But then I wouldn't have anything for you on Christmas."

"Who cares? As long as you don't propose to my sister, you'll still be the best holiday boyfriend I ever had."

I raised my head and laughed. "She is not my type. *You* are my type. I want the sassy, fierce sister with trust issues. You are ten times more fun than any other girl alive and hotter than my aunties' pepper sauce."

She blinked at me. "I changed my mind. I don't even need the gift. Just tattoo that on my ass and we'll call it even."

I kissed her on her red nose. "Stay here a second."

Somehow I heaved my carcass out of her excellent bed. In her bathroom, I made quick work of the condom. Then I tiptoed naked into the hallway to retrieve the shopping bag Lianne had left for me.

Bella clapped her hands when I came back to bed with the bag. But she stopped when she could read the side. "Paragon Sports?" Her eyebrows shot up. "You bought me running shoes! And Lianne tried them on, because we have the same size feet."

"Good guess, but you're wrong." I slid the box out of the bag. It was wrapped in red and green paper, and it weighed more than a pair of running shoes. I'd decided I was fine with giving her the gift now. I could still make her a really romantic card for Christmas. And I'd make her open it in front of me, so I could watch her try to pretend like it was no big deal.

Bella *did* appreciate romance. She just didn't like admitting it.

With big eyes, she gave the box a shake. Then she tore into the paper. Throwing her head back, she laughed out loud. "Hockey skates? God, I'm going to break a limb. Maybe two."

"No you won't."

"I don't skate."

"Sure you do. It's just like walking, but slidier. Just hold on to me."

She rolled her eyes. "Fine. I'll try it. You have to promise not to laugh *too* hard."

"I wouldn't dream of it."

"And this is awesome, because it means I get to choose a present for you that's outside *your* comfort zone."

"What?" It was possible I hadn't thought this all the way through.

Bella gave me an evil laugh. "Handcuffs. No. *Restraints*."

"I think I need to renegotiate."

"Too late!" Giggling, Bella grabbed my hands and lifted them up to the headboard. "Yeah. This is going to be awesome. And a *blindfold*. But I'll take it easy on you, and we'll save the nipple clamps for another holiday season."

"*Jesucristo*."

"I can make you scream that word." Then? She *tickled* me.

"I am in so much trouble," I said, dodging her questing fingertips.

"Yes you are!"

"Then so are you." In a lightning-fast move, I grabbed both her hands and rolled, trapping her under my weight.

And her shriek was not unlike a howler monkey's.

~

Thank you for reading Ivy Years #4!

~

The *Ivy Years* series continues with: The Fifteenth Minute #5 (Lianne's book!)

The Ivy Years is:
The Year We Fell Down #1
The Year We Hid Away #2
Blonde Date #2.5
The Understatement of the Year #3
The Shameless Hour #4
The Fifteenth Minute #5

And Don't Miss the Spin-off Series: The Brooklyn Bruisers
Rookie Move (#1)
Hard Hitter (#2)
Pipe Dreams (#3)

For all the latest news, check the sarinabowen.com, and sign up for Sarina's newsletter.

ACKNOWLEDGMENTS

I am incredibly grateful to the following authors who read this book before its publication. You all swept in at my hour of need, and I am so lucky to know you. Thank you Tammara Webber, Amy Jo Cousins, Natalie Blitt, Elle Kennedy, Kristen Callihan, Megan Erickson and Karen Stivali. You all helped make this the book I wanted it to be.

And thank you to Mari Cárdenas and Silvana Reyes for your help with Rafe's Spanish slang! Those emails we passed back and forth were incredibly amusing. (And #NSFW!)

Finally, thank you to Edie Danford for the excellent editing and friendship. #Vermont#Girl#Power!

ABOUT THE AUTHOR

Sarina Bowen writes contemporary and New Adult romance from the Green Mountains of Vermont. *The Shameless Hour* is her seventh novel.

Contact Sarina:

www.sarinabowen.com
sarina.bowen@yahoo.com

Printed in Great Britain
by Amazon